G000078179

LIZZY MUMFREY

Fall Out

Copyright © Lizzy Mumfrey, 2017
Published by I_AM Self-Publishing, 2017.

The right of Lizzy Mumfrey to be identified as the Author of the
Work has been asserted by her in accordance with the Copyright,
Designs and Patents Act 1988.

All rights reserved.

ISBN 978-1-911079-84-2

This book is sold subject to the condition it shall not, by way of
trade or otherwise, be circulated in any form or by any means,
electronic or otherwise without the publisher's prior consent.

Some names and identifying details have been changed to protect
the privacy of individuals.

 SELF-PUBLISHING

🐦 @iamselfpub
www.iamselfpublishing.com

To Bob my best friend. Sorry for all the late suppers.

Contents

Acknowledgements

With grateful thanks to Marion Deegan and John Boland of Wiltshire Police and Peter Power of Visor Consultants for their invaluable help in providing factual information about a UK response to a fictional major incident. Any errors are mine. Thanks to Alex Wellerstein for his interactive NUKEMAP freely available on the internet which enabled me to map the effect of a 10k uranium enriched device with realistic effect. Thanks to my three sisters Diana Heatly, Sara Hope-Hawkins and Susie Cooper and my niece Erica Stewart-Jones for their feedback and encouragement for my first novel writing endeavour. Thanks too to Leila Dewji of I_AM Self-Publishing for her thorough, questioning editing and Lisa for her proofreading and kind comments.

Chapter 1

"Start by telling me why you are here, Mrs Cole."

"Where do I start? It was May 25th. Look, just look at this letter from school. That is what started it." Susie stabbed at it viciously with a finger.

May 25th? Alarm bells rang.

Susie blurted, "My darling, adored husband had sex with someone else. He is dead, by the way. I caused the death of one of my closest friends. Everyone despises me for that. It's as if thousands and thousands of people have died because of me, which I know is ridiculous. There must be some hope but I really, really can't see it." Susie scrunched up the letter and sobbed uncontrollably.

The counsellor gently took the letter from her clenched fist. Smoothed it out. Read it. It looked innocent enough.

FALL OUT

Charlton Academy
Hartley Wintney Road
Charlton
Reading, RG14 2TB

13th April

Dear Parent or Guardian,

A school trip has been arranged for Year 12 students on May 25th.

The purpose of the trip is to explore democracy in the UK as part of the PGCE syllabus through observation of the State Opening of Parliament, visiting the Churchill War Rooms Museum and taking a tour of the Houses of Parliament and Palace of Westminster. The outcome will be an appreciation of democracy and the process of Parliament set into the context of the fight against fascism during the Second World War.

The trip will leave Charlton Academy at 08:45 and arrive back at school for 16:30. Students may wear their own clothes and will be provided with a packed lunch.

There will be no charge for this trip as the Cecil Watson Memorial Trust is funding it.

In order for students to go on this trip, they must have parental permission. Please complete the slip below and send to: Mrs Davies, Charlton Academy, Hartley Wintney Road, Charlton, Reading, RG14 2TB.

Thank you.

Mr J Barker
Head, Charlton Academy

I hereby give my permission for _____ to attend the school trip on May 25th.

Signed: _____ Date: _____

Chapter 2

Richard Hughes and Pete Cole headed for the bar at the 19th hole at Charlton's unquestionably traditional Golf Club.

"That was pretty crap," said Richard cheerfully. Although both were clearly of similar age, in their mid-40s, they were an unmatched pair in looks. Richard was compact with blond, straight-ish hair, dazzling blue eyes and a bounce in his step like an eager greyhound. He was only averagely tall next to Pete, who was sturdy, solid and commanding, with the steady gait of a strong bulldog that somehow immediately identified him as a police officer. Pete's dark Mediterranean colouring, fierce brown eyes, with dark coils of neatly styled, no-nonsense hair, combined to make a very handsome man indeed.

"Won't be doing much for your handicap, that's for sure," snorted Pete, smiling indulgently.

Richard didn't mind. He always managed to make light of an appalling round of golf that had had so many hooks, slices and lost balls. The scorecard was such an embarrassment that it was crumpled up in the waste bin in the gents' locker room. Pete's had been as steady as a rock.

"Well I may have played like a neophyte, but I enjoyed the fresh air and a nice morning's stroll. Got time for a drink? My Jessica no doubt is sitting around the kitchen table at yours, having a good gossip with your Susie and the lovely Leah, otherwise known as the 'Eternal Triangle'. What are you having? I'm definitely the loser, so I'm buying."

"Half of bitter, please."

Richard was used to Pete's abstemious ways. "Coming up, but watch out for incoming." Richard mouthed exaggeratedly, "Gary Webber," and managed an extravagant gesture with his blue eyes towards a small, pristine man who walked confidently into the bar, dressed in perfect slacks, roll-neck sweater and a Pringle jumper. Not a hair out of place, even the little duck's tail perfectly at the centre of his hairline.

With conscious arrogance, the small man looked around himself unashamedly, a cobra waiting to strike, openly assessing who was scattered around the bar. His mesmerising eyes took in the men lounging in the sturdy chairs, with glasses balanced tidily on drinks mats on low, veneered wooden tables, each with its neatly-folded menu and a jar of slightly dusty silk flowers. Many of the members were shuffling, intently looking anywhere at all to avoid making eye contact with Gary, just like Pete and Richard.

Gary, after a long, slow, considered look round, slithered straight for the secretary's table, where he was deep in conversation with the club captain, pulled out a chair and sat down confidently with, "Good morning chaps. Good rounds this morning?" His esses were sibilant. While the secretary looked alarmed, everyone else looked relieved, relaxed and conversation restarted.

Pete headed for a corner table, behind a pillar so he couldn't be observed, sank weightily into the chair, and stretched out, awaiting the arrival of his beer. Richard returned, placed the glass on the table and athletically leapt into the chair opposite, as Pete tidily centred his drink on his mat.

"I can't believe that Susie is asking Gary to her dinner party on the 12th May, I can't stick him," complained Pete, before picking up his half pint, which looked very small in his hand, and taking a first slurp.

"I thought it was your super-important promotion to Superintendent dinner party, not Susie's," laughed Richard.

Pete glanced over towards the secretary, who sat looking mesmerised, caught in Gary's hypnotic gaze.

"My promotion, but definitely my Susie's dinner party. She is very excited and in complete overdrive, bless her. Thank God you and Jessica are coming. In any case, the last thing that I feel like at the moment is celebrating anything. It seems so, I don't know, trivial."

"Trivial?"

"Yeah. Frivolous, inappropriate, but Susie has set her heart on it. You know what she's like. Between you and me, the situation couldn't be worse. The anti-Muslim attacks and riots in so many major cities and then the counter-threats and terrorist plots. Unconfirmed rumours are just pouring in every day. We are being drowned in information and it is impossible to tell which pieces are real. It's never been this bad before.

"The Joint Terrorism Analysis Centre may have set the threat level to Substantial but we all think that's conservative, but there is nothing we can put our fingers on. Everyone knows that something big is going to happen but when, where and how?"

Richard looked a bit baffled by Pete's "police speak" but he was used to it and just ignored it.

Pete paused, stared into space. "It's got to be London again, everyone realises that."

"I'm surprised they are sending the kids on this Year 12 school trip to London then if the threat level is that high. Alfie wants to go. Should I let him? Is Jack going?" Richard said questioningly.

"Jack wants to go, for sure. It seems a bit unfair not to let him when he knows that I'll be up there. I'm attending as a Tactical Firearms Commander. With so many of the Met officers responding to the anti-Muslim attacks, they have called on us in Hampshire for Mutual Aid to bump up the numbers for the State Opening of Parliament. The Met have committed to specialised anti-terrorist officers but they just can't train them fast enough. They need more boots on the ground."

Richard noted more "police speak", but got the gist of it. Basically, Pete was going to be in London that same day.

Pete took a sip of his beer and continued thoughtfully. "Who knows, it could be somewhere completely different. That is how they are so bloody clever; it always seems to take us all by surprise. Think of all the different places that they strike just when we have scaled everything back and become complacent. Luxor, Tanzania and Kenya, 9/11 and 22/3 in London, Madrid, Paris, 7/7, Delhi, Moscow. Are they really going to strike London again when they know we are on high alert?"

Richard nodded and took a long gulp of his beer. "True enough."

"But anyway, Richard, let us speak of more cheerful and entertaining things. How about a blow by blow account of your remarkable round of golf this morning?"

"Bastard." Richard threw back his head and laughed loudly, the mood lightened.

Chapter 3

Susie looked at herself critically in the mirror.

"Oh gosh, how did that happen?" she exclaimed out loud. "I'm bigger than I was when I was pregnant, even the second time."

Poor Susie, she really had tried everything to try to get her rampant tummy under control. The stuff she got from the chemist had disastrous results with its absolutely revolting, explosive consequences that were coyly described as "treatment effects". If only they had said it like it was, she would have avoided considerable embarrassment that day out shopping. All the weird herbs and things that she'd bought over the internet just made her feel either sick or so wired that she couldn't get to sleep, even though she was knackered.

What else had she tried? Every bloody fad diet ever invented. Atkins, no carbs, just carbs, starving every few days, which just made her very bad tempered, and it was hell cooking for the family, particularly when she ended up dribbling into their food.

It was so depressing. What was going to happen when she turned 45 next month? Did this make her middle-aged? Was she going to suddenly develop even more middle-aged spread? Argh!

It didn't help being the mother of Jack and Amelia, two super-sporty teenagers, fit as fiddles, who ate for England without putting on an ounce, and a husband, Pete, who despite doing nothing active at all outside of his job, except a bit of golf, was the same size that he was when they had got married 20 years ago. Just so frustrating.

When Pete said, "Susie, love, you are not fat, just delightfully cuddly", the endearing words of comfort were somewhat diluted when he squelched her love handles as he said it.

Susie shovelled her wayward flesh into her bra, which seemed to make her ample bosom even bigger, flung on the loosest, baggiest top she could find (they were all rather tight), wiggled into her very largest trousers, the ones with the elasticated waist that had stretched in the wash, making her feel more petite within their voluminous folds.

Once everything had been scooped away, she turned to the mirror and concentrated her focus on her gorgeous, thick, luxuriant, long, blonde hair, which she brushed firmly and soothingly to make herself feel better.

She lavishly applied layers of mascara to her enviously long blonde lashes and suddenly, like magic, her vivid, sparkly eyes looked enormous and her generous and benevolent personality shone out. She looked more beautiful than she could ever realise.

She ambled downstairs, put the kettle on, cleared the debris from everyone else's earlier breakfast and stared into the fridge, wondering what to have herself. She was starving, but after the fright of the examination in the mirror, she plumped for a coffee, black, no sugar, and a bowl of healthy whole bran cereal with skimmed milk, and settled to read the papers before getting on with her day.

Mentally, she noted: one – must ring brother Henry about visiting at half term; two – must plan Pete's big dinner party; and three – it was her day for Riding for the Disabled, which she loved; all those solemn beautifully-behaved ponies and their adorably overexcited riders with all sorts of special needs.

The dinner party was to celebrate Pete's promotion to Superintendent, and secretly, she wanted to show Pete that she was a super hostess, fit for a Superintendent, not just a fat, wobbly wife. She must make it perfect.

She knew that if she planned the menu for the upcoming dinner party, she didn't want to start salivating over her beloved cookery books on an empty stomach, so she topped up the cereal bowl, pouring in more milk with gusto, which splashed over the edge in a wave, and tucked in eagerly.

"Right. Must get down to it," declared Susie, as she heaved herself up, knocking the kitchen chair over backwards, and loaded the dishwasher with her dirty dishes in a rather higgledy-piggledy fashion.

List. Pen and paper?

Susie shuffled through the papers that were heaped on the counters, finding a *Vogue* that she'd promised to return to someone – she couldn't remember who – weeks ago, Jack's school trip permission slip – mustn't forget that either – and joy of joys, the NADFAS subscription that she thought she'd lost and was very, very late.

"The National Association of Decorative and Fine Arts Societies," she read out loud in a faux posh accent, and giggled to herself. She found a piece of paper eventually.

She pottered through to Pete's study, peeped in through the door of his inner sanctum as if he might be there, tiptoed to the desk, and whipped a biro out of the pen pot before scuttling back to the kitchen, where she settled down to plan her dinner party.

"Shit," she exclaimed, as the piece of paper sucked up the wayward bit of milk that had splashed onto the table. She mopped at it ineffectually with the drying-up cloth, adding a bit of greasy, unrecognisable something in the process.

Now, who had she got coming? Basically, it was her two closest friends, named the "Eternal Triangle" by Pete, rather cleverly, she thought. He said it was because they were eternally together, and their husbands, of course. Coincidentally, these friends all had kids in the same class as her own children, Jack and Amelia.

Top of the list was Jessica and Richard Hughes, parents of Alfie and Hannah.

Jessica and Richard's daughter, Hannah, and their Amelia had met on the bus when they had both started at Charlton Academy, the local school. They'd just clicked instantly, which was nice. They were in the same year, both sporty, and fast beginning to turn into girlie girls that took ages getting ready to go anywhere and dabbed on discreet amounts of make-up, even for school.

Over these last few years, their homes had become fairly interchangeable, with Amelia staying at "yours" and Hannah staying at "mine". Hannah had become her surrogate daughter and Amelia, Jessica's. The girls had laughingly made a silly, little pact where they said that if anything happened to one lot of parents then they would share the others. "That's okay with me," Jessica and Susie had said simultaneously, and laughed in accord.

Jack and Alfie got on okay, but not in the same way as the girls. Alfie was one of the cool gang, tall and gangly, trendy haircut, with Jessica's wide face, although he was too cool to smile as much. Despite his aspirations to be stylish, he was studious, ambitious and wanting to go far.

Jack was more of a jock – tall, well-built and practical, like his dad. Neither father nor son wanted their hair sculpted into a trendy style. Jack was somewhat bumptious, with a big, infectious laugh, always ready with a quip and wanting the last word. He cuddled Susie as if she were the family pet and had a tendency to play at being the big man, slightly patronising actually, when Susie still saw him as her little boy. It was rather nice to have Alfie and Jack so well matched in ages though; lots of excuses for the two families to do things together.

Jessica was such a good friend and she and Richard were the loveliest couple in the world. They always brought oodles of optimism and heaps of delight with them, with their sparky humour and self-effacing ways. The only problem with Jessica and Richard was stopping them from trying to help clear the table and do the washing up.

Jessica had one of those wide, smiley faces, big, cartoon-like eyes that made her head look a little too big for her slender body, and a personality that made you feel really, really good to be on the receiving end of her attention. She always made Susie laugh, even at herself when she'd yet again done something stupid or tripped over something.

Richard reminded Susie a bit of Daniel Craig – the same square face, blond mop of hair and blue, blue eyes. When she said it to tease, Jessica would roar with laughter, cover his ears and say, "For God's sake, don't tell him that, it might go to his head," while Richard did a 007 pose. They really were a lovely, lovely couple.

Why did all her best friends seem to have such fabulous figures? Perhaps working stopped Jessica getting bored and diving into the fridge, Susie pondered; perhaps this is what she should do.

Jessica enjoyed her job as receptionist and administrator at the kids' school, and all the youngsters thought she was wonderful, although it made Susie and Jessica chuckle that Alfie refused to go into school with his mum every morning

– "Too early for me, Mum" – and preferred the school bus. Or maybe he just preferred the drop-dead gorgeous Ellie, who got on the stop after his.

Pete and Richard got along like a house on fire, played endless rounds of golf together every Sunday like clockwork, and put the world to rights over many a pint of beer. Richard seemed to bring the conservative Pete out of his shell. Pete could be a bit tricky at social occasions, and was quite picky on who he did and didn't like, so she knew that putting Jessica next to Pete and Richard not too far away would ensure that everyone was happy.

Then she'd asked Meredith and Gary Webber, parents of the much-admired Ellie. Alfie definitely liked Ellie, and she always seemed to be hanging out at the Hughes', but she didn't seem to be having any of it, according to Jessica. Perhaps Jack fancied Ellie too. He was most certainly "seeing" someone, but any attempt at finding out actually who was met with "Mu-um!" and rolling eyes. She and Jessica giggled about the bothersome business of teenage boys and their teeming testosterone, which made Leah put her hands up in horror, as the mother of only girls.

She wasn't entirely sure about Meredith and Gary, but had asked them on a whim because she liked Ellie. They were a very smart-looking couple, always perfectly groomed, perfectly mannered and polite. Gary was the owner of the new restaurant that had opened in what used to be a really rather ordinary pub. Apparently, Gary bought up run-down, loss-making places, transformed them, put the right managers in place, and then at the top of the rise in popularity, sold it on as a going concern at a huge profit. It made sense. Rather clever in fact.

They had only recently moved into the area last autumn to get this new project underway, and Ellie had joined

Charlton's sixth form. Gary had joined the golf club and was a regular fixture there; very competitive, according to Pete, and working hard to get in with the committee.

Susie didn't actually know them at all well; they were difficult to get to know. Meredith rather kept herself to herself and was a bit timid. She looked fragile, wraithlike and a bit colourless – even her hair was a bit nondescript in colour. She didn't seem to find socialising easy and Susie had got the impression that they had moved quite a lot, probably because of Gary's business enterprises. Another reason that Susie had rather taken pity on Meredith and asked her along.

Meredith seemed rather cringingly grateful for being included in the social arrangements. It was a bit unsettling. Perhaps Susie had made a mistake, but she couldn't un-ask them now – that would be far too rude.

Funnily enough, their house was spookily identical, even though it was right at the other end of the ribbon that was Charlton village. It had obviously been built by the same architect, with the exact same layout; the same modern, executive home, with enough of a "run-in" to call it a drive. Both houses had four bedrooms, three bathrooms upstairs and two receptions, an enormous kitchen/diner and a study, discretely tucked away. Except that Gary and Meredith's house, the one and only time she'd visited for coffee with Meredith, had seemed very pristine, clinical and almost impersonal, like a hotel. Pete, who would love to have a house that tidy, always complained about Susie's permanent state of chaos, but she knew that she much preferred the cosiness of their home, even if she always seemed to be losing important things.

Gary came over as a bit hypercritical, but that would be absolutely no problem on the food front. Food was her forte. She was a brilliant cook, even though she said so herself.

Probably the only thing she was really, really good at. Proper training at a posh cookery school, and years of being a chalet bird and cooking directors' lunches, had honed her skills, and they ate a hundred times better at home than at the golf club – and Gary's restaurant, the one time they had tried it out, although she would be far, far too polite to say so.

Susie chewed rather harder than she'd realised on the biro and suddenly tasted the rush of ink in her mouth. "Yuck, yuck," she declared, wiping at her mouth and smearing blue over a much wider area. She rustled around amongst the chaos and unearthed a box of tissues, dabbing her tongue ineffectually on a frantically extracted handful. She guzzled down the last inch of cold coffee to clear it and then shook her head at her stupidity.

Dear Leah, the third leg of the Eternal Triangle, and her husband, Farrukh Ahmed, were coming, which meant she needed to do something vegetarian. They would never eat meat in other people's homes in case it wasn't halal, or rather Leah wouldn't allow it – she was a stickler for her religion's rules.

It was an absolute doddle to create an amazing veggie dish and then serve it with quite plain meat with an alcohol-drenched jus. That solved the problem of Leah and Farrukh not drinking alcohol either, although Susie suspected that Farrukh did when Leah's back was turned, just as he would eat any old meat, or so Pete reported from eating and drinking with him at the golf club.

Gosh, quite by mistake, it had turned into a golfing evening. Now that would please Pete.

She rather fancied doing the delicious potato, fennel and parmesan combo. It always went down a treat, and served with what the boys called "joined-up meat" – a slab of butterflied lamb with a port jus – it was a crowd pleaser all round. She carefully wrote the required ingredients down on her list; she was determined not to forget anything this time.

Leah was such a sweetie – stunningly beautiful with her kohl-lined eyes and gorgeous, silky saris. She was always a fund of hilarious stories about all the exotic places that they'd lived and their travels all over the world, which she told really well.

Leah had the most amazing face that lit up when she laughed, her doe eyes flashing with joy, her mouth opened really wide, and it seemed to make her fabulous cheekbones almost burst with the joy of it. Susie was always looking for ways to make her laugh so that she could enjoy that wonderful, expressive face in its full glory.

She was always so complimentary to Susie, saying how lovely her hair was and stroking it as if she was a cat, telling her what great big eyes she had (a bit like Red Riding Hood's wolf), how charming her children were, how well brought up, how clever, how sporty. It was nice; she liked it.

Leah made Susie think of chocolate; smooth, comforting, soothing, satiating and relaxing. She, Jessica and Susie had become firm, inseparable friends over the last six years, as their children had made their way through Charlton Academy. No wonder they had been nicknamed the Eternal Triangle by their husbands.

Leah's two girls were absolutely stunning too; the most gorgeous, long, shiny-black – really, really black – hair and Leah's striking eyes. Susie thought it a shame that Leah had made Aisha cover her hair with a hijab; Sara as well soon, no doubt. It did make sense, sort of, with the boys becoming so predatory, but Susie couldn't see the point, and anyway, it wasn't their hair that they should be covering.

Other parents were rumbling about the fact that Leah insisted on going as a chaperone with Aisha to any event outside school. It was fine for Leah to be so strictly religious and adhere to every rule, but it did make Aisha stick out like a sore thumb at school in this ridiculously middle-class outpost of commuter land. Leah had been pleading with Mrs Davies to be allowed to go on the planned London trip with Aisha, but Mrs Davies could be very stubborn and was refusing, politely, but very firmly.

Aisha seemed to get on well with Ellie, as they were in the same year and did the same subjects at school, so she'd hoped their parents would get along well too, but Susie had got this a bit wrong. Another reason that perhaps she shouldn't have invited Gary and Meredith.

Gary could be tricky, and very cunningly would provoke Leah when she wouldn't exchange the customary air kisses or even shake his hand when they met. It was a difficult one. Should Leah put her religious customs on one side to satisfy the Garys of this world or should she stick to her guns – or rather the Koran – and refuse to touch men?

Susie suddenly thought that she must take that NADFAS subscription round to Leah's now that she'd found it. It was late; it was meant to have been in at the end of last month at the latest, and Leah, as newly-crowned Membership Secretary, was a bit of a stickler for the niceties of paying subs on time. She added a note about it at the bottom of her dinner-planning list to dig it out later, now that she'd found its hiding place, after phoning Henry, of course.

Let's get back to the food.

Pudding was easy. Her homemade coffee ice cream was legendary, her chocolate mousse superlative, and the moreish crunchy cappuccino tuiles finished it to perfection. When she was next in the Yummy Mummy deli – it was rather nice to have such a variety of scrummy things conveniently in the village high street – she would pick up some of their chocolate coffee beans.

They weren't actually that nice when you bit through the chocolate and met the dry and bitter bean, but they looked the part. It was always quite funny to see people's faces when they solemnly tried to chew and swallow the bits. It made her chuckle. She added all the required ingredients carefully to her list.

Starters were always tricky. The sort of things that she liked, Pete didn't. He just about let her get away with fanciful puds, although his very, very favourite was good old bread and butter pudding, but his list of things that he didn't really like kept growing longer and longer as he became older and older.

Did he always used to be this fussy?

So, no smoked salmon, no pate, neither smooth nor chunky. No "rabbit food", no "hippy food". It went on. Susie sighed. She loved him to bits, but actually, it could be very, very irritating.

Also, do Muslims eat shellfish or was it just Jewish kosher people that didn't?

She would ask Leah. Perhaps it would be safer if she just stuck to a really, really nice veggie soup. She could make it look very, very pretty, do crunchy croutons, a swirl of luxurious truffle oil (add that to the Yummy Mummy deli list).

All this thought of food was making her feel peckish. Having carefully listed it all, underlining her note about the NADFAS subscription twice as a double reminder (had she put it back on the same pile?), she had a good rummage in the fridge and discovered a leftover slice of pizza that Amelia hadn't managed to finish after tennis last night.

If I have that now, I can call it lunch.

As she munched on it solemnly, she didn't notice the blue ink that smeared onto the crust.

Chapter 4

Susie phoned her brother, Henry, which was the next thing on her list.

"Hi Henners, how's Mum?" asked Susie, somewhat tentatively, because such an enquiry could sometimes unleash great fountains of self-pity from her brother. Catch him on a good day and he was funny and conversation flowed. She was regaled with all the doings of her lovely nephew and niece – Arthur, eleven years old and Alice, nearly nine – the crazy cocker spaniels – mother and son of a long line – the best-rat-catcher terrier, and all the comings and goings on the farm. On the other hand, catch Henry on a not so good day and he was a pain in the bottom, moaning about milk prices – and Mum. She wondered whether her dad had been the same.

She really, really missed Dad so much. He had been dead for years, tragically consumed by the dreaded big C, although Mum always forgot and seemed to have invented some weird story about him going off to farm in Scotland. Why Scotland? As far as possible from the farm, tucked away in South Lavington in the Surrey Hills, the only thing in common being that they began with an S. Who knew? Mum was mad as a hatter.

Early onset dementia had nibbled away at her reason over the years and Susie conceded that Henry did have a lot on his plate. It was his choice though; he had taken on the farm as son and heir, moving into the enormous, airy farmhouse with his tribe, while Mum had moved into their cottage, with a live-in carer, Moira, a jolly Scotswoman who sounded like Susan Boyle, and perhaps even looked a bit like her, apart from the hair. On the whole, it worked really rather well.

Despite her madness, Mum still remembered to patently dislike Susie's husband, Pete. She was a bit of a snob and Pete didn't really cut the mustard because he had been to the local comp, was a policeman – "Sorry, my darling Pete, I do mean police officer" – went to the "toilet" instead of the "loo", and used serviettes instead of napkins. Unfortunately, as she got more and more barmy, she wasn't afraid of saying so. Dementia seems to turn off all the tact buttons.

Susie had taken one look at Pete when he had arrived as a chalet guest in Méribel, nearly 20 years ago, and fallen head over heels. She hadn't been able to stop staring at him, open-mouthed –not a pretty sight. He was so tall, dark and handsome, and she loved his confidence, his strong, manly presence, his stillness.

She couldn't believe it though because the stunning Caroline, who worked alongside her, went straight in for the kill, with almost obscenely obvious flirting. Susie hadn't thought that he'd even noticed her. Caroline just had something so sexy about her compared to everyone else – enormous, cat-like green eyes, a wide, generous mouth, let alone the enormous boobs and that indefinable something, like Marilyn Monroe had.

Caroline worked really hard to snare Pete, including parading through the chalet in her black, lacy underwear that didn't hide a thing, with an airy "Just forgot my hairdryer", and Susie really, really couldn't believe her luck when Pete actually chose her instead. It might have been something to do with her cooking; they always say that the way to a man's heart is through his stomach.

For the remainder of the season, they had phoned obsessively. As soon as the season had finished, he had suggested that she might like to move in with him. She had been really, really flattered, and the rest, as they say, is history. Her mum had been shocked by the speed of it.

On the other hand, Mum adored Henry's Fenella, the perfect wife for her perfect son. Yes, yes, Susie was a bit jealous of the beloved Henry, the much hankered after son who had always been so worshipped by her mother, like a blooming gift from the gods.

Susie was always being told how Mum had been convinced that she would be a boy, had painted the nursery blue and got all sorts of little boy's clothes. Susie's arrival had proved a bit of disappointment. It had taken a few weeks before they'd thought up a suitable name for her.

The picture of Fenella and Henry's glorious wedding day, in pride of place on Mum's piano, was stunning. The farmhouse is in the background of the photo because Fenella very sweetly agreed to have the reception there to compensate for Susie's inconceivable decision to get married on "neutral territory". She'd really, really tried so hard to keep the peace between all the parents but it was always so hard to please everyone.

A stick-thin Fenella, in the traditional all bells-and-whistles, to-die-for dress, with her gorgeous, luxuriant hair swept into a chignon and her Julia Roberts smile, alongside Henry, handsome in his morning coat, which he filled magnificently with his hunky farmer's form, his blond hair beautifully cut, and a discrete carnation in his button hole. Susie and Pete's somewhat less flamboyant wedding picture tended to move further and further behind; it would disappear down the back one of these days.

Pete hadn't wanted a fancy wedding; in fact, it was his idea to find somewhere halfway between their two families, and in a registry office, halfway between not getting married at all and the full church kerfuffle. All of this was much to her mother's horror. But they'd had a lovely day, with a great, fun knees-up at a local hotel.

She'd been quite thin then, and in the photo, Pete was looking at her adoringly, in her simple dress, halfway between being bridal-white and controversially coloured (she could hear her mother tutting), and free-flowing, long, blonde hair, which Pete loved to stroke and run through with his fingers. Definitely her best feature. Still was.

Susie always described Pete as film-star handsome – his statuesque figure in his police uniform, his thick, brown, curly hair that was just starting to creep over his collar. The very same photograph was on the dressing table in their bedroom. It made her smile when she remembered that happy day. She thought she was the luckiest girl in the world.

Phew, it was a good phone day and Henry regaled tales of Mum ordering a taxi to go on holiday – where to? Who knows! Arriving dressed to the nines on their doorstep for some grand occasion that had never existed.

The kids were well and, as ever, doing brilliantly at the little local prep school that both she and Henry had gone to yonks ago.

"When are you coming to visit, Susie? Mum hasn't seen you for ages," asked Henry.

She can't remember that I've been anyway.

Susie ignored the subtle, little gibe.

"That's partly why I was ringing. Probably the last weekend of May, if that suits?"

"That would be great Susie. I will just check it out with Fen so that she can load the fridge. We are having the ritual sports day and lunch out with Alice and Arthur when we go and collect them on the 25th May for their exeat weekend. Do you remember when Mum and Dad used to do the same with us? We even go to the same pub, the Crown and Anchor!"

"Oh, that reminds me. Jack's on the school trip on the 25th so we wouldn't be coming down in any case until the morning of the 26th, by the time we get sorted out, if that is okay?" Susie rabbited on. "Jack and Amelia love to come to you. I think it brings out the kids' inner hippy – living off the land – and, although Amelia won't admit it, she loves mummying those two angels of yours, they are so adorable, and Jack would happily become a 'dog herd', if there was such a thing."

"And Pete?" Henry enquired, but not terribly enthusiastically. Susie knew that he found Pete a bit tricky, a bit competitive and, dare she admit it, Pete could be a bit chippy – making little, barbed comments about how charmed and protected Henry and Fenella's life was, safe in the hereditary home, out in the fresh, unsullied air of the countryside.

"I shouldn't think Pete will come. He seems to get busier and work longer and longer hours the more promotions he gets." Actually, she had a much better time without him on these visits because Mum conveniently ignored the fact that he existed and Fenella and Henry were just more relaxed. Was it mean to think that, she wondered. Probably, but it was sadly true.

Sorry Pete, I really, really do love you.

"What great heights has Pete reached?" asked Henry.

"Just been made up to a chief super-duper," laughed Susie. "A sparkly crown and a pip on his uniform now. Very, very proud wife! We are having a celebratory dinner party in his honour."

Susie glanced at her watch.

"Must fly Henners, I'm off to RDA at Hartley Wintney; it is just down the road but I don't want to be late."

Actually, I'm going to be rather late again, if I don't get a move on, but then I always am, she thought, glancing down at her watch.

"Lovely to catch up with you. Lots of love to Fenella, Alice and Arthur, and big hugs to Mum. Looking forward to seeing you for the last weekend of May. Bye!"

Susie put down the phone and carefully wrote down the visit on the 26th May, using the pencil that lived in the family diary, which lived by the phone, only to be moved anywhere else under the pain of death, so Pete kept reminding her.

She tried to remember to keep it in its appointed place, really, really honestly; it's just that if she took it into the kitchen to fill the diary in, it sometimes got left on the table and then moved to the pile by the telly when she cleared the table for supper and, and, and… She carefully laid it back in its appointed place. Ta-da!

She was feeling really peckish and needed lots of energy to charge around with the ponies at RDA, so she drifted towards the fridge to have a rummage for something to eat, something she could easily chomp on in the car on the way.

Chapter 5

Henry fed back to Fenella after his call with Susie.

"Yup, it was Susie and she's thinking of coming for the last weekend of May with Jack and Amelia. Is that okay for you, Fen?"

"More the merrier!" Fenella said happily. She got on well with Susie; they always had a good giggle together. It had been a bit awkward at first when she and Henry had just got married and they had moved into the farmhouse with great ceremony, and Henry's mother was pushed out of the back door.

It seemed a bit unkind as poor Brenda had only recently lost her beloved Neville, but she could see the point. If Henry was taking on the farm, it was only right, and they hoped to fill it with lots of little people as soon as they could.

Fen wondered how Susie felt, particularly as the eldest, to see everything the family owned bestowed on Henry and her. Susie received token items of furniture, the ones that Henry hadn't wanted to keep, like the heavy, old dining table that had been in the family forever and some ugly Victorian paintings that Fen had been delighted to see go. Fen had since seen them hung in Susie and Pete's sitting room, where they looked rather incongruous against the ultra-modern fireplace but somewhat at home in the complete muddle of things that was Susie's eternally happy existence.

It hadn't been that easy for Fenella being the incoming in-law. Fen had been like a rabbit caught in the headlights at first and hadn't dared make any changes to the family home, with its eclectic mix of old and new that had been gathered over several generations. Henry had gaily wafted his arm about, saying that she could do anything she liked, but she felt so tentative just putting away anything that she found hideous or rather "not her cup of tea", as she explained to Henry. She caught him stifling many a "but it's always been…" As a result, they still used a rather groovy 60's style teapot every day for breakfast, alongside a solid silver toast rack.

Funnily enough, she soon realised that Susie was her most conspiratorial ally. She was completely happy with the whole situation of Henry inheriting, and had long ago moved on. Fen had commented in passing to Susie that she couldn't stand cacti – horribly, spiky things that ignored her attempts to starve them to death – every time she went through the conservatory. Susie, with a great flourish, had swept them all into a rubbish sack with lots of silly "oohs" and "ouches" and dumped them in the bin with enchantingly childish quips such as "good riddance to bad rubbish". Fen found Susie such a laugh. Most cathartic.

Henry's mother, Brenda, could still be a bit awkward, and she'd heard her on occasion, in her more lucid moments, complaining to Henry about any changes that she'd initiated, such as, "It was perfectly alright as it had been, that carpet could have lasted another 20 years." It was never to Fen's face, when she was all beaming sweetness and light.

However, Brenda was inclined to sing Fenella's praises to the rafters in front of Susie, extolling what a perfect daughter-in-law she was, which Fen thought was unkind. Fen knew it was only because Brenda didn't like Pete. Mind you, she found Pete not entirely easy herself. He could be a bit pompous and took everything so seriously, and she always felt that he was somehow judging her, with the heavy discussions about "whether it was right in this day and age to banish your children to boarding school", let alone "dairy farmers complaining about the price of milk as they packed their skis for Méribel".

But Brenda seemed to enjoy goading Susie more and more as she became more doolally. She went on and on about how she'd "let herself go", following this up with comments like: "Are you pregnant or just fat?" and how "Pete would be looking elsewhere" if she didn't buck up her ideas. It was relentless, and Fen could quite see why Susie had become more and more reluctant to visit. Henry wasn't at all sympathetic, but then he was out farming all day and Brenda was always on her best behaviour in front of him.

Brenda was becoming increasingly muddled and would wander in through the back door and look around her, frowning in confusion. It was such a shame to see someone who had been a stalwart of the community, a regular and devout member of the local church congregation, in charge of all the church flowers, even on the Parochial Church Council, as well as President of the local WI, come to this.

It was obvious that she couldn't work out quite what had happened, so Fenella had become adept at saying thing like: "Brenda, do you like the new table, chairs, pictures?" or whatever, however long it had been that they had been changed. She hoped it helped, but Brenda would still look round suspiciously, searching out her old, familiar things, as if Fen and Henry were deliberately playing a mean trick on her.

Fen had often got back from being out somewhere to find Brenda searching through the drawers, or she'd been into the study and messing around with the farm records that Henry had to keep meticulously, in search of who knew what. Thank God she couldn't use a computer.

It was awkward and rather irritating, but Henry had refused Fen's suggestion to change the locks and lock up when they went out. His point was that it had been his mother's home so she should come and go as she pleased, that he was never very far away, just somewhere on the farm, and it would be inconvenient to have to remember keys. Also, he liked to leave the door open for the dogs.

It had all become much easier once they had bitten the bullet and employed Moira to move in and look after Brenda on a full-time basis. Moira was a fantastic find; a lovely, cosy and down to earth Scotswoman with a sense of humour and a twinkle in her eye. She kept Brenda occupied, gently put her right on where she was, and who everyone else was, and tried her best to keep her from straying back to the farmhouse.

Chapter 6

Pete and Susie sat with Jack around the dining room table.

Having heard about the great plans for his dad's promotion party, Jack had decided at the last minute that he wanted to do something for his 17th birthday. Susie wasn't very impressed but it did seem a bit unfair not to let Jack celebrate when she was making such a fuss of his dad. He decided that he wanted it on May 26th, but Susie had already promised Henry that they were going to the farm that day and it would be the day after the school trip to London; all a bit much to pack in. She had explained that it had to be on a Saturday to give them all a chance to recover before school and work started again. It couldn't clash with Dad's promotion dinner. It was agreed for the Saturday in between, the 19th.

Jack was very, very clear. Not something infantile like going to Pizza Hut in Reading or skating in Bracknell. Not one of his mum's fancy, over the top dinner parties. Just a party. Basically, he wanted alcohol.

They had had a very, very serious family pow-wow about it around the formal dining room table, in order to give the occasion gravitas. Jack with his grandiose ideas; Pete being very police officer-like, understated, strong and silent; and Susie ready to keep the peace between them. Pete could be quite severe when he chose to be. Ooh, Susie found him very exciting when he was acting all macho.

Jack had very carefully researched the law related to alcohol and under 18s and had printed out the relevant page from his Google search to share and discuss with Susie and Pete. It said quite clearly, *"It is not illegal: For a child aged five to sixteen to drink alcohol at home or on other private premises."* Jack decided on that basis that "anything goes", and had suggested really silly things like champagne or fancy cocktails based on spirits.

Pete had been very firm. "No shots, no Jaeger bombs. Beer, cider and wine only. That is it."

Susie had become somewhat distracted by the fact that it seemed to be perfectly okay to serve up drink to a five-year-old.

Just imagine serving up a bowl of punch at your child's fifth birthday party and having a whole lot of drunk tiny tots racing round your sitting room!

Susie giggled to herself at the thought, but as often happened with Susie, it popped out loud, incurring identical, simultaneous frowns from Jack and Pete.

Gosh, father and son, they looked so alike!

The discussion on how much was acceptable became somewhat heated, Pete erring on the side of "adequate" and Jack not wanting to look like a child in front of his "mates". Jack wasn't very good at negotiating and lost the argument the moment he said, "That isn't fair," in a peevish, whiny voice. Silly boy, thought Susie indulgently; not as mature as he liked to pretend to be.

Apparently, Susie and Pete were most definitely not to join Jack and his guests. In fact, if she and Pete decided to go out that evening, it "would be preferable", after preparing all the food presumably, Susie thought to herself indignantly.

Pete wasn't having any of that however; he had heard of numerous occasions of teenage parties running riot. Jack sulkily agreed that it would be okay if they stayed in, as long as they made themselves scarce and didn't interfere.

They were to be confined to the kitchen apparently, or Pete's study, and most certainly not to greet guests.

"You can be so embarrassing, Mum."

Susie blushed.

Jack refused point blank for his guests to be searched on arrival for spirits. Susie was amazed that Pete accepted that; he even avoided looking at her. She fumed quietly and could only assume that he was keeping his powder dry for later negotiations.

"How many people are you inviting?" asked Pete sensibly.

"Dunno, it doesn't work like that."

"There has to be a limit, Jack. We are not having some uncontrolled occurrence," stated Pete firmly.

Jack looked at the ceiling and sighed.

"Come on, Jack, who are you inviting?"

Jack hesitated and started reciting a list of names petulantly; not exactly an invitation list, more of a stream of schoolmates' names.,

Susie knew some of them – Jessica's Alfie and Hannah, Ellie Webber, Kate's Lily, her Amelia – but not Emily Chittenden, who was in the same year as Amelia and Hannah apparently. Susie had been very surprised when Jack had included both Amelia and Hannah; usually, he distanced himself from their year group and tolerated rather than welcomed his little sister. Perhaps he was actually growing up. When she'd commented as much, Jack had given her a withering look so she hadn't said any more. Susie then started speculating. Perhaps Hannah or this Emily girl was dating Jack? She daren't ask.

"And Aisha?" asked Susie tentatively.

"Nah, she wouldn't be allowed."

"You could still invite her though, make her feel included. It would be nice for her."

Jack shrugged dispassionately, unconcerned about Aisha's feelings. Poor Leah would be sad about that, and it was going to make it awkward when she, Jessica and Susie got together.

Other names dribbled out: Dharmesh Patel, Charlie Powell, Karol Dubicki. The stream of names slowed up and dried up. Actually, it was not nearly as bad as Susie had feared. Visions of Glastonbury-sized masses faded away. She let out a "phew" without thinking, which incurred yet another eyes wide, eyebrows raised, arms folding by Jack. She tried to smile winningly. It didn't really work.

They moved onto food; less controversial and rather less important to Jack, Susie thought, than the booze. Susie's excited suggestions of a party theme based around cars were met with eyes raised to heaven, and the idea of a themed cake for pudding met with a snort. "Mum, I'm not six years old!"

"What would you like then, Jack?"

"I dunno. Pizza, chips, dips, a bit of salad, but not too much, not all your fancy stuff."

You might as well have gone to Pizza bloody Hut.

Susie kept her thoughts to herself and practiced a seraphic smile.

"Could my guests stay over?"

This one Susie and Pete hadn't thought about in advance. Susie glanced at Pete for guidance.

"Where will they all sleep?" asked Pete.

"We can just all bunk down in the spare room, can't we?"

The thought of a Roman orgy popped unexpectedly into Susie's head and she let out an involuntary "Absolutely not!"

They finally agreed that the girls could all sleep in the spare room, in the beds, on the floor, wherever they could squeeze in, but only if their parents gave their absolute permission to Susie or Pete for them to stay over. The boys could camp out in the sitting room. No boys upstairs. Pete was a light sleeper and would be alert for any corridor creeping.

When did things get so fraught with innuendo and difficulty? Susie could understand why the school and Leah had been making such a fuss about the upcoming trip into London. Give these teenagers an inch and they took a mile.

At least Jack's birthday present had not met with such angst and tense negotiation. What would any 17 year old want, other than driving lessons and insurance on the family car? Susie had been dreading the thought of taking Jack out, after the horror stories from Jessica of Alfie missing the gatepost by inches, going out of Tesco car park through the entrance and whizzing round roundabouts the wrong way.

Although she and Leah had howled with laughter at Jessica's hilarious descriptions of the horrendous goings on, it made Susie's hair stand on end. She was secretly thrilled when Jack had said that he couldn't possibly practice in her car because it was an automatic, and he would need to practice his gear shifts in order to pass his test first time.

Hooray! That would all be down to Pete then in his car. God bless Pete, my superstar hero!

She couldn't help but stare at him, her love beaming unashamedly. She reached out her hand, put it on his knee under the table, and playfully worked her hand up his thigh, unseen by Jack. He squeezed her hand gently, his face not changing one little bit from stern father. Oh, but she adored him.

"Right then, that's it." Pete brought the formal meeting to a close. Susie scuttled off to phone Jessica and fill her in, but she couldn't gossip about it with Leah because of the embarrassment of Aisha not being invited.

Chapter 7

The Charlton Academy Year 12 school trip briefing meeting was in the sports hall.

Alfie plonked himself languidly into the plastic seat beside Charlie in the front row, where he had room to splay his long, lanky legs out in front of him.

Charlie said, "Yo, bro", they bumped fists and sat back, arms folded, looking cool, just as Mrs Davies strode purposefully in front of them all and shuffled papers on the lectern.

Mrs Davies was one of those small women who packed a punch just through her presence; it was always surprising to find that she was only five foot two inches tall. She was wearing a suit – a rather old-fashioned one that made her look much older than her actual age of early thirties. Her earrings and necklace were always a bit too large, her haircut too severe, and the whole effect looked as if she'd been raiding her mother's wardrobe to play dressing up.

Ellie shuffled in just in the nick of time, looking hunched and smaller than her long-limbed five foot seven, clutching a pile of books to her chest defensively, her dark, customarily glossy hair looking frizzy and all over the place. Bed hair. She had grey rings under her normally beautiful Elizabeth Taylor eyes. Her wide mouth drooped and not a trace of make-up on her usually plump and glossy lips.

She looked very down today, thought Alfie.

"Yo, sister. Come and join Da Bus Crew." Ellie ignored Charlie's proffered fist and stared ahead, her forehead frowning, her mouth sucked in anxiously, her eyes staring blankly.

"What's up?" Alfie asked. Ellie gestured blandly, shook her head and plonked herself down next to Charlie.

Charlie and Alfie looked at each other questioningly and then shrugged their shoulders in unison. She'd been like that this morning on the bus and hadn't come out of it yet. It happened quite often, but she wasn't saying what was causing it. Not anything they had done evidently, otherwise she wouldn't come and sit with them. They sat ready to listen if needed. They never touched her. She didn't like to be touched.

"Okay – Year 12, please listen. This is important!" boomed Mrs Davies, with an incongruously enormous voice.

She caught sight of the only three kids in the front row, Alfie Hughes, Jessica's son, next to Charlie Powell. They looked like chalk and cheese, yin and yang; Alfie's straight, blond hair and Charlie's black cornrows, except for the fact that they were both so tall and their legs splayed for miles in front of them. Those two seemed to be joined at the hip.

Alongside was Ellie Webber. She wasn't looking at all happy; very down and despondent. There was something amiss there most definitely. As her tutor and first level of pastoral care, Sarah knew she must get to the bottom of it, despite being fobbed off on many an occasion.

"This meeting is to brief you all on the school trip to London on the 25th May. It is essential that you pay attention. Quiet please!"

Mutterings died down quickly.

"Firstly, where are we going? We travel by coach to London, arriving at the coach park in Park Lane in plenty of time to walk through Green Park, in your designated groups of ten, each with two teaching staff, and get a good viewing point of the State Opening of Parliament procession along The Mall."

Muttering.

"What was that?"

Mumbled question from a burly-looking, grinning boy three rows back, who looked around himself, seeking admiration.

"No, The Mall isn't on the Monopoly board, Jack; I'm surprised it isn't," she said, rather sarcastically, as the rest of the class looked at Jack pityingly and exchanged raised eyebrows. Mrs Davies wondered why Jack thought he was so witty when he all he did was get up the noses of all the other kids. "After the procession, we will regroup in Green Park at the place that will be pointed out to you on the way down, the Canada Memorial. You will return to this place directly, and no, not pass Go, Jack."

More groans and sneers towards Jack, with a few hand motions that were not polite.

"We will move onto the War Rooms, again in designated groups. We will then stay together for the museum visit before returning to the park where we will hand out picnic lunches in designated groups. After lunch, we will then go in convoy in..."

A loud chorus of "designated groups".

"To The Houses of Parliament, where we are booked in for a tour.

"Other information: You may bring mobile phones and tablets so you can take endless selfies."

Murmurings.

"Wear sensible and appropriate clothes, uniform is optional."

Mrs Davies ignored shouts of "Thought we was going naked Miss."

"Particularly shoes, there will be a lot of walking." Mrs Davies could not help but notice the sharp movement as Charlie Powell quickly withdrew his feet out of sight under his chair. He was right, they were not in good shape. "Bring a waterproof, and if you need to bring a bag, make sure it is a rucksack – less easily lost. You can bring drinks and snacks but you will be expected to eat the lunch provided by school."

Gagging noises.

"You shouldn't need much money, it is all paid for, but if you want to buy souvenirs, please bring small amounts. All the time that you are on this school trip, all school rules apply, strictly, so no alcohol, no smoking of anything and no vaping, and please keep the designated 15 centimetres apart, I don't want to see you all draped over each other."

A shout of "Yeah, I'm gonna crack out a fag with my TA aren't I."

"Hush now, please," said Mrs Davies, reasserting herself instantly with a simple wave of her hand. "We leave school at 8:45a.m., whether you are here or not. If you are late, you stay behind. Last, but no means least…"

Restless shuffling wafts through the hall. Chairs scrape.

"You must have a permission slip, signed by a person with parental responsibility, before you go on the trip. No exceptions. You will stay at school and work! No slip, no trip. And there are several that I haven't got back yet... Jack Cole, Charlie Powell," she consults her list, "Kieran Maley, Aisha Ahmed, and several others of you. If you have lost yours and need another one, come and see me straight after this briefing."

Murmuring starts up again.

"Okay, any questions?"

Lily Symington sprung up from a row halfway to the back, very upright, challenging, confident, and looked Mrs Davies squarely in the eye. In measured and polite tones, she stated a prepared speech: "Mrs Davies, I think I speak for all of us, but we do feel that you are treating us like kids, making us stick in designated groups with constant adult supervision. Surely we are responsible enough to have free time and do our own thing? Can't we at least have some time to ourselves?"

Murmurs of assent and admiration for Lily's audacity mounted across the room, with a smattering of weak applause. Everyone held their breath; Mrs Davies could be very sharp when challenged.

"Yes, Lily," Mrs Davies could not help but admire Lily's composure, and she was a straightforward, sensible child, so remained restrained, "we do realise that you are all perfectly capable of looking after yourselves, that you go to London on your own outside school, but... and it is a big but, at 16 and 17, you are still officially minors. There is a heightened level of security at the moment particularly after the incident in Westminster and, although we all want to carry on as normal despite it, the school has a duty of care under our child protection policy to safeguard all children from harm.

"Following a detailed risk assessment and taking all factors into consideration, this is what we have agreed for your safety. We would have some explaining to do if we lost any of you along the way. Any more questions?"

Absolute silence. At least Jack had decided to shut up.

"Sure? Right then, thank you for your attention, off you go."

Scrapes and rustles and sudden loud talking as the kids got up to go.

Alfie and Charlie unfolded themselves from their seats, towering over Mrs Davies, waiting patiently for Ellie to arise sluggishly and join them, shielding her from everyone else like bodyguards, and mooched out in their tight-knit, little group. They kept well away from Jack; just because he was on the same bus, he tried to claim to be a member of their crew. He most definitely was not.

Chapter 8

Ellie's stomach dropped.

As she walked the few yards from the school bus stop, Ellie saw her dad's silver BMW, its nose poking out from the garage, crouching menacingly behind her mum's little Smart car.

Oh bollocks. Dad's home.

She heaved her school bag higher on her shoulder, lifted her chin, straightened her uniform just in case, and strode as confidently as she could up the drive, past the immaculate border and the manicured grass, skirted mum's car, slipped down the path at the side of the house, and as quietly as possible, gingerly opened the back door.

Shit.

There, right in the kitchen, was her dad, and he was bang in front of the cupboard with the housekeeping tin, staring in intently.

Shit, shit, shit.

She went rigid. Her heart was thumping loudly in her ears.

Had he noticed? Had Mum said anything?

He turned towards her with a smile on his face.

Phew.

She breathed out long and hard. She always forgot to breathe when she was with her dad.

"Hello Eleanor, my love, did you have a good day?"

Phew again – good mood.

He embraced her in a warm hug and she retracted as much of herself as she could, enveloped by his immaculate soft wool suit, his crisp white shirt and silky, striped tie. Even after a day at work slaving over a hot computer at his newest enterprise, he managed to smell freshly laundered and clean.

Despite his lack of height, he was a handsome man, squeaky-clean shaven, with an athletic body, beautifully manicured hands and a signature little duck's tail. The whole package made him look much classier than he actually was. It had taken a lot of cultivating – she'd seen it emerging over the years, as they moved from place to place, every move heralding slight tweaks to his wardrobe, his accessories, even his haircut, as he carefully observed and learnt from those he perceived to be of superior rank.

He couldn't have been in long as he normally changed straight away, carefully smoothing and hanging each article in its rightful place and placing his shirt and socks in the laundry basket, which gave him the opportunity to check that his wife, Meredith, had kept on top of the laundry, before a shower and a change into his casual clothes with the ubiquitous red trousers, checked shirt and cashmere sweater.

It was Tuesday. A night in for Dad, rather than his usual hectic out playing golf, "Essential exercise and networking, which is why I am so fit, unlike some, Meredith"; at one of his men-only bridge sessions, "Women just don't have the minds and concentration for bridge, do they, Meredith?"; or patrolling his latest restaurant enterprise like a glossy tom cat.

Ellie bent down, shucked off her shoes, neatly aligned them on the rack that was specifically there for that purpose, and slipped into her slippers.

"So, Eleanor, my love, what did you get up to today?"

Ellie racked her brain for the right thing to say. "Oh lots of hard work, thinking ahead to those A-levels, Daddy, you know me!"

"That's what I was worried about, Eleanor, I do know you!" He laughed at his own little joke.

"I've got loads of homework to get through, so I'd better get going on it." She started slinking towards the door.

"Aren't you going to have a cup of tea with me before you go on up? I'm just making one; tell your Daddy all about your day?"

Oh hell, yes or no? What was the right answer? She could feel her heart racing and was terrified that he would notice the guilty look on her face. *For God's sake, pull yourself together girl, it was a simple question.*

"Actually, Daddy, I'm busting for the loo, must dash. I'll just grab a Coke and then I'll fill you in at supper." She whipped a Diet Coke out of the fridge and legged it before he could think about a response, flinging a reconciliatory "See you later", as she dashed through the door, skidded across the hall, nearly fell over the dog, Marmite, who was stretched out on his favourite place on the rug and, being a black Labrador, cunningly camouflaged in the gloom.

Ellie pounded up the smart wooden stairs and met her mum creeping out of the parental suite in her usual mousy way, looking anxious for no good reason at all.

"Hi Mummy, desperate for the loo." She ran into the sanctuary of her bedroom, closed the door firmly, flung her bag on the floor, went into her own en suite, had a really hard and fast, pushed-out pee for maximum sound effects, and flushed the loo as dramatically as she could to make sure they knew that she'd been telling the truth on that one thing.

How did you make a loo flush loudly?

She shook her head at her own ridiculous effort, washed her hands and flopped onto the bed with a sigh of relief. She suddenly remembered poor Pips, her precious, little sister, home all day in bed, sick. She hadn't even dropped in to see her.

I'm a selfish cow.

Ellie bounced up and listened carefully at the door. She heard her dad say something unintelligible to her mum as they passed on the stairs, and then march briskly across the landing – thanks to the characteristic creak on the rebelliously, wayward floorboard that just would not comply with her father's authority – and into their private parental suite. The door closed with a characteristic click. Dad was definitely off for the ritualistic changing ceremony but might reappear at any moment. She would have to catch Pips later.

Ellie, safe in the sanctuary of her room, rummaged in her top drawer and pulled out a box of Tampax. Removing the ones laid casually across the top, she pulled out an envelope that was starting to get grubby and creased from constant use. She took a tenner out of her school bag and added it to the fat wodge of notes.

I think that must be enough now. She stroked the notes affectionately. *It should be more than enough; I can stop nicking the housekeeping. Enough now.*

It had taken nearly nine months to get together this fortune, and actually, it hadn't been too difficult. She'd saved everything she could from her generous allowance of £250 a month, buying enough clothes from Primark to make it look as if she wasn't salting it away, not buying any mags, getting her long, glossy, brown hair trimmed only when her dad accused her of looking scruffy.

By not eating lunch and spending time with friends doing free stuff, such as having film nights with streamed movies, rather than shelling out for the cinema, it was easy to save. Everyone else was saving madly for driving lessons, but she'd decided that her growing pile of secret cash was more important.

The lack of lunches had their benefits too. Her chubby puppy fat had melted away to a model figure. Now that she was 16 going on 17, she had great cheekbones. With her stunning, almost-violet eyes, fashionably bushy eyebrows and sultry lips, Ellie could see that she looked good in the mirror, even if her mum and dad couldn't. Dad still made his remarks and little gibes about her lack of attractiveness. "There is eventually someone out there for everyone, Eleanor, just look at your mother. I was a great catch!"

Her mum never said anything about anything. Ellie hid her body under chunky jumpers and layers so they couldn't see that she had become sleek, deliberately wore not an iota of make-up, and kept her hair in a floppy, boring ponytail.

She'd been taking a twenty-quid note, or occasionally a tenner, each week from the housekeeping tin alongside the tea, when she was legitimately helping herself to her lunch money. It was more from spite than necessity. It seemed the only way that she could exert any power against her father and get back at her mother for being such a wimp. It confused her mum, who seemed to think that it was her own fault that the housekeeping "just isn't going as far as it used to". Her mum was really very stupid, as well as wet and hopeless.

Why couldn't she stand up for herself?

It felt good to count out the notes – she did it twice, £1,245 – and slid them into the envelope that had split along the seam, returning them to the Tampax box, carefully balancing the extras on the top and secreting it back in her drawer.

Smiling with satisfaction, she got changed out of her uniform, carefully folding each item onto the chair, just in case of a random inspection, slipped into her skinny jeans and popped on a voluminous jumper. She then got out her books and stared at them dreamily, shook herself out of her daze, reached for the bottle of Diet Coke, twisted it open with a fizz, took a great swig, and proceeded to look busy and serious in case her parents came in.

"Yup, I'm ready," she said out loud, because it felt so good, and adding a really good and loud, fizzy belch, just because she could without getting told off.

Chapter 9

Charlie let himself in. He was tired and not looking forward to a long shift at the gastro pub later.

He'd had enough run-ins with the owner, Gary Webber, who had ripped him off for "slinking about and not enunciating and speaking properly", whatever that meant.

It was just the way he moved and spoke, man!

Charlie was used to letting himself into an empty house. He turned the key and put a well-practised shoulder to the door – it was stiff on account of it being flimsy and warped; cheap as well as damp. The paint was peeling off it.

He flicked the light switch but nothing happened – either the bulb had gone or there was no money left on the electric – and chucked his rucksack down onto the worn carpet, next to a half-open cardboard box and a pile of magazines that spilt drunkenly across the floor that had sat there for as long as he could remember.

He dropped his rucksack and toed off his shoes. He noted that they were falling apart, which was why he had instinctively hidden them when Mrs Davies had glanced at them at the school trip briefing.

Embarrassing. Everything seemed to be falling apart right now.

God, my feet straight up stink now. I wonder if I can find some clean socks.

He couldn't remember when his mum had last done any washing, and when he had last looked, there wasn't any washing powder, just a heap of clothes festering on the floor, being kicked around the kitchen. He was going have to get his work uniform washed somehow.

It was disgusting. Mr Gary the Main Man Webber would definitely not approve.

No sign of Mum.

It was quiet. He couldn't remember when he'd last seen her, but she was out most of the time anyway, leaving for work before he got home and coming in way after him, even when he came in late. He usually heard her creep in at night, her tread making the same old tune up the stairs, the step, step, long creak, step, step, squeak, rattle of the loose banister, which becomes familiar to people in their own home. When he left in the morning for the bus to school, she was snoring in her bed.

At least her live-in lover, whatever this latest one's name was, wasn't there. He hadn't lasted long. Charlie had thought he was a dick, so wasn't surprised when he upped and left after yet another row. He hoped he wouldn't be back, with the excruciatingly embarrassing making up that always went with it. Charlie shuddered; the walls in this crappy house were too thin.

Mind you, he hadn't been asked to call this one Dad or anything like it. His mum had decided to tell him that her and Charlie were brother and sister. They could be; she was only just over 30. He wasn't sure how far over 30 she was, she would never say. It was almost as if she'd decided that that was exactly what he was, just her brother, and that any sense of parental responsibility had evaporated with her lie. Whatever, she was the only family he had.

She always told the string of inadequate men that drifted in and out of her life that her parents were dead and that she was making her own way. He often wondered about his mum's parents but if he asked her about them, she just ignored the subject. "Best forgotten", "All in the past", was the closest he could get.

There were no pictures of parent-like people anywhere, and he had had a good rummage around when she was out. He hadn't found his birth certificate either, despite a careful hunt. There weren't that many places to look.

He had the distinct impression that she had fallen out with her family when he came into the world, and his best guess was that she would have been a schoolgirl mum and they weren't too happy about it. It made sense.

Perhaps I wasn't even been registered at birth? Perhaps that's why there wasn't no birth certificate?

He had no idea where they had originally emigrated from, or when; she wouldn't even tell him that, which added to his sense of being rootless, not a real person at all.

He padded into the kitchen, instinctively ducking under the doorway because of his height, skirting the mouldering heap of clothes and headed for the fridge. There wasn't anything worth having in it; he wondered why he'd bothered to look. He was always hungry and there never was anything to eat at home. No wonder he had to keep hitching up his pants; he was getting so skinny, his cheekbones were like sharp knives. At least when he had shifts at the fancy pub, he got fed and it was real fancy.

Well decent.

He tried to remember when she had last cooked a meal. He found a piece of cheese sweating in cling film, scraped off the mould with a knife, chomped into it and found he wasn't hungry after all.

Wiping his now greasy fingers down his trouser leg, Charlie rummaged in his rucksack, pulled out the permission slip for the school trip, heaped all the crap that was on the table onto the top of teetering piles where he could, poked the numerous dirty plates, mugs and encrusted knives into the decomposing pile already in the sink, and put the slip in the middle of the kitchen table.

She couldn't miss it, but would she get that she was meant to sign it? *Maybe, maybe not.* He looked round for a pen to put by it as a further clue, but there wasn't one amongst the piles of shit, dirty mugs, pizza boxes and discarded clothes that squatted on every spare surface. He reluctantly took out his only pen from his rucksack, knowing that it was the last he would see of it.

Anyway, at least it was quiet; he'd get some work done before his shift. He'd get on top of it before she got back so she didn't start on at him again. She was always making fun of him, laughing, telling him he was as whack as his dad had been, whoever he was; she'd decided not to remember. He was stupid to think of staying on for sixth form, let alone aiming for university: "All that shit ain't for people like us, Charles."

Fuck Mum and her remarks about his attempt to better himself.

He knew that the only way he was going to get out of this shit hole was by getting an education and getting into college. He knew he could do it. His mates, Alfie and Ellie, "Da Bus Crew", had helped him so much, made him feel better about himself, despite his situation.

When he sat down to do his homework at the wobbly table crammed into his bedroom, his long legs bent almost double, it was Alfie and Ellie in his head, at his elbow, urging him on. That and the support of Mrs Pietruski, the chemistry teacher, who told him he could do it, kept telling him he could do it, meant he knew he could get somewhere if he put the effort in. Maths and chemistry were the easiest, he liked those subjects, he liked the smooth logic, and he didn't have to write loads of pointless sentences.

Chapter 10

A message pinged on Ellie's phone – an invitation to an event on Facebook from Jack Cole.

Ellie immediately scanned it to see who had been invited, who said they were going and the maybes. Jack was a knob, but you couldn't help feeling sorry for him – he tried so hard – and there weren't many parties.

Charlie had already said he was going. Surprising, he always agreed that Jack was a knob too, but a trier.

Ellie messaged Charlie: "Hey dude, why you said yes to Jacks?"

Ellie swiped down the lists. Alfie hadn't responded. Other randoms had said maybe, Daz, Lily. She was surprised to see Hannah had been invited. It wasn't usual to ask people in years below, particularly little sisters. She then saw Emily Chittenden's name, great friend of Hannah and Amelia, and then she got it. Ha-ha, a cunning plan of Jack's to disguise his relationship with Emily.

You aren't fooling anyone mate!

Charlie's reply pinged in: "Jack's mum, renowned cook and nice lady."

Ellie snorted with laughter; Charlie was always hungry and never passed up an opportunity to eat for free.

Ellie messaged Alfie: "Are you up for Jacks? Charlie's going."

Alfie messaged back: 'Yeah, why not, if you and Charlie are. Da Bus Crew on the move. And keep the mums happy in their happy families' fantasy of our kids r best friends and stuff."

Ellie hesitated slightly; she looked forward to an evening away from the tension of her own happy family but would she be allowed? She hit the Maybe button.

"Supper's ready!" Mum yelled from the bottom of the stairs.

"Coming!" Ellie shouted back, as she galloped down the stairs. As Dad was home, she couldn't be late for dinner. By the time she dashed into the kitchen, her little sister was already in her appointed place. Her definitely ill, anxious, little elfin face turned towards Ellie. Ellie gave her a gentle hug.

"Hey, feeling better?"

"Sort of. Good day?"

"Yes, you Pips?" responded Ellie.

"Her name, Eleanor, is Philippa," stated her dad as he sauntered in. He firmly ejected Marmite, who was sniffing hopefully, and took his place at the head of the table.

"Yes, Daddy, sorry."

"Well, Meredith, what delight and delectation have you prepared for us this fine evening?" he asked gaily, as he smoothly removed his starched white linen serviette from its shiny, polished napkin ring.

"Sausage pie, darling, I hope you like it. One of my mother's favourite old recipes."

"Pushing the boat out, aren't you?" her dad enquired sarcastically.

"The housekeeping just doesn't seem to go as far as it used to, darling. I can't think where it all goes."

Ellie stared at her place setting with sideways glances to see if this was going to turn into anything.

Be very careful, Ellie, this is not a good mood. It was starting.

"Really, Meredith, I work hard all day to give you all this fantastic lifestyle; just look at this house, look at the garden, your wardrobe. I do rather expect rather more than sausage pie when I sit down to supper with my loving family round me."

Ellie saw him spit as he enunciated "pie"; it landed just by his perfectly polished water glass. She firmly looked down to avoid any possibility of eye contact.

"So sorry, my darling, I'll make sure that we have a really good slap-up something tomorrow, if you are in?" Looking apprehensively guilty, she placed the sausage pie onto a large plate with a flourish, surrounded it with French beans and placed it ceremoniously on the table, hoping to make it look more important than it was.

Looks like Mum's in for it this evening.

Ellie thought that the sausage pie looked very much like dog food – pink and dense – topped with mashed potato. Mum carefully dug into it, slopped an enormous spoonful onto each plate and passed it somewhat anxiously to her husband and then to Ellie and Pips. Watching carefully for Dad to start, Ellie tucked in. She was starving from missing lunch but unfortunately, the first heaped forkful seemed to taste somewhat like dog food as well.

It struck her as ridiculously funny and made her want to giggle, which was hard to stifle. She caught Pips' eye, who silently mouthed, "What's up?"

Ellie tried hard to smother her mirth but accidentally snorted out loud, because her dad asked softly, "What, Eleanor, appears to be the problem?"

She mumbled rapidly, swallowing her giggle, "Nothing really. Honestly, nothing, Daddy".

"I beg your pardon, Eleanor. I asked you a question?"

"It's hard to explain, Daddy. It's just that I couldn't help thinking that it looks like dog food and then..." She tailed off miserably and thought that as he had already taken her mum to task over their dinner's inadequacies, he wouldn't mind. Sometimes, when she made this sort of remark in criticism of her mum, he would throw his head back, laugh uproariously, and join in, adding to the discomfiture of his wife, but this time, Ellie was wrong, very wrong. He stared at her coldly with a pretend smile on his face. She tried to hold his gaze bravely.

Was that it? Was the teetering crisis over?

He pointedly rose to his feet, slowly and surely, looked Ellie in the eye, a smirk on his face and purposefully marched across the kitchen, out to the hall.

What the hell was he doing?

Ellie was seriously worried. Pips was staring at her, her eyes out on stalks, her knife and fork in her hands, stiff. Her mum was staring at her – her eyes wide, wide open, her body rigid, looking totally shocked. The silence was deafening. They had all stopped breathing. This felt different.

He strode back in, stood behind her, and grabbed her hair. She sat as still as she could, frozen in fear, despite the sudden pressure exerted on her neck.

What was he going to do?

She felt something hard across her throat. She was being strangled. He was strangling her. She tried to scream but was choking and couldn't.

For fuck's sake, someone stop him.

She tried to shout "Mum" but couldn't, and knew that there was no point in struggling. She couldn't help but claw at the ligature with her spare hand. She discovered a hard tag, which she instantly realised was Marmite's collar. He pulled it tight; she was going to die.

Fuck, oh fuck. Oh Jesus Christ. Jesus Christ.

She could feel the pressure tighten sharply and then in a moment, reduce minutely. The little metal bit in the buckle had obviously slotted into the hole in the leather. At least she could breathe now, if she kept it shallow.

What the fuck is he doing? He has never, ever been as bad as this before.

"Now then, Eleanor. Dog food, is it?"

She heard him move over to the cupboards.

Oh my God, he has found out about the missing housekeeping money, he was just biding his time. Oh shit, oh God.

He returned, stood alongside her, a can of dog food in his hand. He ripped off the lid with a pop and a flourish. For a moment, she was relieved.

He grabbed her fork out of her fixed hand – she didn't realise she was still holding it – and spooned the dog food over her plate, gave it a vicious stir, and his eyes holding hers, quietly said, "It looks like dog food, eh? Now eat that. Eat it. Yum, yum." He laughed, a hollow laugh, without one iota of mirth.

She just stared at her plate. *Did he really mean it?* Suddenly, he grabbed a handful of hair again and shoved her forward into the plate, mashing her face into the heap of mush. Her glass of water went flying. Her knife and side plate clattered onto the floor. She felt dog food going up her nose, hot sausage meat squelching into her eyes, she couldn't breathe, it smelled horrible and she gagged.

Her head was yanked back upright. "Now, my love, just eat it. Enjoy!" He returned to his seat, laughed and shook his head with amusement, raising his hands in a magnanimous gesture.

"Now, that was silly," he said, grinning at his family. He calmly spread his napkin on his lap, picked up his knife and fork, and started delicately cutting into his sausage meat. Silence. Absolute silence and the horrified faces of her mum and Pips looking at her – their jaws slack, the pity running down their cheeks like tears of horror and making them look like mirror images.

Ellie didn't know what to do. She couldn't move. She dared to glance at her dad, who neatly forked pieces of food into his mouth, chewed carefully, tidily, and swallowed before repeating the procedure. Marmite pottered in, wagging his tail, grinning at everyone, looking at them all in turn for a reaction to his forbidden presence, and confused by the smell of his food at the wrong time of the day and that distinctive, tantalising sound combination of tin and fork.

"Eleanor, please eat," her dad suddenly said, very softly, without raising his eyes from his plate, forking in the next mouthful, making not just her but her mum and Pips visibly jump, even though it was said so quietly. Ellie shakily followed his lead, picked up her dog food-smeared fork, clumsily cut away a chunk of the mashed-up mess and, hands trembling, put it in her mouth.

She chewed, it tasted revolting, it smelt so strong, the texture was repellent. Waves of nausea flooded through her. She decided to just swallow it, she knew she had to. It wasn't easy with the collar so tight.

How much will I have to eat to satisfy him? How long could this last?

She carefully put together another mouthful, popped it in and tried to swallow it whole without chewing. If only she could wash it down with a swig of water. She daren't ask, she daren't even reach out to place her water glass upright.

She gulped vigorously, mind over matter, and the mess went down, but then immediately, with a massive surge, it came straight back again, gushing through her nose and her mouth with that horrible, uncontrolled feeling of rushing liquid and lumps and acid, and an appalling, ugly, gurgling sound that resonated in the silence. Fuelled by the volume of fizzy Coke from earlier, it surged again, a rising second wave.

A grisly dark liquid with oily specks of dog food splashed on top of the revolting dish like grotesque gravy, down Ellie's front, on her hands, where she'd tried in vain to hold it back, in her hair, where it had become torn from her customary ponytail by his heavy hands. Humiliatingly, whether it was the fear, the muscular spasm, or the violence of it all, she wet herself. She hung her head, tried to hide her head in her filthy, stinking, sick-covered hands, and silently sobbed and gurgled and heaved and shook, and tried not to be sick again.

After forever, her dad started speaking quietly in a measured, soothing tone. "Oh dear, Eleanor. I think that you have now completely spoiled our evening and I have quite gone off my dinner." He then added cheerfully, "I know, let's go to the restaurant to eat, owner's perks. When we come back, I am sure that the kitchen will be spotless and every trace of that preposterous pie, your silly behaviour and its filthy consequences will have gone."

Ellie stayed slumped at the table. She couldn't see her mum and Pips but she could feel their petrified silence and revulsion, and backward glances as they rose up as one, shuffling out before him, their clothes whispering their inner thoughts. She could hear the clack-clack of Marmite's toes as he danced around them all, incongruously happy, out through the door, ahead of her dad.

As he left, he turned round and said, with a jarring, humorous quality to his voice, a fake laugh, "And for God's sake, Eleanor, take off that ridiculous collar."

Chapter 11

Susie invited Caroline and Thomas to Pete's promotion dinner party, but she hadn't meant to.

Bother, bother, bother.

She'd got caught out in the Yummy Mummy deli, where she'd gone armed with her dinner party list and had bumped into both Leah and Caroline.

It was a risk she always took by shopping in the village, as you always bumped into people you knew. Charlton wasn't exactly an enormous place and all the main facilities were concentrated along the High Street, in a tidy, archetypal English village row: the church, with its old Rectory tucked behind it, home of said Caroline and Thomas, the old-fashioned pub, the post office store, the butcher, and the interesting independent shops, selling trendy artisan wares. The ordinary supermarket was deliberately out of the centre, on the way to Leah's, and they had built the imposing, modern Charlton Academy on the outskirts. All the nice shops were here in a charming, traditional strip.

Leah enquired chirpily about start times for the dinner party in front of Caroline. It would have been really, really mean to not then extend the invitation to her. Actually, Susie had been a bit flustered and tried to make out that she'd only just issued the invites and that of course Caroline and Thomas were included. In her usual way, she overdid it and Caroline was perfectly aware that she hadn't been going to invite her.

Oh dear.

Thomas, quite extraordinarily, could actually come, apparently. Usually it was "He is staying up in London", and it always made it difficult with the seating when Caroline came along on her own. She was inclined to overdo the flirtatiousness with the men; it was really, really embarrassing. Pete was stony-faced when she'd put him next to her last time, when she'd yet again somehow wheedled an invitation out of Susie. How did she do that? How did she know that Susie was entertaining? She seemed to have some sort of special invitation-hunting radar.

It was slightly awkward with Caroline. Although they had been at school together, in the same house, and often doing the same activities, it never felt like a really genuine friendship, certainly not the easy give and take way it was with Leah and Jessica. Caroline had always tagged along at school, always wanting to be her partner, always wanting to sit next to her. Susie was too nice to stop her.

Somehow, Caroline had even followed her across Europe to join her as a chalet bird in Méribel.

How had that happened?

She couldn't remember now.

It was where Susie had met Pete when he arrived as a chalet guest. Caroline had obviously been very, very miffed when Pete chose Susie and not Caroline. She'd done her level best to put her off him: "He's not your type", "Your parents will have a fit!", and "You can do so much better than that". It was no wonder they had drifted apart when, at the end of the season, Susie had moved in with Pete.

Susie thought because they'd taken such completely different directions that Caroline wouldn't see Susie as a suitable friend anymore. Susie had married her beloved Pete, a down to earth policeman (oops, that should be police officer; Pete was always putting her right on that) who "Couldn't be doing with all that elitist private school nonsense", and Caroline had married Thomas Hanson-Carr, the Audi-driving, hooray Henry. Actually, that was a bit cruel, he was perfectly nice and sweet; in fact, very little *hooray* about him, and actually, nothing like her own brother, Henry.

Thomas came from a wealthy family and had absolutely oodles of money, but he was a gentle soul. He had the most incredible eyebrows that sprouted madly in all directions, and the kindest puppy-dog eyes and plump cushions for cheeks. He couldn't help it, but he was inclined to be a bit straight-laced and pompous. He had a most endearing habit of getting his words and phrases mixed up. It had caused side-splitting hilarity between Jessica and Leah when Susie reported that he'd told Pete, "You have no contraception what I go through on that commuter train to London."

They'd stayed in Christmas-card contact, when Susie actually got round to doing her Christmas cards.

Quite extraordinarily, when Caroline had unexpectedly moved to Charlton four years ago, she'd pounced on Susie as her long-lost friend and never let her go. Wherever Susie went, whether RDA or NADFAS (must remember that subscription, it had escaped and gone missing again), Caroline would appear too, regaling everyone with stories about Susie at school and tucking her arm possessively through hers. Susie was far too nice to remove it, so everyone assumed that they were the greatest of friends.

She found Caroline a bit too much, parading around her house as if she was the chatelaine of a stately home, graciously inviting everyone to her house-warming to admire her great taste and wealth.

Was it too nasty of her to think it; a bit of a snob for no good reason?

They had been to a private school but quite frankly, it had been a very mediocre one, and not exactly up there with Roedean and Benenden. Absolutely no one had ever heard of it and she doubted that it still existed, but Caroline always tried to make out that they were very much grander than they were.

Caroline was more and more magnificent to look at. Her brown hair had definitely been encouraged in the direction of auburn recently, and fell like a silk curtain around her immaculately made-up face, her big, green, pussy-cat eyes open wide as if she was permanently enchanted by everything, her lush mouth just too sensuous for words. Susie wondered whether she'd been trying Botox; her skin certainly looked far less baggy and wrinkled than her own.

Ouch, Susie, that was a bit mean.

Caroline worked out regularly at her private gym and she would glide around, with beautiful deportment, like a perfect Stepford wife on casters, kindly bestowing her gracious smile on those beneath her. She certainly dressed the part too, carefully observing the things that made you out to be of the right class – the right tweed coat, the scarf tied just so, the outrageously expensive dresses from Hobbs.

Caroline made sure that she did all the right things, went to the right events in season: Henley, the Steward's Enclosure, of course, Royal Ascot on Ladies Day, and somehow, she always managed to wangle tickets for Twickenham and Wimbledon.

How did she do that?

Susie and Pete would love to go to Wimbledon and Twickers, but thought the others were rather phoney events.

Caroline had met Thomas at a house party in Cambridge, set her cap at him, and totally convinced him that she was the perfect marriage material. He had proposed on one knee while skiing in St Moritz. They had had a wonderfully grand wedding at Thomas' family's Scottish pile with kilts everywhere, and every bell and whistle as well as both icing and cherries on the top.

Susie had been surprised to be invited to the wedding with Pete, who stood out, not just for being the most handsome man there, but because he had refused to hire a morning suit and was not going to wear a skirt for anyone. Susie had spent most of the time being extra nice to Caroline's parents, who seemed to have been very much side-lined in favour of the gracious Hanson-Carrs.

She did wonder why hubby Thomas was "away a great deal". He did seem to spend an inordinately long time "in town" but then, Susie giggled to herself, so would I be if I had to put up with Caroline every day. *Oh gosh.* She didn't like to be so mean.

Another reason that Caroline hadn't been invited was that her doted on, one and only son, William, went to the very smart indeed Westminster School, which also set Caroline and Thomas apart from that social circle. It really didn't matter a fig to Susie, but Caroline went on and on about it rather a lot.

Anyway, Caroline and Thomas were coming, like it or lump it. Caroline drove Susie round the twist but she couldn't help but feel a teensy weensy bit sorry for her that she had to go through life trying so hard. She didn't seem to have any friends but Susie. Sad.

The trouble was, with the addition of Caroline and Thomas, it made the numbers suddenly rather large. Eight was a good number, but ten would be a squash. In her calculations when caught on the hop, she'd thought it would be fine, but she'd got a bit muddled when counting up her guests and found that she'd forgotten to include her and Pete. *Oops! Daft as a brush!*

If she put the extra leaf into the old family dining table (Where had she put that? In the garage?), she could sit ten comfortably, but it meant that you could barely get round it in their regular, executive home dining room. At least her waiter and waitress, also known as Jack and Amelia, earning a bit of cash, were so skinny, they would be able to squeeze through.

It was a good thing that Kate Symington hadn't been able to come. Kate's Lily was in the same class as Jack, Alfie, Ellie and Aisha, so it had seemed a stroke of genius to ask her, but she'd already signed up for a shift at Gary's gastro pub, and being such a decent sort, didn't want to let anyone down by cancelling.

For one thing, where would she have sat? On Pete's knee, perhaps, she'd like that; they all agreed he was so, so handsome. My gorgeous man, and he is all mine!

Then she wondered what Caroline would have thought, arriving at a dinner party, dressed to the nines, to find her cleaner there, and Gary turning up to find himself sitting next to one of his waiting staff. He most definitely wouldn't like that. Susie laughed out loud at the thought of it. She wished that Kate had been able to come; it would have been a hoot.

Kate was a great girl and Susie admired her enormously. Kate could always be relied on to be straight down the line and say exactly what she thought. At first, it came over as rather antagonistic, a bit short, until you got to realise that her sharp comments were meant to be ironic and funny. She was a reliable, completely unflappable friend.

Susie felt a bit sorry for Kate being on her own. She'd never actually married Lily's father – "he whose name must not be mentioned". They had been together for ages apparently, until he had just upped and left her soon after Lily was born. Ever since then, Kate had soldiered on as a single parent with not one penny from "Voldemort", who had mysteriously disappeared (it made Susie giggle how they had taken to calling him that; it all seemed so appropriate).

Kate had insisted on working around Lily, always being there for her when she got home from school, and so it had been convenient to clean people's houses. In the school hols, she could always take Lily along, and Lily was such an angel that no one minded a bit.

Now that Lily was grown up, well almost, Kate and Lily had both started taking shifts at Gary's gastro pub. In fact, when she and Pete had been to try it out just after it had reopened, Kate had been behind the bar and Lily serving tables. They had another boy from school actually doing their table (gosh, we do live in an incestuous place), the same year as Jack. Charlie, she thought his name was, although she couldn't remember his second name. A really, really nice boy though, quiet, intricate hairstyle (corn trails?), and a great mate of Alfie's apparently, part of the bus gang, often round at Jessica's with the lovely Ellie, apparently.

Kate must have been very, very young when she had Lily because she was several years younger than the rest of the group, or at least Susie thought she must be. Without her make-up on, Kate looked the same age as their girls. She had a short, sharp haircut and sharp features, and always looked a bit cross. Her dark eyebrows had been plucked into thin slivers above the darkest, longest eyelashes ever seen. She was also stick-thin – probably all that energetic cleaning.

Why was everyone else so thin? It really, really wasn't fair. Anyway, enough of all that, Susie, Kate isn't even coming and Caroline is.

Chapter 12

Caroline was pissed off and upset.

She didn't like being an afterthought. Susie had quite clearly not been going to invite her to Pete's promotion dinner party. Susie had gone very pink in the face when Leah had let the cat out of the bag in the deli.

It was awkward with Susie. Susie always made her feel that she was doing her a favour in continuing their friendship. Perhaps she should have left it at the school gates. Susie occasionally included her in her dinner invitations, on sufferance it appeared, and only when Susie knew that Caroline knew about it.

Who was feeling sorry for whom though? Caroline thought that Susie was getting more and more enormous, and had completely let herself go. She should be careful because Pete, that husband of hers, was gorgeous in anyone's eyes.

Susie's home was a typical executive monstrosity; a muddle of mismatched styles, all shrieking out loud in their garishness, with a minute garden and, she could not believe this, a stand of pampas grass. *How naff can you get!* She'd told Susie with glee that it was rumoured to be the secret code to show you were swingers. She'd even added, "How about it then? Pete is gorgeous!" Susie had gone bright red; she coloured so easily.

It just seemed these days that everyone was ignoring her and it was a very lonely place to be. To be honest, when she said "everyone", it was Thomas that she was bothered about. He seemed to be even more airy-fairy than usual, went along with everything she said without discussion or argument. He would go through the motions of loyal husband but there was no real warmth; it felt like an act.

She would just have to show him what he was missing at Susie's dinner party. She would dress to show off her figure – she spent enough time at the gym working on it – and go overboard with the rocks. She loved to flash Thomas' grandmother's three-stoned diamond ring, letting it do the talking about just where she stood in society. She would make him proud of her.

It was hard to stand out against the naturally beautiful Leah and her gorgeous collection of silky saris, of which she seemed to have masses – something to do with exchange of wedding gifts, she'd once explained in one of her rather earnest "let me explain my culture" lectures.

She knew that Meredith the mouse would be no competition; she always looked grey and her face always twitched anxiously. Whenever Gary made one of his little digs, which he seemed to revel in, she would paw at her face, exactly like a little rodent washing its whiskers. The image made Caroline smirk to herself.

Jessica, although naturally drop-dead gorgeous, and a definite rival in the best figure department, even though she hadn't been near a gym in her life, always dressed very unadventurously and somehow missed the mark. Probably because she proudly proclaimed that she'd found amazing bargains from downmarket stores like M&Co and New Look. No wonder.

Yup, she would make Thomas take notice of her; she would get him to pay her attention if it was the last thing she did.

Pete had developed an off-hand attitude too. He was so drop dead gorgeous, so sexy, and she'd never understood why he had chosen Susie when he could have had her on a plate. Not forever, obviously – he would have been her temporary "bit of rough", a bit of fun. He just had that look about him, that masterfulness, a strong and silent type.

It amazed her how it wound everyone up when she flirted with Pete, Pete especially. He became deliciously steely and she could always see Susie looking on with pathetic Bambi eyes. It was meant to annoy and wind up Thomas, particularly after the little white lie about her and Pete. It wasn't her fault; she'd been goaded into it. There's only so much you can take of a sheepish, lacklustre husband who patronises you like a naughty daughter instead of a wife. He had needed shaking up.

He had innocently – or had it been so innocent, you could never tell with Thomas – commented on how "off" Pete had been with her at a drinks do. She, in a fit of pique at the implied insult, had taken perverse pleasure in blaming it on Pete's wounded pride, providing Thomas with salacious detail of her fantasy encounter with Pete and how it had only been allowed to be a "one-off". It could be so easily true, after all, if you compared her figure, her sense of style, her sophistication, to tubby, messy, clumsy and naive Susie.

Her bombshell hadn't had the desired effect. Thomas had been dignified, hadn't said very much, in fact, nothing at all. She'd watched the emotions crossing his face like a silent movie. He'd stood there stiff and upright, looking somewhere just above her eyebrows, and had then quietly withdrawn like a butler bowing out of a dinner party, and retired to the library.

Had he believed her? He hadn't mentioned it since. Perhaps he had seen through it. Who knew?

It hadn't made him notice her, pay her any more attention, and in fact, he just seemed to have moved to

London and spent less and less time with her. That also really pissed her off.

Perhaps she could surprise Thomas. He never seemed terribly keen to see her in town, but for God's sake, he was her husband, and could jolly well take her out for a nice lunch. He just seemed so preoccupied these days, making excuses to stay up in town, and she needed attention; after all, she wasn't getting it from anyone else! She'd heard that Heston's place, Dinner, in Knightsbridge, was to die for. If she booked a table there and then descended on him with a casual ultimatum, he could hardly refuse. She flicked on her phone to Google it.

If she timed it for a Tuesday or Thursday, she could perhaps drop in on William and see him playing football at Westminster School. You couldn't get much better than Westminster, except perhaps for Eton, but Thomas was an old Westminster, as was his father and grandfather, whose claim to fame was that he was there with Nigel Lawson. Of course, William had followed in their footsteps into the hallowed halls that snuggled secretly behind Westminster Abbey.

She'd become used to calling it "station" instead of "sport", and by dropping this little-known idiosyncrasy into the conversation, she could highlight how William was at such a good school, even though it seemed to fall on deaf ears around here. At least Thomas' parents were appreciative.

Perhaps they should move up to London. There were so many interesting things to do.

She wondered, not for the first time, why on earth she'd thought it a good idea to move to Charlton at all.

She'd never seemed to fit in anywhere that they'd lived, always ending up feeling that she was on the edge of everything, never really accepted by the people that she thought of as "her class", however hard she tried, and by God she'd tried. But at the same time, just not "getting" the hoi polloi, who she just felt nothing in common with. She'd floated about, neither fish nor fowl, and had never made any close friends. It was actually rather lonely.

If only Thomas had been more supportive. She always felt that his whole family ganged up on her, and Thomas took their side. She tried so hard to do the right things, say the right things, but somehow, she felt that they always looked down on her, just a bit.

It was too subtle to make a fuss about, but the odd barbed comment would find its target, such as the time she'd asked her mother-in-law, "What is that lovely perfume you're wearing? It is divine?" The collective wince was so slight as to be almost imperceptible other than to someone as acutely tuned in to such things as Caroline. It was only when mother-in-law had replied, with a delicate emphasis on the second word, "The *scent* I am wearing this evening is Arpege; I am so glad that you like it." Ouch. She'd screwed that one up.

Her mother-in-law had gone on and on about William being an only child. Caroline received no sympathy at all for having had pre-eclampsia and nearly dying to have him, and it was always inferred that she was being rather selfish in not going through a near death experience again for the sake of the Hanson-Carr family proliferation. At least he'd been a boy. A girl would never have done.

She'd genuinely thought that living near Susie would be the answer to her friendlessness. She would have an instant circle of like-minded girlfriends through Susie, without having to make any effort to watch her every word, and would have instant acceptance – perfect! Susie had made the miraculous transition from boarding school, jolly hockey sticks, to ordinary housewife living in commuter land, churning out a boy then a girl, and had seemed eternally and blissfully happy in her somewhat sporadic communications at Christmas.

From Susie's letters, Charlton sounded a fun area, with loads going on with NADFAS, where she would be able meet the right sort of art-loving people, RDA, which seemed to attract Home Counties' girls from good boarding schools, and a decent golf course for Thomas, with an easy commute to London when he needed to get to business meetings.

Idly googling, she'd found that there were a few decent "real" houses in the old part of the village, despite all the ghastly closes of executive homes, clones of Susie's, which tended to sprawl out in a tatty ribbon towards London.

When Charlton Old Rectory had come up for sale, it was ideal. A glorious drawing room opening out onto a raised terrace, overlooking a two-acre garden (with pony paddock beyond), a morning room, an enormous, old kitchen with butler's pantry, a stately dining room with a fantastic gothic-style fireplace, and a library for Thomas to use as his office at home.

They'd needed to rejig upstairs to create proper en suite bathrooms for all of the six bedrooms but she'd enjoyed that. She'd loved the opportunity to redecorate from top to bottom, incorporating their collection of grand and glorious antiques, some inherited from Thomas' family and some meticulously chosen over the years, and Thomas' old family portraits.

The whole project had taken several years, and multiple dashes to London for just the right thing in Beauchamp Gardens and at Christie's sales, but it had been worth it because it was a triumph. It most certainly looked good enough for *Homes & Gardens*, if not too good.

Thomas' parents had been somewhat lackadaisical when it was all finally revealed, and Caroline had been mortified when she'd overheard her mother-in-law saying, "If only she didn't try so hard. It's all just so matchy-matchy. It's positively exhausting!" She didn't tell Thomas she'd heard.

Thomas himself had said it was, "Very nice, darling", and then William had said, "What we need is a good party to bash it about a bit and make it look homely." She didn't really get what they'd meant at all, but boys will be boys. It was just clear that no one appreciated all the effort that she'd taken to make it look so nice for them all.

When she'd invited Susie to her housewarming, she'd seemed oblivious to all her hard work and creativity, not really listening to all the trials and tribulations that Caroline had overcome to get it just right, and then of course, Susie had promptly spilled her champagne on the new cream carpet. Thank God it hadn't been red wine. Caroline had very sensibly anticipated that in advance.

Apart from the inbuilt clumsiness, or even despite it, everything had always seemed to go right for Susie. She'd always been just a bit better at everything than Caroline at school and always so meekly self-effacing. She sang in all the choirs, was super-fit and sporty, always in the first team for everything; it was a long time ago. Susie played piano well and violin in the orchestra, was always given parts in plays and was always so popular. She'd romped through her GCSEs, getting four more As than Caroline, and then straight As at A-level, although they were in arty-farty subjects. *Could drama really be classed as an A-level subject?*

Even after leaving school, Susie had found life easy, excelling as a star pupil at Ballymaloe, the world's best cookery school, before hitting Méribel for a season. She skied like a dervish and cooked like a Michelin-starred chef, and was always receiving unctuous letters of intense thanks from all the enchanted chalet guests. At least being Susie's friend had got her the job in the chalet, but not as cook, more the housekeeper, or in truth, more as the cleaner.

And then Susie had grabbed Pete right from under her nose. *How had she done that?* Caroline had the looks, the charm and knew how to work it. Susie had had a better figure then, and her crowning glory, the blonde hair, but she was so scatty and giggly that surely it shouldn't have been enough to win top prize in the man hunt. She'd rapidly pumped out Jack and then Amelia with great gusto – "They just pop out like peas" – and revelled joyously in her motherhood.

But look at Susie now, going to seed, middle-aged spread, whatever you wanted to call it, but despite her rundown appearance, she still managed to be so bloody happy. Unlike her and Thomas, Susie and Pete still seemed so in love. Thomas called Caroline "darling", opened car doors, bought her nice presents, kissed her dutifully before leaving and on his return, but he didn't really give her any genuine affection or warmth.

Pete clearly adored Susie in his understated way; fiercely, almost like a wolf protecting his pack. He never actually touched her in public, but was always hovering nearby, watching her. Susie openly worshipped Pete as if he were some divine being; no wonder Susie's mother always called him God!

Was she a bit jealous of Susie? Perhaps a bit, but look at what she had in comparison. A fabulous lifestyle, a wonderful home, incredible holidays all over the world, designer clothes, handbags and shoes, and her bright, handsome boy at an excellent school.

It had surprised her when she'd moved to Charlton that not one of Susie's other friends had their children at private schools. In fact, the calibre of Susie's friends had been a bit of a disappointment altogether. They all seemed to go to Charlton Academy down the road. A fancy name for the local comprehensive school. "Why pay for it when you can get a good education for free?" Susie had chortled happily.

As comps go, Charlton's was a good one, but, all the same, she was frankly amazed that Susie had sent Jack and Amelia there – her father would be spinning in his grave. She would bet that Susie's brother Henry's children wouldn't be going to their local comp; they were probably at their old prep school, but then he had "married well".

Perhaps it was a bit of envy on Susie's part that she'd been so tardy in extending me an invitation to the promotion celebration?

It must be difficult for Susie when she saw Caroline, and similarly, Henry with his Fenella, and realised what she'd foregone by choosing to marry policeman plod Pete.

Caroline sighed. But even so, after being such close friends for all this time, she'd had the temerity not too ask her to her sodding dinner party until she'd been caught on the hop.

Bugger that!

Chapter 13

Pete was exhausted.

There were persistent rumours at police headquarters of an "unspecified terrorist threat". It kept rumbling around; it wouldn't go away but had no substance, no fact, attached to it. It kept being brought up at meetings, but then set aside. The threat level throughout the UK had been raised to Severe, and the response raised in turn to Heightened.

The riots and anti-Muslim protests, the so-called tit for tat killings and unprovoked attacks on mosques were enormously disturbing.

Poor sods, just ridiculous and completely out of order. Who was behind them?

It seemed like a co-ordinated effort, but they were occurring as lightning strikes in random cities, even large towns. It was the response from the victims that didn't feel right. Whole communities were rightly indignant and apoplectic with anger, but it wasn't just that; it felt that there was something more sinister looming.

It was like chasing shadows and was exceedingly frustrating. If it came to anything, would the police be blamed for not taking any specific action? Yes, he was attending the State Opening of Parliament, but would extra boots on the ground make any difference?

They were as ready as they could be. The Commander on duty each day in the Control Room was alert, on his toes, ready. They had learned so much after 9/11, when the Gold System had been put in place. A whole set of rooms were labelled in readiness, should the force need to respond to a threat. Pete's own office had its alter ego, "Gold: Fire Service", inscribed on the door, underneath "Tactical Firearms Unit".

The rota for instantly setting up telephone helplines was in place. The BBC were primed as key communicators. They had sorted out the mobile network across the whole of the country to ensure automatic and instant priority to service calls.

Pete sighed in frustration. No matter, nothing more to be done, and there was tonight to get through.

Dear Susie, in her inimitable way, was making an enormous song and dance about this dinner party. It had been designed as a celebration of his promotion, but he wasn't clear whether it was meant to be for his benefit or hers. The guests were what Susie described as the "school crowd", who had very little to do with his work but who all happened to be members of the golf club. He couldn't think why they were appropriate to celebrate this occasion, if it needed celebrating at all.

And Caroline was coming. *Why?* Susie always felt sorry for her, but she didn't have any reason to do so whatsoever. It was always tricky when Caroline came. He just hoped that Susie hadn't put her next to him; it was just too much to cope with for a whole evening – the pasted-on smiles, the general enquiries, the polite conversation, and the stories told too brightly and not knowing how to look when Caroline placed her hand on his arm in an overly intimate way. She'd been kept in their lives beyond her sell-by date. He wished Susie would wipe her out and make her disappear from their lives.

He hung up his uniform on the wardrobe knob so that it could relax, stretch and air, brushing off imaginary fluff with a firm hand before having a long shower, with the water turned on as hard as it could go, revelling in the jets of spray pounding his shoulders and massaging his scalp. He towelled himself vigorously, ran the electric razor over his stubble, and went to the wardrobe to get out his clothes.

The dress code was lounge suits, apparently – what planet was Susie on? Of course, his preferred shirt was still in the laundry pile in the corner of the bedroom.

Darling Susie, she could be just so irritating. What did she do all day?

He rustled through the rack, finding a half decent shirt that he wouldn't be ashamed of wearing in company, checking carefully for the right number of buttons. Another simple enough job that Susie never got round to.

Scrutinising his appearance in Susie's long mirror, he flattened his curly hair slightly and went downstairs towards the increasingly frantic clattering and banging that was coming from the kitchen.

"Anything I can do, love?" he asked, more out of politeness than desire to get involved in the chaos. Susie was best left to her own devices. He marvelled at the way she could conjure up the most over the top, gourmet cuisine from a kitchen that looked like the Battle of the Somme. No wonder she wouldn't let anyone help clear the table or get within an inch of the kitchen. The only people who were allowed to see the Susie's mess and disorder were Jessica and Leah. Quite a privilege, he thought, ironically.

Receiving no coherent response from Susie, and a shrug of the shoulders and "Don't ask me!" look from Amelia, who seemed to be doing something very important with some vegetables, Pete called out, "I will go and sort out the drinks, okay?", as he wandered into the relative calm of the dining room.

The table looked wonderful, all laid up with the best cutlery that Susie's parents had given them as a wedding present, and the navy-blue striped dinner service that had been on their wedding list for Susie's posh friends and relations to buy.

Each place had been carefully laid, due to Susie's Ballymaloe training. With the vases of lilies, navy candles and crisp white serviettes, it looked nice. Well done, Susie, and at least she had tidied up in here, although some of the piles of God-knows-what were getting precariously high out of sight in the kitchen. He reached for the drinks tray and started to get out the glasses and bottles.

Chapter 14

Pete and Susie were clearing up the aftermath of the dinner party.

"How did you think it went?" asked Susie anxiously.

"It was fantastic, love. You did me proud. Thank you. The food was delicious as ever, presentation exceptional, and you know I love a great big lump of meat. Here, give me a cuddle." She was quite pissed, her cheeks were flushed and her eyes bright. She hadn't held back on the vino, but he had been, as ever, circumspect; he liked to stay in control.

He wrapped his arms round her, thinking that he would need longer arms if she put on any more weight. His chin resting on her blonde head, stroking her hair. He gave her a squeeze, kissed her forehead soundly, pushed her away and turned back to the matter of restoring order. He liked to get it all done and dusted before going to bed, although Susie always pleaded with him that she could do it all in the morning. He wasn't entirely convinced that she would, and hated to get up to all the mess and to have it still there when he got home from work.

"I thought Caroline was on good form!" chirped Susie.

"Hmm, yes."

What else could he say?

"Thomas is away a lot again apparently. She was moaning about it over the drinks. It's crazy how he feels the need to stay in London when it is only such a short distance on the train. He always makes the excuse that he can't drink with his clients if he has to drive home from the station, and whenever Caroline suggests that she join him in London, he tells her that it's all business and she'll be bored. She can't win, poor love. No wonder she's starved of affection."

"What on earth makes you say that," Pete asked, genuinely puzzled.

"Well, she can't keep her hands off you for a start, and it always makes you look really, really uncomfortable. Let alone the looks Thomas gives you!" Susie laughed, as she wrapped the cheese. She'd carefully kept all the individual wrappings but seemed to be putting them back in all the wrong ones.

Pete made a non-committal grunt and Susie burbled on.

"Leah looked stunning as usual. I'd love a sari!" Susie swished around an imaginary sari and did what Pete assumed was meant to be an Asian dance. A vision of a baby Asian elephant inadvertently popped into his mind.

"Leah is a hoot. She brought me and Jessica a copy of the Koran, not a proper one, but a paperback version, translated into layman's English. She tells me she's scared that one day, something will happen to us all and if we haven't converted by the time we die, we won't go to Muslim heaven because we are infidels or something like that. I wish she'd stop giving me the lectures but apparently, she fears for her friends."

Pete managed to fit in another grunt.

"Actually, I might have a go at reading it; it will be interesting and then I can understand better where Leah is coming from when she won't shake hands with you men and suchlike. I really, really can't help but love Leah's complete and utter all-consuming faith, but it can be very, very hard to understand.

"She was so sweet the other day, telling Jessica and I all about it. I can't remember very much of what she said but she was saying that it was quite opposite to all the stuff that keeps being spouted on telly whenever they go on about the terrorists. Islam means peace, kindness and compassion. Apparently, you are meant to lead a healthy, active life and be kind and chaste, honest and forgiving, and I can't quite remember the rest. Patient? Anyway, it all sounded very much like everything we were taught as children in Bible Studies, but that is why she brought us the Korans. Jessica can't be bothered, says she doesn't go much on the whole Christianity thing. I think she's an agnostic or an atheist; actually, I'm not sure of the difference, let alone taking on board Islam."

Pete knew that Gary made a big thing of Leah's beliefs, had held his hands up saying, "Hello Leah, I know, I know, don't touch." It was very rude, made Farrukh look livid and made Meredith cringe like a hurt mutt. For God's sake, we live in a multicultural society. Pete thought that it was fair enough, make a point of it in your own home, but did not appreciate Gary doing it in his.

Farrukh was so polite and dignified, a really good man, and Pete didn't like Gary. Gary was obviously a city boy, born and bred like Pete, in a similar terraced house in a very ordinary street.

Why couldn't he just be himself instead of putting on airs and graces?

His latest affectation seemed to be a signet ring on his pinkie, like Henry wore, and that pink shirt was just OTT. At least Henry's ring was genuine and had come down through the family. Pete wouldn't be seen dead wearing jewellery, except his wedding ring of course.

"I think they loved the food. Gary, eat your heart out with your fine fancy restaurant! Leah is always super complimentary anyway, bless her."

Again, Pete didn't know what to say so sort of muttered encouragingly.

"You boys woofed down that lamb. I had hoped that there would be some left for cold lunches for the rest of this week!" Pete couldn't help glancing at Susie's burgeoning stomach and thinking that it was probably a good thing that they had despatched it all. She used to have such a great figure. He used to be the envy of all his mates, but even so, he still loved his quirky, eccentric girl, just wished that she had a bit more self-control in the eating department.

"Wasn't it hilarious when Jessica started talking about Ellie and how all the boys fancied her? I thought that Gary was going to have a fit, and then when Jack came in to help clear the table, Gary glared at him. If looks could kill. Fortunately, Jack didn't notice. He is a good boy, and he and Amelia did a really, really great job as waiters."

Pete assumed that this didn't require a response and carried on loading the dishwasher. "What was Jessica saying about the school trip?" Pete intervened, to get the conversation away from Gary.

"Oh, I thought I'd told you! I am really, really excited. I have been asked to go along on the trip as a responsible adult." Pete tried to suppress a smirk. "Zoe has had to drop out and there aren't any other staff available, so Mr Barker asked Jessica if she could think of a parent who had been security cleared."

Pete wondered if he should know who Zoe was. He knew Mr Barker though, the head of Charlton Academy, but didn't like to interrupt.

"Because I have been DBSed for RDA, I can go on it." It just wasn't the police force that had its three-letter acronyms but Pete was well on top of them all. DBS –

Disclosure and Barring Service and RDA – Riding for the Disabled.

"I'm pleased for you, love, but what does Jack think of you going along? Won't you cramp his style?"

"Oh dear, I hadn't thought of that." Susie bit her lip and stopped wiping the mats in mid-air, but her face cleared and she said with delight, "I will ask Sarah Davies to make sure that I am in a different group! Phew, that was nearly a faux pas. Poor, old Jack, who'd have me as a mother?" She resumed wiping mats and plopping them into the drawer, some still somewhat smeared.

"And I thought Leah had wanted to go. Won't she be a bit miffed?" added Pete. Pete had seen the wretched look that had passed across Leah's face before she got it back under control.

"Oh gosh. Poor, poor Leah. I was so pleased about being asked that I had sort of forgotten how much she wanted to go. Oh dear, what I can do? Nothing really now. I did rather go on about it too. Did she say anything to you? I hope she won't mind too much. I don't think she would be able to get DBSed in time anyway."

"Where are you actually going on this outing?" Pete interrupted Susie's self-flagellation. He was meant to know all about the trip. Jack was going, he knew that it was the 25th May and that it was London, which worried him enough, without going into the details.

Susie babbled excitedly about the procession of royals and dignitaries, the visit to the museum and the visit to the Houses of Parliament themselves. Pete was surprised that they still allowed visits on the afternoon of the State Opening of Parliament. With all the rumours about terrorist plots going round, he thought it inappropriate, but didn't want to dampen Susie's enthusiasm.

With the threat level hovering between Substantial and expecting it any moment to rise to Severe, the continued rioting, the fear of reprisals, Pete was surprised that they were holding the State Opening of Parliament at all. Security was going to have to be very tight; he knew that they were sending a team from the County Headquarters to help out. It was all hands on deck. His name was on the duty list. Perhaps three of the four of them would be there, with only Amelia left at school.

"Is Jessica going too?" he enquired.

"No, poor, old Jessica has to stay chained to her desk in Mr Barker's office all day. Apparently, she's part of the Home Contact Protocol to these outings. Honestly, who would have known that a school would have to make such a song and dance about a bunch of teenagers going on a trip to London? It is more like a secret mission. The kids all go up there all the time on their own, without any fuss from us parents. What a to-do!"

Pete didn't think it worth commenting on the school's duty of care and responsibility for a group of minors, particularly with the current level of threat. He knew that she wouldn't really listen anyway, and was just happily burbling away as she does, particularly when pissed. He started putting the glasses away, wiping each one carefully, and then he could hit the sack. God, he was tired.

"Come on, love, that's all done, let's get you to bed."

"Ooh, Pete, are you after some celebratory fornication!" Susie giggled hysterically.

"Maybe," he replied, with a predatory grin, running his hand through her fabulous, long, blonde hair and cupping a burgeoning breast. He flung an arm around her shoulders and shepherded her, stumbling, up the stairs. Despite being so weary, he would have a go; he couldn't resist his voluptuous wife.

Chapter 15

Leah sat at the dining room table to write a thank-you note to Susie for the lovely dinner party.

Susie was a most excellent cook and it had all looked so pretty, but she just couldn't settle to the task. Leah didn't know what to do. She was furious. She was in a rage and she was also panicking. The school trip was in a fortnight and she still hadn't convinced Mrs Davies that she needed to accompany Aisha.

What had really made it so infuriating was Mr Barker inviting Susie to go on the trip, through Jessica, in front of her, at the dinner party. A member of staff had dropped out at the last minute and they had asked Susie, the only parent allowed on the trip, to step in, just because she had her DBS clearance. Jessica knew that Leah wanted to accompany Aisha. Mr Barker knew that she wanted to accompany Aisha, Mrs Davies knew most certainly and, most certainly of all, so did Susie. It made her really angry. It was completely and totally wrong, but she hadn't liked to make a fuss in Susie's home when Susie was the hostess, and it was such a lovely party, except for that ghastly Gary.

Farrukh agreed with her that it would be totally unsuitable for Aisha to go on her own, particularly in mixed groups with the boys, as had been suggested, but he didn't seem to be as passionate about it as she felt. Despite what Mrs Davies kept saying, on and on, that she and Farrukh were quite happy for Aisha to be with those same boys every day at school, it just wasn't the same.

Goodness knows what children could get up to when away from the safety of the school environment.

She had begged and pleaded but Mrs Davies was immoveable.

In any case, it was unfair of Mrs Davies. Leah and Farrukh had tried very hard to find a single sex school for the girls, but out here in Hampshire, there was no such thing unless you paid an absolute fortune for it. She and Farrukh were comfortable and had a nice home, and Farrukh was doing very well in the engineering industry, but just not enough for the girls to be privately educated. They had looked at Claires Court, it was not such an expensive school, but even that they couldn't manage. So frustrating.

Leah knew in her heart that her feelings of dissatisfaction weren't just about the trip, it was about everything – everything about living in the middle of a narrow-minded, white middle-class community and knowing that she wasn't allowed to complain about it without being ostracised further. It got on top of her sometimes. It was the just subtle nuances. "Is it like that in Pakistan?" "Do you know about the State Opening of Parliament?" When people asked her where she was from and she quite deliberately answered, "Charlton in Hampshire", there was always a double take.

She had to smile and be nice, even when that ghastly man, Gary, was so insulting about her not shaking his hand or embracing him, as all the other women did. That had been so embarrassing. She could not forgive him for that. Everyone just stood awkwardly and said nothing, did *nothing*, not even Susie and Jessica. That was the worst part about it. She thought they were her best friends!

She also knew that Susie was having a party for Jack. She and Jessica were pretending it wasn't happening and had only mentioned it by mistake. For some reason, Aisha was not going to be invited when everyone else from Year 12 was. *Why?* It was just so hurtful that even her best friends, the Eternal Triangle, were keeping things from her, and Susie had not even had the courtesy to tell her why Aisha hadn't been invited. She was certain that Aisha was very hurt too, although she denied it.

She was beginning to feel very sorry for herself and found herself trying very hard not to cry about it, the same feeling of embarrassment, shame and discomfiture rising again, as if it was happening right now – sometimes, she felt so helpless. She'd discovered that her smile could be used as the best disguise whenever she chose, her protective mask to hide behind; it seemed to delight people and make them smile back, but she lived on the wrong side of it.

Leah adored both of Jessica and Susie's girls, Hannah and Amelia, who were in Year 10 with Sara, and she loved it when the girls came over to play. Last time they came, they had such fun trying on Leah's saris and she'd made up both of them with kohl. They had looked enchanting. They had cooked kheer together and ate it up like ravenous puppies.

If she was safe to look after Jessica and Susie's children then she was surely safe to go on the school trip with Aisha and her classmates. Why did she need this DBS thing to prove that she was harmless?

Leah didn't like to even think of it but she could only conclude that at the bottom of all this was her different culture and religious customs. If that was true then it really was totally unacceptable. She was furious; she was hurt and felt powerless to redress the situation. The tears started oozing from her beautiful, kohl-lined eyes.

What she found really difficult was trying to explain to them all, however kind and interested they appeared to be, about her faith. They just did not understand. They were such dear people and she wanted everybody to have Allah's protection and the opportunity to go with her to Paradise on the Day of Judgement. Allah, may his name be praised, was merciful and forgiving, but he could not forgive shirk.

She yearned to find a way to help them understand their duty, their need to turn to Allah, to protect their children, not just themselves. Susie and Jessica were her best friends, so she had a duty to show them the way of Islam, for the sake of all their spirits, for Susie, the innocent, little Amelia, for Jack and for Pete and Jessica, Richard, Alfie and Hannah. They just could not seem to understand that it could be saving their lives, their very existence.

Leah wondered if Susie and Jessica would look at the Koran and leaflets that she'd given them. She desperately hoped so. She decided to give in to the emotion and had a good sob, hoping that saas, happily ensconced in her studio bedroom doing whatever it was that mothers-in-law did all day, could not hear.

She sat and let go until she felt a bit better, the tension flowing with the tears. She blew her nose noisily and thoroughly, wiped her eyes, and decided that instead of feeling sad, it would be much better if she felt determined. Whatever happened, she was thoroughly convinced of one thing. No one could supervise Aisha at all times on a school trip like that, no one. She was determined to be there to keep Aisha safe. Mrs Davies just was not listening to her.

Perhaps if Farrukh were to talk to Mr Barker, man to man?

She would ask him about it this evening.

Chapter 16

Caroline hadn't enjoyed the dinner party particularly.

She knew she must write her "bread and butter" letter to be polite. The food looked excellent and Susie was a fantastic cook, but she seemed to have no concept of healthy nutrition. By the time Caroline had avoided the enormous quantities of carbs and heaps of gluten, there wasn't a great deal left to eat.

The soup was laden with cream, had added oil and croutons, the potatoes were impossible, and were swimming in butter and parmesan of all things. At least the meat was straightforward, but Susie was certain to have slipped some flour into the jus. Caroline wasn't a coeliac but she did like to avoid gluten whenever possible – the effects on the body, the brain and the possibility of addiction were all well known.

Pudding was a cacophony of everything in the world that a healthy living person simply should not touch: sugar, cream, flour, chocolate, and then not even decaf coffee or herbal teas to finish. Caroline had politely declined offers of coffee from the cafetière.

Caroline dreaded to think how many calories Susie had managed to dole out in just one meal. No wonder Susie was so tubby; she'd tucked in with horrifying gusto and scraped every morsel from her plates, except for the bits that she'd spilled down her front in her haste.

Jack and Amelia were on waiting duties, but clearly had absolutely no idea about how to go about it. Surely Susie had drummed into them "serve from the left, take away from the right". Apparently not, and they cheekily shoved themselves into the conversations when they should have been invisible.

When they took away the plates and squelched them on top of each other, noisily scraping the food that she'd left onto another plate, she thought she might scream with disgust. At least when she'd used Kate and Lily Symington to serve at dinner parties, they had been trained correctly and behaved impeccably.

It had been rather embarrassing when she and Thomas had arrived to find the other guests dressed as if they were going to the pub. Even Susie was in a very casual dress with minimum make-up, a lick of mascara and smudge of lip gloss, which was extraordinary for the hostess of a "dinner party". Thank God Thomas had settled for a suit rather than black tie, although he had been a bit bemused, particularly when Pete suggested he took off his tie and put it in his pocket. Caroline had thankfully gone for a subtle silk shift, which clung to her curves fabulously, although she'd had to wear her pull-you-in knickers that weren't especially comfortable.

Caroline wondered why it mattered that she felt so overdressed when it was everyone else that was under-dressed. She always seemed to get it wrong, however hard she tried.

At least the Ahmeds looked the part, with Leah in one of her glorious saris with her beautiful doe eyes, alongside Farrukh in an exotic sherwani that most certainly showed off his assets. He was a fine figure of a chap, with his smooth, black, oiled hair, distinguished, long, regal nose and glowing eyes.

Gary had been his usual bumptious self. She couldn't believe it when Meredith piped up to join in his anecdote about a useless waiter, and he had literally put up his hand to stop her like a traffic policeman, and said coldly, "Meredith, please be quiet, I am telling this story, do not interrupt." Meredith just smiled weakly, shut up docilely, and carried on as if he had said nothing at all. How rude of Gary, how pathetic of Meredith. Gary was a pill.

Pete had been less than communicative, as usual. He looked tired, and answered all her cheerful enquiries with one-word answers, and hadn't asked her a thing about herself. Boring and hard work. He had almost flinched when she'd casually placed a hand on his arm, and Susie, sensing that something was amiss – her Pete antennae were extraordinary – had stared at her with eyes like a frightened Bambi. *For heaven's sake!*

Caroline found that she just didn't have very much in common with the other guests and their ordinary suburban lives. What on earth was she meant to talk to Jessica's Richard about? He may be good looking, spookily like Daniel Craig, but he was so anodyne with his boring job in Victoria as a middle manager for a middling-sized organisation, doing middle of the road things.

Apparently, he was keen on football, which is why he and Gary had so rudely talked across her, despite her interventions and attempts at diverting the conversation to more cerebral things. They had also spent endless time discussing the finer points of the train service into London; Richard on his daily commute from Winchfield station at the crack of dawn and Gary for "business meetings", which weren't very clearly explained. It was utterly, mind-numbingly boring.

She'd tried to divert the conversation. Richard and Gary couldn't remember when they had last been to an art gallery and looked at her blankly. She tried theatre. "Years ago and far too overpriced." None of them had been to any of the live screenings, even though they were on regularly, only a few miles away, and cheap as chips.

Their book choices seemed to be airport thrillers, if they ever got round to reading – far too busy. Neither of them had been skiing and their holidays seemed to be those all you can eat and drink places, walled off from the local culture in places like Ibiza and the Canary Islands.

It was like getting blood out of a stone. How could people live such mundane existences? In fact, the whole evening had been such a let-down that she wasn't sure why she'd worried at all about not being invited. *Really silly in retrospect.*

She picked out a postcard that she had bought at the Royal Academy, especially for writing thank-you notes, a Monet, that exhibition was years ago, She hadn't used many of them because the social life round here was exceedingly slow.

She took the cap off her fountain pen and started to write delicately, her head tipped to one side in her bold style. "Darling, what a triumph. So marvellous to see you and Pete and celebrate his triumphant promotion."

Bugger, two uses of triumph. Should I start again? Why bother, it was only Susie, she wouldn't notice.

"What a clever man. Of course, you are the hostess with the mostest and dinner was a feast to behold. Well done you! Much love, Caroline x"

She blotted the writing on her desk-top blotter, wrote an envelope, popped the card in, removed a stamp from the drawer, stuck it on carefully so that it was at right angles to the edge, arose with dignity, even though there was no one to see, and popped it on the hall table, from whence the postman kindly collected their post on a daily basis.

She consulted her to-do list, striking off "Thank you to Susie", and moved on to the next item: hairdresser's appointment. That was becoming quite urgent; her roots were beginning to show. She consulted her diary, looked for a free day when she could get up to Megan's salon in London.

She wouldn't dream of using anyone else, certainly not round here; they were all the most dreadful modern monstrosities of places where all the stylists seemed to have metal sprouting from every orifice and hair dyed quite the wrong, common-looking colours. She'd tried out Susie's acclaimed hairdresser in an emergency, but it had taken months for Megan to put it back to rights.

May 25th. She could go on and see William afterwards. That would cheer her up. She started dialling.

Chapter 17

Susie was regaling Jessica with all the finer points of Jack's party in an endless stream.

They were sitting around Susie's kitchen table, a mug of herbal tea at hand. Susie had gone off proper tea apparently. Probably one of her new diet things, or perhaps it had been Caroline's bitchy gibes at the dinner party about caffeinated drinks. It seemed odd not to have Leah there, like missing a sister from a family gathering, but it would have been inappropriate, as Jack, for some reason, known only to himself, had declined to invite Aisha.

Jessica couldn't get a word in edgewise, but was almost paralysed by giggles as it all just came pouring out.

"Why on earth did Pete and I let Jack have a bloody party? It was a nightmare. The only good thing about it was not too many children turned up for it, despite Jack saying that he had six yeses and forty-five maybes, whatever that means. He seemed a bit disappointed that only about a dozen came in the end, but that was plenty to make a mess, and far too few for the amount of booze that Pete and I had allowed for them."

Jessica screwed up her face in distaste and sipped at her tea that in truth, she didn't actually like very much, but wouldn't say.

"But why do they have to drink themselves silly and puke everywhere? Why not in the loo like civilised people? I couldn't stay hiding in the kitchen when people were vomiting in the hall, horrible noises. Yuck, yuck. And it made me throw up clearing it up, which didn't help, and it all went down my front.

"Thank heavens I decided to have it after Pete's party; I would never have been able to face any sort of entertaining ever, ever again. And the sleeping arrangements were bonkers."

Jessica managed to squeeze in a quizzical "Alfie?" in an "Oh my God, I hope he wasn't part of all this trouble" tone.

"No, no, not Alfie. He seemed to be in a permanent huddle with that nice boy, Charlie, who works at Gary's, and the adorable Ellie, such a nice girl. They are extraordinarily protective of her – it's as if she were royalty. I saw them sneak upstairs and take over Jack's room, but Pete and I turned a blind eye because they seemed to be sensible, and reasonably sober. I feel I can trust Ellie, she has something about her, nice girl, something vulnerable, something bothering her, unlike the rest of those, those, those… drunken floozies."

Jessica nearly choked on her tea. "Not Hannah?"

"No, no, not Hannah. Your children seem to be angels. Hannah was taking the role of holding people's hair back when they puked. Actually, it is my bloody children that were appalling. Jack was snogging the face off a girl, Emily, in the dining room, and wouldn't go to bed, and not in that way either – it looks as if he would have, given half a chance, little bugger, but we weren't having that. She is only 15! Pete and I had to patrol the bottom of the stairs to stop the boys shooting upstairs. Little shits."

Jessica struggled to keep down another wave of giggles.

"And Amelia was off her head. Pete and I had to put the silly, little idiot to bed in her room in the recovery position with a bucket. It is useful having a policeman as a husband, his first aid skills are brilliant. Silly, silly girl. Pete was livid. And don't tell Kate, but Lily was nearly as bad. Thank God Aisha didn't come. Leah would have had a fit." Susie stopped to draw breath.

Jessica managed to squeeze in a comment. "Poor Leah, she was upset that Aisha wasn't asked though."

"I know, but what could I do? That was really, really embarrassing, and you know how hopeless I am at keeping my mouth shut. Poor Leah, I feel quite dreadful about it. She isn't happy about me going on the school trip either when they won't let her go. I feel really, really awful about it but what can I do? I did offer to chaperone Aisha myself, but I don't think that that helped very much.

"But anyway, where was I? Oh God. Then parents started arriving to collect their little darlings. I managed to prise Jack off Emily when her granddad came to collect her. She was furious and very rude to him… told him he was meant to wait for her outside and not come in. Poor chap looked mortified."

"That's because he is her stepdad, not her granddad." Jessica was helpless with laughter. "Poor, old chap; he is always being mistaken for her granddad."

"Really? Really? He looked very, very old, and if looks could kill, I'd be dead."

Jessica patted Susie on the shoulder, helpless with mirth.

"Why did I ever agree to go on the school trip with that little lot? I was really chuffed but I'm dreading it now."

Jessica just laughed even more. "Oh Susie, I do love you!" she managed to squeeze out.

Chapter 18

Bernie knew he was an embarrassment.

He couldn't help being so much older than everyone else. He squinted at himself in the hall mirror through his thick spectacles, tidying up the remnants of his grey, lank hair, leaning over his portly belly, rubbing at a new mark that turned out to be one of those liver spots, a hideous sign of his age, before standing up straight and pulling his trousers up with a shimmy.

He wished he could go back to wearing his braces, but Evie had laughed at them and they had been banished with anything else in his wardrobe that she considered made him look old-fashioned. If the truth were to be told, she actually meant just old. He had managed to hang on to his favourite old, leather slippers, even though they were very much the worse for wear.

He had collected Emily from an evening out. It was the residence of people called the Coles apparently, their son's 17th birthday party, according to Emily, when she had actually strung more than two sentences together. He was "just a boy from school", according to Emily (said rather dismissively, he felt), but there were so many "friends from school" that he taxied Emily to visit that he had rather lost track of them all.

As requested, Bernie had phoned her when he had got there, fumbling awkwardly with the intricacy of the too small keys on his ancient mobile phone. Her phone kept ringing and went to the answering service: "Hi, it's Em, leave a message…" He tried again. And again. He didn't know what to do. He tried to look at his watch but the light was too dim. It was getting very late. He tried just once more.

Giving up, he heaved himself out of the car – he was stiff from just sitting there – and shuffled to the door. It was easy to see which one it was, lights blazing, loud music crashing. He leant on the bell.

The door was answered by a mad-looking woman, hair all over the place, a manic grin on her face, with a rather suspicious-looking streak of something unmentionable on her blouse. "Hello, hello," she beamed at him. "Who have you come to collect?"

"Emily," he muttered.

"Pardon?" She couldn't hear him above the riotous noise.

"Emily," he piped up, as loud as he could, but had to cough to clear his throat, which ended up in one of his long choking incidents.

"Oh righty-ho. I'll go and winkle her out," the mad woman shouted unnecessarily loudly, and swivelled round, her curtain of hair taking some time to catch up, skittering down the passage shouting, "Emily, Emily!" at the top of her voice.

He stood on the doorstep, not sure whether to step in or stay on the mat.

Emily had appeared eventually. She looked weird, her eyes too bright, her face sort of squashed, and her hair all awry. She'd come out and climbed into the car, without so much as a hello or thank you, just a strange sort of mewing sound, and immediately stuck headphones over her ears.

Emily had obviously had far too much to drink, which he thought completely inappropriate; she was only 15. He thought it best not to express his disapproval. He avoided confrontation at all costs. Her eyes were very unfocussed and she smelled strongly of alcohol. It had pervaded the car so he had opened his window just a little, but Emily had turned to him and glared, wrapping her arms around herself exaggeratedly and slumping awkwardly against the door.

The Coles must be very lax people to allow that sort of thing. He wondered if they had even been there to supervise; people did things so differently nowadays. One heard such horror stories.

The moment that they had got home, Emily had opened the car door, nearly fallen out in her hurry to escape, and staggered up the crazy-paving path, swerving from side to side, missing the rose bushes by inches. She'd forgotten that she hadn't got her keys, so slumped against the porch until Bernie caught up, smartly inserted his key, twisted it somewhat viciously and pushed open the well-oiled door.

Emily bolted up the stairs, tripping as she went. Bernie sighed and wandered into the hall, carefully placing the car keys in the special little pot and staring at himself in the mirror as he pondered.

He fancied a cup of tea, not so much the tea itself as the comforting ritual of boiling the kettle on the hob, warming the pot, spooning the exact amount of leaves into the teapot, the roll of drums as the boiling water poured in, and waiting for it to steep. The ritual complete, he went and sat in the sitting room, in front of the fireplace, nestled into his customary chair.

As he sipped at his perfect cup of tea, his thoughts wandered, going over what had just happened.

Bernie had an uneasy relationship with Emily. He knew it was hard for her, having to accept him as a stepdad; she clearly didn't like him very much but who would? He knew he was such an old man, getting very doddery, old enough to be her grandfather, or even worse, her great-grandfather.

He was a useful taxi driver though and was always willing to fetch and carry Emily when Evie was "doing her thing" elsewhere.

He tried not to get in the way between mother and daughter, and would quite happily potter off with his cup of tea into another room when they had their heads together, giggling. He knew that he wasn't welcome in these female tête-à-têtes. If he came across them deep in conversation, they would look up simultaneously and stare at him, waiting for him to wander off again. Fair enough – women's chatter.

Emily occasionally answered his gentle enquiries politely but monosyllabically, at least when she bothered to listen at all and wasn't wearing those wretched earphones, but she always dashed upstairs to her room the moment she came in, if Evie wasn't in. She didn't seem to want to be in the same room as him if she could help it. There wasn't very much he could do about it really, he didn't want to interfere or offend, but it was quite hurtful.

Bernie had met Emily's mother at his late wife Helen's wake, of all things. Evie had been one of the waitresses, helping out her friend Daisy-May apparently – ridiculous name – bustling about energetically, doing her job with vigour, but at the same time, she'd been so kind and sympathetic to him when he had been so clearly distressed, having lost Helen. A little pat, a shy, little smile, she was so charming.

It was one of those occasions that had gone horribly, horribly wrong. It still made him sick to the stomach when he thought of it. The caterer, Daisy-May, Evie's boss, had presented him with a bill as she prepared to leave, her duties completed. Bernie thought this somewhat inappropriate and tactless in itself, being a wake, particularly in front of his guests, but then had glanced at the bill.

The bill was enormous and far more than he had budgeted for. Unfortunately, Daisy-May seemed to have added all sorts of sundry items to the bill that he had not anticipated. Tactfully, he had invited her to discuss it in the kitchen. Best deal with it straight away.

Daisy-May had squared up to him in the kitchen, a belligerent look on her face, and claimed that when she'd discussed with him his requirements, that he had verbally agreed to all sorts of little extras that she'd suggested. He had not realised that she was not merely explaining what he would receive for the agreed price. She went on and on about it. He had tried to explain that it was a misunderstanding. She became louder and he was certain all the guests would hear. He had shushed her, which seemed to make her even angrier.

It had escalated, he had got rather upset, and he was already rather upset, understandably, under the circumstances. Shaking with annoyance, he had given her the envelope of cash that he had carefully assembled to the exact amount as quoted, with a bit extra as a tip for the staff. He had virtually thrown it at her. He had told her in no uncertain terms that that was all she was getting, to go away and never darken his door again. He had been unpardonably rude – most unlike himself.

Daisy-May had stormed out in a huff, throwing back, "You will hear from my solicitor", and Bernie had nearly collapsed with the distress of it all. He had sat at the table, anguished, his head in his hands, still shaking, his farewell to Helen tainted and besmirched. He felt awful.

Evie had come and sat next to him, bearing a cup of tea, calmed him, soothed him. It had made him feel a bit better. She had sat there in silence for as long as he needed.

Evie had turned up on his doorstep a week later, saying that she thought she'd left behind a scarf or something. He had invited her in, offered her a cup of tea, "my turn", been warmed by her solicitude, as they sat in the low-ceilinged, beamed sitting room in front of the inglenook fireplace. Secretly, he was so enormously pleased to see her again. He had noticed her because she'd stood out like a candle in the gloom, and seemed to be the only person who genuinely seemed to notice his distress under the polite façade, and had so kindly come to his rescue in his hour of need.

She had sat there, curled up in Helen's favourite Parker Knoll armchair, and listened to him burbling on about Helen, waffling about his daughters, Nicola and Gillian, her heart-shaped, little face alert, her perfectly straight fringe nodding, her blue eyes shining with understanding, and he hadn't wanted her to leave, ever again.

Evie was a tiny slip of a thing, barely five-feet tall, a slight and dinky girl, but with a huge amount of energy and love and passion to give. He had nicknamed her Mini from the very first moment that she had let him kiss her. Her big, round eyes would look at him, and only him, with such tenderness. She filled a gaping hole in his existence and filled him with a warm glow.

Her nickname for him was "old codger". It was meant endearingly but it did annoy him a bit, a little demeaning, but he didn't want to make a fuss about it and would take it on his chin; after all, he had been the first one to use it to reference himself. "What would you be wanting with an old codger like me?"

How she had fancied him enough to actually "you know what" with him, he could not fathom, but she did and she had weaved her magic, entranced him, enchanted him and he could not believe his luck. He had worried terribly about that whole business; to be truthful, it had been rather a long time, but he seemed to be firing on all cylinders, which was a mighty relief.

She didn't mind that she was younger than his own two girls, neither did he, and anyway, they were both living their own lives so far away, in Edinburgh and Australia, and he had rarely seen them or the grandchildren. They always invited him to their houses, but it was such a long way to go and he liked to stay in his archetypal, roses around the door, chocolate box thatched cottage with all his familiar things around him. It was home, and he was a bit of a homebody.

Both girls had come for his and Evie's wedding, at the registry office because Evie had been married before, twice, and their disapproval was clear for everyone to see. They'd stood there po-faced throughout the ceremony and the reception, the only people wearing hats, looking old and old-fashioned, graciously flopping out their hands to be shaken by Evie, and smiling politely when introduced to Evie's sister, Liz, but delicately withholding any vestige of warmth. He didn't want to mind that they couldn't see how wonderful Evie was, but he had been upset. He wasn't going to let them spoil his elation at his newly-found happiness.

He could only be relieved that Evie didn't have parents. They were long gone to horrible diseases. It would have been a real blow to have had them lined up with him; the same age, if not younger than him, everyone comparing them.

His beloved Evie, his Mini, was the centre of his universe. She was exhausting; she was so full of vitality and ideas. She made him feel so alive and young in the mind, although he could do nothing about the state of his wrinkly, old body. He wanted to live forever.

As soon as they were married, she'd swept through his and Helen's cottage, turning it all upside down. Swooping through, her arms full of who knew what, which seemed to have been buried deep in the hidey holes of the place, she would dash out and dispose of years of accumulated debris at the charity shops. "Might as well do some good with all this stuff," she would say gaily, as she shovelled it into the boot of the car before dashing back, reaching up and giving him a noisy kiss.

She'd plotted and planned and, with enormous enthusiasm, brought the place up to date with new furnishings. She ripped up the old curtains (and she was quite right to do so, as they fell apart in her eager, little hands), tore up the carpet in the bathroom, and put in a power shower, which he never used as he still preferred his bath. It was all very jolly and bright, and it brought a smile to her lovely, little face.

It had cost quite a bit, but he hadn't spent very much for years so his money was there, sitting in his bank account, doing nothing. Helen had been housebound for her last agonising years, and to tell the truth, a bit crotchety, so they hadn't spent very much at all. He was well aware that Nicola and Gillian were a bit anxious about Evie spending their inheritance, but sod it, he was just so happy to indulge her and bring that glorious, impish grin to her lovely face.

He did rather miss some of Helen's old-fashioned ways. He'd become accustomed to his meat and two veg for lunch and a light supper at 6p.m., before a comforting hot drink and a biscuit just before bedtime. He didn't like all the modern pasta and pizza, stir fries and takeaways. They gave him awful indigestion, particularly as they seemed to eat so late, and usually off their knees in front of the television, slumped uncomfortably over a precariously balanced tray. It was a small price to pay for having this unexpected joy so late in his life.

He had to tuck a serviette into his collar to catch the debris that would inevitably fall on the long journey of the fork from tray to mouth. Mini and Emily would laugh about it and referred to it as his bib. He joined in the merriment and would make baby noises to make them laugh even more.

He also wished that Mini didn't dash off to so many places without him. She always seemed to be out and about, hither and thither; he couldn't keep up with where and when and with whom. She was always left him with an affectionate hug and a kiss, before dancing out of the front door with a "see you later, 'old codger'".

When she got back from wherever she'd been, she would dash in, give him an enormous hug, flit around doing a million things at once, between throwing away snippets of the funny things that had happened to her along the way. London was a favourite haunt and she would return laden with bags. "Show me!" he would ask in a hearty way but often, she would say, "It's a surprise" or "It's for Emily" or "Nosey, nosey, these are women's things", and laugh at him with deliberate coyness before tripping off up the stairs.

To try and keep track of all of her comings and goings, and after much cajoling and reminding, he had started a family diary. He had used the excuse that he needed to record when and where he needed to fetch and take Emily, explaining that he got in a bit of a muddle otherwise and was worried about forgetting her. He hadn't yet, but was terrified that he might. Emily would be furious. It was on the hallstand below the mirror and Bernie glanced down at it. He nagged Mini to write in where she was going but she rarely did.

Today recorded Emily's outing to the Coles. Mini, Pilates. What was happening tomorrow? Mini Book Club, which it seems was more about catching up with her various young girlfriends, all as young and vital as she, and having a good gossip. For him, nothing. Emily, swimming after tea. Looking ahead, Mini had actually recorded a weekend visit to London with her sister, Liz, 25th May, or rather scrawled it in her favourite bright pink ink. It was a miracle that she had done so. She was improving, good girl! Underneath was a further comment: "Emily to Hannah". Phew, at least he wouldn't have to be alone with Emily for a weekend. That would be extremely awkward. He must count his blessings. He was so very lucky to have found love at his ripe old age. He and his beautiful, quirky, little Mini had settled into their married life together very happily. All was right with his world. A few liver spots weren't going to get him down!

He stretched out, bending and straightening his dodgy back to each side like the physio had told him, flexing his stiff knees, and padded, in his slippers, to the kitchen to make another comforting cup of tea, while he waited for Mini to get back from goodness knew where.

Chapter 19

Charlie had stayed over at Jack Cole's after his birthday affair.

He hadn't said anything to his mum, just to see if she'd notice he was gone. She obviously hadn't. There wasn't even a missed call on his mobile.

He hadn't really wanted to go to Jack's – the guy was a bit of a knob – but he was curious to see Jack's gaff, and the thought of some decent food was always an incentive. Ellie and Alfie were going because he was. It would be a laugh, they'd thought.

It had been okay, plenty of food, but he didn't touch the hooch, as it was not his thing. He couldn't believe how crazy those kids were after necking all that stuff like they were dying of thirst. Puking everywhere. Insane. They made him feel so old.

At least he, Alfie and Ellie had managed to get away from it all and sleep in Jack's room, leaving a drunk Jack to show off to his other mates. He hadn't slept too badly and breakfast was awesome. Plenty of it too, as most of the others were so hung over, they looked as if they were going to throw up at the sight of it.

He liked Jack's mum too. She was one of those warm, nice people that he wished was his own mum. She had patted him on the shoulder as she'd placed that humongous, heaped plate in front of him. He couldn't remember when he had last been patted with affection like that. *Nice.* He yearned for a motherly hug.

He glanced across at the permission slip on the table, expecting it to be sitting there like it had for the last few days, where it had simply been moved about like a pawn on a chessboard.

The school trip was next week, for fuck's sake. For fuck's sake, all she'd to do was sign it.

To his amazement, alongside the permission slip was a heap of cash, loads of crumpled notes and a miscellaneous collection of coins.

Fucking hell, this is a first. Well done Mum, at least you've done something right.

The pen wasn't there, but he hadn't expected it to be. He'd get another one from Alfie, a good mate. He picked up the slip with an amazed grin on his face, ran his eye down it, but this unexpected stirring of happiness broke; he groaned, hopes dashed, put his head in his hands.

Fuck it. She hadn't signed it. *For fuck's sake.*

It wasn't difficult. She'd written on the back though. In her pathetic, babyish writing, she'd scrawled, "Gone away for a bit, babe. Back soon. Left you something. Mum." He couldn't even fake her signature now, with all that stuff on the back.

Shit. I can't fucking go.

He stopped to think. He was used to fending off awkward questions about his mum and her whereabouts.

I could try and wing it, but Mrs Davies had been straight up about signed slips. I could just stay at home, not go in at all, but that wouldn't look good, might count as non-attendance, which isn't good for my record on uni applications. Perhaps I could call and say I was sick, but Mrs Hughes would see straight through that.

Fuck, what to do? I'd better just be too late for the trip, run in carrying the slip as if I got caught up, look mad at not going. What time did Mrs Davies say? 8:45? I'll "miss" the bus, jog in and get in for 9:00 'cause that isn't too late for registration.

He would be wearing his regular clothes so he wouldn't sweat up his school uniform by jogging.

He screwed up the permission slip, threw it at the wall, howled with rage, and suddenly remembering that he needed it to carry through the performance, he picked it up and attempted to smooth it out.

Shit man. Life sucks. It just goes from bad to fucking worse.

He vaguely wondered where she'd gone, who with and for how long. He was hungry. He couldn't be arsed to trek all the way to the shops. He smeared the Hungry House icon on his cell, "the easy way to takeaway" with his long, elegant fingers. Where they lived, they wouldn't deliver without an up-front payment. They would if he paid online with his debit card.

Chapter 20

Caroline was in a rush.

She'd overslept and had not heard Thomas get up. She'd thought that he was working at home today so she had absolutely no idea where he had gone. London, she assumed. He must have left at the crack of dawn, deliberately creeping around so as not to disturb her. He seemed to be avoiding her more and more these days. Presumably, he would be back this evening so she would catch up with him then.

Caroline leapt out of bed and dashed for the bathroom, where she threw a flannel and soap over the important bits, reminding her of the daily ritual at boarding school.

She dressed in a hurry, grabbed a matching handbag, the Louis Vuitton, and piled in her keys, her wallet, a handkerchief, her diary and a fountain pen. She rushed down the stairs, hastily scribbled a note to Kate, and dashed out of the door in order to catch the train. Megan hated if she was late for her hair appointment. She would get very snippy in all senses of the word and she couldn't risk that, her hair was too precious.

Chapter 21

Susie was excited; it was the much vaunted school trip today.

It was really exciting because she loved the Royals, couldn't wait to see them in the procession. She had also never been to the Houses of Parliament in her life, and this was the first time she'd ever been invited to go along on a school trip. She was very flattered that she'd been deemed suitable for such an important role. She wasn't the first person that people usually thought of. She'd been convinced that the head, Mr Barker, thought her a bit scatty, and maybe she was. In fact, she must be really, really excited, as well as a bit apprehensive, because she felt a bit nauseous.

Susie suspected that her being asked was Jessica's doing; such a dear, kind friend, she knew how much Susie would love to go on a trip like this and she knew that she did already have her DBS clearance thingy from RDA. She was only sorry that it had upset Leah so much. She still felt terrible about that.

Poor Leah still hadn't convinced Mr Barker that she should go, however much she had pleaded. Susie would make sure that she was with Aisha's group and then she, Susie, would be her chaperone. Susie was pleased with this satisfactory compromise. Now that would make Leah happy and make her feel better about it all. She would sort it out when she got to school and bring that lovely smile back to Leah's beautiful face.

In her usual chaotic way, still in her dressing gown, Susie had kissed Pete and sent him on his way to London, part of the enhanced police presence for the State Opening of Parliament apparently, and returned upstairs for a shower, forgetting to pick up the pack of loo rolls that she'd placed there, ready to go up.

It struck her as amusing that she too was heading that way when Pete had been lined up for this duty for a week or so, something to do with the increasing anti-Muslim riots, a quite ridiculous carry-on, a heightened security status or something and his specialism in Firearms. She wondered if, perhaps, she would see him there. She imagined waving proudly to him from the crowd as he strutted about looking important, drop-dead gorgeous in his uniform. "That is *my* man and isn't he just magnificent?"

She'd better get a move on so she was ready to take the kids to school in time. Now where was her "going on a school trip" outfit? Damn. She'd left the shirt in the laundry room. If she was going down, she might as well take the washing down with her; it seemed to be growing rather menacingly huge in the corner of their bedroom.

She flung on her dressing gown. Jack always groaned dramatically if he caught her wandering around in her undies – it wasn't a pretty sight apparently: "Gross". She bundled up the washing, fighting to get all the sleeves and things into a manageable ball, and sighing when knickers and socks kept escaping. She struggled to pick them up without other items absconding too.

She staggered out onto the landing and headed off down the stairs, gingerly taking a step at a time because she couldn't see a thing over the pile. She wasn't sure how it happened but her feet slipped on the smooth, plastic packaging of the forgotten loo rolls and she bounced down the stairs like a skier going straight through a mogul field. As she landed at the bottom, the pain that shot through her ankle made her shout out loud.

"Bugger, bugger, shit," she exclaimed, her teeth clenched in agony, making her sound like a ventriloquist. Dirty clothes cascaded all around her.

Jack and Amelia both shot out of their bedrooms.

"What the hell is happening, Mum?"

"Are you okay?"

"Shit."

Jack and Amelia slithered down the stairs, exclaiming as they went, picking their way over the trail of clothes, Jack grimacing at the sight of Mum's dirty underwear displayed so unashamedly.

"Oh hell, it really, really hurts," mewed Susie pathetically, clutching her left ankle. In a matter of seconds, it had already started ballooning alarmingly and her toes were rapidly looking like a packet of sausages. Amelia put her arms around Susie, not being sure what else she could do to assist.

"What do you want us to do, Mum?" asked Jack practically.

"I don't know, I don't know!" keened Susie. The children stood and watched her closely.

Once she'd got her head round the pain, she went through her mind what the consequences of this were. There was no way she was going to be in any fit state to go on the trip. She couldn't face even trying to stand up, let alone start yomping around London with a bunch of lively teenagers.

Her Mum-mode kicked in and she thought for a moment before stating, with unusual authority, "Right now, you two, you had better get ready as quickly as you can and go and catch the bus. If you rush, you will make it. While you get on your way, I will phone school and tell them what has happened and sort something out with them. Okay?"

Gosh, I am being efficient.

Nods from Jack and Amelia and then they turned tail, dashed up the stairs, disappeared into their rooms. Susie could hear Jack's being turned upside down, as he grabbed his rucksack out of the cupboard. No problem, she could deal with all the mess later, she just didn't want him to miss the trip.

Using the banister as a crutch, Susie heaved herself up. It was at times like this that she wished she was sylph-like. She hobbled into the kitchen, leaning heavily on the table, picked up her phone, had a brief think and then called Jessica.

Jessica answered after a couple of rings with her usual efficient school secretary manner. "Charlton Academy, Jessica Hughes speaking. How can I help you?" As soon as she realised it was Susie, her tone instantly took on a warmer and friendlier tone. "Hi Susie! Are you on your way?"

Susie explained in a great rush.

"Oh pants," said Jessica, most un-school secretary-like. "Are you okay? What can I do? Do you want me to come round and rescue you?" Susie explained that the best thing that Jessica could do would be to sort things that end, tell Mr Barker and Mrs Davies what had happened and let them take it from there.

"So you definitely won't be coming?" asked Jessica "That's such a shame, you were really looking forward to it. And you are sure that I can't dash round like an administering angel?"

"Absolutely," responded Susie. "Much better if you try and put things right that end and..." hesitating, "my first reaction was to ask Leah to step in. I know that she really, really wants to go but I am guessing that she won't be allowed to because of the whole DBS thingy?"

"That's right, Susie. Poor Leah. It's a bit ironic really but you're right, she won't."

There was a pause before Susie blurted, "I know that it is a huge ask but perhaps you might even go on the trip yourself?" Her cunning plan fell out in a rush. "Hannah could come home with Amelia if you are late back, so that won't be a problem. Alfie will be with you and can drive home with you, and you can drop Jack off when you pick up Hannah. I won't be good for anything looking after the girls, other than a friendly smile, but hey, that is better than nothing!" Susie took a breath at last.

"Now, that's a great idea. I will ask Mr Barker and Sarah Davies. I have always fancied a visit to the Houses of Parliament, and they are going to be hard pressed to find anyone else DBS checked at such late notice. Yippee, I can play hooky!"

"Thanks, Jessica, you're the best, best friend in the whole wide world."

"Okey-dokey, my eternal friend, let me go and sort something out. In the meantime, you look after yourself and I will drop by this evening, bearing grapes, magazines and a bottle of medicine, also known as Shiraz. Take care and think of me having a great time at your expense! Must go. Love you, bye!"

Susie was so relieved when she put down the phone. She hated to think that she was letting people down, and Jessica had such an uncanny knack of making it sound like an adventure rather than a bore or inconvenience, bless her. She did feel bad about Leah though.

Jack and Amelia swept through the kitchen, grabbing handfuls of fruit as they went. It wasn't much for breakfast, but at least they wouldn't starve. She gave each of them a giant bear hug, trying to avoid squashing the fruit, and as they sped out of the door, shouted after them, "Have a great trip, Jack! Have you got enough money? Have a good day, Amelia!" They barely looked back.

She eased herself into the chair. Leaned back, put her poor foot onto the chair opposite and groaned.

"Ouch, ouch, bugger, bugger, ouch," she said out loud.

Chapter 22

Ellie woke up and with a stomach lurch, remembered that today was the day.

The school trip and the beginning of the rest of her life. It was quite scary, but she was ready.

She got up, showered, washed and dried her hair, straightened it carefully and started to get dressed. She put on her bra, two pairs of knickers, a pair of tights, her jeans, two strappy tops and a shirt. Her cardigan and waterproof jacket lay ready on her chair. Already rolled up and in her rucksack were more knickers, a bra, a pair of smart trousers and her favourite shirt, a skirt, thick tights, another top, another cardigan and a pair of pumps. At the very bottom was her wash bag, bulging with products, and the box of Tampax.

She'd already worked out that if by any chance, anyone wanted to search her rucksack, she would say that she was on her period and was worried that she might leak, and therefore needed stuff to clean herself up, a change of clothes and, here was the clever bit, she wanted two outfits in case the weather was hotter or colder than she had thought. The worst that could happen was that they would make her leave one of the outfits behind.

She suddenly felt reluctant to go downstairs, so she clenched her fists, closed her eyes and took a deep breath. "Let's go, Ellie," she said, with conviction.

Entering the kitchen was really weird. It was going to be the last time. She patted Marmite and fondled his ears in the way he liked, reluctant to stop. Now, Marmite, she was going to miss, a lot.

Mum was fiddling and farting around at the sink, looking like a scuttling mouse.

"Morning Mummy." Her mum turned suddenly and looked at her, surprised and wary.

"Um, yes, good morning, love." She seemed distracted, her eyes staring and a bit vacant.

Ellie took her usual place at the kitchen table. A shiver of revulsion passed through her that just wouldn't stop; it happened every time she sat down on that chair at that fucking table, and gave her a horrible adrenalin rush every bloody time after that "thing".

It made her ask, "Has Dad, I mean Daddy, left yet?"

"No dear. He is still in bed. I think he must have caught Philippa's virus. He isn't happy about it; he says he is feeling terrible. He has gone back to sleep probably so don't disturb him," her Mum wittered on .

Ellie stopped listening and couldn't help but sigh with relief that she wouldn't be seeing Dad. Despite everything, she felt a tiny little disappointment that she wouldn't be able to say goodbye.

How ridiculous. After everything.

She calmly reached for the muesli as Pips arrived. She looked up guiltily. Oh dear, Pips. She still hadn't fully decided what to do about Pips. They treasured each other, were closer than any other sisters she knew. Would she give the game away if she told her? Should she just contact her on Facebook? On the other hand, how would she feel – abandoned? Let down? Did it matter what she felt – she was going to feel bad whatever.

The time came to leave for the bus. A wave of dread swept over Ellie. She could still not go. As she gathered up her stuff, Mum remarked, "Only you, Eleanor, could look as if you were going for a month for a trip to London! Haven't you got anything smaller? Borrow Philippa's rucksack."

"No thanks, Mummy. This will do fine, and I'm the one who has got to lug it about so no worries." Hitching it onto her shoulder (actually, it had turned out to be really heavy), she went to hug her mum. She couldn't help squeezing a bit harder and a bit longer. Her mum seemed to almost push her away and Ellie noticed a surprised look flicker across her face. Ellie supposed it was a bit unusual . "Bye Mummy."

Pips was half out of the door already. Ellie turned back and looked at her mum, storing a final snapshot. They meandered down the drive, past her mum's Smart car and her dad's BMW, which squatted alongside each other in the garage.

They walked to the bus stop in companionable silence, as usual, and stood at the bus stop, not speaking. They never did, never had, it was always their time to be completely relaxed and peaceful, just the two of them. Ellie was aching to reach out and hold onto Pips, talk about everything all at once, but knew that she couldn't, it would be odd.

The bus arrived, they boarded, and Pips buffeted her way to the back, bouncing off the seats to find Hannah and her friends.

Ellie took her usual seat, second row in, next to Alfie. "Mornin' Alfie."

"Hey man," replied Alfie, laconically, flicking back his too-long blond fringe and easing his too-long legs to make space for her. He tried so hard to be cool. It made Ellie smile to herself. She liked Alfie. She knew that Alfie liked her, but she suspected that he liked her in a different way than she did him. Complicated.

They were good mates though. Da Bus Crew. They looked out for each other and were comfortable, although Ellie never told them about what happened at home. Too personal. They knew something was wrong but being boys, they didn't pry.

Ellie knew that Alfie, Charlie and she were in the same "designated group" for the trip, which was good, but she wasn't sure who the adult leaders were going to be. Rumour had it that it was Jack's mum, a last-minute substitute for a teacher, apparently. She was really nice, a bit airy-fairy and eager to please, but in a good way.

It turned out that Jack was on the bus today. Odd, Ellie thought. She thought that he was coming in with his mum. Turning round to the back, Ellie noticed that so too was his sister, Amelia, deep in conversation with her best friend, Hannah. Ellie shrugged and thought no more about it.

After the routine stop and start at every stop, the same as every day before, Ellie mentally ticked them off as they went, thinking, "The last time I stop at..." The last stop was where Charlie got on, but he didn't. Alfie and Ellie craned their necks to seek him out, asking the driver to wait just a bit, which he obligingly did for just a minute or two, even though it had a reputation as being a dodgy area to hang around. Charlie had never been late before.

The bus swung into school. It took Ellie by surprise when her stomach lurched again. Fear? Excitement? She wasn't sure.

As they piled off the bus, Ellie hung back. As Pips bounded down the steps, she nearly fell into Ellie's arms as Ellie stepped forward. Ellie enveloped her and hugged her tight. "Pips, you won't understand what I am saying but please remember that whatever happens today, I really, really love you. Always will. You got that?"

"What are you saying, Ellie? What do you mean? I don't get it. What is happening today? Ellie, you are scaring me!" Ellie just couldn't let go. Tears started forming and she squeezed her eyes to stop them escaping and bit her lip.

"Ellie? What's going on?" pleaded Pips.

"Don't worry, Pips. Please don't worry. I shouldn't have said anything. I just... I just love you, right? Now off you go, you'll be late." Ellie pushed Pips away, stood for a moment, and then turned and ran towards the hall where they were to meet. God knows what Pips was doing. She couldn't look back.

Chapter 23

Sarah Davies bustled onto the podium.

"Right, now, is everyone paying attention? Are we ready to leave?"

An anxious shout came from Alfie at the back.

"I know that Charlie isn't here, but that is just tough. I told you all quite clearly that if you weren't here on time, you didn't get to go. And that also applies to those of you who have not, despite my nagging endlessly, brought your permission slips. No slip, no trip."

Sounds of protest.

"You have all had plenty of time, plenty of warnings. There cannot be any exceptions. Could those of you therefore not going, please go to the chemistry lab and meet Mrs Pietruski, who will be supervising you today. Yes, now, please go and we will see you later!"

Jack hung back. Sod it; it wasn't his fault that he hadn't got his shitting permission slip. His mum was going to bring it with her and now she wasn't coming. Mrs Davies knew that, for Christ's sake; she knew that his mum was even meant to be on the sodding trip. Talk about unfair. He glared at Mrs Davies, except she didn't even notice, turned and stalked out past Ellie. He glared at Ellie for no good reason.

"Hey Jack..."

He carried on walking. He caught up with Aisha of all people. Awkward. "Why aren't you going?" he asked.

"Mum, what else?" Aisha said dejectedly. "She was totally adamant that I couldn't go. We had a big row about it this morning once Dad had left for work. She refused point blank to give me my signed permission slip." Aisha wasn't too happy to be spending the day with Jack after he hadn't even bothered to ask her to his party, but she had got used to being excluded from stuff over the years. It didn't stop her feeling hurt, but she had got used to hiding it.

"Why, what's she objecting to?"

"Mrs Davies wouldn't let her come on the trip and therefore, no chaperone, no trip. You boys are obviously very dangerous when let loose and I could come to all sorts of harm. I seriously don't get it, but you know what Mum is like." In all fairness, she knew that her mum was perhaps why Jack hadn't bothered to ask her. She probably wouldn't have let her go to the party anyway.

"Why wouldn't Mrs Davies let her come? My mum was supposed to be coming and Mrs Hughes has had to step in at the last moment."

"No DBS check. I think Mrs Davies thinks that Mum has some dark and mysterious secret past and can't be trusted just because she's a Pakistani and a Muslim. Deadly combo, obviously a terrorist sympathiser. Honestly, it's mad."

"Who else hasn't got their permission slips then?" asked Jack.

"Don't know really. We will see who else is there when we get to Mrs Pietruski's room. I wonder when Charlie will deign to turn up. Not like him to miss an educational trip; he is such a nerd."

Miss Chawla came in, striding purposefully in her super-efficient manner, and approached Mrs Davies. "A message from Mrs Symington: Lily is not at all well and isn't coming. I guess it is this nasty bug that is going round. She won't be at all pleased to miss the trip."

The remaining happy students milled around like sheep, and with much *baaing*, eventually found their "designated groups". Ellie looked out for Alfie – he was easy to spot his blond hair hovering above the rest – and she sidled in next to him. "Still no Charlie?" she asked.

Alfie shrugged.

They were confused. He hadn't been on the bus this morning, he wasn't answering his phone, and he hadn't answered their texts.

"It turns out that one of our group's responsible adults is Mum." Ellie looked confused. "Seriously, Mum is coming on the trip. It was meant to be Jack's mum, but apparently, she'd had a fall or something. Jack is obviously not pleased about the whole thing; she didn't send his permission slip with him. If looks could kill."

It was good that it was Mrs Hughes though, Ellie reasoned; she was really nice, and Alfie wouldn't mind, he got on well with his mum. But then they also had Mrs Davies. No one ever called Mrs Davies nice, but they respected her. She was okay but it made Ellie nervous, as she was very thorough.

"Well hello, Da Bus Crew," said Mrs Davies heartily, as she came and joined them. "Except Charlie, of course. What's happening there?"

Ellie and Alfie shrugged in unison.

"For heaven's sake, Ellie, what on earth have you got in that enormous thing?" Ellie looked suitably abashed and didn't want to make her explanation sound too rehearsed.

"Seriously, Ellie, do you really need such an enormous bag?"

"It's awkward, Mrs Davies."

"I can see that. Couldn't you have found a smaller rucksack?"

"Well," said Ellie, casting her eyes dramatically around and looking embarrassed. "It's just that I'm on my period at the moment," she whispered exaggeratedly, "and I need extra stuff in case I sort of leak."

"Oh good grief, Ellie. Just please don't moan when you are having to carry it around with you all day. And don't try and sweet talk Alfie into carrying it for you either."

Suddenly, they were on their way. They shuffled and jostled out of the hall, funnelling through the door quietly, in their anticipation of a day out. As they followed the tail end of the flock, Alfie and Ellie hung back, expecting Charlie to turn up. As Ellie looked back, she murmured, "Bye-bye!"

Chapter 24

Ellie's rucksack was getting very heavy.

She was exceedingly hot in her extra layers of clothes and couldn't wait to strip down. It had seemed miles to walk from the coach park, around Hyde Park Corner, through Green Park. "Here is the meeting point, the Canada Memorial," and down to The Mall. Dear Alfie had of course stepped in and taken Ellie's rucksack for her, despite Mrs Davies' protestation.

The Mall was very crowded, far more than Ellie had expected. She stuck with her designated group like glue; she didn't want to get separated. Alfie had her rucksack, and using Alfie's blond head as her beacon was convenient and reassuring.

They passed some fancy gates, very tall, covered in gold, and obviously not ever used – crazy – and they could see Buckingham Palace looming ahead. Helicopters were buzzing overhead. The sound of traffic could be heard in the distance, brakes screaming, emergency vehicles shrieking urgently. Funnily enough, the people themselves were quiet, subdued, and moved along, muffled and muted.

After endless dodging of great droves of wandering humanity, the inimitable Mrs Davies managed to find a less dense spot and had no hesitation in assertively worming her way through the foreign tourists to get the group really close to the front. Ellie thought she was amazing.

With Mrs Hughes herding them in from behind, they squeezed in and found a really good position from which they would be able to see the procession clearly, as it made its way down The Mall. Cool. They had already lost sight of the other designated groups. It's incredible how large crowds could swallow up people so easily.

They hung about, settled down, and took swigs from their drinks. Alfie handed around a packet of crisps and Maudie shared out her snack of choice, Everton Mints, as old-fashioned as her name. Crisps and mints do not mix but hey, whatever. Ellie was getting waves of butterflies and couldn't settle, so she ate without thinking. She tried not to look anxious. She was worried about saying goodbye to Alfie. She was worried about not saying goodbye to Charlie, let alone worried why he hadn't turned up.

The pavement was packed. There was a really mixed bunch of people around her. A lot of foreigners. It was amazing how she had absolutely no idea what they were saying. A young mum with a headscarf like Aisha's leant over her fractious child's pushchair. The baby was getting cross, not enjoying being still, and kept thrusting away the proffered bottle of milk. Ellie realised that you could hear crossness in any language.

A mum-to-be, her belly straining at her t-shirt – you could even see her belly button sticking out; rather weird – was stroking her bump in the way that pregnant women do, and looking dreamily into the distance.

A rather beautiful police horse clopped by with a tiny policewoman on its back, looking bossily into the crowd as if expecting them to all behave badly at any moment. There seemed to be loads of policemen about, eyeing them all up suspiciously; she'd never seen so many in one place. Apparently, Jack's dad was here somewhere, which was ironic really when Jack and his mum were not.

The policemen in the dark grey uniforms looked really scary, identical with their helmets covering their faces like an army of robots in a sci-fi movie. They carried guns, armed and dangerous, with CTSFO emblazoned on their sleeves.

If they are meant to make us feel safe, they are not succeeding.

A cute, little spaniel with a waggly bum wiggled through the crowd, sniffing bags with enormous enthusiasm. It so obviously loved its job. Adorable. She wanted to give it a pat, but thought it wasn't probably the right thing to do. It made her think of Marmite. She loved Marmite. She would miss Marmite. She tried not to think about dog food.

They'd been there some time; conversation in the group had died to the odd murmur. Nothing more to say really. The crowd was starting to get noticeably restless, pointlessly straining to see if anything was coming yet.

She got out her phone to check the time.

Should I go now or wait until later?

She had butterflies in her tummy. She dithered. Alfie, from his great height, shouted loudly like an excited, small boy, "They're coming!" He promptly looked really embarrassed.

It made Ellie snigger and she biffed him on the arm. "Not cool, mate!"

She decided to hang on and just see the procession go by.

Chapter 25

Kate let herself into Caroline's house.

Through the back door, of course, otherwise known as the tradesmen's entrance by Caroline, and only Caroline. She called out, "Hi, only Kate." She expected both Caroline and Thomas to be there, but was greeted with complete silence. Kate cocked her head on one side, listening out for movement anywhere, and shrugged.

"I've got Lily with me, hope it's okay but she wasn't at all well and I didn't like to leave her on her own. I left you a message."

Pause. Still no answer. *Phew.* she could just get on with the cleaning without hearing all Caroline's tales of woe. The "I was clearly not invited to Susie's big dinner party" thing, the cold, unloving husband, the school fees, and how the gardener had put up his hourly rate.

Get a life, Caroline!

Being certain that Caroline was actually out, she called out to Lily, who dragged herself in, clearly not well at all. Lily immediately flopped out on the pristine white sofa in the kitchen, where it was nice and warm from the navy blue Aga, propped her head on the silk cushions, wrapped her coat tightly round her and closed her eyes.

Kate felt her forehead; still very warm but obviously just this virus that was going round. "Okay, love?"

She received a grunt in reply. Kate took off her coat – Lily obviously wanted to keep hers on – and hung it in what Kate called the back passage; a name Caroline did not find at all amusing.

She spotted the note on the granite counter, written with a proper fountain pen, of course, in swirly, curly lettering.

"Dear Kate, Please could you make up William's bedroom, ready for half term. The sheets will need to be changed because they are rather stale from non-use. Could you also have a go at the Aga top – it seems to have become much stained. Is there something else you could use on it? Perhaps just a bit more elbow grease? Gone up to town. Hairdressers. Back later so please put the casserole from the fridge into the top left of the Aga so that it is there when we return. Many thanks, Caroline HC."

Alongside was Kate's cheque.

Caroline had managed to pack in a jibe about the beds and the Aga all crammed into one note, but it was the "HC" that made Kate snort.

Why did she bother? Why not just Caroline, like an ordinary person? Did she not realise that everyone called her Madame Holy Cow? Silly woman with her airs and graces.

Kate left the note and, with a last pat on Lily's unresponsive shoulder, she walked through to the study to double-check that Thomas wasn't in. She knocked, opened the door and peered round. Nope, he wasn't. She turned away and started on her weekly routine. She would spritz a bit of spray starch in William's bed, Caroline would never know the difference.

After rushing about non-stop for two hours, polishing, hoovering (although it was a Dyson), chasing cobwebs, 8,181 steps recorded on her Fitbit, she had a break, made herself and Lily a cup of green tea (none of that dreadful caffeine allowed in this house), and popped outside the back door for a vape – Caroline didn't like her to vape indoors.

Her phone was running out of juice and she hadn't brought her charger with her, but she had enough to flick through if she was quick. No new messages, usual junk on FB, although there was a hilarious post from her little brother about a new device to keep Muslim illegal immigrants out; basically, it was a pack of bacon. It was probably a bit racist, but it still made her chuckle.

The main topic trending seemed to be pics of the crowds at the State Opening of Parliament.

Nice carriages! Lovely horses. Poor Lily missing it like this.

The last bit of charge dried up. Kate quietly vaped to the last drop, enjoying the sunshine on her face, and opened the door to go back in and resume her duties.

It was very odd; there was a sudden glow of light, as if the clouds had suddenly stepped back, almost like a reverse eclipse, if such a thing was possible. She shrugged and set off up the stairs, two at a time, can of spray starch in hand to tackle William's bed with a loud "Yee-hah."

Take that Madame Holy Cow!

Chapter 26

Ellie found the whole procession thing to be a bit of a disappointment.

It didn't look real. Perhaps it was her mood, but Ellie just couldn't really see the point of all the fancy coaches, the crazy crowns, the people who by some strange accident of being born were famous for being just famous and all that crap. It was a bit like a pretend Disneyland parade, without the music and fireworks. She had liked the horses though. They were real enough and some were behaving very badly. *Cute.*

Ellie got up the app, *Great British Public Toilet Map*, found her nearest one and caught up with Mrs Davies as they headed back towards the meeting point.

"Mrs Davies, Mrs Davies. I need the toilet urgently. I've found one really nearby up by the tube station."

Mrs Davies sighed and raised her eyebrows, looked at where Ellie was pointing on her screen, and looked over her shoulder, as if she would be able to see it through the trees of Green Park. Ellie could see her going through it in her mind but had obviously remembered what she'd said earlier.

"Okay Ellie, but be quick. We'll meet you back at the meeting point, okay?"

Ellie hoiked on her rucksack. Turning to Alfie, she gave him an enormous hug and a quick little kiss on the bottom of his chin, it was as high as she could reach.

"Thanks, Alfie. Thanks for everything."

"No sweat. It was only carrying your rucksack, Ellie – any time!" he grinned.

Ellie checked her phone screen, looked up and headed off towards the toilets, squeezing through the crowds that trailed slowly into the park, looked all ways, turned back to the group, hesitated, waved, and then strode off determinedly along the wide tarmac path towards the toilets. Within moments, she'd been absorbed by the crowd.

Chapter 27

Sarah Davies was concerned.

Ellie hadn't come back from the toilets.

Surely the queue couldn't have been that long.

At the meeting point, all the groups had miraculously converged together again, wandering about between the two wings of the memorial, lots of familiar faces gathering and bumping and tousling like a pack of dogs that hadn't seen each other for ages.

There was a lot of banter about the procession. "Come on, how can you fancy her? She really is pug-ugly!" "Don't be an asshole!" Mrs Davies was normally onto that sort of language in a flash, but she didn't even bother to intervene.

They waited. Mrs Davies rang Ellie's phone but it just rang and rang and cut to the answering service. She'd a bad feeling about this, very bad. They waited and waited and all the kids were getting very restless. They all gathered round Ellie's group, questioning them as if they should know where she was: "What had exactly happened? Where had Ellie gone? To the toilets? When?"

Alfie was looking thoughtful. What had Ellie meant? It kept re-running in his head. That enormous hug and the quick little kiss on the bottom of his chin. *"Thanks, Alfie. Thanks for everything." "No sweat, it was only carrying your rucksack, Ellie – any time!" OMG.* He didn't know whether to say anything. *Best keep shtum for now and see how it shapes up.*

Mrs Davies was now seriously worried, but made a precise decision. Ellie's designated group would be reallocated to other groups. She would contact the head, Jon Barker, for advice, wait at the meeting point and liaise from there. The rest of the trip would continue as planned. She called Jon; it took him only a second to pick up the phone, and they had a long conversation, her bringing him up to speed. He agreed with the plan.

"Bye, Jessica, see you later," Mrs Davies called after her friend and colleague.

"Bloody kids!" Jessica shouted back, a grin on her face. "Come on you lot. Let's go!" she said, laughingly herding the kids off like a flock of sheep. The school party moved off towards the War Rooms, still talking about it. Nothing much happened in their lives so they were buzzing with it.

Sarah was left standing there, abruptly alone, peering around as if Ellie might suddenly appear, dialling Ellie's phone once more, just in case. She pursed her lips and, as agreed with Jon, called the police. Was she over-reacting? Instinct said not.

The police were vaguely helpful but not as worried as Sarah. "She is 17? She has gone missing for how long? She said she was going to the toilet? That is probably where she is then! Look, Mrs Davies, I am sure that she will turn up; it sounds as if she is probably having a great time and has bunked off to go shopping in the West End, or something like that."

Sarah was getting a bit shirty and she knew that she sounded it.

"Yes, we do take all such reports very seriously. We agree that you should wait exactly where you are. We will send officers to take details and take it from there. We have pinpointed your location on satnav so please just wait. Please do not wander off."

Wander off? Good grief, who do they think I am?

"Obviously that area is very crowded and busy at the moment, so it may be some time. In the meantime, keep trying her phone. Your incident number, if you could write it down please, is 3-1-4-9-8-7."

Sarah found them rather patronising. She really was not an idiot.

The school procedures said that she should now get the head to contact Ellie's parents. She was quite comfortable about talking to Jon Barker, but Ellie's parents were another thing. She couldn't put her finger on it but something told her that it could get Ellie into very hot water. She would talk it through with Jon. She guessed that he was feeling the same way. It was his decision at the end of the day.

How long were the police going to be?

Sarah once again looked anxiously at her watch. A small aeroplane, not an airliner, odd sort of thing, incongruously passed overhead, between the helicopters.

That's really low.

Chapter 28

Meredith received a phone call from Jon Barker.

"Mrs Webber? Mr Barker here. I am sorry to trouble you but we need to meet and speak about Ellie." Meredith's heart was racing, her stomach sank.

Oh dear God, what has Eleanor said? Was this it, the moment that she'd been dreading, when it all came out?

She stood frozen, everything going through her head as if in slow motion. She turned aside, hiding the phone, as if Gary was watching her reaction and listening, even though she knew he was upstairs in bed. "When, Mr Barker?" Meredith could barely speak, her throat had closed up, and she couldn't breathe very well.

"Straight away, if that is okay. This is extremely urgent."

"Yes, okay, that is fine. It won't take me than 20 minutes to get round to school. I will come straight away."

It suddenly dawned on her that Eleanor was on the school trip.

Had she been confiding in her teachers? Oh God, Susie Cole was on the trip, she'd been crowing about going at her dinner party. Perhaps Eleanor had said something to her; Susie was that sort of person, a person you felt obliged to tell confidences to.

She put her coffee mug in the dishwasher, wiped the work surfaces with a trembling hand and straightened the chairs out of habit. Meredith was suddenly desperate to go to the toilet and took longer than necessary over it, washing her hands meticulously and drying them carefully on the hand towel, her stomach churning. She checked herself in the mirror. "You aren't going out looking like that, surely?" she could hear Gary saying in her head.

Did she dare tell Gary where she was going? He would ask questions. He might want to come too. Should she just creep out? She listened carefully at the bottom of the stairs for any sign of any noise. Best do this on her own. She grabbed her bag from the hall table, carefully opened the front door, shutting it quietly behind her with just a gentle click. She tiptoed to her car.

She fumbled clumsily in her bag for her car keys and trying to breathe, turned on the ignition. Music blared out so loudly that it made her tattered nerves ping, so she instinctively hit the off button before easing her little car around Gary's – "Be careful, Meredith, watch out, you can be so careless" – heading off to school, crunching the gears and bunny-hopping down the road in panic.

She parked with exaggerated care, hoping to waste time and put off the meeting, sat for a moment, her eyes closed and her fists clenched. Her whole body was trembling and cold.

Big breath now, Meredith, you have to do this for Eleanor and sod the consequences.

She climbed out, closed the door carefully – "Don't slam the door!"

Please Gary, get out of my head.

Taking small, slow steps, she moved, her head bowed in shame, for the main entrance.

She buzzed the bell and was let in by Mr Hubbard. Meredith didn't know him very well. She had seen him occasionally at previous school functions, but he looked very odd, wild almost, and out of control. Normally, he was a bit offhand and superior for no good reason and made Meredith feel stupid.

"Mrs Webber? Oh my God, you are here! We weren't expecting... so quickly... Mr Barker has asked for all Year 12 parents to be directed to the sports hall. You are the first to arrive... He will be down... He has to sort things... He has to find out..." Meredith tried to get a word in edgeways but seemingly failed. He looked as if he was about to burst into tears.

What a strange man.

Meredith meekly headed for the sports hall. All very odd and not what she'd been expecting at all. Why all Year 12 parents? Mr Barker had definitely said that he needed to speak about Eleanor specifically. Perhaps it wasn't what she'd dreaded after all. She let herself relax, just a little.

Chapter 29

Susie didn't know what to do with herself; she was just sitting at the table with her throbbing ankle.

After having a couple of bowls of cereal, eating all of the drugs out of the first aid cabinet, all the odds and ends out of multiple half-used packets, and finding a packet of frozen prawns – there didn't seemed to be any peas – to put on her throbbing ankle, she read the paper, did the Sudoku, the Kakuro, and all the other puzzles.

To be honest, none of the maths ones had seemed to turn out quite right, and she always ended up with more than one of the wretched numbers in a square where it shouldn't be. Maths was not her strong point. Crosswords were better. She'd managed to finish the cryptic one in half an hour, with only a tiny bit of cheating using the Crossword Solver that she'd googled.

She was still fretting over the call from Jack. He had been incandescent with rage. It had completely slipped her mind that in the heat of the moment, she still had his school trip permission slip in her own bag. She'd meant to take it in with her when she went into school.

It was all because of the sodding fall down the stairs. It was a bit much that they wouldn't let him go. They knew that he had her permission, otherwise, she wouldn't have been going on the bloody trip with him, would she? Sarah Davies was very, very efficient, but she could also be a pain in the bum. *Sod her.*

How was she going to make things right with Jack? This could fester for days, weeks, even years. He could be a bit like Pete in the way he would bear a grudge for days on end.

May the 25th would always be the day Mum forgot the sodding permission slip. What would Pete say? Probably just "Oh, Susie", the way that he did when she yet again did something hopelessly daft.

Fretting about the permission slip suddenly reminded her that she still hadn't taken her NADFAS sub to Leah. Leah at least wouldn't be quite so furious, but she'd reminded her at the dinner party and when they met for coffee in town and when they had been round at Jessica's. It had sounded a bit like nagging, but she did realise that it had been the nth reminder.

Bloody hell. Slips had become her absolute nemesis. The curse of all mothers. The deadline of all deadlines for NADFAS was tomorrow; it had already been extended twice. She couldn't post it, it wouldn't get there in time, and anyway, Leah only lived just down the road, so to post it would be madness, even for herself. She could pick up some more pain-killing drugs and frozen peas at the supermarket as she drove past.

She thought about it carefully as she worked her way down the packet of Pringles that she had bought as a snack for Jack on his trip and forgotten to give him. The ads were right, once you popped, you really couldn't stop. Thank heavens it was just a small snack-sized tube.

She pondered some more. Her car was an automatic. Her injury was to her left ankle. She could drive round to Leah's if she could hop into the garage. What she really needed was a walking stick. Dad used to have a whole umbrella stand of the things, all shapes and sizes, some with beautifully-carved and painted handles. They stood in the hall of the farmhouse. a magnificent display as you came in through the front door, caught in a spotlight of sunshine from the fanlight window above the door. Susie could see it in her mind's eye, one of many happy memories of a charmed childhood. By coincidence, a flare of bright sunlight lit up the kitchen as the thought went through Susie's mind.

Anyway, I digress, I will just have to improvise.

Licking her salty fingers one by one, she buried the evidence of the unscheduled snack at the bottom of the bin, where Pete and the kids wouldn't spot it.

She hopped to the utility room.

Broom or mop? Mop or broom? Broom is probably easier.

It certainly did the trick, she decided with a grin, leaning on it with determination. With her handy new crutch, she found hopping about so much easier. She hopped into the hall and even up the stairs and wrestled herself into yesterday's clothes – the school trip special outfit was side-lined.

She couldn't fit any shoes over her puffed-up foot so she just put a deck shoe onto her right foot. She carefully brushed her hair, while balancing with the broom tucked under her armpit – it was just so soothing when she felt agitated. She smoothed on mascara to make herself look more presentable, Leah always looked immaculate, and her face burst into life.

She took ages carefully hopping down the stairs, one step at a time, careful that it was not going to happen again, eventually arriving at the scene of the crime, somewhat breathless from all the exertion. The clothes were still spread all over the place and she leant down and flicked them feebly into a semblance of a heap. She would deal with them later.

She hopped about in the kitchen, the sitting room, the dining room, flicking through important-looking piles of paper, and eventually found the NADFAS form, with the Electoral Roll form that she'd promised Pete she'd sent in. She imprisoned it in her bag.

Car keys? Car keys?

She hopped about in the kitchen, the sitting room, the dining room, vainly looking in all the usual hiding places. They were found eventually in the loo, on top of the spare loo roll. She couldn't understand why, until she remembered dashing in, desperate for a pee, after shopping the other day.

Yes she knew there was the special key dish just inside the door from the garage but, well, just "but". Pete always looked at her, head cocked to one side, one eyebrow raised, every time she lost the keys. He had placed the dish there for her especially, but she always forgot to use it.

It was harder than she'd thought to get into the car. In the end, she sat down, swivelled round and manhandled her left leg into the foot well, being very careful that it didn't make contact with anything on the way. She knew it would hurt – it was throbbing still.

She carefully stowed the broom behind her, placed the subscription envelope on top of her handbag on the passenger seat so that she could keep an eye on it – she wasn't going to lose it again – started the car and breezed out of the garage. A rousing chorus of *The Phantom of the Opera* shouted from the speakers. Her favourite. It was fine just using her right foot. *Phew.*

It usually only took a couple of minute to get to Leah's, but as she drove down the main street, she was surprised to see it so busy. Everybody in the world seemed to have decided to descend all at once. It looked as if they were all having parties, the way they were piling stuff into the boots of their cars. It was most unusual for a mid-week day.

Have I missed something?

She edged her way through tentatively. People seemed to be parking in really weird and rather stupid places. The mass of cars suddenly tailed off and Susie was able to speed up as she headed out of the centre. She turned right at Gary's newly-refurbished pub – it did look very smart actually – and halfway down, swung into Leah's drive, parking behind Leah's Mercedes.

She chuckled to herself, remembering how Amelia was always complaining about Leah's terrifying driving. Apparently, she would accelerate away at great speed, and then brake heavily to stop before racing off again. Leah's mother-in-law was a permanent fixture in the front passenger seat and apparently flopped backwards and forwards like a rag doll. Amelia, in the back seat, said it made her feel quite sick, but the whole mother-in-law thing was hilarious, particularly as she didn't speak a word of English but was always very friendly, smiled a lot and nodded like a family dog.

She opened the door, grabbed her stalwart broom, grasped the subscription form and swung out of the car, using the broom to lever herself up. She realised that she must look quite a sight. She smiled and started the hop to the front door, where she leant on the bell. The smile stayed on her face as she waited for the surprise that Leah was going to get when she opened the door to see her and her trusty broom.

The door opened. Susie grinned, waiting for Leah's face to light up in the way that it did, but instead, Leah starting shrieking and wouldn't stop. Tears poured down Leah's cheeks and she flung her arms round Susie – this was not easy when balancing on a broom – sobbing into Susie's shoulder, raising her head intermittently to almost howl, babbling in what Susie assumed was Pakistani.

There seemed to be a lot of "Allah, may his name be praised" amongst it all. It was bit bizarre and just went on and on.

"Leah, for God's sake, what is the matter? Please, please, what is happening? Why are you so distraught?"

Leah continued to wail and gripped her tighter.

After what seemed ages, Leah looked Susie in the eye, her hands on her shoulders, shaking her roughly and kept saying, "You're alive! You're alive!" over and over again, almost knocking her over as she thrust her back and forwards.

"I only fell down the stairs!" Susie responded, very puzzled. Looking around to see if anyone was witnessing this extraordinary behaviour, Susie suggested that they go inside, and attempted to bundle Leah in through her own front door.

"Now, Leah, please talk to me. Tell me what on earth is going on." She was so concerned at the hysterical behaviour that she forgot to take her shoes off – well, the one shoe – which was strictly taboo. She wasn't thinking about shoes, just Leah's extraordinary emotional display. Leah tried to speak through her distress and Susie tried really hard to make out what she was saying.

"London... I thought you must be dead. I thought you were in London, on the trip. The bomb. Everyone is dead. It's horrific. It's terrible. It's indescribable. But you are alive!"

Leah gasped. "Now, Leah, slow down and try and tell me what happened. Did you say bomb? What bomb? Where? Who is dead? When?"

"They don't know who did it; of course, they are immediately blaming it on Muslims, but thousands, maybe millions are dead." Leah collapsed into racking sobs again.

Susie was uncharacteristically beginning to get a bit annoyed. "For God's sake, Leah, take a deep breath and tell me slowly and carefully."

Leah was always somewhat prone to drama and exaggeration when she told her magnificent stories, but this was something else.

Leah turned and went into the sitting room, and flapped her hand towards the TV while babbling incoherently. A newscaster that Susie had never seen before was sitting looking serious and intoning in a hushed voice in front of a plain blue screen. Words were bouncing along as subtitles along the bottom of the screen.

Susie couldn't hear above Leah's wails. She looked at Leah's mother-in-law, who was sitting on the sofa, rocking crazily and clutching the remote.

"Turn it up, Leah, please."

Leah grabbed for the remote and increased the volume frantically, stabbing at the button.

"I repeat," intoned the newscaster, "this is an emergency broadcast from BBC Salford. Please remain calm. Today, at 11:30a.m., a small nuclear device was exploded in Westminster. It is assumed that there may be further attacks in major cities and towns throughout the UK. You may be at risk if you are within the M25 around London, or within 25 miles of any city or town centre. Please take shelter immediately. Stay indoors, close all windows and doors, and barricade windows where possible. Do not leave your home, even to collect children from school; they will be taken care of. You are safer if you remain indoors. Do not go outdoors where you may be exposed to radiation. Radiation will kill you. If you are in a vehicle, leave it and find a place of safety nearby, but do not obstruct access by emergency services. Tune to your local radio or television and await further instructions. Do not use your phones, as the networks are required for use by the emergency services. Please remain calm, stay indoors and await further instructions."

The presenter took a deep breath and stared down at the pieces of paper. A woman's voice started in a foreign language and unintelligible words floated across the bottom of the screen.

Icy water trickled down Susie's spine. The hairs on the back of her neck bristled. She looked at Leah, her eyes wide. "Jesus Holy Christ!" Her eyes turned back to the TV, and after a moment, she muttered, "London – a bomb. Westminster. Nuclear device. A nuclear explosion. Sweet Jesus."

She stared at the TV as a man's voice started talking in another language, and more hieroglyphics drifted across the screen. Then it dawned on her. "Jesus Christ, the school trip. The children. Westminster. All the children. Jessica! Pete! All the children!" Her stomach rolled over and she felt adrenalin surge through her body. "And Pete, my Pete." She thought she might have screamed, as she sunk heavily onto Leah's sofa without being asked; she was just so shocked. She suddenly understood why Leah was so distraught. "Oh Jesus, Oh Jesus!"

Susie stared at the television, aghast, her mouth hanging open unattractively, and waited for the bulletin to start again to try and understand it, to take it in. She tried to think, but she couldn't, she didn't know where to start. She felt sick. She needed to pee. Thoughts kept piling in.

All those people dead. All just suddenly dead. But Jack was safe. Thank God. But Pete, Pete!

I escaped by the skin of my teeth. Jessica! Dear, sweet Jesus, Jessica. Jessica went instead of me. Alfie was on the trip. Aisha was on the trip. No wonder Leah was so distraught. I bet Richard is at his office up there. Oh my God. Hundreds and thousands of people. Unbelievable.

What about Henry? Mum? Was Surrey affected? And the children? And Caroline's William is at Westminster.

The names kept piling into her head: The kids that had come to Jack's party... nice Ellie, that lovely boy, Charlie, she couldn't think of all their names, there was a Daz, a Jordan, and there was Kate's Lily and... just thousands of others. She couldn't make any sense of it.

She sat icily still, her mouth working as she tried to take it in. The names were like a roll call. Leah was moaning and clutching her arms around herself.

"Leah, Leah, I am so, so sorry. Leah, what can I say? Aisha? Aisha?" Tears suddenly burst out, flooding Susie's cheeks.

Leah seemed to pull herself together. "No, you don't understand, Susie, Aisha is safe. I would not let her go unchaperoned. She didn't go. And you. You didn't go? You are safe. Allah, may his name be praised, has saved my child and he has chosen to save you."

Susie stared blankly at Leah. "I don't understand".

Leah turned to Susie, her eyes bright with fervour "The Holy Prophet Muhammad, may peace and blessings be upon him, informed mankind of God's message, which is found in the Holy Qur'an, and he warned us about God's punishment if we did not follow that message. This..." Leah waved her arms so expansively that her covering fell from her head, "this is a Divine punishment, warning mankind. God has brought about the destruction of non-believers. It is up to mankind to turn to following God's way!"

Susie shook her head and looked baffled and amazed by this lecture, this outpouring. "You can't mean that, Leah? Surely! You can't think that! Leah, think of all those innocent kids and children and…" Susie's voice tailed off and names kept piling up in her brain, names of people who were in every likelihood dead.

Jessica was innocent. Alfie was innocent. What had Pete ever done wrong?

She looked questioningly at Leah. Leah stared back defiantly, with a set look on her face.

"But, Leah, Aisha was meant to be there. I was meant to be there. Jack was meant to be there. Jessica has gone instead of me."

"Jessica. You made Jessica go instead of you? Susie, she will have been killed. She will be dead too. What have you done? How could you? Jessica! You sent Jessica?"

"For God's sake, Leah, I didn't know. Poor, poor Jessica, but I didn't know, Leah, how could I know? It was just pure luck. It is just some really, really mad stroke of luck that I didn't go, or Jack."

"Luck?" Leah responded "Luck!"

Susie was baffled, hurt, angry. What could Leah mean? They were interrupted by waves of moans and cries from the mother-in-law.

Susie looked at her, looked angrily at Leah, shocked, hurt. "I don't know what to do but I think I had better go to school, see Jack. Find out what is happening."

"But they specifically say to stay indoors."

"Sod that, we're miles away," replied Susie, heaving herself to her feet. She forgot about her ankle, a vicious pain reminding her – it made her feel sick again. She hobbled out of the sitting room in a daze, found her broom, which seemed even more ridiculous now, and shuffled to the door.

She turned to speak to Leah but just couldn't think of anything nice to say.

Divine bloody punishment and sending Jessica to her death. How dare she? How dare she?

She let herself out, hobbling clumsily, closing the door as quietly as she could. It was up to Leah to follow if she wanted to.

Chapter 30

Moira was standing at the kitchen sink, peeling tatties ready for lunch.

She was looking dreamily through the cottage window, out onto the yard, and listening to Radio 2.

It was a bonnie May day so all the doors and windows were flung wide open in the cottage to let in the sunshine, and a nice, refreshing breeze was blowing in from the open back door, wafting in the honey scent from the deutzia, which was flowering profusely alongside the path.

Moira hadn't noticed Brenda sneak out of the front door to go to the farmhouse, yet again. It was one of her current obsessions. She looked up when an extra bright shard of sunlight flashed from behind the clouds, catching her attention. She saw Brenda shoot across the open yard at a rapid rate for someone who was 75 years old. She was sound in body, if not in mind.

The chickens gave her away by squawking indignantly as she scuttled by, as did the three dogs who leaped up from their sunbathing and greeting her with their madly wagging tails. They caused a great visual disturbance, the little terrier squiggling with pleasure.

"Och, bother that woman! *The Great Escape*!" Moira exclaimed indulgently, as she saw Brenda scurry furtively over to the farmhouse and nip in through the back door.

Should she go and round Brenda up? Henry and Fenella weren't due back until mid-afternoon so it was nae bother. She had seen them leave and understood that they were going to watch the children at a sports day, before bringing them home for an exeat. Following a long-standing family tradition, going back to when Henry and Susie were at the very same school apparently, they were having their lunch at the Crown and Anchor.

Moira was looking forward to seeing Alice and Arthur; they were adorable, wee things.

Brenda had taken to rummaging around over there in the main farmhouse, which annoyed Fenella, but Moira didn't think it did much harm. It did keep Brenda calm, and she was getting very muddled indeed these days. She would come back from her rummaging, very piqued; bearing things that she claimed Fenella had taken from her "without even asking!" – Moira just returned them once Brenda had forgotten about them again.

Moira was fond of Brenda. Moira liked working for people like Brenda, rather than those who were always feeling sorry for themselves, despite the odd situations caused by the dementia. She'd looked after a fair few during her career and was used to it.

Moira's first patient had been her own mother, crippled with multiple sclerosis, widowed young and just not able to look after herself at all from when Moira was a wee, young bairn. Social Services had designated her as a "Young Carer", which indeed she was, but she didn't like labels, too definite. Moira had fallen into taking care of her mother and had never been able to do anything else, more from not ever considering that anything else was an option than intent. It hadn't really struck her that she could move away.

By the time her mother had eventually passed away, life had already passed Moira by, and she wasn't really equipped for any other jobs. Living in the remote Highlands, she found herself suddenly alone. She opened her eyes and her soul and, feeling like Braveheart, bravely stepped out to meet the rest of the world. It had been easier than she'd thought, and she soon discovered that carers with her skills, her personality and, probably most importantly, no dependents, were very heavily in demand.

Despite her dementia, Brenda was a tough, old bird, down to earth and amusing company. Old school. Physically, she was excellent for her age, standing tall and straight, her skin fighting back the age wrinkles from the Oil of Olay cream she diligently applied every day, sometimes several times when she'd forgotten that she'd already done it. She went through gallons of the stuff.

Brenda insisted on keeping her thick, grey, wiry hair long, and tied it back firmly in a film star chignon, showing off her strong cheekbones, jutting below her startlingly-coloured, aquamarine eyes. She'd been blonde once upon a time, like her daughter, Susie, who had inherited both her magnificent mane of hair and the startling eyes. Brenda was indeed still a handsome woman.

Moira, in comparison, was a bit on the short side and rather plump – homely, she liked to think. Her Celtic colouring marked her out as a true Scot, and she was rather proud of her red hair, although it was inclined to have a mind of its own, and proved very wayward. She was more than glad that it had held its own and stayed red; well, mainly, once she'd got to 50, as she'd been worried that it would fade to a dirty grey like her mother's had.

"We are interrupting this programme to give you an emergency bulletin." The sudden change of tone from good, old, cheesy tunes to deep, sombre voice caught Moira's ear immediately, and she stopped to listen. "This is an emergency broadcast from BBC Radio 2. Please remain calm. Today, at 11:30a.m., a small nuclear device was exploded in Westminster. It is assumed that there may be further attacks in major cities and towns throughout the UK. You may be at risk if you are within the M25 around London or within 25 miles of any city or town centre. Please take shelter immediately, stay indoors, close all windows and doors, and barricade windows where possible. Do not leave your home, even to collect children from school; they will be taken care of. You are safer if you remain indoors. Do not go outdoors where you may be exposed to radiation. Radiation will kill you. If you are in a vehicle, leave it and find a place of safety nearby, but do not obstruct access by emergency services. Tune to your local radio or television and await further instructions. Do not use your phones, as the networks are required for use by the emergency services. Please remain calm, stay indoors and await further instructions."

Good God Almighty! The Saints preserve us!

Moira dropped a potato into the sink in horror and the water splashed back onto her face, making her jump with another spike of adrenalin. It sounded appalling.

How could this be? It was monstrous.

Her heart was racing.

Dear God in Heaven.

Some rather odd music came on, more Radio 4 style. Perhaps it was just a radio play trailer, like *War of the Worlds*.

Not very clever, if you ask me, frightening people half to death with that sort of thing.

The radio blared out again. A repeat of the same message. Moira stood stock-still. *Perhaps it was real.* She waited, staring at the radio, her hand holding the potato peeler, still poised in the air. More sombre music. Then, there it was again.

Good grief. It must be real. What on earth was going to happen?

She vaguely remembered a film about it. *The Day After*, she thought, or was that about the seas rising? She stood there, rooted to the spot.

What did it mean? Did it mean that lots of people would have been killed?

How bad a bomb could it be?

Being practical, how far are we from London?

She'd absolutely no idea but it must be about 30 miles. They were certainly well outside the M25.

Surely we're safe out here in the countryside? Thank God for that.

She let her breath out. She hadn't realised that she was holding it.

It was hard to restart peeling the tatties. She was just so shocked, mesmerised. She wondered what everyone else must be thinking just now. She couldn't help but peer out of the window to see if anything had changed. No. The sky was still blue, with a lot of clouds floating about, going about their business, the sun shining and it was still a lovely day.

The chickens were fine, wandering about, pecking randomly. The three dogs were back settled in their favourite spots, basking in the sunshine. Rags, the elder of the two spaniels, was lying on his back, his legs in the air, his private parts on full show, with a ridiculously saucy grin on his face, occasionally wriggling in the grass.

They repeated the news bulletin and added emerging information. It was still just London, nowhere else as yet. They explained that it was not an enormous bomb, smaller than the one that had hit Hiroshima, about zones of destruction at varying distances, and the expected spread of destruction from the epicentre of the bomb.

It may not be an enormous one to you, pal, but it sounds appalling enough, shocking, horrific.

In her mind, she ran through where each of the family members were: Brenda across the yard at the farmhouse, Henry and Fenella at school with the children, Susie and Pete and their children near Hartley Wintney, Dave the cowman and wife Heather at home in their cottage. Having decided that everyone she knew was safe she'd gone back to peeling the tatties in slow motion, in shock, watchful and listening obsessively, waiting for more information.

She wasn't entirely sure what else she could do.

The bulletins developed. The area hit appeared to be the Houses of Parliament, and today was the State Opening of Parliament. All the MPs, the whole of the Royal Family, the lords and the bishops; all of the most important people in the land were crammed into the Houses of Parliament, all together. Moira gasped.

Dear God! All of them! Each and every one of them? Dear God!

It was a grand occasion and there would have been a whole bunch of foreign visitors strung along The Mall. It seemed that they would have all been wiped out; it was that sort of bomb, an enormous, great, vile, radioactive thing. It was too big, too fantastic, too grotesque to take in.

Moira looked out of the window again, towards the general direction of London, and couldn't believe it had happened so close and yet so far. The sky still looked exactly the same as it had all morning – slightly cloudy, and the sun was still beaming as if completely unconcerned. She was tempted to close all the doors.

Her heart was fluttering, she felt trembly and out of sorts, and decided to ring Henry just for someone to talk to about it. She dried her hands on the tea towel and reached for the telephone, but after dialling five times, she gave up. It just kept giving the engaged signal. She tried Susie and Pete.

She tried phoning Dave and Heather. Engaged, engaged, engaged.

"I am guessing that all the world and his wife will be trying to phone someone right now. I'll try again later."

She shook her head in an attempt to rid herself of thoughts of this awful cataclysm, and picked up an unpeeled tattie that suddenly looked very reassuringly normal and solid in her grasp, but the thoughts wouldn't stop whirling in her head. Should she go and round up Brenda or was she overreacting?

Chapter 31

Bernie sat in front of the TV.

The hair on the back of his neck prickled. He felt as if someone had just fast-frozen him; a strange trickling feeling ran down his spine. He thought he had better breathe because he seemed to have forgotten to do so. The noise of it was so loud and it felt so fresh that another burst of adrenalin shot through him like being stabbed by an icicle.

He wanted to yell out loud. He wanted someone there with him. He felt isolated, alone, as if floating in a sea of icebergs. A pathetically unmanly whimper oozed out instead. He still couldn't move, just sat cold and numb, staring at the man on the telly, listening to the words that fell from his mouth, through the strange whistling sound that had invaded his ears.

He staggered up, headed into the hall and, with shaking hands, rifled through the diary to 25th May. It was there in black and white, pink lurid writing actually, London, with a great big messy arrow going through to Sunday. Mini had definitely gone to London.

"No, no," he groaned. "No, no," he said, in a wintry whisper.

He couldn't think what to do, so he wandered back into the lounge, sat in his armchair. His hands clutched the arms of the chair, frozen. Emily was at school. She was meant to be going to Hannah's. They would be taking care of her, they said so on the TV, but would she realise? He watched as the story unfolded.

"Nuclear explosion... Please remain calm, stay inside... Do not use phones."

Mini, Mini? His head had sirens going off inside. It hurt. *Perhaps she was in a safe part of London.* How could he find out? Surely she would ring and let him know as soon as she could.

Despite what they were saying, he would try her mobile telephone. He levered himself up and picked up the house telephone. His mind went blank and he couldn't think what Mini's number was. He flipped up the index by the phone, the one that Mini had laughed at for being so old-fashioned, but he had managed to hang onto, thank heavens. It still had Helen's neat, cursive handwriting in it, with the addition of Mini's mad pink ink for her entries.

With trembling fingers, he dialled, but had to make several attempts because his fingers always seemed to be too big for the buttons and were shaking uncontrollably. *Big breath, dial slowly, carefully.* Eventually, his inadequate poking and prodding worked, the call went through, but went straight to the irritating message "Sorry, the person you have dialled is not available. Please call again later." *What did that mean?*

He had kissed her goodbye this morning, enveloped her fragile, wriggling, little body in his arms and kissed her on the top of her silky, little head. She'd darted away, skipped out of the door, blowing him a kiss as she went with her adorable little giggle and her girly little wiggle. "I must dash or I will miss the train. See you on Sunday."

He had let her go. He should have stopped her. He should have known. If only he had hung onto her a moment longer, she would have missed the train, she wouldn't have been in London. She would be here. *Dear God. How was he going to tell Emily?*

He rifled through his index, looking for Liz's number, her landline, as she always called it. Perhaps they were together or something and they were safe. He found it in Mini's favourite bright pink pen, scrawled across the page, the last numbers curling back and crawling down the edge because of her enthusiastic writing running out of space.

He dialled very carefully, despite his shaking hands. It went through to Liz's answering machine but he didn't know what to say; he needed to plan it in advance, so he just put the phone down. Should he leave a message? Surely they would know to get in touch with him to say that they were safe? Surely?

He knew that Mini definitely had her mobile telephone with her because she'd telephoned him from the train. "I'm on my way! Very excited to see my sis. Will try and phone this evening but we will probably be going out so don't bank on it." The line hadn't been very good and he wasn't very comfortable on the phone anyway; he always worried that it must be costing her a fortune, and the conversation had been short. "Bye old codger."

"Goodbye my little darling Mini," he had replied.

Bernie howled with pain.

Chapter 32

Henry and Fenella were watching Arthur in the shot put.

He was quite good actually for such a small chap, the shot went miles. Then they tried to work out where Alice was and what her next event would be.

No one was entirely sure who heard or saw it first, but word spread hesitantly at first, in disbelief, but rolled into a wave that washed over the whole crowd. A bomb. London. A major incident.

It was shocking but seemed remote, far away, and it seemed right to try and carry on watching the children's inter-house athletics. All the same, everybody scoured their tablets and phones for updates as the horror unfolded, glancing north towards London, as if they might be able to see what was happening.

It was a bizarre situation, whole herds of parents anxiously swiping their screens, sharing the latest news whilst trying to act as if nothing out of the ordinary was happening, so as not to disturb the family atmosphere, so British. Great gasps and crescendos of chatter would suddenly ripple through the tense crowd as the latest bulletin revealed the full ghastly extent of the monstrous act, each new announcement adding to the enormity of it. The tense atmosphere was palpable.

Firstly, there were just rumours of a bomb, but not what sort of bomb. Then the fact that it was a nuke, a "uranium-enriched, improvised device" apparently, that immediately labelled it a terrorist attack, became evident and the level of panic rose. Where it had actually struck suddenly became clear: right at the heart of London. The size of it started to sink in. Virtually five square miles devastated! Gasps everywhere. The consequences started to ooze out.

They were safe outside Chichester, not a target for a bomb; it would only become a crisis if there was another bigger one on one of the major coastal cities, and they were miles away from the unfolding horrors. Everyone was going through everyone they knew, relieved when families were well out of range of London, and moaning when potential victims were identified.

Henry consulted Fenella urgently, running through their nearest and dearest, and were hugely relieved that no one in the family would have been caught up in it. Mum was at home on the farm with Moira; Fen's family were all "up North"; Susie and Pete and their children were in Charlton, so they were well out of it. Most farming friends and all their neighbours were likewise safe in the countryside.

But what if there **was** *another one? There usually was with these terrorist cells. Where else might they strike? Should we cut and run or wait and see?*

Henry immediately tried phoning home to reassure Moira, let her talk it through with someone sane, and check that Mum wasn't too upset by it all, but the networks were unsurprisingly engaged. Everyone must be doing the same thing. They would be home by teatime so there didn't seem to be much point worrying about it now. They could have a good "blether", as Moira would call it, over a drink this evening.

When everyone remembered that it was the State Opening of Parliament, the full implications started to dawn. On such a grand occasion, absolutely everybody who was anybody would have been at the Palace of Westminster. Everybody. There was the realisation that each and every

Member of Parliament had been wiped out, every single one in the Commons and the Lords.

Everyone was asking each other what would happen now, who would take over governing the country.

Then the full impact on the Royal Family started filtering out. There had been so many of their members at the ceremony. Buckingham Palace was annihilated, St James Palace wiped out. There was a frantic scrabble to identify which of the Royals had been there, and it transpired that this year there was a mass turnout.

The Royals not attending were holed up at St James Palace, all the little ones included. Whoosh. A whole dynasty assassinated. It was worse than the Russian Revolution. There was frantic scrabbling around to find out, from the line of succession, who had to stand up to the plate. It seemed that it was the Duke of York, and people were not happy.

He had blotted his copy book too many times over the years, and just was not the sort of man that anyone could think of as a monarch. He had become increasingly seedy over the years, and still seemed to hang out with his sleazy ex-wife. Racing ahead of themselves, not even letting the dust settle, the chatter was "I'd rather be a Republic than have that man as our King". Henry thought this a bit crass, but was inclined to agree.

Each report that broke escalated the swell of hysteria. People seemed to find it hard to absorb just how bad the situation was, the sheer volume of people who were potentially along The Mall, all the people in their offices, pupils at Westminster School, people in Westminster Abbey and in the Methodist Church and Hall, an Art Exhibition there apparently. So many people. Thousands. It was surreal.

There they all were, standing in a playing field in Chichester, with the sun shining, the children calling and encouraging each other, while stunned parents watched them compete through dismayed eyes, fake smiles, pretending it wasn't happening, a conspiracy to stop it reaching the children, while wave upon wave of horror surged through them.

The match finished prematurely; the headmaster quietly engineering it without causing a fuss. Calmly, he invited those who should be heading to London to wait in the dining room and have more tea. Each family was weighing it up, deciding what to do. Everyone tried to behave as normal, although it wasn't easy. Suitcases were collected, cars packed.

Henry had loaded up Alice and Arthur with warm hugs and chatter about how brilliant they had been at their sports events, while his head was miles away. The whole thing had a dreamlike quality.

Could such horror be happening somewhere else when, looking around, everything seemed just so normal? What shall I tell the children? How do you tell your children something like this?

They drove to the Crown and Anchor, ready for a slap-up lunch, with lots of false and hearty conversation, although the adults did not feeling like eating anything. Would it be open? Should they go? They felt like going straight home. Henry was uneasy and unsure, but he and Fen had decided that it was better to carry on as normal. There was nothing they could do for the poor souls in London, nothing that would make any difference at all. What else could they do?

The pub was abuzz with the calamity, a TV was on full blast, intoning the dreadful news via presenters who were exhausting to watch in their sheer intensity and fervour, and the effort they were making to contain their alarm. Henry thought it completely inappropriate to be blaring out such horrors; there were other children there, besides Alice and Arthur. The children didn't really need to know about it, innocent children bombarded with this adult horror. Henry tried to find the landlord to ask him to turn the TVs off, or at least turn them down.

As he glared crossly at the inappropriate screen, Henry caught sight of a map, with the animation of a yellow streak blossoming out from London, in a roughly south-westerly direction, pointing effectively towards where they stood. He stopped in his tracks, stumbled towards the TV, suddenly listening very carefully to the overexcited voice. His blood ran cold.

"Jesus Christ, we need to get out of here. That is fallout and it is headed this way." Henry grabbed Fen. "Its fallout, Fen. It's coming this way, blown by the wind."

"Wait, Henry, wait." Fen held back her head, twisted towards the screen. "Look, look, where it is going. Home... the farm... home... where..."

Henry cottoned onto Fen's thoughts. The yellow streak smeared past Morden, over Epsom, across the Surrey Hills, skirting the South Downs, and fading out between Chichester and Bognor Regis.

"Oh my God, oh my God. We'd better get back there. It only takes just over an hour. Try Moira again and tell her to get her and Mummy ready." He dragged her, more roughly than he had meant to, towards their table, and their innocent, oblivious children, who were happily giggling and joshing and hitting each other with their menus.

"Alice, Arthur, I'm really sorry but we have to go now." He bundled up their coats and hauled a protesting Alice by her forearm, and lurched out to the car. "Quickly, quickly, we have to go and get them!"

"Daddy, stop it, you are hurting me," protested Alice.

Fen started dialling Moira frantically as she ran along, but the network was still engaged.

"Turn the radio on, Fen, we might hear some more."

Henry had zoomed out of the car park, crashing the gears in haste, headed into Chichester and immediately found themselves caught in total congestion; everyone seemed to have taken to the ring road in sheer panic, but God knows where they were all headed.

"Jesus Christ!" exclaimed Henry. "We have to get back!"

Alice and Arthur were bewildered, getting upset as well as hungry. "Daddy, what is going on?"

"Hush now, we will get sorted out as soon as we can, but we have to get home," responded Henry, not really knowing what to say.

"What did we do wrong?" wailed Arthur, and burst into tears.

Fen hushed him soothingly. "Nothing, my darling, nothing. It's just that a very bad thing has happened and Dad and I need to decide what to do for the best."

They listened anxiously but it was hard to work out what was going on without a map. There was no 4G so Fen couldn't access Google Maps or any of the information websites. Scrabbling around, Fen found an old road map with curled-up pages stuffed in the glove box, and frantically turned the pages to get an idea of which area they were talking about on the radio and where they were relative to it. The radio newsreaders weren't very helpful in their level of detail and not very precise.

They crawled through the traffic, getting increasingly anxious. Frantic hand signals of the posse of policemen that had suddenly emerged from their secret burrows to deal with the emergency made them turn north up the A286. They were insistent. Henry needed to carry on round the ring road to get to the A27 that took them home, but they simply weren't allowed to.

They crept along the A286, just one of a total flood of cars, working out how they might head east to get to the farm. Every time they passed a side road, they could see swarms of policemen manning barricades and talking anxiously into their handsets, moving on cars that tried to go down forbidden side roads leading eastwards.

They diverted the streams of traffic west on to the B2141, presumably to get further away from the dangers of the fallout, pushing Henry and his family even further away from their desired destination. Fen searched for a way to loop back.

It wasn't just Mum and Moira that he was worrying about. What should he do about the cows? They were out at pasture in open fields and would bear the full brunt of anything blowing in. He had to get them all into the milking parlour and the overwinter barns. Dave Easton, the cowman, and his wife, Heather, were there too.

Henry was trying really hard to remember an article that he had read in the *Farmer's Weekly*, years and years ago, or was it at Cirencester College, about what to do in such a situation. He remembered some of it. Get all the livestock under cover, preferably in closed barns. Reduce their feed so that they didn't produce as much milk and they were able to use the bottom of the silage clamp, just not the top few feet. All that was doable.

Come on, come on, think. What else?

He couldn't remember; it was the sort of article that you read out of curiosity, not intent.

What about milking?

The cows were in agony if they weren't milked, particularly now that they were at their peak yield. He would have to keep milking them, particularly this time of the year, their most productive time. Obviously, the milk would have to be ditched, it would surely be contaminated.

Where though? It couldn't go down the drains.

Would Dave know what to do? Would Dave just stay inside, as they seemed to be advising?

He was frantic with worry and indecision, and they still couldn't get through to anyone on their phones. Fen kept trying pointlessly. It made no difference whether she called Moira, Dave, Susie or her family. It was the network that was engaged, or down. The radio kept telling them not to use their phones anyway.

The road became marginally quieter, as were the occupants of the car. Fen had explained simply and quietly to the children what had happened, without frightening the poor things to death. They hadn't really taken it in, and were still oblivious to the consequences of this crazy nightmare that had all the adults in such a meltdown. They continued to chat about school, about their friends, about what they were planning to do over half term, what they were going to show Jack and Amelia and Auntie Susie, and complaining that they were hungry and thirsty and needed the loo.

Every time a fresh bulletin came on, Henry would shush the children and lean an ear in towards the radio, as if it might make a difference to what he heard. His mind was racing. It seemed that the cloud of radiation was spreading, inexorably, to the south west of London, from a north-easterly wind. It was hard to predict where it would spread because of winds at different levels of the atmosphere. The Met Office were desperately modelling a predicted path.

More detail was coming in of its expected spread. They were evacuating towns either side of an imaginary strip, all the way from Richmond down to Chichester on the west side, and Croydon down to Angmering on the east side. They were quite clear that people within the zone itself should take shelter, shut all doors and windows, and stay inside until further notice.

Jesus!

Fen moved her finger from the map and suddenly said, "Henry, what on earth are we thinking, we can't go home. We would be driving right into the radiation cloud; it will kill us all. For God's sake, stop. We can't go there!"

Henry concentrated, tried to think clearly.

What to do for the best? Risk it? We can't – the children. Where can we go? Susie and Pete's? They were already heading in that general direction.

He turned to Fen, who frantically moved her finger round the map on the hunt for Charlton, checking that it was not within the yellow streak area. "We will head there and keep trying to get hold of Moira. Perhaps she and Mum are already on their way there too, it is surely where Moira would head for."

If they hadn't already left, Henry presumed that Moira and Mum would be listening to the same bulletins. Surely they would have heard? If they weren't on the way to Susie and Pete's, they were probably holed up in Mum's cottage, as instructed.

But were they safe? Would they get exposed to the terrible radiation? How much would fall in their area? Suppose they hadn't heard and were still pottering around in the garden, oblivious to it all? Jesus, so many questions.

He was feeling so full of panic but knew he had to appear calm, otherwise he would worry the children, who were already het up.

Henry shuddered and drove on, his hands gripping the steering wheel so tightly that his knuckles looked fit to burst, and his teeth were clenched so tightly that they grated against each other. The traffic was so dense, so slow. He felt like shouting at them to get a bloody move on.

Jesus Christ. God preserve us.

Chapter 33

Diverted into the sports hall, Meredith was confused.

She'd plenty of time to look around, as other parents wandered in, in dribs and drabs. She sat at the side, not even on one of the chairs that had been laid out in rows, tucked away next to a long curtain thing that hung from the high ceiling. It smelled of sweat. She sat, her hands gripped in her lap, her back ramrod straight with tension.

As parents came in, everyone was buzzing with something – something that was obviously awful. They were looking anxious and gasping and yelping and crying openly. People turned to other people and held them in their arms, stroked their hair, women hugging women, men hugging men, it was all very intimate. It was extraordinary.

What on earth had happened? Why were all the parents getting together?

"Bomb... nuclear explosion... London..." She could only catch snippets because of the strange echoing acoustics of the hall and the way everyone was jabbering madly. Meredith's skin prickled.

She looked around for people that she knew. She didn't know many; she wasn't good at making friends. She only really knew the people that had gone to Susie Cole's dinner party, so she looked out for Susie, she was always friendly, but remembered that she would be on the school trip. She looked out for Jessica Hughes, she was nice too, but no sign of her. She was probably working in some office somewhere deep in the school. No Leah Ahmed either.

So it wasn't a meeting for all the parents then?

She sat back, protected by the curtain, and tried to listen in. Suddenly, Mr Barker strode in purposefully, his eyes staring at the floor. He looked very strange; his eyes were sort of bulging. He was a nice man, cosy-looking, like a favourite uncle in his tweed jacket and knitted tie, thin-rimmed specs and greying hair, so it seemed odd for him not to have his usual wide-mouthed, generous smile on his face and a jovial greeting.

The whole room went silent, except for one woman's piping voice that was hushed immediately. Mr Barker didn't even have to call them to order.

Mr Barker stood straight, took a deep breath, swallowed hard, cleared his throat, swiped at his nose with a hankie and started. Solemnly and quietly, in measured tones, staring glassy-eyed, alternating between a piece of paper wavering in his hand and a window high at the back of the hall, he read out what had happened to the school trip.

Meredith was aware of the absolute silence. Missed beats of total and absolute stillness before the first person cried out the name of their child. This gave them all permission to let their own expressions of horror escape – their howls of despair.

Eleanor, Eleanor.

It went on so long and every time it started to die down, another bereft parent would wail and set them all off again.

Awful, awful. Eleanor, Eleanor.

A vision of Eleanor came into her head.

That awful, awful day. Gary's smirking face.

Meredith put her hands over her ears, digging her fingers into her tense scalp.

Mr Barker just didn't have enough to tell them to satisfy their hunger for information. They were dissatisfied. All of them. They sat waiting for more. He didn't have any more, just this too-short, factual statement. They were left helpless and didn't know what to do next. A whole roomful of inconsolable, angry parents. Turning to each other, outraged. No one knew what to do next.

Then the questions were launched at Mr Barker. Angry demands for answers were thrown at him furiously as if it was all his fault. He looked stupefied at first, wincing and dodging each thump like a boxer, but composed himself, took it like a man. Raised his chin and absorbed their anger.

"Why did you let them go?" tearfully.

"Why didn't you cancel the trip?" wailing.

"Why didn't you go on the trip if you thought that it was safe to go?" hysterically.

"What are you going to do about it now? Resign, right here, right now!" angrily.

"What sort of man are you? It's outrageous, it's disgusting," furiously.

"You just wait. You haven't heard the end of this," venomously.

He kept referring back to the written statement in his hand; it wasn't enough, but he stood his ground and calmly took it all on the chin. He suggested that they reconvene tomorrow at 11a.m., same place, when there would hopefully be more information. He would do his very best to keep them informed.

Meredith didn't want to leave the united mass that milled around confused, afraid, baffled. For some reason, there was comfort in just being with other people in the same boat, where you were allowed to cry and shout when you were all in it together, even if you didn't.

She wanted to scream and shout but she couldn't. She hadn't taken it all in. She hadn't spoken to anyone. She had just sat there alone, not attempting to share the hugs. Meredith sat there and turned to salt.

Eleanor, Eleanor. That incident, that hideous thing.

Immobile. Silent. Her fingernails had indelibly marked her palms and her teeth broke the skin on her bottom lip.

It was just awful, just terrible, unbelievable.

The feeling of unreality was totally overwhelming. She was trembling, she felt sick.

Not just Eleanor. Susie? Susie's Jack, presumably. Jessica's Alfie? Leah's Aisha.

She didn't know any of the other children.

Dear God, so many people just... just evaporated, it seemed. Not just the school trip, but everyone. How many people had died just like that? So many. Chaos. Who would know who had died?

Parents were leaving the sports hall in dribs and drabs. Everyone looked pale and drawn in shock. Hardly surprising. Nothing, nothing would ever have prepared her for that nightmare. Nothing.

A vision of Eleanor came into her head, sitting looking down at the mess of dog food mixed with vomit in front of her. Gary's face gloating. Meredith groaned out loud eerily, almost a howl. Meredith, head bowed, was deep in thought. She was thinking, thinking her mind was boiling in contrast to her inert body.

Mrs Chawla put her hand on her shoulder, which made her jump out of her skin. Her ears were singing and she felt paralysed, but she did as she was told and, like a zombie, left the hall for the reception area.

As she sleepwalked her way towards reception, Mr Barker singled her out.

What now? She couldn't help feeling a bit sorry for Mr Barker, the bearer of bad news. Biggest understatement ever. He looked like a ghost.

"Mrs Webber." She turned and looked through him. "Mrs Webber, please may I have a word?"

What more was there to say? She needed time to get her head round the whole thing, not more words. She stared at him blankly, exhausted. Drained. Empty.

"Please, Mrs Webber, there is something I need to discuss."

Good God, not that, please not that, not now. Wasn't it enough to have to take in the biggest catastrophe that had ever hit this planet and darling Eleanor was gone now... and all those poor children and just so many people?

"Mrs Webber, shortly before..." He hesitated unable to speak the words again, and then tried again. "Mrs Hughes rang me from London." He swallowed hard. A vision of Jessica Hughes, laughing delightedly at Susie's dinner party, flashed through her mind.

Why Jessica Hughes? She wasn't going on the trip.

"Ellie had not met up at the meeting point. They were waiting for Ellie to turn up when... when it happened. That is why I phoned you and asked you to come in. I know it doesn't make a lot of difference now, but I felt it my duty to inform you. I am so sorry. I am just so sorry. Once things are clearer, we will talk about this again, but I thought you should know." He looked as if he might cry, but Meredith admired him for his strength and professionalism. He had been superb, poor man. How awful for him.

"Thank you," muttered Meredith. "Thank you for everything today, Mr Barker." She grasped his hands in hers and pumped them up and down, grotesquely relieved that it was just that, not the other thing, as they stared into each other's watering eyes. She wondered briefly "Why Jessica?"

So many people gone. So many missing. So many unaccounted for. Such a lot of confusion. Will they ever know who actually died in that maelstrom? She wandered away like an automaton, thinking intensely.

I have to go home to Gary.

Chapter 34

Susie roared around to school, her head reeling.

She plugged in her phone and kept trying to connect to everyone: Pete, Henry, Mummy, Fenella, Jessica, their mobiles, their landlines. Each and every one she selected to dial, the phone just gave the network busy signal. Frantically, she kept trying over and over again. Hopelessly.

She parked haphazardly in the car park, grabbed the broom – she was past caring how ridiculous it looked – hobbled up to the main door and lent on the buzzer. The intercom clicked and she shuffled in.

A white-faced, red-eyed Mr Hubbard greeted her, shouting over the sound of the phone ringing urgently behind him on the reception desk. "Mrs Cole? All the Year 12 parents are meeting in the sports hall. Mr Barker is going to talk to them, but I don't think it would be appropriate for you to..." He tailed off, looking embarrassed.

"What on earth do you mean, 'I don't think it would be appropriate'?"

"Well, Jack is... and you..." Mr Hubbard tailed off again.

"For God's sake, Mr Hubbard, what do you mean? "

Susie made a move towards the sports hall and Mr Hubbard side-stepped, as if to block her way. "Jack is with Miss Pietruski in the science block. Room S4. I think if you were to go there. It would be better... Do you know which way...?" Susie frowned at Mr Hubbard's strange coyness, but was desperate to see Jack, and Amelia, for that matter.

"Yes, yes, I do," and she sped off along the corridor, surprisingly fast for someone propped up by a broom. Mr Hubbard watched her with a strange look on his face, before he returned to his desk, fielding the telephone, which just kept ringing off the hook, and dreading the next buzz on the door. *Who would it be? Whose parent?*

He reached for the list and ticked Jack Cole, but it felt really odd. The list didn't distinguish between those who were... who were... and those who were sitting, very much alive, with Miss Pietruski in the science block. He felt like weeping but it wouldn't do.

Susie fell into Room S4, normal social niceties of knocking politely abandoned, saw Jack and launched herself at him, flung her arms round him, the broom flying, and wept into his shoulder.

Miss Pietruski intervened. "Now, now, Mrs Cole, that is not helping. Please calm down and sit down."

Bossy cow.

Susie just clutched her beloved boy tighter to her. Miss Pietruski physically pulled at her shoulder, which made Susie so angry that she nearly squashed poor Jack to death.

Raising her head, she could see Aisha, her huge, dark eyes round in her surprisingly pale face, and Charlie Powell staring at her as if she'd gone mad. She thought that she probably had. She looked at them again, her eyes travelling one way and then back, as if hoping that some other child might miraculously appear.

Only the three of them? Jesus Christ!

"Aisha, I've just come from your mum's. I'm sure she will be on her way."

Jack then asked the question she'd been dreading. "Have you heard from Dad?"

She pulled herself together, but couldn't stop holding onto his sleeve to make sure that he was still there, tried to meet his eye with reassurance, but couldn't help but let her gaze fall to the floor. "No, lovey, not yet. I am sure he will be far too busy sorting things out to phone."

Turning to Miss Pietruski, Susie asked, "What do we do now?" as if the teacher might actually have a sensible plan and magic everything back to how it was just a few hours ago.

Miss Pietruski consulted a slip of paper. "Please come into school tomorrow at 1p.m. and meet Mr Barker. This is going to be a meeting of just the parents and guardians of the students that didn't go on the trip. The other parents are being invited in at 11a.m. for an update. Mr Barker will then answer any questions that the parents and guardians of any other students have at 3p.m."

Susie hadn't really taken it all in, but replied, "Yes, yes. So 11a.m. tomorrow."

"No, Mrs Cole," exclaimed Miss Pietruski, rather hastily. "1p.m., please. Mr Barker is also letting students leave school early if collected by someone with parental responsibility. If you want to collect your children, you need to sign out with Mr Hubbard at the main entrance. All students are being held with their class tutor in their meeting rooms, so if you wish to collect Amelia then please return to reception and Mr Hubbard will send her to you."

Susie stomach took yet another plunge as she suddenly remembered Hannah.

Dear God, her mum, her brother. Richard worked in London. Was he alive? What must Hannah be thinking? How must she be feeling? She must be distraught.

She'd told Jessica that she would look after Hannah if she was back late. Hannah and Amelia had their silly pact about what happened if their parents ever died, dear God. She should take Hannah home with her! She must look after Hannah, where else could she go?

She found that she was still clutching onto Jack. She turned to Miss Pietruski and said, "We will go now, if that is okay?" She cast around for the broom that Jack, following her eye movements, bent down and retrieved, and hobbled to the door, tugging at Jack's clothes so that he followed like a dog on a lead.

Jack was reluctant to come with her; perhaps he seemed to feel safer staying where he was, so that he could believe that nothing had changed, in the middle of it, in touch with what was unfolding. Whatever his reason, Susie was hurt by his reluctance. She'd saved him. She needed to hold onto him and never let him go. She determinedly flung an arm over his shoulders.

Back in reception, Amba Chawla, who was urgently talking on the phone, had joined a harassed Mr Hubbard. Susie explained that she needed to collect both Amelia and Hannah because she'd promised Jessica that she would look after her. Just saying Jessica's name out loud nearly finished her off again, and she held back another rising sob.

Had it really happened, this nightmare? Please stop, please make it go away!

The door buzzed and Kieran's mum, Danni Lewis came in, wild-eyed, her cheeks streaked with tears, gabbling hysterically. She took in Susie and Jack standing there and for a moment, looked momentarily confused then suddenly, went all spiky, stopped still and raised her hands in a gesture full of hope.

Mr Hubbard stepped in and quietly ushered her to the sports hall with sympathetic murmurings and, "They didn't go, Mrs Lewis, they didn't go." As she scuttled off down the corridor, Danni Lewis kept looking back over her shoulder at Susie and Jack and then back at Mr Hubbard in abject confusion.

Mr Hubbard picked up the phone and spoke quietly to Amelia's tutor. After a while of just standing there, phone in hand, the tutor obviously came back on the line and Mr Hubbard then spent a good deal of time nodding and saying "yes" and "I see" and "understandable" and "okay", with the odd glance in Susie's direction, then turning his back and whispering into the phone. Susie stupidy strained as if she might hear both ends of the conversation.

Eventually, Mr Hubbard put down the phone and sauntered over to Susie and Jack. "Amelia is on her way, but please be aware that she is rather upset."

Of course she is bloody upset. She must be wondering what the hell has happened to her dad and all those poor kids, let alone everyone else in the whole of bloody London. It was a nightmare taking part in full daylight. Everyone was "rather upset"!

"What about Hannah?" enquired Susie.

"She is staying at school," responded Mr Hubbard, with an odd hardening of his lips and what looked like a glare. Had she just imagined that?

"But her dad... Jessica... Alfie... they're..." How did she put this so that Mr Hubbard would understand. "Poor, poor baby, she must be..."

"Thank you, Mrs Cole, but we will take care of Hannah," he said, rather more firmly than necessary, Susie felt.

For God's sake, it suddenly dawned on her; the bloody man was blaming her! How dare he! First Leah blaming her and now him.

She rose in indignation.

At that moment, Amelia erupted from the corridor, threw herself into Susie's arms and wept wildly. "Mum, Mum!" she sobbed. A couple of parents buzzed and came in. Susie didn't really know them, but knew they had a child in Year 12, you could see from their distressed faces. Her heart went out to them and she clasped her daughter to her as they were ushered down the corridor to the sports hall. She was still holding onto Jack rather awkwardly, almost dragging him away. These parents too turned back and looked at her quizzically.

Amelia was now blubbing, "Dad, Dad!"

Susie just patted her and said soothingly, "He'll be very, very busy. The networks are all busy. We'll wait to hear from him," and murmuring anything else that came into her head, while actually, she just wanted to scream and throw up, all at the same time.

She was still worrying about Hannah, poor, poor Hannah. She still thought that she ought to come home with her. She didn't dare ask Mr judgemental bloody Hubbard but thought it would be okay to ask Amelia how she was faring. Susie wished she hadn't.

Amelia wailed really, really loudly and howling, and kept saying, "She hates you, she hates me, she hates us. It's been awful. She keeps saying it. I thought she was going to kill me," over and over again. Susie tried shushing her and rocking her to quieten her down.

Dear God, poor Hannah, and it dawned on her. She could see it from Hannah's perspective, she really, really could. She, Susie, had sent Jessica to her death. *It should have been me.*

Could she ever live with herself? She was stricken by overwhelming guilt and her eyes brimmed again with tears.

CHAPTER 34

"Come on, Amelia, Jack, my loves, let's get you home and we'll wait for Dad to ring." Her arms around her children, Susie hobbled to the door, leaving the broom incongruously in the middle of the hall. She dare not seek out Mr Hubbard's condemning eyes.

Chapter 35

Charlie sat in Mrs Pietruski's class, his eyes staring, unblinking.

His gaze came to rest on a periodic table on the wall. To his horror, he found himself staring at element 92, U, Uranium, relative atomic mass 238, melting point 1,132°C. His head was banging and his brain felt like it was swelling and pushing against his skull, making everything ache. His stomach kept plunging. He felt sick. He felt cold, and shivers kept slicing through him. His teeth were clenched so tight, he thought they might snap.

If he let the thoughts free in his head, he would start to scream. If he started to scream, he didn't think he would stop. He was clutching a pencil, clenched in his fist, his veins pulsing in tracks across the back of his hand. He was turned to solid stone. He had a sudden urge to stab himself with the point of the pencil, anything to stop the feeling that was suffocating him.

Alfie. Alfie. Ellie. Alfie.

Why have I escaped? Why? Why have I, of all fucking worthless people with a fucking useless mother, lived when Ellie, Alfie and his mum are all dead? Dead, gone. They were all fucking dead!

"Charlie? Charlie?" Mrs Pietruski's voice seeped in. He didn't want to look at her, or at anybody. Jack's mum had swept into the shocked silence of the chem lab like a comedy clown, clutching a broom, for fuck's sake, and whisked Jack away in a cloud of hysteria. She and Jack had had a close escape. They didn't seem as happy about it about it as you would think. Mrs Cole had seemed oblivious to him and Aisha standing there like spectators at a show, and just threw away a comment to Aisha.

Am I invisible?

Mrs Ahmed had similarly swept in with great drama, swooping on Aisha, her sari flowing like wings, and flown out again, fluttering and twittering.

"Charlie? Mrs Chawla can't get hold of your mum on the contact number in the office. Does she have another number?"

Charlie couldn't give a shit.

"Charlie? Please!"

"Nah."

"Okay then, what do you want to do? What time do you expect her home? I am not letting you go home to an empty house." He wasn't too keen on going home to an empty house either, and he didn't know how long it was going to be empty for.

He was booked on a shift at the pub tonight; he had banked on getting fed.

I guess that won't be happening, inappropriate like, but would I stand to lose the job if I don't turn up? Should I phone in and speak to Ellie's dad? For fuck's sake, he won't want to speak to anyone after this. Ellie. Ellie. Dead, gone.

The world had stopped dead in its tracks.

"Charlie? Are you listening to me?" He shook his head to clear the smog. It was as easy as fuck to lie; he'd been doing it for years to cover up for all his mum's weirdness. He pulled himself together, the professional actor, ready to deliver his lines.

"No problem, Mrs Pietruski. Mum will be probably be at home when I get there. In fact, I'd like to go now, if that's okay. Go find her, like." He pushed back his chair, grabbed his rucksack and fled before Mrs Pietruski could say or do anything.

"Charlie!" called Mrs Pietruski. He heard as he legged it along the corridor.

He ran all the way home. pounding the pavement as hard as he could.

Alfie, Ellie, Alfie, Ellie.

He tried to pound the black, seething. crappy thoughts of element 92, U, Uranium, relative atomic mass 238, melting point 1,132 °C, out of his head.

Chapter 36

Moira had assumed at first that it wouldn't affect them at all, physically.

Why would it?

They kept saying on the radio that the bomb, although horrific and devastating in its impact, was actually smaller than the one that was dropped on Hiroshima all those years ago. The area directly impacted in London was thought to be in the order of only five square miles.

Only five square miles!

Moira was astonished that they could say that.

As the bulletins developed and became more informative, they started talking about "fallout". She sort of knew what that was, a cloud of radiation blown by the wind, silently and invisibly along in the breeze from the centre of London, like the breeze that was blowing through the cottage right now.

It was a north-easterly wind today. A cloud of nuclear radiation was drifting away from London and it was heading south west. Towns along its path were being evacuated. Towns mainly to the north of them.

Moira was concerned. She needed to find out more about this. She abandoned the tatties that she'd been scraping like an automaton, with an ear glued to the radio, to turn on the TV in the lounge.

A solemn man was sat behind a desk, looking shocked and intoning the latest update. A film of a landscape of billowing smoke and dancing flames was behind him, obviously filmed from high above. He looked as if he was in hell. Moira was taken aback.

Was that a part of London?

The camera angle changed. A diagram replaced the man and flames of hell. The wind direction highlighted with an arrow on the map of the South East of England. What was really sinister was the red, orange and yellow smear, a tongue with an almost ghostly glow to it that was marked on the map, centred on London and heading to the south west. The predicted levels of radiation, according to the prevailing winds at different levels of the atmosphere, being carefully monitored by the Met Office and plotted as they became clear.

Did it affect them? Would it affect them?

Moira unconsciously stepped forward to the screen and leaned in for a closer look. She could see the yellow smear, stretching out towards the coast. She could see the towns labelled clearly. She could see Guildford; she could see Hartley Wintney, well out of danger. She tried to place her finger on where she thought South Lavington must be. It was definitely heading this way, right over them.

They seemed to be on the edge of the glowing area, but it was hard to tell. The scale of the map was too large to show the minute hamlet of South Lavington. She carried on staring watchfully. Her skin prickled, was that radiation or fear? Before she'd had a really good chance to look at it, or examine it in detail, the picture was replaced by the sombre man and then footage of static queues of cars and lorries on unknown main roads. With sudden resolution, she decided to act as if they were potentially being exposed to radiation. Better to be safe than sorry. But then there was the dilemma of what to do for the best.

Should she hunt out Brenda, bundle her in the car and head for Susie's, which was definitely outside the danger area, according to the map. But then the map hadn't been that clear and the advice on the radio and TV said to stay indoors, as there may be radiation already in the air. She imagined it as an invisible mist. The roads were reportedly chaotic everywhere.

Should they just shelter as soon as they could? Moira umm-ed and aah-ed and then made her choice. She hesitated for a moment and then abruptly galvanised into action; "Right then, let's go!" She switched off the TV.

Thinking quickly, Moira dashed across the yard to the farmhouse to find Brenda. She hadn't run anywhere in years; it wasn't as easy as she'd remembered, but the fear made her feel that she could run forever, and she tried not to breathe in case she was sucking in poison. *Run, Forrest, run!*

The chickens scattered, squawking, the dogs leapt up and pranced around her, jumping up excitedly at the sudden rush of excitement, their eyes shining, their tails wagging madly, grinning from ear to ear, the terrier dashing back and forth, yapping.

She looked up to the sky; it still looked normal.

Should she get them all inside? And what about all the cows out in the fields? Her first priority was Brenda, so she continued on to the farmhouse, calling up the dogs to follow: "Come wi' us!"

They pottered after her with absolutely no sense of urgency, no inkling of anything untoward, just hopeful that there was something in it for them. Moira wondered whether perhaps she was making a fuss over nothing.

Arriving panting at the farmhouse back door, she yanked it open, called the dogs in. "Barney, Rags, Mutt, come on quickly." She firmly closed the door, dropping the deadlock; goodness knows why, it just seemed to help her peace of mind.

The farmhouse back door opened into the boot room, also the dogs' quarters. Striding across the wooden floor, Moira opened the door into the kitchen, commanding the dogs to stay. They looked at her eagerly but being obedient, little souls, did as they were told.

She closed the door solidly behind her. "Brenda? Brenda! Where are you?" Moira yelled, trying to tone down the panic that she could hear in her own voice, but failing miserably.

She skittered across the stone floor of the tidy kitchen, looking frantically to the right towards the sink, the navy blue Aga and the run of wooden units, and hastily left towards the dresser and the table with vase of jolly tulips, as if Brenda might be there, and burst through into the hall.

Pushing open the door to the bright and cheerful family snug, poking in her head, withdrawing, pulling the door to with an extra sturdy tug, she urgently worked her way down towards the office, doing the same with the dining room on the left, and the sun-filled drawing room on the right, weaving her way along the brightly-coloured rugs, glowing in the light that streamed in from the fanlight above the front door.

As suspected, Brenda was in the office, sitting in Henry's captain's chair, her back to the large French windows that looked out onto the burgeoning garden. The peonies were beaming from the border; the tulips were standing smartly in their tubs, all flooded with warm May sunshine.

Brenda was lazily swivelling herself from side to side, while reading a letter that had been picked at random from Henry's in tray.

"Hello dear," greeted Brenda cheerfully. "You look a bit dishevelled!" Brenda always called her "dear". Moira wondered if Brenda could actually remember her name.

Moira hadn't actually thought through what to say to Brenda, so taking a deep breath, calming her heaving chest, swiping her unruly hair back from her freckled, now rather red, face, she decided on a straightforward resume of the situation.

"Brenda. There is a problem; a poisonous, radioactive cloud is coming this way from London. We have instructions to batten down the hatches and stay indoors. Can you help me now by closing all the curtains and doors, please?"

Brenda arose from the chair unhurriedly, without any hint of alarm or concern. Had she understood?

"All right, dear. If you say so. Whatever we have to do. We had better get on with it." She turned and pulled the heavy curtains across the windows with a triumphant flourish, promptly dousing the view and turning the sunlit office to instant darkness. Had she understood the gravity of the situation? Did she understand what on earth was going on? Who knew? With Brenda, you never did.

Together, they went through the ground floor of the house, pulling curtains, closing shutters and yanking all the doors thoroughly closed, until they were totally cocooned and muffled in the dark. It brought to her mind an old film that she'd enjoyed. It had Nicole Kidman in it as a rather manic mother, and it had ended up with a surprise twist that she and her children were in actual fact dead. It had been very clever and at the same time, rather troubling.

Not as troubling as this situation. Dear God!

Moira had stood at the bottom of the stairs, anxiously eyeing up the pool of light, radiantly shining on the landing like an alien spacecraft. Should they go up there, nearer to the sky, closer to danger? Probably best avoided.

Where would they be safest and most comfortable? Moira scuttled into the drawing room and turned on every light that she could to dispatch the dark. At least the electricity hadn't been affected. Yet. It did feel odd to be in the dark in the middle of the day. She could hear the birds cheeping without a care in the world. Would they be alright if they were exposed to the radiation, wondered Moira.

Brenda sauntered in after her, reached for a magazine from the pile on the coffee table, sat elegantly on the cream sofa, and nestled herself in. "A tot of Scotch would be rather nice, dear," she said, without looking at Moira, and indicating with her head towards the tray of decanters on the occasional table.

"A wee dram might be just the thing indeed." It was a bit early but she was at a complete loss for what else to do.

Chapter 37

Henry reached Susie and Pete's.

He swept into the drive much too fast, and pulled up suddenly behind Susie's erratically-parked car. Pete's car wasn't there. Neither was Moira's.

Henry climbed out, stiff from the tension of the long, slow, stressful drive, helped Alice and Arthur to clamber out, and hurried them along, as he waited impatiently for Fen to get herself sorted. Together, they marched to the back door.

Henry didn't bother to knock, he never did with family, just strode in with a shout, "Susie, Susie?" To his surprise, Jack and Amelia rushed through from the front of the house and threw themselves at him, howling and crying.

"We thought it was Dad."

"We hoped it was Dad, but it isn't."

They were beside themselves, poor loves.

"Where's Mum?"

"In the lounge." They stepped aside and he continued through to the hall, stepped over an incongruous pile of laundry that was heaped at the bottom of the stairs, and found Susie on the sofa, her face red from crying and her eyes all puffy, facing the TV that was blaring urgently. She didn't get up.

"Oh, Henners, I twisted my ankle, you see, I really, really did, I'm not pretending, I left the broom at school, and I couldn't go... and I forgot Jack's slip because I thought I was going, and so he couldn't go either... Jessica went instead and she's... she's dead... and Pete went to help out because of the threat... and we haven't heard from him… and all those poor, innocent children… and they are innocent, whatever Leah says. And we haven't heard from Pete, and I have a horrible, horrible feeling that…. Oh, no, please, not Pete!"

It was hard for Henry to make head nor tail of all this, as it spewed uncontrollably out of Susie's mouth.

Suddenly, Susie pulled herself together, looked at Henry and said, "Where's Mum? Where's Mum, Henners? How's she coping? Is she coming?"

Henry was disturbed. "She isn't here? Oh my God, we thought, we assumed, we hoped that Moira would bring her here. I wonder if they are on their way. Surely they must be on their way here, where else would they go?" He paused. "If not, she must be at home, Susie. We can't get through to her on the phones though; we've tried and tried and tried. God knows we've tried. South Lavington might actually be in the danger zone, in the area of fallout."

Susie stared at Henry, her mouth open. "Dear God. What do you mean? What zone? Why have you come and not brought Mum?" Henry did his best to fit an explanation between the outbursts to explain, but Susie was just looking at him, her puffy eyes wide open.

"Oh Henners, poor, poor Mum, poor, poor Moira. We'll have to go and get them. We have to go and jolly well fetch them, right now!" She struggled to her feet, wincing as her foot hit the floor too hard.

The queasy feeling of guilt rose in his throat. Was he just abandoning Mum, Moira, all of them in that area, and all his livestock, to save his own skin? He weighed it up. "Look, I will try and get through. As you can imagine, I am worried about the whole farm, about Dave and Heather, about the cows, Roscoe the bull, the dogs, and the chickens. I will see if I can get through, but please, could I just have a break, a cup of tea or something, then I will get going. It is all a complete nightmare!"

"Oh Henners, thank God. Poor, poor Mum. What must she be thinking?"

Fen came in with her arms round Jack and Amelia's heaving shoulders, trying to wrap herself around an increasingly-distressed Alice and Arthur too. She caught the end of the exchange and looked at him aghast.

"Seriously, Henry, you can't go in there. You have us to think about us, your family. It will be too dangerous!"

Henry looked her in the eye, looked at Susie, staring at him pleadingly, turned back and groaned. "Fen, I just don't know what to do."

Chapter 38

Meredith went in search of Philippa.

Philippa ran up to her, her dear, little face puffed and red, and looking ugly. Tears poured down her face. She was raving on about Eleanor, about Hannah, about kids Meredith didn't know. Meredith was just too traumatised. A searing headache had built up. She pulled at her hair to make it go away. She was trembling. Philippa wouldn't stop asking questions and she wanted to scream.

"Please, love, let's just get home. I can't talk right now."

Their journey home was in silence, except for hiccupping sobs from Philippa. Both of them stared ahead. The traffic was so slow. The high street was packed with cars parked higgledy-piggledy, their owners piling armfuls of stuff into their boots.

"Mum, Mum, this morning, Ellie…" whispered Philippa.

"Not now, love, not now." Meredith squeezed Philippa's little hand.

Pips could only keep quiet for a few seconds, her head racing with shock and horror. "Mummy, why didn't Daddy come and collect me? What did Daddy say?"

Meredith stared ahead for a moment. "Daddy got an urgent call this morning and had to go out."

"But why would he do that?" persisted Pips.

Meredith sighed. "I don't know, Philippa. You know Daddy. He does what he wants."

"But, Mummy…?"

"For heaven's sake, Philippa, please stop asking questions," Meredith snapped.

Startled, Philippa jumped at her mum's out of character behaviour and curled in on herself, wrapping her deep sadness in her own arms.

At home, they were all out of kilter, on edge. What were they meant to do now that they were in their house, at a time of day when they shouldn't be there? Without Eleanor. Marmite was oblivious, just annoyed that he wasn't having the usual fuss made of him, as Meredith and Eleanor crept in, hand in hand. He pushed his nose into their legs and skittered around in circles, looking ecstatic instead of devastated.

Philippa and Meredith's instincts were the same. Without saying anything, they went up the stairs, still hand in hand, to Eleanor's room, and lay on her bed, inhaling her scent. They wrapped their arms around each other. Philippa sobbed quietly, her whole body shaking with the pain of it. Meredith was too cold and broken to cry any more. They lay there, in mutual silence, not wanting to leave.

Philippa didn't mention her father for ages, until she said very timidly, "Daddy doesn't know. Daddy doesn't know about Eleanor. How do we tell him? Mummy, how do we tell him?"

Meredith stared at the ceiling.

Chapter 39

Bernie sat in his armchair, staring into space.

Emily was now up in her bedroom. She hadn't really stopped sobbing since she'd got in. She wouldn't come out and she wouldn't let him in. She had her earphones on and pretended she couldn't hear him.

He had eventually decided that he ought to collect Emily from school. She couldn't go to her friend Hannah's as scheduled if Mini was missing, she had to be told. He had to do something.

It had been the hardest moment in his whole, long life, having to explain to Emily that since her mum had gone to London with Liz, he had not been able to contact her, although he had tried and tried... It had been left hanging in the air. Hopeless.

Emily was in hysterics and not really listening. She was raging on incoherently about Hannah, Hannah's mum, Hannah's brother, all dead. Even Hannah's dad. She was shrieking about all the children who had been on a school trip to London. She was inconsolable and he didn't know what to do. He tentatively patted her on the arm but she swung away violently, and he was left feeling inadequate and lost.

He tried again, staring fiercely into her face, and eventually got through to her, made her listen about her mum. She screamed, really screamed. He was terrified. Thank God that a really nice lady stepped in, he had no idea who she was, enveloped her in a motherly embrace until she eventually calmed down. He had stood there in the middle of the school lobby, feeling alone, at a loss, ineffectual, and only just managed to hold onto his stiff upper lip.

He shuddered as he remembered the long journey home in the car.

Chapter 40

Moira felt secure, holed up in the drawing room.

The combination of old-fashioned, solid, wooden shutters and heavy curtains made her feel that nothing would be able to seep in. They had the TV there and had it on permanently, much to Brenda's disapproval; she thought it rather common to watch daytime television.

Moira continued to consume at all the TV bulletins for ideas, but the only advice seemed to be to stay where you were, stay indoors and batten down the hatches, against the invisible, deadly mist that was trying to get in. Moira shivered.

The TV reported that the army and the police were putting up barricades across all the roads into the potentially affected areas, to stop any traffic moving in, but they didn't say about moving people out. The traffic was madness.

Whole towns were being evacuated along the length of the yellow smear: New Malden, Chessington, Epsom, Ashtead, Box Hill, Dorking, Coldharbour, Clemsfold, Five Oaks… and so they droned on. All of these towns were to the west of them. It confirmed her belief that they must indeed be in the danger zone.

Perhaps we should have gone? Should we still contemplate going? How can I know what to do?

Moira truly regretted her first instinct to stay.

She wondered whether they should have hoofed it to Susie's while they still could, but it was probably too late now. It seemed that the best interpretation of the jumble of conflicting information was that they should stay put and follow all precautions.

They advised that they should fill as many water containers as possible, in case the mains failed, use water only for drinking and cooking, and they weren't to flush the toilet.

Moira had umm-ed and aah-ed about what to do about going to the toilet. The downstairs cloakroom had flimsy curtains and thin walls so she didn't feel safe in there. She was reluctant to go upstairs because she similarly felt exposed walking through the airy hall; she didn't know where the draughts were getting in and what they might contain.

What decided it for her in the end was the advice on the radio that they should remove any clothes that might have been contaminated, especially shoes, and shower carefully, thoroughly soaping their bodies and shampooing their hair, but definitely not to use conditioner, she didn't really understand why. It all seemed a bit contradictory to their edict on saving water.

This meant going upstairs for certain, so she and Brenda had sped through the hall, taken the stairs 10 at a time, and dashed round upstairs pulling curtains, closing doors, settling on using the master bedroom as their dressing room and en suite bathroom for their ablutions. All this tumult was just so exhausting to both mind and body.

When Moira had explained what she was planning to do, Brenda insisted that she too must be thoroughly cleansed, even though she hadn't been outside at all, and must wear fresh clothes. Brenda seemed to be enjoying the melodrama.

Moira had shivered as she'd showered. She felt her flesh was crawling with the contagion and vigorously washed herself over and over again, her hair four times, to get rid of any possibility of invisible dust remaining. She remembered that bit in that film with Julia Roberts, where she'd been exposed to nuclear waste or something. They had scrubbed her very thoroughly. Moira scrubbed under her fingernails with the nail brush and continued to scrub at any part of her body that might have been exposed, until she was satisfied that she was unquestionably clean. It took a long time until she felt cleansed.

Brenda had scrubbed away at herself theatrically under the shower with a loofah, until her poor, old, crinkled skin had gone bright red.

This whole decontamination drama then gave Brenda the excuse to have a good rifle through Fenella's wardrobe to find something "suitable to wear", while sporting a towel wrapped glamorously around her old body like Mrs Robinson in *The Graduate*.

Brenda had settled, eventually, on a rather nice and completely inappropriate peacock blue cashmere suit. Anyone would think that they were on a shopping spree at Harrods, the way Brenda was carrying on. The suit was a wee bit tight, although fortunately, it was stretchy enough to cover Brenda's curves, but looked very odd where it flattened her old chest.

There was no way Moira was going to fit into anything of Fenella's – Fenella was stick-thin – so she'd tentatively rummaged in Henry's drawers until she found a Tattersall check work shirt and a pair of jeans. She took them from the bottom of a pile so that they could not have been exposed. She had to roll the sleeves up on the shirt and the legs up on the trousers. She knew she must look ridiculous, but at least she felt cleansed. It felt most peculiar not wearing underwear though, but even in these dire straits, she didn't fancy someone else's smalls. She felt terribly embarrassed at wearing Henry's clothes at all.

They scurried back downstairs and returned to the haven of the drawing room, rushing through the hall, which seemed to be especially dangerous, because the sun still streamed through the fanlight above the front door, glistening on the rugs and on the hall tables, making them look as if they were aglow.

On the TV and radio, they had moved on from talk of destruction and escape and protecting oneself, to the symptoms that would indicate radiation sickness. The first symptoms of radiation were nausea and vomiting, which neither she nor Brenda had succumbed to as yet, nor the dogs or even the chickens (if they could be sick). They advised people to "see a doctor if they were worried" but had no solutions for dealing with the now and then of being stuck inside a farmhouse.

The phone was to hand and she'd kept trying to phone Henry, Fenella, anyone really. Every time that she dialled and dialled, it was continuously and irritatingly engaged, with an infuriating woman intoning that "The network is busy".

The TV eventually advised something sensible amongst all the fluff – that it was fine to eat food that had remained inside, as long as it was carefully washed, especially the tin surfaces on the canned food, before opening it. They could use water from the taps, as long as they ran it for a while.

Moira knew that she ought to go and make some food. In all the commotion, they had completely missed lunch, her tatties abandoned in the sink in the cottage, and she was now getting very hungry. It was nearly teatime.

It took Moira some time to get up the courage to risk going to the kitchen. She was a bit worried that she had left a trail of radiation on the kitchen floor when she'd come in and it might get back on to her. She took the biggest steps possible to the sink to avoid touching the floor more than necessary. She rummaged underneath for Marigolds to put on before she dared touch any surfaces. Feeling marginally more protected, she opened the fridge and was delighted to find it packed with food.

Of course, it was the children's exeat weekend, and Susie and the family were supposed to be coming for the weekend as well.

There was enough food in the freezer and the fridge to keep them going until doomsday, unless this was doomsday, and she just hoped that it wasn't contaminated or would become more contaminated as the hours went by.

She took out the makings of a salad, ran the tap for as long as she could, washed every leaf and every vegetable under the running water, rubbing at them with a scourer. Moira got out knives, forks and plates, similarly scrubbed, and laid out a very late lunch – or was it an early supper; the whole day had gone awry – on trays, which she had also scoured clean, ready to take back to the sanctum of the drawing room.

As she prepared the meal, she heard Dave, the cowman, draw up in the yard in his Land Rover.

Dear God, what did he think he was doing? What a dunderhead!

She raised the corner of the kitchen blind, rapped on the window and waved her arms frantically to attract his attention. He stopped in his tracks, looked at her quizzically and strolled towards the back door, as if he had no cares in the world. He was a big man with a broad, smiley face and an enormous Brian Blessed bushy beard. He had worked for the family for donkey's years, and was getting on a bit now, although his hair and beard were still dark, belying his years.

Moira had an uneasy relationship with Dave. He seemed to be a bit put out that Brenda treated Moira like a friend more than a servant, whereas Brenda was inclined to be rather patronising in her dealings with Dave. Moira was allowed to call her Brenda. Dave had to call her Mrs Hillier.

Moira didn't know what to do. She rolled down her trouser legs and sleeves to cover her arms and legs completely, and tottered out through the boot room to the back door, squirming to keep away from the dogs, who surrounded her eagerly. She could almost see the radiation gleaming off their coats. She imagined the radiation as a shimmer of yellow, ephemeral dust, like the smear on the TV maps.

Lifting the letterbox and bending down, she found herself looking straight at Dave's private parts. She winced and shouted, "Dave, Dave! What on earth do you think you are doing? You must get indoors at once."

Dave bent down and his eye appeared within inches of hers. "What are you on about, you crazy Scottish woman? Look about you." His head turned to look up at the sky, which indeed did not look at all ominous. "There's no problem. We're miles from London. They're just trying to frighten you with all their crap on the telly. Scaremongers, the lot of them." He laughed, waved his arms about and said, "We're all doomed!" in a very bad imitation of a Scottish accent.

"But, Dave, you can't be too careful," Moira pleaded.

"Don't be daft. I have cows to milk and chickens to feed, and there you are, a grown woman, hiding in the house, trembling like a scared, little mouse. What about those poor dogs that you have shut in?" He laughed again. "And what will Mr Henry and his missus think when they come home and find you cowering in there?"

"But, but…" spluttered Moira, but Dave had sauntered off towards the dairy, chuckling to himself and swinging his substantial arms, like great haunches of meat, jauntily.

Actually, he did have a point about the dogs. What should she do? She decided to let them out, they would be happier, and they wouldn't be there to bounce all over her with their contaminated fur.

She held her breath, opened the back door and whooshed at the dogs with her arms. They all leapt up happily from their beds, their claws scrabbling on the wooden floor, and sped out of the door at crazy angles, following Dave in the direction of the dairy. The moment the last tip of tail had whipped through, Moira dashed back into the kitchen, slamming the door shut with relief. Should she go and shower and change again? She stood, her arms raised, feeling contaminated. She would, just in case. And change her clothes.

But first, she needed to clean the kitchen floor and surfaces… get rid of the evil dust.

Returning eventually to the drawing room, kitchen scrubbed, passageway to the drawing room scrubbed, shower done, clothes changed, she found Brenda had happily settled in front of the TV, obviously abjured to the novelty of daytime TV. Perhaps being in the false, cocooned, curtained twilight made it okay to watch it. She was very excited to find so many more channels on Henry and Fenella's TV than the Freeview box at the cottage. Brenda kept flicking through to non-British channels, awful, canned American laughter, sudden violins scraping away at music to raise tension, explosions, and lots of "Let's Go!" yelled by soldiers. She would then find the British ones, sombre, doom-laden or populated with hysterical panicking people, speaking in spiky voices

Brenda didn't want to listen to that, and flicked on with a "Tut! What are they going on about?"

Sitting with nothing else to do, Moira had suddenly panicked about the chimney, open to the heavens, and stuffed blankets and duvets up as far as she could go to keep out the deadly mist. They seemed to have stayed there okay. She'd taken another shower afterwards, you couldn't be too careful. The water still seemed to be working; it was nice and hot from the Aga back boiler and they had plenty set by.

The time ticked by slowly.

There was still no joy with the phones; she couldn't get texts to send. She felt very isolated. She felt unclean, contaminated. She shivered. While the rest of the world was hurtling around, beating its chest, howling with the anguish of it all, shouting out its anger, Moira and Brenda sat quietly in the gloom with the flickering TV.

Chapter 41

Pips timidly traipsed down to the kitchen.

She pushed the door open tentatively, holding her breath, and put her head cautiously around the door in case her dad was up and about. She thought she had heard him come in in the middle of the night, thought she had heard a car, had certainly heard Marmite clattering about. Only Mum was there, at the sink, drying up a plate.

Pips' face was pinched and her eyes puffy with dark circles underneath.

"Mummy?"

"Yes, Philippa, dear. Are you okay?" she asked, keeping her eyes firmly on the plate.

"Not really."

Pips snuggled up to her mum, suddenly realising that she had not done this for as long as she could remember. Her mum didn't snuggle back.

"Mummy?"

"Mmm?" Her mum seemed shut off.

"About Ellie, I woke up this morning and I can't believe that she has gone like and I was wondering about what she said…"

"Hush now. I know it is just so hard…" Her mum squeezed her shoulders momentarily, but seemed reticent and uncommunicative, as if she was holding back. Pips sighed, tears welling up again, frustrated that her mum didn't want to talk about Ellie, or hear what she had to say. Pips tried again.

"Mummy?"

"Mmm?"

"Is Daddy getting up? What did Daddy say about Ellie?"

Her mum tensed, her eyes flew open, and she replied, at first hesitatingly, "He hasn't come home yet. He has obviously been delayed, caught up in the catastrophe. It must be madness out there. He said he was going to London, but I don't know where."

"Why didn't he come home last night, like? I thought I heard his car last night. Has he phoned you? Will he be coming home today?"

Her mum was silent for ages, stared at the ceiling, breathed deeply, and exhaled loudly.

"Philippa, I just don't know what to think. I will try and find out more today." A pause. "I will investigate, I promise." Pips fell silent, dissatisfied.

Mum didn't seem to be too bothered about her dad. Perhaps because she was dreading telling him about Ellie. They had fallen asleep on the settee together, waiting for him to come home last night. So many other people must have been doing the same, waiting to tell their family members about people who had been killed. All those dads of people in Year 12. The families of all those other people who had been wiped out: mums, dads and people's kids. Pips shuddered and felt tears welling up again.

"What is going to happen now?" Pips exclaimed suddenly.

Her mum pursed her lips. "What do you mean, Philippa?"

"Well, the whole London destroyed thing, all those dead people. All of Year 12. Poor Hannah Hughes. It's just so... It's just so huge! I can't get my head round it."

Her mum tapped her on the shoulder, almost a pat. "We will be fine, Philippa." Marmite interrupted, pushing in, wanting his breakfast. Sighing, Pips wandered towards the utility room to get Marmite's bowl.

She picked up a mess of plastic bags, strewn unusually across the floor, and shovelled them back into their sock, where they were usually neatly stored.

Chapter 42

Susie woke up with a crashing headache, her eyes gritty and sore, her cheeks aching, her chest tight and feeling queasy, her stomach cramped from crying herself to sleep.

Susie's face was crumpled against Pete's pyjamas, which she clutched in her hands. Their wedding photo was also tangled up in the duvet. She was surprised to realise that she was on Pete's side of the bed, her head on his pillow; she could smell his delicious, woody, masculine scent. It was disorientating.

It took just a few moments before it all came back to her. A horrible bolt of adrenalin went through her, releasing waves of despair that flooded through her sleep-befuddled mind, making her eyes open wide in horror. She was once again drowning in awful shock. She gasped then groaned out loud, and a torrent of tears cascaded onto the damp material clasped in her taut fingers.

"Pete, oh dear God, Pete." She sobbed uncontrollably, burying her head in his pillow, both to stifle the sound and to breathe in his dear, dear, precious aroma.

She let herself howl, her arms wrapped tightly around her body, roaring her despair, relieving the oppressive pressure inside her head. The anguish gushed out with her tears.

She let the pain pour out of her until she was exhausted. Her deep, heart-breaking sobs became involuntary hiccups. She lay still, hoping that by not moving, the world and its sudden, grotesque transformation into hell on earth would turn out to be just a vile nightmare.

It wasn't. It was real.

The hiccups became quieter and less frequent. Susie gradually calmed. Suddenly feeling guilty at her egotistic self-indulgence, her maternal instincts kicked in and she thought of poor Amelia and Jack.

What must they be feeling? They must be feeling really, really awful about their Dad.

They knew as well as she did that he wasn't coming back. Had they heard her outburst? She really, really hoped that they hadn't.

Must pull myself together and be strong for them. Poor, poor darlings.

Had Fen and Henners heard from the spare room? And Arthur and Alice, they were so, so worried and upset about all that was going on. Would they need breakfast? In fact, what am I going to do about feeding everybody?

She hadn't done a big shop because they were going to Henners and Fen's for the weekend.

But would the shops be open after such a catastrophe? What would people do – the day afterwards? It seemed to be too soon to be doing anything ordinary. And what about people still in the midst of it all, in London?

The TV had reported last night that they were sending in drones to scout around, but they couldn't risk actual people. There were reports of signs of life amongst the devastation; apparently, it could actually happen.

Was Pete, by some miracle, in one of those places that would have kept him safe: the shadow of a building, below ground?

Susie's mind continued racing.

And what about the fallout area? And what about poor, poor Mummy and Moira – where were they, what were they doing? Were they feeling abandoned and frightened? She wondered whether she should still try to go and find them.

And Hannah – dear God, that poor, poor, darling little girl, waking up to the sheer horrible dreadfulness of what was facing her. And Jessica... and Alfie. All those poor, poor, innocent children.... the MPs, the Royal Family, all the London commuters, Richard, and all those blameless foreign visitors.

A picture of a fervent Leah popped into Susie's head. Susie angrily shook her head to rid herself of it. It stopped her tumbling thoughts in their tracks.

With sudden determination and a "I must be strong for the children" attitude, she kissed Pete's pyjamas and popped them under his pillow, gave it a pat, swept back the covers, and got out of bed thinking, "on the wrong side". She remembered to be careful of her twisted ankle, set her shoulders, ran her fingers firmly through her curtain of hair and rose determinedly to face the challenge – after she had had a pee.

Chapter 43

Jonathan Barker had never experienced a media ambush before.

Nothing had ever happened in his life that warranted it, and he was frankly amazed. He had had no idea how threatening it was, how stressful, the raw hostility and aggression. It was as if they were inhuman, an army of zombies moving in, showing no emotion or reaction to anyone's distress. Nothing, absolutely nothing at all, would stop their relentless predation.

For some reason, only known to themselves, every media organisation across the region had pounced on the story of the school trip that had ended so tragically, as if it was the main event of 25th May. It had started with the local radio, but it had escaped like a virus, and within the day, a seething mass of media organisations from all the surrounding counties had besieged the school and anyone associated with it. It was quite frankly terrifying.

The press onslaught when he arrived at school this morning had reminded him of the old newsreels of the miners' strikes, with the police holding back the pickets to let the buses through, the shocked, white faces of the passengers staring ahead, looking terrorised, braving a frenzy of flashes and writhing and people and shouting.

Good God, how could people behave like this? The parents and students were shocked enough as it was, without all this crap.

You couldn't possibly go on foot. They had swarmed in on him, poking cameras at him from below, shoving their microphones into his face, with no regard to personal space, dispassionate faces looming in on him with impassive eyes and hard, strident voices.

"Mr Barker. How do you feel about allowing so many of your pupils to go to their deaths?"

"Why did you send your students to London, into such danger?"

"Why did you ignore all the warnings?"

Had he ignored the warnings about security levels? Should he have stopped it? Was he indeed culpable?

He couldn't move forward because of people crouching in front of him, fighting amongst themselves to get up close, and the constant feeling of trepidation that you might accidentally make contact with them, even though it was impossible not to because they held their ground. He could see the headline in the local rag: "Murderous Head Assaults Photographers". Surely they must know how repugnant they were being?

Poor Amba Chawla, now holding the fort in Jessica's office, was finding it impossible. If she answered the phone, it was usually one of them pretending to be a parent or an official. They were cunning and clever and persistent

Jon was extremely stressed anyway. He was horrified and distraught about the whole thing: the children and the staff. Should he have seen it, prevented it? Flashbacks. It had taken minutes for the horror to truly sink in and then it just kept coming back, wave after wave. Total disbelief. Feeling detached from the world, with a ringing in his ears. He knew that as head, he had to do something, but this was overwhelming.

At least last night, when he eventually got home in the small hours, he could stop pretending he was the stone-faced stronghold that he had had to be. Thank God for his darling

Fran, who had enfolded him in her love and rocked him back to sleep when he howled out his anguish in the privacy of their bedroom.

He just hadn't been prepared for the level of responsibility that would fall on his shoulders; it had stretched him beyond where he had ever believed that he could go. Years in education could not have prepared him for this. He had drafted and implemented so many procedures over the years for the safeguarding of his students and his staff, but no one could ever have written a procedure for dealing with something as massive as this. So many risk assessments. Useless. He was already exhausted and finding it very difficult to keep the calm façade going.

He had tried to sort through the consequences rationally, logically, and do the right thing. He had consulted the Critical Incident Management Plan, created years ago to meet the criteria for Ofsted, but suddenly real and actually useful.

Trying to focus through the onslaught of raw emotion had been hard enough, but trying to break it down into sensible, manageable chunks that could be tackled had been nigh on impossible when waves of disbelief and horror kept sweeping any sensible thoughts away.

Dear God. A nightmare of colossal proportions.

Jon had immediately read that communication was the most important thing. He scheduled immediate meetings for the parents of Year 12 students, with a follow-up for the day after, an opportunity for other parents in the school to come and ask questions and get information, and a separate gathering for the survivors' parents. Between all those meetings, he could frantically gather any information that he could. The local police were being amazing in this respect, but they seemed to know so little.

He had set up a telephone rota, using willing teachers for late into the night to answer the phone to parents, guardians and students. Everyone other than the intended audience choked it within seconds. He had set up a monitored enquiry email address, swamped within seconds. The "Contact Us" facility on the school website was engulfed. The Facebook information page had been inundated with comments immediately

For some reason, the media had sniffed out some vague facts and concocted a bizarre interpretation of the reasons that certain children had survived. They had found out that Susie and Jack had meant to be on the trip but Susie's fall had resulted in neither of them going. For some strange reason, they thought there was "more to that than met the eye" because of Pete's access to intelligence in his job as a police officer. They speculated as to whether she deliberately saved herself and her child and sent her so-called best friend in her place.

They had found out that Aisha was a Muslim, and that her mother had, at the very last minute, prevented her from going. Anonymous people had already called the Terrorist Action Line, talking about the coincidence.

There was rumoured to be a terrorist, who was thought to be associated with the plot, with some tenuous link to Leah Ahmed, through a distant cousin in Pakistan. Even without that, just being a Muslim appeared to be enough of a reason to be somehow to blame.

The trolling had been shocking. He had logged onto the Facebook page this morning as soon as he had got in and uncovered the most appalling messages, scattered explosively between the sincere messages of condolence for the Year 12 students.

Facebook seemed to attract the very worst of humanity. "What total twat sends his pupils to a terrorist hotspot?" That had made him wince. He was surprised that the language wasn't censored in some way. But it wasn't just attacks on him.

"You may have got away with it this time, you muslim cunt but watch out, your next." Did they allow that sort of language? Why didn't they delete it?

"Muslim pig bitch."

"Fucking raghead, just die.".

"Murderus cow"

"Everyone nos that you new, bitch."

Why would anyone want to attribute blame to guiltless parents at a school in the middle of Hampshire, rather than the perpetrators, the terrorists who had committed, and admitted to, this appalling act? People were so racist and quite frankly weird, and the teacher in him also just couldn't help but pick up on the fact that the trolls' spelling was appalling, even though it seemed petty in the scheme of things.

It was going to be really hard to defend these poor, innocent parents, and their kids, from these most obnoxious claims, particularly Susie Cole and Leah Ahmed, to whom most of the trolling was blatantly targeted. He had to assume that Jack Cole and Aisha Ahmed accessed Facebook, and he dreaded to think what they must be feeling when they read all the vitriol.

The 11a.m. meeting with the bereaved parents had been heart-breaking. What can you say to people who have lost their beloved children? There was nothing more to say than had been said the evening before. "Your children are missing, presumed dead." It sounded so callous. Each parent was required to phone the police helpline and describe their child and what they were wearing, in the minute glimmer of hope that they might be found just injured or irradiated. Jon could read between the lines; they were hoping to match names to bodies – if any trace of bodies remained.

They tried to focus instead on something more positive – a memorial service. When, where? The parents had left, weeping and distraught, baffled and torpid, walking back to their cars under fire of the waiting press.

The 1p.m. meeting set up for the survivors' parents had proved nearly impossible, with the close watch of the predatory press. Their meeting had become farcical with the poor souls, Mr and Mrs Ahmed, Kate Symington, and Susie Cole having to run the gauntlet of the school car park, bodily fending off the attacks from press and hangers on, both verbal and physical. There was nothing that could prepare you for that and, as he had experienced himself, you were defenceless. Naked. Exposed.

Leah and Farrukh Ahmed – unusually without his mother, perhaps she had stayed at home with Sara – had stormed through the human barrier, looking as disdainful and dignified as possible. Jon had watched them with admiration from his first-floor vantage point. They had arrived promptly.

Poor, old Susie Cole, hampered by her sprained ankle, which made her walk like a cringing, culpable criminal, had eventually only managed to reach the goal of the buzzer, thanks to the defence of the fearsome Kate Symington. By the time she'd been let into the sanctuary of the hallway by the stalwart Amba Chawla, the poor woman was in pieces. She was 15 minutes late.

When she came stumbling into the meeting room, full of apologies and excuses, she looked at the Ahmeds. Just looked at them. She grimaced, cleared her throat, mumbled a greeting to Farrukh but said nothing to Leah. This was odd, as he thought they were good friends.

Leah Ahmed, sitting bolt upright next to her husband, Farrukh, seemed tight-lipped and accusatory. She stared with her kohl-lined eyes into the distance, with a look something like indignation. She wouldn't look at anyone else.

Perhaps she had heard the nasty, little gibes from the press, the whispers and racist taunts, and God forbid that she had seen some of the horrendous remarks on Facebook.

Perhaps she was still angry because he had fully supported Mrs Davies on not allowing Leah to go on the trip, on the basis of there being no parents allowed on the trip – and then somehow, Susie Cole got invited. For heaven's sake, it had been that decision that had saved Leah's life, and then consequently, that of her daughter, but she seemed to be furious with him and Susie Cole instead of relieved.

Perhaps it was because of losing Jessica. He had understood that Susie, Leah and Jessica were all three very close friends. He realised it must be complicated that poor Jessica Hughes had gone in Susie's place, but instead of Susie and Leah comforting each other at the loss of their mutual friend, as he had expected, there was an icy coldness there. He was baffled, but had too much on his plate to dig any deeper, and he too was devastated by the loss of Jessica and the rest of his faithful team of staff. An echo of Sarah Davies' larger than life voice popped into his head.

Jon couldn't help but feel that Leah was being somewhat reticent on condemning the whole terrorist atrocity; in fact, he couldn't remember her saying anything about it at all. He couldn't voice this to anybody, even to Fran; head teachers had to be so careful about any trace of implied racism. He hardly dared admit it to himself.

Susie had just sat hunched over throughout, looking at her knees, her eyes screwed up, her lips sucked in, her hands clenched so hard that they were shaking. It wasn't surprising really. The poor woman had lost her husband, the only one of this tiny group to have actually lost anyone.

Thank heavens for Kate Symington, sitting alongside Susie Cole, her hand placed comfortingly on her rigid shoulder. Kate was brilliant, immensely practical, and said exactly what she thought, about the press hysteria, and the weird sense of their children having survived something so monumental, and the feeling of guilt when faced with the grieving parents of their classmates. She certainly made every attempt to lighten the intense atmosphere, and asked intelligent questions on how best to support their children through this crisis, but nothing could dispel the glacial mood.

They discussed at length, well, at least he and Kate discussed at length, the merits of the surviving kids coming into school on Monday. It seemed that the consensus was that they should. Mind you, they were not a full compliment. He was baffled as to the absence of Charlie Powell's mother. He had tried every way that he could to get through to her. Perhaps she would join in at a later get together, if they had another one.

So, the whole parents/survivors group meeting hadn't exactly proved to be a success. Perhaps it was too soon. Perhaps it had been too traumatising, going through the press barrage. Jon decided to hold the next meeting in secret, arranging an obscure venue away from the predators – the coffee shop in the out of town John Lewis perhaps.

They should get about half an hour of clear space before they were sniffed out, hunted down, spotted, and the hounding commenced. He hated to say so, but Leah Ahmed was inclined to stick out like a sore thumb, in her gloriously-technicolored saris. Her faithful mother-in-law, who was equally exotic, always obediently walking to heel, didn't help.

The meeting attendees had appeared to agree to this suggestion. It was hard for Jon to tell whether the grunts through gritted teeth were of assent, when given the chance, they couldn't get away fast enough. Leah Ahmed raced for the door without so much as a backward glance, Farrukh shaking Jon's hand firmly, thanking him for making the time to see them, mumbled condolences to Susie, before running to catch Leah up.

Susie, assisted by Kate, lumbered to her feet and staggered from the room with a mumbled goodbye. She looked close to tears.

Jon sighed. He was doing his best. Looking at his watch, he found he had plenty of time to prepare for the next gathering. It was the general parents and guardians meeting for those without children in Year 12. That would be much easier.

God, that sounded crass.

He sighed, emotionally exhausted, rubbed his tired eyes, looked out of the window, and caught sight of Susie Cole and Kate Symington battling through a pack of mean-looking media.

There was the memorial service for Year 12 and the staff to think about.

What was best to do about the survivors on Monday, if they came in? What will I say to the rest of the school? Should the survivors be part of that gathering?

Nothing, nothing at all had prepared him for this. He took a deep breath, flexed his cramped and tense shoulders, and went in search of his stalwart Amba Chawla to plot and plan.

Chapter 44

Bernie had sat all day, obsessively ringing Mini and Liz's phones in turn, between watching endless footage of desolation and destruction on TV, apart from his one excursion into school.

Everyone was truly relieved that the bomb had been a one-off; they kept going on about it as if it was a good thing, but just one bomb of an estimated 10 kilotons of uranium had been enough to cause unspeakable devastation, loss of life and chaos, just unbelievable in scale.

A whole square kilometre of London reduced to literally just nothing. Centuries-old landmarks just evaporated. Tens of thousands dead, hundreds of thousands hurt, horrible injuries from flying glass and debris, and many more expected to die, particularly from the radiation.

Bernie had faced a dilemma. Should he go into school for the 3p.m. briefing offered by Mr Barker, to help all the parents of students at Charlton Academy come to terms with the loss of their world, as they knew it?

Was it safe to leave Emily alone in such a state?

She was ensconced in her room, refusing to come out. She was 15, going on 16, so theoretically old enough to leave on her own.

He had needed help, he had needed information, and he could do with some contact and guidance on what to do next with Emily, and he didn't have a clue where to start on the missing Mini.

In retrospect, he wished he hadn't gone to the meeting. He had wandered into a Slough of Despond, awash with raw emotion, everyone seeking sympathy, but they seemed to not be able to give it.

What had happened to people nowadays that they just fell apart? Where was their dignity?

He was devastated about Mini, he was completely helpless about Emily, but for heaven's sake, he didn't need to make a song and dance about it in front of everyone else. Bernie's group weren't the parents that had actually lost their children. They'd been dealt with elsewhere. Most of them had not lost anyone at all, and seemed to be wallowing in the grief and loss of others. It reminded him of the aftermath of Princess Diana's death.

When he had arrived at the meeting, everyone seemed to ignore him. He was just an old bloke, wandering aimlessly between the young and agitated parents. No one had sat next to him. It was funny how people would always leave a space next to you in a row of chairs, just like at the pictures, they always did that. They had no inkling that he had lost Mini. No one bothered to ask.

After the briefing from the solemn Mr Barker, they'd been offered tea. Tea didn't help, but British people always offered it to those in a state of anxiety. He had stood awkwardly, alone, supped down the tea, which was weak, too milky and tasted of dust.

The stories about the group that had gone on the school trip were appalling. He could hear them swirling around. So many young people from Charlton Academy dead, the whole of Year 12, it was harrowing. Everyone was so shocked, but at the same time, outraged. Strange conspiracy theories, fantasies and feverish agitation abounded.

They were saying that Mr Barker should never have allowed the trip to take place. They were defaming a mother who happened to be Muslim, because her daughter had not gone on the trip and had therefore lived, questioning whether she knew.

They seemed to be heaping blame on a woman who had apparently decided not to go on the trip after all and sent one of the staff members instead. They seemed almost to be basking in it all, trying to wring every bit of feeling out of it all, almost revelling in it and rending their clothes, and wailing like people out of the *Old Testament*.

Extraordinary. How could people be so malicious and so parochial? Thousands and thousands of people had perished.

At least he had found out what he was meant to do about Mini being, oh God, it was so unbearable, missing, presumed dead. He had to ring some helpline apparently and tell them where they thought she might be, what she looked like and what she was wearing. It made him shudder, the baseness of the information in order to endeavour to name the dead, if they were ever found. Many would have evaporated or be charred to anonymity. He tried not to think about that.

He had, rather quietly, left as soon as he was able. He felt his age, as he staggered back to the car. He had stiffened up and everything; just every muscle ached and he felt cold to the bone.

He couldn't help but drive back via the station, a wide sweep of a diversion. He cruised along the ranks of cars until he found Mini's Mini, which had been a birthday present from him last year, his little joke. He got out and touched it, tried the doors, but they were sensibly and firmly locked. He didn't even know why he had done it. Despair washed over him again, and he had crept back into his car and crawled away, wondering how many others of those cars would still be left morning after morning, unclaimed by their dead owners.

Back at home, he had let himself in, cocked an ear for any sound of Emily, and heaved himself up the steep, narrow stairs, knocking on her stripped pine door with its iron furniture.

"I'm back! Would you like something to eat?"

No answer. He had pottered down into the kitchen, leaning heavily on the stair rail.

He had attempted to sort something out for tea, but he didn't know what there was or how to prepare it or cook it. His Mini had always done all that.

In the end, he made himself a sandwich, but it hadn't gone very well. The butter was too hard and wouldn't spread, and he made great holes in the thinly-sliced bread. The cheese was too thick and stuck in his false teeth, and caught the back of his throat. It nearly made him cry, but he was damned if he would.

He heard Emily leave her room and thought she was coming down, stopped and listened, but she was evidently just using the toilet before returning to her room, the door slamming behind her.

His attempt at swallowing his monstrous, chunky tea was interrupted by the doorbell, a slurred version of Big Ben's chimes; it made him wince. He slowly dragged to his feet, shuffled to the door, wondering and worried who it might be.

It was a large, dark-haired boy, older than Emily, who introduced himself, quite politely, as Jack Cole. He hadn't seen him before; he was a complete stranger, presumably from school. He wanted to see Emily.

Hang on a moment, wasn't he the boy who had had that disgraceful party?

Bernie had left him on the doorstep – *you can't be too careful* – and had once again climbed the stairs heavily to knock on Emily's door. She didn't want to see this Jack apparently, or so he gathered from the muffled shrieks and insults, so he had staggered down again, being careful not to fall in his increasingly unstable state.

Jack looked at him gormlessly and didn't seem to want to go, so Bernie said a brisk "Goodbye then!" and closed the door. He presumed that he had gone.

He sat despondently, staring at the space where Mini always sat, wriggling and squirming and jumping up and down in her exuberant way, always on the move. Always a smile, always a pat on his arm, accompanied by a chortle, a kiss on the top of his thinning hair.

Oh God. Mini. Mini. Mini.

He felt numb. Heartbroken. He wasn't sure what to do, and so sat immobile, staring into space.

Chapter 45

Moira had decided that they would sleep in the drawing room.

It had become their sanctuary, their place of safety. She and Brenda had hunkered down on the two cream sofas, after removing all sorts of crazy-coloured, patterned cushions, which sat either side of the glorious inglenook fireplace, now blocked, hopefully. It was surprisingly comfortable.

Moira awoke in the early morning to the incongruous sound of Dave driving in, Land Rover doors slamming, and the dogs barking challengingly as they ran helter-skelter from the boot room through the back door that Moira had left open for them.

Then she heard the slight squelch as Dave wandered across the yard in his too-roomy wellies. "Morning chocks!" he cried, as he let out the chickens. "It's a lovely morning, sky's as clear as a bell!" he said very loudly, in his booming Brian Blessed voice, followed by a guffaw, obviously to be overheard by Moira.

Then there was just the sound of his receding footsteps and general muttering, as he started about his regular morning milking routine.

Moira however stood firm. She might be making something out of nothing but was it worth taking the risk? The fact that Henry and Fenella had never appeared made it absolutely clear that the problem was genuine.

On his own head be it! Stupid, stupid galoot of a man.

Moira woke Brenda, went through their regular morning routine of shower, wash and then dry hair, but

Moira stupidly hadn't brought Brenda's drugs or her toiletries, her powders, creams and lotions, over with her. Should she risk going back to the cottage? Having been so very cautious so far, she decided not to, but then worried about the consequences of Brenda being off her chemistry set of medications. Could she ask Dave to get them? That would probably be inappropriate, given his pantomime performances.

At least the cows were being milked. That was one less worry for her. She understood that leaving cows not milked was a catastrophe, and left the poor dears in terrible agony. It wasn't her problem, but she did wonder what he was going to do with the milk. She'd listened out for the familiar rumble of the milk tanker but had not heard it at all, another pointer that all was not well. No newspapers, no postman either, and they always had mail for the farmhouse.

Her thoughts turned to breakfast. She didn't like the thought of cereal. Radiation would surely be able to penetrate cardboard. She wasn't sure about the eggs either. Thankfully, Fenella kept the bread in a pottery crock, which was more substantial, so she'd opted for toast with butter and marmalade from the safety of the fridge.

Her next worry had been the dogs. Mutt enjoyed his ratting forays into the barns and Rags and Barney seemed happy to mooch about, rolling in anything disgusting they could find, and endlessly licking their bits and pieces. Typical farm dogs.

They usually drank from the pond, rather than the nice, clean water that Henry and Fenella faithfully provided for them, so all Moira had to do was provide them with food. *But were they safe outside?* They looked perfectly fine. Perhaps she was wrong.

She'd discovered a nice, big overcoat, scarf, gloves and a hat in the downstairs hall cupboard that let her build her own protective suit against the evil brume. She put them on to dash into the boot room and shovel out the dog food, the sound of which of course made them come running. She felt protected against any bad air that might have drifted in, and from the dogs' polluted fur, but could not bring herself to actually pet them.

Moira was keeping careful track of how they were both feeling as the day progressed. It had limited itself to slight bouts of nausea after supper yesterday, which worried Moira to death, but was probably psychosomatic, and some horrible headaches, but she was not sure whether they were imagined because of all the hype on TV, the effect of radiation or just the stress.

She wasn't entirely sure how long they would need to stay holed up. They seemed a bit vague on the TV – "remain indoors until you are told it is safe to go outside". She still couldn't get through to anyone on the phones, and the internet wasn't working at all, even if she knew how to use it. If only she could email someone, she wouldn't feel so much at a loss.

Dave Easton came again at half past four. He shouted from outside the kitchen window, "All the cows look perfectly fine, the chickens are fine, in fact everything looks fine. in fact, everything looked fine. I feel fine, the wife feels fine and the dogs are fine." She couldn't be entirely sure but Moira was sure he had added that she was "as mad as Henry's mother". Moira started doubting herself, but decided to err on the side of caution and wait it out.

Every quarter of an hour, she had another go at phoning, using both her mobile and the land lines, but still nothing; all means of communicating seemed obstinately busy. She stayed glued with one ear to the local radio and an eye on the local TV station, waiting for anything new in the bulletins. Waves of anxiety and helplessness swept over as time dragged by interminably.

The TV updates were pretty much more of the same, but focussing more on the consequences of the whole ghastly mess in London. Footage from drones flown over the site were overwhelming. It was just a mess of charred rubble, odd spikes pointing out of the dust and rubble. A sombre voiceover intoned solemnly, explaining more about the explosion and the consequences:

"As we approach the City of Westminster, at about five miles out, we can see evidence of window breakage. Within two miles, we encounter the Light Damage Zone. We know we have reached it because of the increasing prevalence of broken windows. Shattering of windows and the consequential devastating effects of flying glass has occurred at up to approximately three miles from Ground Zero. Many victims that have survived are being treated for terrible injuries.

"As we move towards Ground Zero, rubble and litter has increased considerably. We can see crashed cars. The damage to buildings has increased considerably, affecting roofs and gutters. Emergency services are moving in and have been able to rescue some survivors from this area.

"As we get closer in, the damage to buildings is enormous. Utility poles have been downed, cars are overturned, there are fires burning everywhere. It is getting impossible to see where the streets are because of the muddle of rubble, although very few buildings remain standing in part, but unrecognisable. We are now approaching one mile from the epicentre. There is very little left standing. There are so many fires, and thick smoke is billowing from the remains of collapsed structures."

Moira was mesmerised. It seemed unbelievable. The sombre voice continued:

"The drone is now coming within half a mile from the centre of the blast at Big Ben. Within this area, the No Go Zone, the infrastructure has been completely destroyed, with unlikely survival of anyone in the area. The whole area has been reduced to impassable rubble. There is a slight chance that those in the underground network may have survived, but with very high radiation levels, the zone is gravely dangerous to survivors and responders.

"The No Go Zone itself has been reduced to a sea of rubble, with an enormous hole in the middle. There seem to be less fires burning here, but the fireball from the blast has incinerated everything. There is absolutely nothing that is recognisable and no evidence of any survivors."

The TV overlaid the images on maps. It was totally mind-boggling. It seemed like a remote planet, unreal, unable to comprehend. Thank God it had only been the one in London, though the whole country remained on alert, very sensibly.

The TV coverage then turned to the matters of law and order.

The remains of the Privy Council had formed the Cabinet Office Briefing Room emergency committee – mainly old men who should have retired years ago. Interim martial law had been declared until elections could be held, quite obviously really due to the extinguishing of every MP in the country, bar one from Scotland, who had escaped simply because he had been struck down by food poisoning at a constituency dinner the day before. They seemed to spend an inordinately long time going on about him, interviewing his constituents, his office staff, and even the caterer who had managed to poison him so opportunely. He seemed ridiculously pleased with himself, to Moira. It was sickening.

Wiltshire Police, for some unknown reason, were on some rota to take on responsibility for all the communications, and they had efficiently and quickly set up helplines for reporting people missing and safe.

Well done the boys in blue.

The agreement had been unanimously made that all local councils were to take charge of their own counties, in conjunction with the police; apparently, they all had a plan for such an eventuality, with lots of talk of Gold teams, whatever that was all about. Everything must go on as normal, everyone droned at every opportunity, in sepulchral tones.

Easy for you to say, sitting far away from it all, and what the hell are Surrey County Council daein'? They don't seem to be daein' anything, from where we are sitting.

There was great speculation about what would happen next in terms of restoring a parliament; not just a building, but the whole hierarchy of people, which seemed extremely and distastefully premature to Moira. For God's sake, the poor people had only just been annihilated!

The replacement of the Royal Family was taken as read. Prince Andrew had been declared the new King by the media, before the dust had settled, or been blown to the south west, and the new "court" would be based in Sandringham, well out of harm's way.

The reports were robotic; they seemed to be totally devoid of any humanity, just factual "how it affects the status quo", rather than being about more than 25,000 real people that had just suddenly left this world, the nearly 150,000 reported to be injured, and only God knew how many more irradiated and ill and dying. It was appalling. The TV just seemed to be churning out gruesome speculation and ghoulish tales to titillate those not involved. It was unspeakable.

The local news came on. There was sudden interest in a school trip that had turned out badly, choosing that very day to visit London. Indignant reporters reporting live from the gates of a school were frankly amazed that the head had allowed the trip to go ahead and were calling for his resignation. There were interviews with a rather pretty Indian lady about her daughter having survived, except that they seemed to be implying that she was somehow connected to the terrorists.

What was it with these people? Why were these poor people in any way to blame?

Moira's jaw nearly dropped to the floor when suddenly, there was film footage of Susie.

Susie looked hardly recognisable, dreadful, a puffed-up face, her lovely hair tangled and dishevelled. In her astonishment, she missed a lot of the commentary, but it seemed that she'd withdrawn from the trip at the last minute and sent one of the teachers instead. They seemed to be implying that she'd done so deliberately to save herself and her son. Jack!

"Good grief" exclaimed Moira. She was muddled.

So was Jack at that school, was he on the trip? How was Susie involved?

Hearing Moira exclaim made Brenda wake up from a doze and turn to the TV. She piped up, "Gosh, that woman looks just like Susie." Moira hushed her and missed the rest, but could have sworn that she saw Henry and Fenella's car in the driveway behind Susie.

Had she really just seen Susie or was she hallucinating? Frustrated, she tried phoning out again. Still nothing.

They were facing another night, feeling increasingly isolated, baffled, not quite knowing what to do next, how long to shelter, forgotten and very lonely. At least Henry, Fenella and the children were safe.

Chapter 46

Susie pulled the curtains even tighter.

She was determined that there wasn't even a tiny, tiny chink that anyone could see through.

She couldn't think how else to shut them out. They were besieged. There was a whole herd of them mooching on the drive. They looked so unperturbed, so casual and relaxed, but she knew that the slightest movement or even the phone ringing would set them off, running around like a startled wasp's nest, fully alert, tense and whirring.

She could only just hear them through the double glazing, when they shouted their questions that weren't really questions at all.

"Hey Susie, what does it feel like to have survived when your best friend didn't?"

"Why didn't your son go on the trip then?"

"How's your 'injury'? It looks fine to me."

They were always there, a buzz in the background, staring, focussing on her, targeting her. She was convinced that they had the technology to pick up every word she said in the house, and she used all the tactics that they always use on films if she wanted to say anything at all that she didn't want listened to. Actually, she didn't want anything listened to, and was adept at turning on the taps or turning the music speakers up to really, really loud.

Henry and Fenella laughed gently at her, patronisingly, and kept saying that it was highly unlikely, and that phone tapping had been made illegal, but you just couldn't be certain, they looked so untrustworthy. Henners and Fenella looked at her indulgently, as if she'd retreated to being a small child.

Jack was not afraid to say that she was being utterly ridiculous about the whole listening thing. He just laughed falsely and shouted very loudly, "Fuck off, you nosy bastards!" He would never have sworn like that if Pete had been there, but Susie was a bit afraid to pull him up on it, as he just became nasty. She had tried to admonish him, but he had just looked at her, stared at her challengingly, and mouthed "Mrs Hughes". It made her crumble. She couldn't believe that her son could be so very, very cruel.

Jack insisted on going out as if nothing had happened. He had left the house yesterday and again today, without saying where he was going. He had swaggered through the mob, a smirk on his face, bestowing unctuous smiles as he went, and saying good morning sneeringly to anyone who made eye contact.

The press never mentioned Pete and his bravery. In fact, no one seemed to want to mention Pete, not the children or Henners or Fen. Susie was the only one holding out for a miracle, and received meaningless murmurs and platitudes from Henners.

"I can't talk about it," fretted a tearful Amelia, "and don't mention Hannah or I will scream."

Jack just said, "Stop it, Mum, for fuck's sake, just stop going on about it."

They looked at her pityingly, their common sense attitudes and acceptance, facing reality, versus her wishing, longing, for it not to be true.

Susie retreated to her bedroom to obsessively watch the footage on TV, on the alert for stories of survivors from the conflagration. The pictures from the drones were appalling. Total devastation. Obliteration. In her heart of hearts, she was resigned to the fact that her darling Pete was unquestionably gone. She held his pillow, stroked his face on their wedding photo, and wept as quietly as she could, so as not to upset the children.

I'm allowed to hold out hope, surely?

Neither did they mention poor Mum, in danger, perhaps dead or dying. If she brought it up, Henners and Fen retreated in unanimity, reached out for their children, went very quiet. Henners said, "I have done all I can, Susie. I have reported Mum and Moira's situation to the helpline. What else can I do?"

Should I mount a rescue attempt? Henners most certainly wasn't going to. *I will talk to Jessica and Leah about it and see what they think.*

Susie suddenly remembered all over again that she couldn't.

Chapter 47

Kate was somewhat miffed.

It was crazy but somehow, it was just a tad annoying that Susie and Leah were getting all the media attention. She didn't know about the Powells, she hadn't even seen Doreen or Charlie.

I wonder why Doreen didn't come to that meeting. Mind you, don't see her much at anything to do with school.

The press had all descended at first, a dark cloud of them, poking their noses in, terrifying poor Lily: "How does it feel to have survived?", "How do you feel about all your classmates?" A teeming swarm surrounding them, the moment they set foot in the street. They had gone away very quickly... no story... the living were not as interesting as the dead to those flesh-eating vultures.

It was obvious that in the case of the Ahmeds, the press were picking up on the Muslim angle. The strange thing was that none of them around Charlton had ever seemed to give a stuff about the Ahmeds being Muslim.

How on earth could they now make just being a Muslim a sinister connection to a clearly lunatic terrorist group's atrocity? Crazy minds, and who were the vicious idiots doing all the trolling on FB?

They were saying bizarre things like "Had she known?", "Why hadn't she let Aisha go on the trip?", and asking about some Pakistani bloke that was apparently tenuously related to Leah. A fourth cousin three times removed. *Ridiculous.*

The hunting pack seemed to have picked Leah out as their chosen victim from the family, the vulnerable member of the herd, easy pickings.

Aisha, Sara and Farrukh just managed to look bored and dignified, but Leah's agitation made good telly, her sari billowing, her arms held up in supplication, covering her face, her mewling cries of, "Please, just leave us alone, we haven't done anything at all", which had the opposite effect.

Poor love.

Leah's mum-in-law was a hoot, just gabbled at them in Pakistani, and it quite clearly was not very polite!

Good on her, a tough old bird.

Kate chuckled to herself.

For poor Susie, they were going on about "What was it like to have sent Jessica to her doom?", "How do you think Hannah is feeling?", "Has Amelia visited Hannah to comfort her, weren't they best friends?"

Horrible, horrible words with implications.

They didn't ask about Pete, who was a victim, dying because of his brave role, defending scum like that. They didn't even ask about Susie's mum, holed up, vulnerable, on her brother's farm, possibly dying or even dead.

It was just so awful, all the thousands of people who had perished. Those that were dying slow and horrible deaths.

Just so many people had died and the telly was saying that many more were dying horrible, nasty, painful deaths soon afterwards. No doubt there would be thousands more. Kate shuddered at the enormity of it, all the fallout from such an immeasurable catastrophe. She could only hold tight to her Lily, such a near miss, such an incredible bloody miracle, all because of a virus; she must have done something right in her life to deserve this.

Perhaps she would go and see Susie tomorrow, once she had dropped Lily off at school. It must be bloody difficult for her. Lily didn't want to go in, not very surprisingly really, but Mr Barker had stressed at the meeting he had called that all four survivors should. Presumably, Jack and Amelia were going back as well, poor loves; what sort of reception were they going to get?

Kate pondered about that meeting. Susie and Leah were behaving really strangely. They were unable to look each other in the eye, not a word of comfort between them. It was dead uncomfortable to be there with them behaving like that.

*What was going on? Not like Susie at all to fall out with people, and Leah is the most positive and considerate person I have ever met. What **has** happened between the remaining two of the Eternal Triangle?*

Chapter 48

Leah harangued Farrukh.

"Can't you get rid of them? They are driving me mad." Leah stomped into the kitchen, followed meekly by saas, who pottered over to put the kettle on, wafting her sari as she skirted the island, as if she was doing a little dance.

"*Kiya aap karayn gay chai, baita?*" Saas asked Farrukh, with an adoring smile.

"*Jee haan, ammi,*" replied Farrukh, somewhat indulgently.

"Farrukh? Farrukh? Stop talking about tea. How do we get rid of them?"

"Just ignore them, Leah. They will lose interest soon and go."

"But they are not going, are they? They just hang around all the time, and it is impossible to get in and out. One of them touched me, Farrukh, a man, he touched me!"

Farrukh looked at Leah enquiringly over his glasses.

"Perhaps he didn't mean to, but he did and I won't have it. You can't allow that, Farrukh."

Her mother-in-law reached up for the teapot, her bangles jangling, and clattered cups around noisily.

Leah continued, her voice rising in anguish. "I am so worried about the girls. They don't like it at all. Sara is very frightened. Farrukh?"

Farrukh seemed more intent on his imminent cup of tea.

"I am going to run one of them over. Not deliberately, of course, but they just keep crowding round the car. I have to drive really carefully and they just stand there in front of us, pointing their cameras at us, shouting stupid questions."

Farrukh still seemed to be ignoring her. "And they are blatantly racist and blasphemous. How dare they talk about Allah, may his name be praised. They are blaming us, Farrukh, for this monstrous act. Surely you can't allow that?"

The kettle popped off automatically, loudly, making everyone jump a little. Despite appearances, they were all on edge.

"And we have had to hide in our own home, live in the half darkness, curtains closed." Leah started counting off the inconveniences on her long, elegant fingers. "Tape up the letterbox, unplug the phone, turn off the door bell, lock ourselves in, or them out; I really can't be sure which sometimes." Leah was getting into a state, trembling with rage, indignation and exhaustion. It really didn't help that Farrukh just seemed to not care at all. Tears were very close.

She suddenly realised that the only people that ever took her side against Farrukh and her mother-in-law, in the world, the universe, were Susie and Jessica, the Eternal Triangle. Jessica was dead. Susie wasn't, but Susie had completely ostracised her. She missed Susie so much. It was at times like this that they had always helped each other get through, supported each other. Leah felt a total outcast, desolated, alone.

"Leah, please calm down, you are upsetting Ammi." His mother leisurely poured the tea, looking completely peaceful. "Just learn to ignore them. The girls know what to do. Don't make eye contact. Don't listen to what they are saying. Walk briskly and purposefully. Just pretend that they aren't there. You must learn to be dignified, like Ammi."

Leah seethed inside. Farrukh knew how to score points She said, through clenched teeth, "I am dignified. I am far more dignified than saas."

She whisked out of the kitchen, her silky skirts rustling, into the dark hallway, not really knowing where she was going, the tears dripping onto the white carpet, crying for the loss of civilisation and the loss of both of her only true friends.

Chapter 49

Charlie retreated to his bedroom.

Hurriedly tiptoeing in his socks up the stairs, anxiously looking behind him, although there was nothing to see, he curled up on his bed and tried to make himself small.

The bastards were out there again. He felt trapped. He sat still, silent, alert, breathing as quietly as he could, which was ridiculous because they wouldn't be able to hear. The house was so inadequately built that it was as if there was nothing between him and them, and when he had tried pulling all the curtains, they were so flimsy and crappy that they didn't fit properly. He felt they could look right through the walls and see him.

With his senses on full alert, his ears reverberating with the strain, he could hear their steps on the gravel, their shoes scuffing on the ridges of the concrete, the tiny kerchink as something metal caught the gate, which hung off its hinges and was welded immoveable to the path.

"He's got to be in there." The strident voice made him jump.

"Huh?"

Definitely a twat.

"I said," the voice repeated, with an annoying, sing-song sarcasm, "he has got to be in there. Where else could he be? He ain't at the pub and he's easy to spot." Harsh laugh. The pounding of an impatient fist on the door suddenly thundered through the house – they'd already worked out that the bell didn't work. The letter flap was lifted with a muted creak and an impatient "Hello? Hello? Are you in there, Charles?" wafting through suddenly loud and too close for comfort, invading his space. Charlie shrank back into the corner.

"We're here to help you, Charles. Can we help you?"

You want to help me? You're fucking kidding!

He shifted position, carefully.

"Hello?"

Silence.

"Charles?"

"Is your sister home, Charles?"

"He's not answering. What do you want to do?"

"Forget it. It is all a bit old hat now anyhow. Let's go back to the Muslims. There is more potential there."

"I'll leave him a card."

Then there was just the noise of the letter flap creaking and then snapping back sharply. The stiff, rusting spring was potentially lethal. They shuffled away, their noise retreated, but Charlie didn't dare move. He sat in the silence, breathing. He wouldn't bother to look at the card, it could just stay with all the other crap that littered the hall.

Chapter 50

Bernie woke from a light doze.

He hadn't slept at all well last night, alone in their big bed, and he had now nodded off in his comfy armchair, just for a moment.

The key was turning in the front door lock. Someone was coming in, but he wasn't sure who. It made him instantly alert and he hauled himself out of his chair as quickly as he could, a rush of fear speeding his lumbering rise. Just as he reached his feet, a cheerful voice, Mini's cheerful voice, said, "Coo-ee, I'm home!"

He was astonished. He was stupidly rooted to the spot. As he stood there, gawping, in bounced Mini. "Hello! How are you? Did you miss me?"

He carried on goggling, a gasping cod. She wrapped her arms round his belly – she had difficulty getting her tiny arms right around – and laid her head on his chest. He stood immobile and breathed in her clean, fresh, soapy smell, as if she'd just walked out of the shower. He rather incongruously, in such a revelatory moment, thought that she didn't smell the same as usual, a rather manly perfume.

Just a different soap from home?

Sensing his rigid stance, she turned her little face up to his. "What's up, old codger? What is it? Aren't you glad to see me?"

He didn't know what to say. She stood back, frowning.

"Hello! Is there anyone at home?" She flapped her hand across his face with impish gaiety. "Cup of tea? I'll put the kettle on." She gambolled off towards the kitchen, leaving him standing.

He caught up with her as she was reaching into the cupboards on tiptoes to grasp the tea bags.

"Where have you been?" he managed to squeeze out, in a silly, little, tiny voice that started turning into a pathetic whine. "How was your sister? I thought... we thought that... we've been... What is going on? You are back."

"We had a wonderful time, thanks. I said I'd be back today! You look like you've seen a ghost!" Evie continued cheerfully.

"Have you not...? Surely you have seen...? You couldn't miss it..."

"What, love? What are you on about?"

In steady steps, he explained, each word coming out rhythmically, like a beating drum. As he unwaveringly let it all come out, he stared her firmly in the eye and watched her closely. He watched her face lose its smile, her eyes widen, her frown deepen, her mouth gently fall open, total astonishment. She turned pale. He gripped her tightly.

"I can't believe that we didn't hear about it. That is madness. We... I didn't even have an inkling... How the hell could we, I, not have heard about that? You must have thought..." She tapered off, stopped, the realisation dawning on her. "Emily? Dear God, what on earth did Emily think?" she murmured.

Bernie wanted to shaker her, hard. "Emily is upstairs, not at Hannah's, she is naturally distraught. However, Emily can wait, I think, just a little bit longer. We both need to work out what is happening here before we give her this astonishingly good news," said Bernie sarcastically.

She took a deep breath and held it. He watched expectantly. She tried to turn away. Wouldn't meet his eye.

He could hear her mind whirring. He could feel his own heart beating in his throat.

"Well... we decided not to go to London after all." She whipped around, stared at him hard and scanned his face, anxiously, he thought. "We... Liz and I... found a lovely, little Airbnb in Wiltshire, out in the middle of nowhere." He detected a slight question in her tone, and could see her eyes darting, looking about for further things to say.

"Wiltshire?" he echoed. "And you didn't think to tell me of this change of plan? You have no idea what we have been going through! Emily..."

"I'm sorry, really sorry. We decided to have a weekend away from it all, right in the middle of nowhere. A little, thatched cottage, two up, two down. Really cute. No TV, nothing, no Wi-Fi, not even a phone signal, just glorious countryside. I don't believe it." She paused, puzzled. "How could we have missed something so.... so monumental!" She stopped for a moment, looking completely and genuinely shocked.

Bernie held her eyes, waited for her to start again. She embellished.

"We went for walks, drank cocktails. Chatted. We had long lie-ins..." She was warming to her story, almost gabbling, but she was still watching him very carefully. His hairs stood up on the back of his neck.

"And why was your car at the station?"

"We met there when our plans changed and it seemed silly to take two cars to Wiltshire, so I left mine and came back to it this morning." This, again, sounded more like a question than an answer.

"But why the station? Why not meet here?"

Evie didn't seem to have an answer and just continued to look at him.

They both heard Emily yell from upstairs, "Mum? Mum!" She clattered down the stairs like a whirling dervish, bounced off the walls at the bottom of the stairs and threw herself at Mini. "Mum? Oh God, Mum."

She enveloped her, somewhat towering over her, as she was averagely tall and Mini so small, her hair flopping over Mini like a smothering blanket in her frenzied elation.

Emily sobbed and just couldn't seem to think of anything else to say, other than "Mum!" over and over again. Emily pushed her mum away, looked down at her, tears of joy streaming down her own face, and a rather unattractive smear of mucus, and then pulled her mum back in and rocked her madly from side to side, laughing wildly, lifting her bodily from the ground and twirling round with her like a rag doll.

It was at that moment that the telephone rang. Mini peered at Bernie, looking dazed from the bundle of arms and legs and hair. It rang several times before Bernie squeezed past, keeping as far away as possible, stepped into the lounge and lifted the receiver.

"Hello, 7-4-2-5-6-8," he said quietly. "Liz? Yes, hello, Liz. Yes, yes we are all just fine, thank you, dear. Where are you? Safe, I hope? Well out of the zone? No, we didn't hear or see a thing." He nodded uselessly.

"Yes, yes, I know. It's terrible. Absolutely ghastly. Yes, Emily's school, Charlton Academy. Yes, you heard correctly, a whole class of them. No, no, she's distraught, but she will be alright now her mum is … err… is back. Missed calls from yesterday and today? You've only just got back? Oh yes, I did try to contact you. No, not Evie, me. Yes, Evie is right here beside me. Phew indeed." Bernie laughed, a bitter, little guffaw.

This mention of the school trip set Emily off. "It's true Mum, loads of them, the whole of Year 12... except Jack didn't go, but neither did his mum... and so Hannah's mum is dead, as well as her brother and her dad, so can we..."

Evie had disentangled herself from the incoherent Emily, crept over to Bernie, leading Emily by the hand. Unusually still, she looked into his face, her glittering eyes wide as saucers and her pretty mouth hanging open, a bit of spittle shining on her lip, hers or Emily's, he couldn't say.

"Had you forgotten something, Liz?" Bernie held her look. "What do I mean?" Bernie continued quietly looking at Mini. "Nothing, dear, no, no, don't worry, I must be getting muddled. You know what I'm like, an old codger like me. I never know what is going on. Anyway, dear, I must go. I will hand you over to your sister. Cheerio."

He broke off. "Evie, it's for you, it's your sister, Liz." the emphasis clearly on Liz. He handed her the receiver, his dismayed eyes focussed on hers, desolation washing over him, his heart breaking. He wondered if it could it break any more.

Evie took the receiver from him, her eyes not leaving his and said cheerfully, "Liz? Hi. Look something has come up. Can I talk to you later? Yes, we're all fine. Yes, I'll ring back. Take care."

"It's not what you think," she said hurriedly, staring at him, unwaveringly.

"What do you think I think?" Bernie croaked.

"I have no idea, but I can see why you might be confused." Evie smiled encouragingly, detached herself from Emily, stepped forward, wrapping herself around him, burying her head in his chest.

"Go on," Bernie said coldly, standing rigidly, resisting Evie's embrace.

"Well, you see, it's like this." She looked up into his eyes with a winning smile. "I did lie about being with Liz. I know that you disapprove strongly of me hanging out with Daisy-May." Bernie gasped involuntarily. "I know that you hate her after the incident at the wake. So I lied about being with Liz. I know that it was unforgiveable of me. I lied." She squeezed him. "You can see why I lied. You would have been furious if I had told you. You have, in effect, banned her from my life. You know you have." She punched him gently, playfully.

"The rest of it is true. We went to Wiltshire. Daisy-May has just broken up with her boyfriend and wanted to lick her wounds. We talked and talked and had too many cocktails, etcetera, etcetera. I cannot truly believe that we didn't hear anything about such a heinous act. It is incredible! That is what comes from being holed up in an ancient, old cottage in the countryside." Evie looked at him, expectantly, a sweet smile on her face. Bernie didn't know what to believe.

"Daisy-May dropped me back at my car just now and I came straight home."

He needed to take it in, mull it over. He wanted to interrogate her, ask her more, demand proof, but with Emily standing there, gawping at them, what could he do? Daisy-May? He hesitated, angry, confused, lost as how to proceed.

Had she been with Daisy-May, that… that…? Or was this just another lie?

"I tell you what, old codger," chirruped Evie, looking sly, "we can ring Daisy-May now. You can speak to her and put your mind at rest."

Bernie sighed. He could not and would not speak to that woman, ever. He knew that Evie knew that. He stood rigidly staring over her head at the wall. Silent. He could feel her eyes staring, challenging him. What sort of a fool did she think he was? What if Mini hadn't been with Daisy-May? Who had she been with? Should he call Mini's bluff? What would Emily think? He left it too long.

"Well, that's all sorted now. Silly, old codger, I have no idea what you were thinking. Let me go and put on the kettle and we can have a nice cuppa. It's your answer to everything!" She reached up on her tiptoes, kissed him under his chin, patted him on the cheek and skipped off into the kitchen, with a defiantly-pleased look plastered across her elfin, little face.

"Come and help me, Emily, and I can put your mind at rest too. I am so very sorry, you poor, little darling, you must have been horrified, but here I am now. Come and tell me all about it. What a palaver!"

He was left standing there, drained, cold, in shock, feeling like a cuckolded, old fool.

Chapter 51

Leah took Aisha and Sara into school.

Mr Barker had said that they should carry on as usual to make it easier for the children. She wasn't really sure that he was right in this respect, but felt that it was really important to show their faces. The traffic was very dense. It seemed that all the parents were taking their children in today. Not unsurprising really.

Saas was in the front of the car of course, staring ahead with a defiant look on her face, as if they were going into battle, rattling off words of encouragement in Urdu to the girls in the back, inciting them to stand firm in the face of opposition. In a perverse way, she seemed to be revelling in it all. Perhaps they were heading into enemy territory, it certainly felt like it.

Leah wasn't entirely convinced that Sara and Aisha's grasp of Urdu was sufficient to understand everything saas was saying, but hey.

The press were still there. *Why wouldn't they just go away?* Leah was determined to remain expressionless, immune to the stares and the cameras. She must not crumble.

Once they were through the cordon of evil parasites, Aisha leapt out, grabbed Sara by the hand and legged it into the foyer.

Leah was so proud of Aisha. She was a remarkable, young woman, and coping far, far better than she was. She couldn't help look out to see if Susie was there. She couldn't see her.

As they crawled their way out of the car park, saas held her hand up, put the tip of her thumb behind her teeth and flicked it towards the assembled press pack. "Cutta!" she shouted, with a rather frivolous grin. Now that was going too far, much too far. If Farrukh could see his mother now… most certainly not dignified.

Chapter 52

Pips was finding it impossible to be at school.

Those in authority, all adults, seemed to have decided that it would be best to "guide a return to full normality as soon as possible", whatever that meant, but it seemed to include getting everyone, literally everyone, except the people that were dead of course, back to school on Monday. Pips wasn't entirely sure that normality was doable; she thought that it would have been better to ask the kids themselves what they thought best.

She most certainly hadn't been able to face the bus, that would have been unbearable, and her mum had given her a lift. Pips thought that her mum was still acting very oddly, but she guessed that it was because she was so distraught about Ellie and worried about her dad being missing. It didn't help Pips feel any better.

Normally, when she felt bad about things, she had always talked it through with Ellie. Just thinking about Ellie made her want to cry again, but there were so many people weeping and wailing and carrying on, who hadn't even been affected personally, that she couldn't bear to join in. Her grief was so deep-seated and private that she didn't want to make it into a public performance. It sort of belittled it somehow.

She had tried to catch up with Charlie to test her theory that by some faint, miraculous chance, Ellie might have escaped, but he was totally zoned out. He looked really scary. She had backed off, scuttled away.

Chapter 53

Charlie looked around at the four of them in the chemistry lab.

Mrs Pietruski was talking to them, all softly, gently, calmly. It was soothing, pacifying.

He had got through the ordeal of an assembly of the whole school, or what remained of the school. It had been humiliating; the four of them felt they were being paraded like mutant monsters at a freak show.

For fuck's sake, Mr Barker, was that a good idea? It definitely were not Mr Barker, it were not. Stared at. Gossiped about. Gawped at like transmuted fucking automatons.

He felt inexplicably ashamed.

For some reason, Mr Barker had decided that the four of them would be better in the chemistry lab, not in their regular classroom.

What was he on?

It made Charlie feel trapped, caged, and corralled, his eyes seeking out all on their own that fucking periodic table and that fucking uranium. Shadows of Alfie and Ellie, laughing, joshing, danced tantalisingly somewhere out of sight.

Fuck, fuck, fuck.

To be fair, the world had imploded and no one knew what to do.

Jack sat there, his leg jittering up and down, arms folded, chin defiantly tipped with a creepy sort of smirk on his face.

Weirdo.

The more people muttered and whispered about his mum and the martyr, Mrs Hughes, the more belligerent he became. He was bristling, angry.

He wondered what Emily Chittenden made of it. Were they still dating? It didn't look like it on the bus. She had totally ignored Jack when he had got on, clearly scanning the back of the bus for her, but she was deliberately staring at her friends. All the way to school, she then did that irritating girl thing where she was talking to her friends, muttering loudly, while staring at Jack angrily. Her friends kept looking at him furiously too. Whatever. He didn't care.

Aisha sat there, looking at Mrs Pietruski with intense fascination. Static, dignified, her hijab framing her face. A random shaft of sunlight lit up her face, and she looked like the Madonna.

Charlie had seen the trolling on Facebook.

Had she? Must have. Couldn't miss it.

He and Lily had been lucky to totally avoid all that shit. His weekend had been crap, Aisha's must have been excruciating.

Lily sat, looking pale, and not properly well yet, staring at her hands, shifting awkwardly in her chair. Somehow, because she had been genuinely ill, a valid reason for missing the London trip, she was exonerated from everyone's interest.

His own story baffled people.

Complicated. Least said.

His ears whistled. His head pounded.

This was too fucking hard.

He clasped his hands over his forehead, squeezing, squeezing to make it go away.

Chapter 54

Mrs Pietruski hadn't been able to get through to Charlie.

She was the only person that could always been relied upon to interpret this strange, introverted boy. Charlie was so bright and diligent, and impeccably polite, yet so reclusive and cautious.

All the staff knew that he had been bullied at his primary school, all the usual racial taunts, monkey noises and chocolate references, but all the way through Charlton, he had seemed to be reasonably popular, under the wing of Alfie, Jessica's sensible son. He was part of the cool gang, respected rather than vilified for his academic endeavour, and had made friends, admittedly very few, but rock solid ones.

When Ellie had been permitted to join the tight-knit inner circle, he had progressed and become less cautious, more outgoing, less defensive.

God, it must be awful for him to have lost both Eleanor and Alfie. No wonder he was so distressed and looked haunted. Poor lad.

She felt powerless to do anything to help.

When interrogated, Charlie was inclined to put on a blank face and stare just one centimetre above her right eyebrow. It wasn't insolence, just no contact.

Charlie recited that his mum's phone contract had run out, she hadn't renewed it – no, they didn't have a landline – and reported that she didn't want to speak to anyone or get involved in all that stuff. Jon Barker had told her that his emails had been ignored.

Mrs Pietruski wasn't sure what else she could do, but there was something niggling her. It didn't seem right. Perhaps they should intervene, but there was just so many agonising stories playing out.

Chapter 55

Susie was really quite hurt that Jack and Amelia had insisted on getting the bus to and from school.

Jack had said very firmly that he didn't want her anywhere near the place. She had apparently done enough damage anyway.

Susie, as a result, was sitting in the kitchen, pretending that she wasn't waiting for them to get back. Fen had kindly joined her, and was being very sweet and dear, gently babbling away about everything and anything, except the immense, great, big nuclear elephant in the room that was Pete, Mum and Moira, abandoned at the farm, the disappeared Jessica and the totally hurtful Leah.

Henners was holed up in Pete's study. He seemed to have taken it over without even asking, and he had moved all Pete's stuff aside. Susie didn't like to say anything. She thought he was actually hiding from her because he was ashamed about Mum.

Arthur and Alice were playing in the sitting room; a noisy game with cards, seemingly untouched by the heavy atmosphere that pervaded Susie's hitherto happy, haphazard and contented home.

Amelia was the first to trudge in through the back door, looking despondent. Jack followed, looking belligerent. Susie leapt up.

"How did it go? Was it really, really difficult, do you need to talk about it? Can I get you a cup of tea or a snack or something, supper won't be until six-thirty. Oh my darlings, let me give you a hug, you look like you really, really need it."

Jack glared at his mother. "Have you any idea what it has been like? The full assembly of the school was a nightmare. It was bad enough for me, Charlie, Emily and Aisha, but you should have seen poor Hannah. It was grotesque. Have you any idea what you have done?"

Susie flinched. "But, Jack, you know it was an accident, you know I didn't mean to fall down the stairs…"

Jack stomped off through the hall, up the stairs. She heard his bedroom door slam.

At least Amelia flung herself at Susie for comfort, crying into her shoulder and going on about poor Hannah. Susie wrapped her arms around her and tried not to cry herself.

She wondered if she should try to ring Hannah. She had rung everyone else she could think of, and that she had the numbers for, to offer her sympathies.

Perhaps she should try and see poor, little Hannah… comfort her… she had promised Jessica, after all… or perhaps she had better wait.

Chapter 56

Moira wondered just how much longer they would have to hibernate for.

It had been exactly three days but it felt like three weeks. She felt completely isolated and incredibly alone. Thank God the TV was still working, otherwise, they would have been totally cut off. They had watched with horror the footage from London, the endless programmes about the creation of martial law, the interviews with people clearly dying from radiation. Interviews with Prince Andrew, who was now King in waiting.

They had been a bit more forthcoming about the dangers of radiation. Moira pricked her ears up, but at the end of the day, she was really none the wiser. The presenter, a woman this time, was asking some expert or other about the effects. A man, far too young-looking to know anything about it all, lectured:

"Scientific estimates, based on the premise that the bomb had been a 10-kiloton uranium-enriched device, have calculated that the No Go Zone will remain radioactive for several months."

Moira couldn't help thinking that this was not very scientific but rather vague.

He droned on:

"Within the Dangerous Fallout Zone, fallout particles that are most hazardous are fine sand-sized grains. Fallout descends within 24 hours of the blast and would have extended from 10 to 20 miles from Ground Zero. An exposure rate of 10 rads per hour is used to delimit the Dangerous Fallout

Zone. Winds of varying speeds and directions at different levels of lower and upper atmosphere push radiation in directions not evident from ground level observation, so some areas could be more or less radioactive."

Well, that's not very helpful.

He continued, "Beyond 20 miles, which we call the Extended Fallout Zone, still requires shelter and/or evacuation orders. Monitoring ground radiation levels is imperative. Indeed, fallout in areas 100 miles or more from the centre of London may warrant protective actions."

Moira wished that he would make more sense and actually provide some practical assistance. In frustration, she turned over to the local news.

The Charlton Academy story was still showing on the local news. They hadn't been able to find anything else of sufficient human interest, it seemed, and it had been surreal for Moira to be seeing Susie on the telly, the same footage of her leaving the house repeated with a voiceover. At least she'd been able to clearly identify Henry's car. She knew for certain he was there and safe, with both children presumably.

Why the TV was working but the telephones not was a mystery. They had been saying on the telly that all mobile phones were automatically immobilised so that the bandwidth could be used by the emergency services.

Very clever, but why wasn't the landline working?

She'd developed a nervous habit of picking up the phone, pressing redial, over and over again, but it never worked. She felt at a loss. Very lonely, worried and afraid.

She had woken with a headache this morning, and yesterday as well. Brenda too. It was very alarming and worried her. Had they picked up some radiation? She'd tried to be so careful. She had showered and showered and changed their clothes regularly. She'd scrubbed every bite of food. She'd run the taps as long as she could before drawing any water.

Brenda was getting restless and had completely forgotten that they had to stay inside, or indeed why. It was a bit like Groundhog Day. Dementia was a very wearing condition for the carer. Moira seemed to spend her time steering her away from the doors, the front door, the back door, the French windows onto the terrace, and stopping her from throwing open the curtains and the shutters. She'd locked each and every door and removed the key into her safekeeping like a gaoler.

Dave had arrived like clockwork every morning and every evening, taken to wandering into the boot room and feeding the dogs, a relief for Moira; she didn't have to venture outside her place of safety, and carried on as if nothing at all had happened. He'd continued to taunt Moira all weekend, making his cheeky, derogatory comments, pretending he was talking to the chickens and the dogs, and Moira had just as doggedly continued to ignore him.

Moira was concerned though. Things had changed gradually over the weekend. Dave had seemed to slink into the yard, sneaking in, rather than his usual bold entrance. He had levered himself out of the Land Rover gingerly, not stood up to full height in his usual cocky way, and was moving more slowly towards the chickens without saying anything. He had let them out in silence, feebly dribbling handfuls of corn onto the ground. Lifting the automatic waterer, with effort, he had become more and more lethargic.

Moira was deeply worried.

Should I try and make contact with him? What could I do, in any case? If he has been irradiated, there is nothing I can do, but shouldn't he be seeking medical help? What was his wife, Heather, thinking letting him out?

She felt helpless.

Moira had watched furtively from the kitchen window this morning and seen Dave wander apathetically towards the dairy, where the cows were assembled, waiting patiently for him. If only she could use the telephone, she would be able to do something, at least phone Dave's wife, Heather, and talk to her about her concerns. Moira was guessing that Heather had stayed inside, like a sensible soul.

It wasn't just Dave either. All three dogs had slowed up noticeably, but Mutt was looking particularly unwell. She could hear her being sick through the kitchen door. What could she do? Helpless, so helpless, and without any way of getting help from anyone else.

Moira looked out for Dave again for the afternoon milking and was relieved that at least he had made it in.

Chapter 57

Kate opened Caroline's back door with her own key.

She stepped in and sniffed the air. It smelt of bonfire. Perhaps Thomas has been lighting the fires? Wrong time of year, surely? Shouting her customary, "Hi, only Kate!" she hung up her coat and stepped into the kitchen. No answer.

I wonder where Thomas is.

It had been exactly a week since Doomsday, and she'd been undecided whether to come at all. Thomas probably didn't even know that her day for "doing" was Fridays, but she thought it was the least she could do for him. You know Caroline, William and all that. It would have been more odd not to.

Thomas was a sweetie with his shy manner and beetling eyebrows, and she wasn't sure who else would be looking out for him. She hadn't dared contact him before this, as "just the cleaner", it didn't seem quite right somehow to intrude on his grief.

How did all these people cope with losing their wives, their kids, their nearest and dearest?

She knew Susie had tried contacting him, she'd said so, but they were old friends.

Kate decided that since Thomas wasn't in, she might as well have a cup of tea before she made a start. Caroline would never have allowed it, but she was finding it hard to get going.

To be quite selfish, she had only really come to work to make things seem a bit more normal, doing the same things that "we did before", but now she was here and Thomas wasn't, she felt a bit cut off. It had been hell on earth all week, totally chaotic, completely mad.

There had been great outpourings of grief for those that had died, a tsunami of grief around the world: shock, horror, wailing and indignation. Every monument across the globe lit up in red white and blue, endless candlelit vigils in cathedrals, synagogues and mosques, and every other place of religious reverence. Silent marches through undamaged capital city centres. There were mountains of flowers everywhere, already rotting, a waste of money that seemed pretty pointless to Kate.

The kettle clunked as it reached the boil. Kate dunked a posh tea bag into a mug, mashed it with a spoon and absent-mindedly dropped it into the waste bin.

There had been hysterical rantings from defensive policemen, covered in silver braids, army generals who spoke patronisingly about having taken charge, security people spouting from their not so secret hideout in Cheltenham, all of them saying, "How could we have known?" The media shrieking back frenziedly that they should have.

It may have been the most enormous catastrophe in the history of the world, but strangely, the chaos seemed to be localised. As soon as everyone realised that it had been just a "one-off" and that "only London" had been hit, everyone had sighed a collective sigh of relief, and carried on almost as if nothing had happened at all. Overall, on a day-to-day basis, it hadn't seemed to have made any difference whatsoever to the rest of the country overall.

The utilities all worked. There were no shortages in the shops. The buses and trains ran outside the M25. The weather was ordinary. There was just the awareness of a remote black hole in the centre of London, into which so many thousands had disappeared.

Kate leant on the kitchen island and took a sip of tea.

The actual area affected was a small dot on a map of the United Kingdom. Kate had been very surprised when some programme or other had shown it on a map – the devastation area in red, with a yellow smear showing the areas affected by radioactivity. Apparently, the actual area of the UK affected was a mere 0.01 per cent of the whole land mass. A weird statistic to even come up with, but that was just so miniscule. Yet, the whole thing was colossal and had affected everyone in the world. Everyone mourning strangers.

Kate sipped at her tea.

It seemed to her that the mourning for those that were known personally was more pertinent, more private, unseen from the eyes of the wider world – too small in the scheme of things to be of note. *And a whole year group of kids from one school?* There would have been other school trips than just Charlton that day. Other communities grieving like their own.

Charlton had advised that the survivors go back into school as soon as they could, to distract them from dwelling on things, and to give them the comfort of being together, all in the same boat as such. Sensibly, they had created a special classroom for the remaining year 12s in one of the chemistry labs, so they didn't have to look at the sea of empty desks and the rows of named lockers that stood there in their serried ranks like a world war cemetery.

It had been surprisingly hard for Lily, being a survivor. Lily was distraught about the others, of course she was. It was like the biggest horror story ever, all her friends disappearing in a blaze of destruction. Just so shocking. Thousands and thousands of people she didn't know, but a nucleus of people that she knew really well. Kate shuddered again.

Poor Lily wasn't coping that well, endless tears and refusing to eat. She didn't seem to be getting much comfort from the other survivors. She didn't know why, but instead of clinging together, as she would have expected, they seemed to be wary of each other. Kids could be funny like that.

The survivors had, to a certain extent, been made to face up to the reality that they were alive when others were not. She could not imagine how they must have felt at the big assembly at school, with its wall of wailing and sobbing schoolchildren. They had been offered counselling very swiftly, but Kate wondered if the counselling would do more harm than good, as it forced them go over and over it. Sometimes, she felt it was least said, soonest mended.

Somehow, everyone just seemed to need to talk about it a lot, to make sure it had really happened and that it wasn't a crazy personal nightmare, but you had to pick who you spoke to very carefully, so as not to cause further distress. Essentially, because she hadn't lost anyone, she was not entitled to an opinion, or even entitled to feel sad.

Obviously, for Jack and Susie, it was a very different experience to Lily's. No wonder. Susie was so overcome with guilt about Jessica. It must truly be an enormous, indeed insurmountable, burden for Susie to carry, and without her rock, Pete. No wonder she looked so terrible. Her showpiece hair, which was normally her pride and joy, didn't look as if it had been washed, and was becoming rather greasy and stringy.

Poor Jack was finding it so hard to cope with all the venom that was being poured on him. Apparently, he had had to delete his Facebook page because of the vile trolling. It wasn't his fault, poor lad. Rumour had it that Hannah and the rest of her class had completely ostracised Amelia, who also had to delete her Facebook page, due to more trolling.

Crazy! Rude! Cruel.

It was really no wonder everyone was rallying around poor Hannah, orphaned in one fell swoop, through no fault of her own, and to lose her brother too. A nightmare. She had been staying with Amba Chawla for the time being. They thought it best that she stayed on at school until the end of term, but Kate had heard that she was eventually going up to her aunt's in Manchester for the new academic year.

At least Susie had been distracted by the arrival of Henry and his family. She wondered what on earth they would do next. Susie and Pete's was a big house, relatively speaking, but it must be quite a squash with all of them together.

It seemed that Susie's mum and her carer had been abandoned by Henry and Fenella at the farm. She wondered how that would play out.

It had been very surreal, trying to work out who was dead and who was alive, who was irradiated, who had escaped; like a horrible guessing game, with the most sinister and spine chilling answers – a horror movie come to life, and real.

Kate drained her mug and out of habit, rinsed it under the tap and dried it carefully, before returning it to its appointed cupboard.

It was Kate that had told Susie that Caroline had gone up to town that day. Kate was surprised how well Susie had taken the news. She'd always assumed they were best friends. Whenever she'd seen them in town together, they were always arm in arm, always socialising together and reminiscing about school days. Perhaps she was just shell-shocked over Pete, Jessica, and just so many other people that they knew, let alone the thousands of strangers.

Talking of Caroline, odd that Thomas had left Caroline's note on the table. She would have thought that he would have put it out of sight, so it didn't cause him any further anguish. Looking around, it dawned on Kate that the whole place was still exactly as she'd left it. Not only the note, but everything was just so, the way she always left it. A prickle went up Kate's spine.

Perhaps Thomas just hadn't been back.

He had family elsewhere that he would have gone to; Scotland, she thought, the place where he and Caroline had got married. The wedding photos. The arrays of kilts.

Thomas in a kilt, hilarious!

He would probably have gone straight there from London, or wherever he had been that day, as soon as he could. Knowing that William had perished. Realising that Caroline had passed away. She would have done, if she'd just lost her whole family in one fell swoop. She shuddered again.

Must stop doing that.

Pondering, she wandered into the hall and saw the heap of post piling up below the letterbox, mixed with the last few days' papers. It amazed her that everything could go on as normal, only a matter of tens of miles from complete destruction, with the post and papers as usual.

The answerphone light was flashing, but then it often was. Perhaps there was a message from him there, saying where he was. She assumed that he knew that Caroline had passed away, but perhaps he didn't? It was so complicated. Should she listen to their private messages?

A thought struck her and she returned to the kitchen, made for the Aga and opened the top left oven door with a flourish. As a waft of cremated meat puffed in her face, she coughed. The casserole was in there, reduced to ashes. A horrific thought flashed through Kate's mind: *like Caroline, William and all the others*. She reverently lifted out the charred remains and, not knowing what else to do, bore them out to the back door.

I'd better phone Susie and consult.

It took Susie only 10 minutes to come round, and Kate let Susie in.

"You can see why I called you. It's all a bit of a mystery and I don't want to go poking my nose in and getting into trouble for it."

"Gosh, don't worry, Kate, I quite see your dilemma. It is really, really complicated." Susie suddenly went pale. "Oh golly, the smell, it's..." She dashed over and retched into the sink. Kate thought that it wasn't surprising under the circumstances. The smell of incinerated meat was enough to put all sorts of awful thoughts into a person's head.

She reached for a glass from the cupboard and handed it to Susie, with a sad look in her eye. She didn't dare say anything, there wasn't anything left to say; everyone was in the same boat, except her. Kate hadn't lost anyone.

"Oh, thank you so much. It just caught me by surprise, I wasn't expecting..." Susie ran the tap vigorously, let water into the glass where it whooshed up like a fountain and over Susie's sleeve. She sipped at the glass, poured the remainder down the sink, hopefully flushing away any sick that may have escaped. She wiped her mouth on her already-wet sleeve and turned to Kate.

"Better now?" asked Kate gently.

"Fine, thank you. Sorry, that was really, really silly of me."

"What do you think, Susie, should we listen to the messages? It might shed some light on the matter."

Nodding, Susie headed for the hall. Once at the machine, she hesitated, looked at Kate, looked back to the machine. "If a message doesn't appear helpful, we can just skip them so we don't hear anything confidential by mistake. It's really embarrassing enough, don't you think? It makes me feel uncomfortable." With sudden courage, Susie boldly pressed the play button.

"You have 19 new messages," the machine intoned. "Message one…" it continued. Message one happened to be Kate herself.

"Hi, only Kate. Just phoning to say that I have Lily at home with me as she is rather poorly. Would it be okay if I bring her with me today? I don't want to leave her on her own. Give me a ring if it's not okay, but I'll be over very shortly. Thanks."

Message two: "Hi Caro, it's Katty. Just wanted to catch up with you on your birthday next week. Are you coming up? Any brilliant ideas for pressies? I'll catch you later. Lots of love, bye."

"Caroline's sister," Susie explained to Kate.

Message three: "Caroline, darling, it's Thomas. Thought I'd catch you. Um. Err. Just to let you know that I've decided to go up to the office in town today after all, and I will stay up in town this evening. Terribly important dinner and all that, you know. Sorry it's such short notice but... anyway... um... I'll try and call again later, if I get the chance. Bye, darling."

Kate and Susie looked at each. "Shit a brick," exclaimed Kate.

"Oh my God," breathed Susie.

Simultaneously, they said, "Thomas was in London too!" That explained it. Thomas was gone. Another one consumed by the fireball, one more unidentifiable shadow on the pavements given a name.

Message four had started. "Hi, it's Katty again. Sorry to ring again so soon. I'm not nagging it's just I just heard about the bomb... it's London ... I was worried about William... I... Oh, just ring me when you can please."

Message five: "Caro, it's Mummy. Can you ring me please... William... Katty told me." She could then be heard sobbing. It was heart-breaking.

Message six: "Thomas, it's your father. Look, old chap, I am so sorry – that is an understatement, obviously. William. I am sure that you have plenty on your plate but please telephone us, if we can help... Just let us know what is happening. We can't be sure."

Message seven: "Congratulations. You are a winner..."

Susie hit the delete button angrily. "For God's sake."

Message eight: "Thomas, it's your father again. I'm sorry to bother you, old chap, I've been trying to leave a message on your mobile but it keeps going straight to messages, is it off? Look, dear boy, please ring us. Mummy is beside herself with worry about you all. What's that, dear? That's all very well but what else can I say? Sorry about that, your mother interrupted. Anyway, oh dear God, just telephone us please."

Message nine: "Caro, it's Mummy. Darling, please call... just please call... oh dear God."

Message ten: "They still aren't picking up. What shall I do, dear? What? No point. I don't know..." Thomas' father again.

Message eleven: "Hello, Thomas. It's Susie here. I am just so terribly, terribly sad about William and Caroline. Gosh, it's an awful thing to say in a message on an answering machine. I just wondered if you were okay, sorry, that is an understatement, um, ah. I've left a message on your mobile. Anyway, give me a ring when you get this message. Come over. Um. You've heard about Pete? Or I can come over to you. Bye."

Susie cringed.

Message twelve: "Caroline or Thomas. For God's sake, tell us what is happening. We've left messages everywhere, on all your mobiles. Just call us please, we want to help. William? Anyway, please, please just ring. It's Katty, by the way, and I'm now up with Mum and Dad, who are extremely distressed. Please ring."

Message thirteen: "Thomas? It's Susie again, just wondering if you were home and in need of help or anything. Give me a ring when you get in. Bye."

Message fourteen: "For God's sake…" A sigh. Difficult to recognise.

Susie, getting increasingly distressed, hit the pause button. She didn't want to hear any more, it was too ghastly for words.

"Susie, we have to listen to them all, just in case there is something from Thomas," Kate said gently.

Susie was crying and gabbled, "For God's sake, Kate, the whole family obliterated. What on earth should we do? Who is going to call Thomas' family and tell them? Does Caroline's family know about her yet? Why should they? Someone has to tell them. Which authorities should we tell? The police did all that sort of thing for Pete. I haven't a clue what has to be done. I really, really don't think I can face doing the phoning myself."

She turned to Kate, her face a picture of woeful shock, and said, "I think I'm going to throw up again," and rushed to the sink.

Chapter 58

Moira was making Brenda yet another cup of tea, when she heard an unrecognised vehicle turn into the yard and stop.

Moira looked askance, lifted the edge of the blind and peered out. A big, silver people carrier had drawn up alongside Dave's Land Rover.

Who on earth is it?

She continued to peer out. The passenger door opened and two ghostly figures reared up and out, dressed entirely in white. When they turned round, she assumed one was a he, he was very tall indeed, although he had a mask over his face. The tall one stalked over to the front door, enormous strides and enormous feet, and rang the brass bell. The sound of the bell was strikingly loud after so many days of unreal quietness, confinement and solitude.

Moira dashed down the hall to the door, beating Brenda by a whisker. She opened the letterbox and said excitedly, "Hello, hello! Who are you? Where are you from? Can you help us please?"

The apparition spoke, muffled by his mask. It was extremely surreal but just so exciting to find a white knight standing on the doorstep. She childishly felt like jumping with joy, which was something she'd never had the urge to do before. This was the best thing to happen in years!

The spectre leant down to the letterbox and Moira was able to hear him. He explained that he was there to rescue them... Hooray! "We're surprised to find you at all! It's not easy to find this place tucked up here, and the satnav took us on a wild goose chase. Sorry we have taken so long. We have just picked up Mrs Easton and she pointed out where you were hiding out. She was worried about her husband, who apparently has been coming to work as normal, crazy man."

Oh, hooray, hooray!

He was going to fetch them protective suits. Moira and Brenda were to change into them and then he would escort them to the vehicle and thence to safety.

"Now, let's get you sorted. How many of you are there in the house?"

He strode like a spaceman back to the vehicle, opened the doors, slipped out two parcels and came back to the front door, expecting Moira to open it. She couldn't bring herself to do so, out of habit, so he kindly poked them through the letterbox, one at a time, and they slithered onto the mat.

Moira went and got the Marigolds, returned to the drawing room and clumsily undid the envelopes, which was difficult, given the slippery packaging and rubber gloves, and discovered all-in-one suits, like Babygros. She knew what to do, stripped off, slipped into the Babygro, and put the mask over her face. Then she repeated the process for Brenda.

"Right Brenda, let's get out of here! Thank God!"

Opening the door boldly, and with trepidation, Moira deliberately took a deep breath in to get it over and done with. She and Brenda stepped out, looking ahead, as if going to the scaffold, heads held high. She was feeling shaky, but courageously took Brenda's arm and led her towards the white people carrier. Her skin crawled. She could feel the radiation tickling her skin, and she had to convince herself that the Babygro was as protective as the nice man had said.

They passed Moira's car, which was covered with a fine layer of what looked like sand. Moira didn't like the look of it. She remembered what they had said on the telly.

The dogs immediately ambushed them. They didn't look too good, in all honesty, sort of tired and floppy, particularly Mutt. Moira yanked Brenda back from touching them.

"Can we take the dogs wi' us somehow?"

"Sorry, love. That just isn't possible. Now, I must go and find this other chap, Dave, you said his name was? Where would we find him?" Moira waved an arm towards the dairy. The path was well worn and obvious. The two apparitions vanished into the distance.

Moira opened the car door and helped Brenda into her seat, and was surprised to find another ghost already on residence.

"It's me. It's me, Heather," the ghost squeaked. "Thank God you're okay. Dave told me that you were hiding in the farmhouse. But Dave... dear God, what has he done to himself? Have you seen him? He wouldn't stay indoors, however much I pleaded. He told me I was overreacting but, oh dear God, have you seen him?"

Moira wasn't sure how to reply, so concentrated on getting Brenda comfortable. The dogs were still pushing at her with their noses, demanding attention. With a sigh, she decided that the best thing to do was to go back to the house, get out their food and at least leave them great bowls full.

Surely they could be rescued in a few days?

At this point, the white suited men reappeared with Dave between them. He was staggering rather than walking. He looked dreadful, he had a nose bleed, and his usually thick hair was all patchy. It looked bizarrely as if the men in their white suits had beaten him up, but why on earth would they have done that? Brenda started fretting and tried to get out of the van. Moira wrestled her back. It was quite a fight and it was difficult to be reasonable and soothing when dressed from head to toe like a beekeeper.

The men stripped an indignant Dave, and dressed him into his all-in-one white suit, before persuading him into the van, where he took a seat next to his wife, collapsing like a sack of tatties. As he clambered in, Moira flinched. She couldn't help it. Would he expose her and Brenda to more radiation? Dave slumped back in his seat, clearly unwell and exhausted by his exertions. He wouldn't even look at Moira or Brenda, and ignored his wife.

She could hear him breathing heavily. He wasn't saying much but she could feel his tainted presence behind her. It made her flesh crawl and she scrunched up her body as small as possible to protect herself.

Dave started moaning, "The cows, the cows…"

"What about the cows?" Moira asked Dave to stop him moaning.

Hesitantly, he intoned, still not meeting her eye, "I've let them all out. They're fine. They've got self-filling troughs for water and plenty of grass. There will just be all hell to pay when it's milking time. They will bawl the place down." He appeared to lose interest and, still not admitting to the danger they were in, he whined plaintively, "Can we get out of here now?"

One man slammed the doors shut and jumped into the passenger seat, the other bounced round to the driver's seat, leapt in with great energy, switched on the engine and they were off. It was surreal. Moira didn't like to look out of the window; she could see the chickens sat lethargically on the grass and the dogs swarming after the unknown vehicle.

"What about us?" they seemed to be asking. She had to close her eyes.

The van set off and they careered down the lanes, obviously not expecting to meet any other traffic coming in the other direction, onto deserted main roads and headed for Guildford. Moira had never seen the roads completely empty before. They trundled on along empty lanes, out onto the empty main road, with not another soul in sight.

The sunlight flashed off silver machines that had sprouted along the edges of the roads. "Geiger counters," the driver said.

He threw back the odd comment on where they were going and what was going to happen, but his passengers weren't being very attentive. Moira was too worried about Dave behind her, imagining him dissipating his evil smog around the inside of the car. She daren't open a window in case that let in even more from outside.

Dave kept fretting, saying he felt sick. He had better not be sick on her that was for sure! Heather was murmuring to him and patting him on his hefty thigh. Brenda seemed oblivious to everything, as far as Moira could see through her veiling, and sat upright and calm, her hands folded ladylike in her lap.

After miles of emptiness, Moira was surprised to see an ant's nest of activity ahead, except that the ants were all white, behind red and white barriers, armed men with machine guns. *A Checkpoint Charlie?* They zoomed up to it and stopped with a jerk, which had them all flopping backwards and forwards like crash dummies. It turned out to be a sort of border crossing, which was odd in the middle of the Surrey countryside.

Jets of water were fired at their car. The sudden, loud volley was quite terrifying, as the water hit the car's bodywork. Moira, her nerves already jangling, ducked, covered her head with her hands and gasped out loud. The driver laughed and said, "Sorry about that. I forgot to warn you. It's just to decontaminate the van before we return to civilisation. It's a good thing because it means that we are out of the woods, in a safe area, and nearly at your destination!"

All of a sudden, there were other vehicles on the roads: family cars, lorries and people wandering about. It was quite extraordinary. As they got to the outskirts of Surrey, everything just seemed to be carrying on as normal, busy with cars, busy with people. Moira wondered whether they had been on another planet.

Was it all some nasty joke?

The van slowed on its way towards Guildford, skirting around the A3, which seemed to have as much traffic as ever, driven by more real people, masses of them, still alive, to the Royal Surrey County Hospital. They passed Guildford station, which was besieged by cars, and along Madrid Road, where people popped in and out of the Co-op. She even saw a woman in ordinary clothes, out in the open air, dragging along a small dog on a lead. That gave her heart a lurch.

Barney, Rags, Mutt. I must stop thinking about them.

As they came up to the roundabout at Egerton Road, they had to queue to get on. Amazing. So many cars. So many people, all alive and going about their normal activities.

They swooped through a back entrance into the Royal Surrey Hospital, the sudden turn throwing Moira into Brenda, who seemed to stand as solid as a rock. After they whipped round the corner and parked next to an entrance, yet more white-suited people greeted them. Moira couldn't help but wonder where they had found so many white suits from at such short notice.

A miniature, white-suited person opened the door and said cheerfully in a little girl's voice, "Out you come, you are all safe now. You can relax. Just follow me, let's get you showered and comfortable and then I will take you to be examined by the doctor."

Moira complied obediently, feeling like a prisoner being delivered to a court hearing. She helped Brenda alight, and dashed in through the open door to get out of the exposed open air as soon as she could. More white suits herded them towards a door on the left, marked Female Shower Rooms in a laminated notice, which had slipped jauntily to one side.

Moira shuffled in, feeling a bit nervous in this unknown place, and was met by another white suit with an older woman's voice. "Now, dears, just strip off those suits, step into the showers, they are nice and warm. We need to give you a good scrub down. Now, I know this is not very nice, but we do need to make sure that you are clean and decontaminated. You can pretend you are in a fancy spa and being exfoliated, it might make it easier for you."

It felt like arriving at Auschwitz, stripped of their identity, stripped of their dignity. Moira was nervous – she most certainly had never been exfoliated in a shower by a stranger before. She remembered that Julia Roberts film again.

What was its name?

"It won't take long and then we can give you a nice, fluffy bathrobe and a cup of tea."

After the absolute indignity of being washed like a small child, Moira couldn't look anyone in the face. If that was a spa treatment, she wanted none of it. The robe was nice though. They had obviously got them from a hotel. Hers had GF embroidered on it, and it was soft and fluffy and cosy and soothing. The slippers were similarly adorned in blue thread, but a bit insubstantial. She was looking forward to the cup of tea.

The cup of tea proved to be a bit of a let-down after the luxurious robe. It came in a polystyrene cup, looked rather orange, and didn't taste very nice.

Och, at least it is wet and warm, as Mother always used to say.

It was better than nothing, she thought, as she sat with Brenda and filled out their respective forms. They needed to know her full name, date of birth, brief medical history, any allergies, what she wanted to be called by the hospital staff – "Mrs Hillier of course," declared Brenda pompously. "What on earth else would they want to call me?" – address, date of birth, next of kin, where she lived.

A nice, pert, little nurse wearing real clothes – not actually clothes but blue pyjama things, but at least they weren't white – took a good syringe full of Moira's blood, "just a small scratch" but it never was, took her blood pressure, using a cuff on her wrist; a new-fangled machine, the nurse explained, which measured central aortic systolic pressure, much more accurate apparently, and finally, measured her temperature through her ear. Moira liked it when nurses talked to her like an equal.

The next step was meeting a doctor, one by one. Moira shuffled into his room in her fancy white slippers. He was meant to be a doctor but he looked suspiciously young, little baby cheeks under a thatch of gingery hair, and he also looked very tired, with great bags under his eyes. He was a nice enough lad, also in blue pyjamas, and politely asked her loads of questions from a long list, in a soft and strong northern accent.

The first thing apparently was to establish their exposure to radiation. The doctor had a map on his computer, coloured with the ubiquitous glowing yellow streak, from which he pinpointed the expected level of radiation at their exact location. He asked Moira to be as precise as she could be on the time that she had gone into the farmhouse and the exact time that they had left.

He questioned Moira very carefully about what they had done when, how many times Moira had been outside, what they had eaten, what they had drunk.

The doctor then gave a whole list of terrifying-sounding things – nausea, vomiting, nose bleeds, diarrhoea – Moira was relieved to be able to say "no" to most of them, except a bit of nausea, headaches, some diarrhoea, and possibly some blood in her stools, but then though, that could have been the beetroot.

She then had to rate how nauseous she had felt on a scale of one to ten, and the frequency of it, then the strength of her headaches on a scale of one to ten, as well as their frequency and duration. That was difficult.

How did you decide the right number?

Moira wondered how the doctor would cope with Brenda: no weakness, no fatigue, other than that expected under such the circumstances, no hair loss, no bloody stools, no bloody vomit, we've already established that, young man, no sores. The list was gruesome.

The unnamed doctor did a quick calculation on the computer and came up with a meaningless figure of 950 mSV, whatever that meant, which he wrote down openly and clearly on their notes.

Was it good? Was it terrible?

The doctor was giving nothing away, not even much in the way of empathy. She felt like one of Henry's cows, going through a TB test.

She wondered if she should be there when they asked Brenda the same questions. She was always disorientated, but that wouldn't be down to the radiation exposure. She hadn't seen her since they completed the forms together; she hoped that she was coping okay. Mind you, she seemed to have been coping better than anyone else through this whole malarkey.

The adolescent doctor then explained the medication that he was able to provide "to reduce the risks associated with the level of exposure" that they'd received, and recommended "Granulocyte Colony Stimulating Factor: a protein that promotes the growth of white blood cells, Prussian blue and DTPA –diethylenetriaminepentaacetic acid."

Apparently, the men in white suits should have already given them today's dose of Potassium Iodide, but they hadn't. Depending on their blood test results, they may be offered a transfusion. He shook out the tablets from the collection in front of him into a cup, handed them over with a plastic cup of water, and Moira obediently drank them down.

The youthful doctor then asked if she'd any further questions. Moira had loads but couldn't quite rally them into any semblance of sense or order. It was all happening too fast and the doctor seemed exhausted by it all, and she didn't like to trouble him anymore.

Poor, wee lad.

She did remember about Brenda's medication, and lack of it. Moira recited the list of medication and doses that Brenda took – she knew them off by heart, she had been dealing with them long enough – and persuaded the doctor to write them down carefully. He didn't seem to understand just how demented Brenda was. They would be retrieved from the pharmacy after being checked with Mrs Hillier – *I just told you she wouldnae remember* – and independently reviewed, whatever that meant.

The doctor finally handed over a brightly-coloured pamphlet, more of that yellow, headlined *You and Exposure to Radiation*, and recommended that she read it carefully. Moira hoped that this would tell her what she needed to know.

Apparently, that was the final part of the process. She was dismissed, as the doctor got his head down and scribbled more on his printed piece of paper. Wandering out, she bumped into the girl in blue pyjamas, who asked her where she was going.

"I have no idea," seemed the only possible response.

She was escorted to a ward with four beds in it, where she was to receive medication and "stay in for observation". Brenda was being helped into one bed and Heather was sitting up in the third. She had tears streaming down her face.

"It's not good with Dave, it's not good at all," she sobbed noisily.

Moira didn't know quite what to do, there was very little she could say. She looked around for some tissues, and remembered that she had nothing in the world except the robe and slippers that she stood in, and could only find some blue paper towelling.

Tearing off a fistful, she padded over to the distraught Heather, handed her the paper and gingerly patted her on the shoulder, on a bit of towelling bathrobe. "There, there," she murmured.

Moira hoped that they had decontaminated Heather properly; she felt uncomfortable about touching her. As soon as she could, Moira went and washed her hands, thoroughly.

Chapter 59

Leah was determined to go to the next NADFAS meeting.

After just two weeks since London's greatest disaster ever, everyone in the country, according to the media, was determined to "keep calm and carry on", and show a "stiff upper lip", whatever that meant in reality. Such ridiculous, old-fashioned pseudo-British pronouncements.

What did they think this was? The Second World War?

It also seemed rather ironic that a similar-sized "dirty" bomb, in fact two, concluded the Second World War itself. The Americans, presumably the majority Christians, because they were always going about their God and country, were the first and only people to have used a nuclear bomb in war. It wasn't whole religions that were the problem, just the overwhelming evilness of men.

"Everything should continue as before, we must not give in to the terrorists." Leah couldn't help but think that despite this rhetoric, nothing could ever be quite the same again, ever. It was too monumental.

Leah knew that she needed to show her face at the scheduled meeting and demonstrate that she wasn't reacting to all the whispers and murmured words behind their hands, the hysterical, anti-Muslim rubbish that was being written about in the papers. Leah was the formally-appointed membership secretary of NADFAS. She would rise above any silly nonsense, ignore it, keep her legendary smile plastered on her face like a shield.

Taking a deep breath, she pushed open the door to the Charlton Village Hall, a serene look in place on her face.

She looked around and tried to catch people's eyes. It was uncomfortable when people's gazes slithered away.

She had hoped that Susie might be there; she truly wanted to make her peace with her. Leah missed Susie so much and realised how much she depended on her at occasions such as this. They had always sat together, giggled together, and chatted to the other members as a pair, a united front.

Poor Susie. She must be hurting so much at the loss of her beloved Pete, terrified about the consequences for her mother, and she would be missing Jessica too, just as much as me. Could she still be so very angry with me? Is our friendship irretrievably lost? Why can't we share our grief, like we have shared everything else before?

The meeting didn't start very well. Leah took her usual seat in the second row. It was idiosyncratic how people always tended to sit in the same places at every single meeting. Woe betide anyone who sat in the wrong place. No one sat beside her in the seat that had been occupied by Susie for the last five years. Leah felt a bit foolish, sitting all on her own, and exposed.

The scheduled topic on the published programme was: "The development and spread of Islam led to the adoption of one particular building type for all Muslims, the mosque. The lecture begins with the astonishing spread of Islam after his death. The early Islamic monuments of Jerusalem and Damascus will be examined, as well as the spread to North Africa, from where the religion spread to Spain, and the building of the great mosque at Cordoba."

A bristling and indignant branch chairwoman stood up to announce that this topic had been replaced, in sensitivity to the recent atrocities. She was quite sure that they would "all understand why". Leah flushed in discomfiture, vexed by the bigoted implications, and aware that all eyes were being turned on her, as quite clearly the only Muslim in the room.

"Instead," the chairwoman announced, "we will have a lecture on 'Bestriding the World like a Colossus': The Life and Works of Sir Joseph Paxton (1803-1865), the ultimate Victorian example of rags to riches: the child of a Bedfordshire farm labourer, who became MP for Coventry." The chairwoman looked around the room, as if expecting dissent, but everyone looked up and muttered and nodded at each other in acquiescence.

The chairwoman didn't look at Leah, who looked firmly ahead and tried very hard to look interested in this new topic.

Chapter 60

Henry and Susie went to collect Moira and Brenda from the hospital.

The poor things had been there for five days, monitored, processed, and given handfuls of drugs before being declared able to leave. Susie had insisted on coming along. It clashed with some meeting of one of her society things that she dabbled in, but she asserted that this was far more important.

Henry had visited Dave first on his own, as he felt it would get too complicated otherwise – it always did once Mum was involved. In any case, he didn't think it wise for either Moira or Mum, or Susie, for that matter, to see the state of Dave.

He had been in to see Dave on his last few visits and had been horrified to see how quickly he was deteriorating. Dave's appearance was quite revolting. His thick head of hair was all patchy. He had weird sores, and seemed to have blood oozing from his gums and his nose, and he coughed and coughed until he retched pitifully, leaving slimy, bloody trails across his straggly beard.

Really and honestly, he had expected Dave to have died by now, but he seemed to be fighting on. Perhaps Dave thought that he might actually recover. It couldn't be long now, surely.

Henry could barely speak. He wondered whether Dave wanted him to keep visiting; he wouldn't want to be seen looking like that himself. He only ever stayed for a moment; it was hard to keep up the charade of being cheerful and optimistic. He carefully made no mention of the farm, but only thanked Dave again and again for what he had done, so courageously and selflessly.

Poor Dave had basically given his life for the sake of Henry's cows. At least Heather seemed okay. Should he now be offering Heather refuge? They could hardly fit anyone else into Susie's once Moira and Mum were there too. He felt worn down by these burdens of guilt.

Leaving Dave, quite probably for the last time, Henry went down the maze of corridors to find Susie, Moira and Mum.

As Henry had walked onto their ward, Mum had instantly turned away from the hovering Susie, been very quiet, very dignified, and enfolded Henry in the warmest, most natural, motherly hug that she'd given him for years. "There, there, Henry, everything is alright, I'm all repaired now and I'm feeling marvellous." She sounded very much like her original "before going bonkers" self, and patted him gently on the shoulder like a baby.

Henry wondered what on earth she'd thought had been going on. He looked enquiringly over her shoulder at Moira, who smiled wanly and shrugged her shoulders, and made one of those "Don't ask me" faces. Susie was just looking at him like a rabbit caught in the headlights. "Now, let's go home now, shall we?" said Mum briskly, taking Henry's arm and heading for the door.

At first sight, they'd looked absolutely normal, apart from a rather eclectic mix of clothes that were nothing like their normal attire, provided from donations apparently.

Henry wondered just how much they had been damaged by the radiation.

Surely they must have been affected in some way?

Fortunately, they looked nothing like Dave, and Moira was clutching an advice sheet and what appeared to be a sack full of drugs. She didn't seem to be too concerned.

Susie was concerned, as she shepherded her mum along the corridor, arms linked and firmly holding her hand. Her mum seemed to be a bit reluctant, and kept straining over her shoulder to seek out Henry.

Henry was determined to get Moira on her own. He hadn't liked to ask but someone had to. "What can we expect, Moira, for you and Mum?"

"It's hard to say. It is entirely dependent on exactly how much we absorbed. The bottom line is that your mother is classified as level six, which is slight danger: moderate nausea, headache, and a very low probability of... och, you ken... death. It's a case of wait and see."

"What about you, Moira?"

"A wee bit higher, at a level seven or eight. I was outside a bit more, exposed at the height of the intensity of the fallout. It is the same danger of nausea, headache etcetera, but a five per cent probability of the other thing."

Henry leant across and clumsily wrapped his arms around Moira.

"Come on, laddie, dinna fash yerself. Just think of Dave, he'll be at least a nine, that's who you should be worrying about."

In the car, Moira quietly, in her soft Scottish burr, explained calmly and sensibly to Brenda what had happened in a simple way that she hoped Brenda would understand. It was clearly not the first time she had tried. She explained that they needed to go to Susie's and would stay there until they could go home.

Brenda took it very calmly, nodded and looked out of the window, not saying or asking anything at all, as if it was all an everyday occurrence. They motored on in silence. Henry hadn't switched on the radio, as he thought it might upset everyone; there were still some really shocking horror stories coming through. They still kept going back to the Charlton Academy outing, which had ended in such tragedy that was far too close to home. Calls for the head to resign, poor Susie vilified, and her friend, Leah, seemed to have become a target for just being a Muslim.

Best not let Susie hear that rubbish.

"So has all the cancer gone?" Brenda suddenly piped up in the silence.

Henry and Susie were bemused. Henry wondered whether she knew what had happened or whether this was just one of her wild guesses. Perhaps she had just remembered being in hospital.

He said, as convincingly as he could, "Yes, Mum. You still have lots of medication to take and you are safe with us now." He hoped that he'd said the right thing. They all shared "don't ask me" looks and lapsed into silence, each with their own thoughts.

Brenda started getting very restless when they came in to Hartley Wintney and she recognised where they were going. It's strange how her decaying brain still had some random spots of connecting memories. "I thought we were going home!" she declared bossily. "Why are we going to Susie and… God's?" She often called Pete that, even in front of Susie, never understanding how it hurt poor Susie.

Moira caught Susie's eye in the mirror, raised her eyes heavenwards and said, "We're going to stay there for a wee while. A bit of a holiday for you, Brenda."

"It's not much of a holiday staying there, can't see any fields, and I suppose God will be there, graciously welcoming us to his humble home?"

Henry cringed.

Ouch. Mum is getting really spiteful these days, and I can't entirely put it down to the dementia.

"And I am not dressed for a visit! What on earth am I wearing? Look at it, dear. I'm sure that I wouldn't have bought such a dreadful skirt, it's hideous." Henry, Susie and Moira exchanged glances. Their attempts, all of them, over and over again, at a simpler explanation, clearly hadn't worked.

"Mum," sighed Henry, trying for the nth time, "there's been an accident. Unfortunately everything at home has been destroyed, rather like a massive fire. We can't go home and the hospital have kindly given you some clothes to wear until we can get you something nicer. We are going to stay with Susie and... and... the children." He didn't want to go into the whole Pete situation, far too complicated to explain. "It's just until we sort things out."

"But I don't want to stay with Susie and that officious husband of hers. Why can't we just go straight home?"

Susie bit her lip, turned to the window in distress.

Henry decided that the only way he was going to get through the rest of the journey was to cheat. "Mum, we are dropping in at Susie's and then we will go home as soon as we can." It wasn't strictly a lie after all. He could see the tears welling in Susie's eyes.

Chapter 61

Mrs Pietruski sat opposite Charlie.

"Please speak to me, Charlie. You have to talk about it. You can't go on like this."

He sat there resolutely silent, his eyes staring past her at the periodic table. He couldn't help it, he was just drawn to element 92, U, Uranium, relative atomic mass 238, melting point 1,132°C. The trouble was, it just triggered the same suffocating vibe. He wanted to stand up, tear the obscenely-colourful thing down, rip it up.

Charlie knew if that she mentioned Alfie or Ellie by name, he could not cope.

Mrs Pietruski tried again. "Charlie, please just say something, anything. I know you won't meet the counsellors, but please talk to me. It will help, truly."

Charlie took his eyes off the chart and looked Mrs Pietruski in the eye, and projected all his despair, anger, hurt, horror, guilt at her in one look. Mrs Pietruski flinched; it would have been impossible for her not to.

She gathered herself. "Charlie, I know that this sounds stupid, but at least start working again. You were doing so well and on track for brilliant results. It will provide you with a diversion, a way of carrying on. Your life isn't over; it has only just begun. Everyone is working towards getting this country back to normal, and the universities are defiantly continuing just as they were. That part of your life is still there for the taking. Please take it."

She'd very deftly and deliberately not mentioned Alfie and Ellie. Perversely, he wished she would. His stare went back to the periodic table, element 92, U, Uranium, relative atomic mass 238, melting point 1,132 °C. He decided that this was the last time that he would ever set eyes on the thing. He got up, reached for his rucksack, shrugged on his jacket, stuck his chin in the air and walked out. He couldn't be here ever again.

Fuck the death and destruction. Fuck Mum. Fuck everything. Fuck it all.

Chapter 62

Meredith was living in dread.

Every day, she was on tenterhooks. Every car that passed by, or slowed down, set her nerves racing. If anyone came to the door, or rang, or even just walked by, catching her eye. Every nerve was stretched, as if she was being tortured. It had been weeks of tension.

Meredith sighed from deep, deep down. She did everything as if Gary was going to just casually walk in through the back door as before, cooked enough supper for three of them, laid the table carefully and neatly, put out his serviette in its silver ring. She kept his portion of dinner hot in the warmer drawer, "just in case". She only threw it away, or gave it to Marmite, when she and Philippa eventually went to bed, late, on edge, and unable to settle to sleep.

She'd gone to Gary's restaurant tentatively. She felt a bit stupid asking Chloe, his super-efficient, hoity-toity manager if she knew where her own husband was. Chloe had shown her that his diary had absolutely nothing in it. A blank page. Chloe expected him to return at any moment. "He will turn up. You know Gary and his madcap schemes," she'd said unctuously, with a look on her face that said, "Poor, pathetic Meredith, doesn't even know what her husband does or where he goes." Why did everybody look at her that way?

Chloe informed Meredith that he hadn't been in touch with her. Chloe had free access to his email account, LinkedIn, and any other networking site that he subscribed to. She checked, but there was nothing to indicate where he might be; he could have gone anywhere. There was nothing personal on his work computer, according to Chloe, although she wouldn't let Meredith touch it. Confidential, apparently – *even for his wife?*

Meredith sat at the kitchen table, a cup of tea at hand, as she had for day after day, a very long fortnight, her anxious face working with stress. She was distraught about Eleanor, but most of all, she hated herself for that one single, tiny moment. It would haunt her forever. She just couldn't stop it popping into her head, over and over again, making a hot flush rise to her gaunt face, that moment when instead of being horrified at what had happened, she'd been relieved that her summons by Mr Barker hadn't meant that Eleanor had spilled the beans about the "incident". She hated herself for that and relived it every day, that split second before Armageddon unfolded. She hit her palms against her face in remorse.

Eleanor. Wiped out in just one horrible split second. Such a terrible thing. Gone in a flash.

There was comfort in knowing that she wouldn't have known a thing about it. Even so, she had left Eleanor's room exactly as it was, she couldn't bear to empty it, and still crept in to bury her face in her duvet. Her smell had all but gone now.

Going to all the memorial services without Gary had been difficult, as everyone kept asking where he was. Meredith didn't know what to say. She'd planned to say, "Gary has been missing since that day and we are making enquiries to find him." It got stuck in her throat and didn't want to come out. She found herself staring blankly at them instead. They must think she's nuts.

People kept asking stupid questions in a patronising way, as if she was completely thick.

Of course I've tried to phone him. Of course I've asked Chloe at the restaurant what she thought. Of course I've told the police. Of course I can't think of a reason that he wouldn't come back. What sort of an idiot do you think I am?

Meredith started doodling with a biro on the *Financial Times*, which still arrived like clockwork every morning, despite everything; some things had just gone on and on as normal. Bizarre. She'd picked it up from the mat, carefully folded it and put it at Gary's place every morning, just the way he liked it.

She'd eventually got up the courage to go through his desk in the study. She was carefully to replace everything in exactly the same place that she'd found it, just in case, out of habit. She found nothing of any interest. A pension. No will. No life insurance. All the records for the BMW and the Smart car.

Every bill was in Gary's name; all the utilities, the car, insurances, everything. Gary Webber, Mr Gary Webber, just Mr Gary Webber. No Mrs Webber anywhere. She was a nobody; in the eyes of the world, she simply didn't exist as a person in her own right. She hadn't been able to find even one thing in his desk that included her name. She'd replaced it all meticulously.

She wondered whether she ought to try and track down his parents, although he hadn't been in touch with them for years. They had "done something unpardonable" years ago. She'd never found out what exactly, and certainly had never been introduced to them.

Anyway, where did you start when you had no idea about their first names, where they might be, no past addresses, not even which part of the country?

He had no siblings that he owned up to. "That is all in the past, Meredith. I have moved on," he would say mysteriously and inconclusively. She'd idly googled Gary's name for the want of anything else to do; perhaps she might find other family members or connections. Nothing, just a whole lot of other Gary Webbers, rather a surprising number. She clicked through the links and found one that, for no good reason, had a picture of Superman as his profile picture – most odd.

Susie and Kate had helped report him missing. They had had to find out how to do it for Thomas and Caroline HC, who had both perished in 25/5. She felt a bit tentative asking them how to go about it. Although she'd been to Susie's socially, she didn't feel that she knew her at all well, and there was enormous awkwardness about the whole Jessica Hughes thing.

In any case, Meredith wasn't sure that she would be able to cope with the whole pity about Eleanor thing, particularly after Susie and Jack's fortuitous escape. Susie was inclined to gush and overdo the sympathy, and went on rather. She'd felt very uncomfortable when Susie had pounced on her, enfolding her in her ample bosom. She knew that she'd stiffened and Susie felt it. Just so embarrassing. Susie was a bit overpowering, to be honest.

Kate was easier, more practical, and obviously in a different position than Susie and Meredith. Kate was a survivor's parent too, but she hadn't lost anyone at all, she hadn't lost her man. It sounded careless to have "lost your man".

Meredith had, after a few days of heart searching, reported his absence to the helpline. Over and over again, she gave the same answers to the same string of questions, repeating his full name, date of birth, last known address, what he was wearing, like a well-trained parrot. They were a bit vague and, although very business-like, not empathetic. "I am sure he will turn up. Lots of people have been turning up."

After a few days, the police had come round and asked her questions, aggressively, she thought. Who had picked him up that morning? At what time? Who else saw him leave? What car did he leave in? Which direction did they go? Why had she decided he might have been in London rather than anywhere else that day? Did he have any life insurance? It made her increasingly anxious. Her head reeled. She repeated the same things over and over again, word for word, every time. They noted it all down.

They made house-to-house enquiries about the mysterious car that had picked him up. No one had seen it. People never looked anyway, each in their own little bubble.

Of course they interviewed Chloe too. Nothing came of that either.

They interviewed a terrified Philippa, who was so horrified by the whole thing that she had barely been able to speak through the tears. Meredith held her breath and was relieved that Philippa didn't reveal anything at all that was untoward, nothing about "the incident". Philippa could not add anything useful or shed any light on the matter.

They couldn't interview Eleanor.

Meredith heard one of the policemen mutter, "If everyone whose husband had disappeared…" The implication that he thought that Gary had done a runner was crystal clear.

Meredith clutched the pen and her strokes became harder and bigger and bolder as her doodle grew.

Meredith had been in touch with the bank, who were less than helpful. "Data Protection, Customer Confidentiality," they spouted at her in capital letters. They would only respond to queries on bank account usage from the police. The police were less than helpful. "We are extremely busy, Mrs Webber, there have been no cash withdrawals, no transactions other than regular direct debits from your husband's accounts, and you are not a signatory on any of them."

They didn't seem to realise that she had no way of getting at any money at all, not even cash. She'd had the meagre remains of the last week's housekeeping in the tin in the kitchen and that was it. She felt foolish.

With enormous embarrassment, she'd got up the courage to tell Chloe. If it hadn't been for Chloe giving her some money from the business, she, Philippa and Marmite would have starved. Chloe was a co-signatory on the restaurant accounts, so could happily access them. Chloe wasn't even his wife and she was allowed that privilege. It didn't seem quite right.

The biro dug into the newspaper and she raked at it vigorously, back and forth, round and round.

Abruptly, her head fell into the spoiled remains of the paper; she banged it harder than she was anticipating and howled with grief, not for Gary, but for her lovely Eleanor. She wanted Eleanor back.

Eleanor.

She missed Eleanor so much that it felt like an angry bruise that flared with pain every time you touched it, but she couldn't stop poking it.

Chapter 63

Pips was finding it ever so hard to carry on living like a normal person without Ellie.

Pips ached for Ellie; she carried it round like an overfilled school bag every day, way too heavy to manage, but she still had to drag it about. She'd no idea how you could miss someone so badly.

Somehow, doing your mourning with a whole bunch of other people at school had made it easier than at home. Everyone understood how you felt and were eager to share comforting hugs. She'd never been hugged by so many people in all her life. You were allowed to talk whenever you wanted and share stories: "Do you remember when…?" No one was embarrassed or changed the subject.

She didn't want to talk about Dad, but she liked to talk about Ellie.

The horror still hung around like an all-pervasive bad smell. However hard you tried, you couldn't get away from it.

How the fuck were we meant to get up, go to school, learn anything, hang out and muck about with that evil stink hanging over us. If I smile I feel bad, if I laugh, I feel worse. If I chat about something that doesn't reference that day, it feels like treachery.

Just seeing those four kids every day was like it was happening all over again. You couldn't look at Aisha Ahmed, Charlie Powell, Lily Symington and Jack Cole without thinking about it.

Poor sods, I wouldn't like to be in their shoes. They were wandering around like zombies; they were avoided like zombies too, which was a bit weird.

The competition element had died down now. That had been dead odd. *Who can miss their loved ones most! What was that all about?* She didn't really like it.

Obviously, Hannah Hughes was right there at the top of the list. She seemed to have won the competition outright by losing everyone in her family. She'd attracted a cult following in a really bizarre way, the Hannah worshippers who turned and glared at Amelia Cole, as if she was the evil perpetrator; Amelia the responsible criminal, sent to Coventry.

Poor Mrs Cole too. She just walked round on the edge of everyone else, tears in her eyes, but no one really wanted to know about her.

She'd lost Mr Cole, but she'd escaped herself because of her ankle (if that was true); Jack had escaped 'cause of the no permission slip (had that been deliberate?). It must be really strange for her, but had she known something? Some sort of premonition or something?

The rumour was that Mrs Ahmed had known too, as they were thick as thieves. Being a Muslim, perhaps she'd been given advanced warning. Was it a coincidence that their children had not gone?

In her heart, she knew that that the whole conspiracy theory was rubbish, but the whispering hadn't stopped.

The stories were tailing off; there had been enough of them on telly, in fact, endless bloody stories, endless misery, endless people damaged horribly. She was actually sick of it by now.

Why couldn't everyone just shut up about it now and get on with living?

She would never, never stop missing Ellie every day of the rest of her life, but that was her business and she presumed the personal business of every other one of the hundreds and thousands of people in the same boat who had lost loved ones.

Pips knew that it was fantasy, but sometimes, she couldn't help hoping that maybe Ellie had survived. Mum had said something about Ellie not meeting up with Mrs Hughes on "that day", and she fantasised to herself about Ellie getting away from the maelstrom. She'd tried testing out her theory on Charlie, but he had just looked at her as if she were insane. But after all, the newspapers were reporting that some people had reappeared out of the blue, perhaps others would too.

Just hope Dad doesn't. Ouch, that's so out of order, I shouldn't be thinking that.

Sometimes, she thought about Dad. She remembered his handsome features – he was good looking, if nothing else, and he had a nice laugh.

He was nice to the dog. He was usually nice to me. It was just Ellie and Mum that caught the brunt of it.

She thought it best to try and remember the nice bits.

On the other hand, he was a fucking bastard. She daren't say it out loud, what would her mum's reaction would be, and she wouldn't dare use the f-word out loud anyway.

Was he actually and totally dead?

A little shiver ran through her. She hoped it was not a premonition.

Chapter 64

Charlie trudged in through the back door.

His clothes, soaked by the rain, smelled so bad that it made him gag. He was trying to keep his stuff clean but it was hard. He flopped into a chair at the kitchen table and wondered just how long he could go on like this. The cash his mum had left was long gone. They had stopped his debit card. He had told so many lies that it was hard to remember what the truth was.

What was the fucking point? It had been fucking weeks, almost seven.

His mum had never gone for this long before. She'd never bothered to keep in touch before when she went off on her own, and had just turned up again out of the blue, as if she'd just been out to the shops. But he had to accept that this time, she wasn't coming back.

Was she dead? Did she die in "it", alongside Alfie and Ellie and all the rest of Year 12? Fuck knows.

He wasn't sure whether that would make a difference anyway. He sighed loudly, making himself jump in the silence.

He didn't turn on any lights to bring any sympathetic gleam into the house; he didn't want to waste his meagre earnings on cash for the electric card. At least he had enough to eat. The pub seemed to sense that things weren't right. They had given him more meals than they did before, and more shifts. Mind you, this change of heart wasn't surprising, given that fucking Gary had gone, the mean bastard, and there were "vacancies" to fill, missing souls, burnt to a frazzle. It all helped him, but it made it feel worse – dead men's shoes.

Gary's non-reappearance was a mystery too. If Ellie were still here, Charlie would have texted her, shared how he was feeling about it, let it all come out and let the heat of it escape. Charlie couldn't text Pips about it as she was a baby. When he was at school, she'd even asked him if he'd heard from Ellie.

For fuck's sake, what was she on? Ellie was fucking dust, and it made him mad when she was wittering on about it. A total fucking fantasy.

The water was still running, but it was cold. It cost a fortune to heat it up; he could see the meter figures flying round. He wondered how long the water would last though; the pile of demanding-looking mail was building up – there was one from Thames Water. His phone contract had expired and it cost too much to keep it going.

What the fuck was the point? Who was there left to text him anyway? There was no banter pinging in from Alfie and Ellie.

He longed for Alfie and Ellie, wanted to say stuff to them about it all, wanted to talk through the options, what he should do about his mum's disappearance.

They always knew what to do but they were both fucking ash. And Alfie's mum. Perhaps Mum? Perhaps Ellie's dad? They were all just fucking dirt.

Fucking element 92, U, Uranium, relative atomic mass 238, melting point 1,132 °C. Don't go there. Don't go there. Don't go there. Stop. Stop.

He couldn't stop, and he keened and howled and sobbed his heart into his mouth until he was spent, empty. He slumped forward onto the table and, starved of every last thing that mattered to any boy, cold and exhausted, he slept, wrapped in his own arms.

Chapter 65

Bernie was obsessively scanning the long, drawn-out list of names of the dead in the newspaper, each with their town of residence next to it.

They published all the latest ones once a week. They gradually seemed to be getting fewer. He didn't actually seem to spot any that he knew, but he would see familiar surnames and nearby towns, giving him a jolt. Each line was a real person, with a life, perhaps a family, a whole story to tell. *Just so many names.*

The doorbell rang again. Not just once, but twice. It was particularly inappropriate, as it chimed like the lost Big Ben, and it brought to mind the destruction and loss of life as we had known it. He really ought to get a new one. He knew who it would be.

This love-sick boy kept turning up on the doorstep and just wouldn't go away. Jack Cole, apparently. He came along, rang on the doorbell and pleaded to see Emily, but Emily wasn't having any of it. It was very complicated, but was something to do with Emily's new best friend, Hannah, who seemed to have moved in, to all intents and purposes, and Hannah's mother.

Hannah came home with Emily on the bus after school more days than not. Emily let herself in with her key, shouted, "I'm home", scurried into the house, followed by Hannah, and they would dart up the stairs, into Emily's bedroom, and slam the door noisily.

Jack's mother had somehow been instrumental in Hannah's whole family being killed in 25/5, but he couldn't see how. In Bernie's humble view of life, it was simply the terrorists to blame.

It had got a bit out of hand with Emily, shrieking in a very unladylike fashion out of her bedroom window at this boy, Jack, below, Hannah presumably hiding behind her, telling him to eff off. He couldn't bring himself to even think the complete expression. He didn't like confrontation, because it reminded him of the situation at the wake, which made him feel prickly and uncomfortable.

At least Mini was in more often now, so she could usually handle the boy. Ever since 25/5, she'd been overly attentive in all ways, not going out as often, and snuggling up to him at every opportunity, soothing him, stroking him like an anxious dog. She said that other people such as Hannah losing their loved ones had made her realise how lucky she was to have him, and Emily, and that she was so sorry to have betrayed him. He remained suspicious of her motives.

He genuinely hoped that it was Daisy-May, a quite ridiculous name for such a vile woman, that she'd been with. *But that distinct smell?* The doubt remained and niggled. It gnawed at him all the time. When he was sitting there comfortably in his armchair, with a cup of tea, watching something good on television, it would nip him and he would jolt with anxiety and find himself staring at Mini to try and see inside her head. He wasn't sure that life would ever be quite the same. Trust was a fragile and delicate thing.

Should I answer the door or just leave it?

He lumbered to his feet, shambled towards the door in his battered, old slippers, peered through the spy hole, a legacy of an anxious Helen, who had been through a stage of being terrified by news reports on vulnerable, old people, and done up the place like Fort Knox.

Yes, it was him.

CHAPTER 65

Bernie sighed. *Was there any point in speaking to him?* Shaking his head, he shuffled back to his armchair and settled back down, his finger running down the roll call of the departed.

Chapter 66

Susie was sitting on the side of the bed in the spare room.
Mum was downstairs with Moira, arranging some flowers or some such other pastime that Moira used to keep Mum amused. Susie had noticed that Moira was wearing Marigolds – she seemed to for everything these days. Moira also kept washing and washing her hands at every opportunity, had showers in the morning and every evening, flinched when anyone touched her, as if in terror of being contaminated. Moira spent hours at the sink, scrubbing vegetables, and was paranoid about where any food had come from.

Susie hadn't said anything to her about it directly because she thought it might be a bit insensitive; she seemed to be treading on egg shells with everybody.

Susie had realised very, very quickly that Amelia would do anything to stop anyone, people at school especially, actually seeing her with her mother. Really, it was a relief not to have to go into school herself; she couldn't take the looks that ranged from pitying to murderous from pupils, staff and other parents. It was far, far worse there than anywhere else. Perhaps it would die down by the time the new term started in September after a long break; she hoped so, at least.

She never, never wanted to be a celebrity. The attention was terrifying and she couldn't go anywhere at all without being stared at, people turning to each other and saying in stage whispers, "It's her, isn't it?"

How did our story become so public? It was everywhere!

There seemed to be no sympathy, no understanding that she'd lost her beloved Pete, that she missed him with every fibre of her soul, that every night, she silently cried herself to sleep, clutching their wedding photo, that every morning, she woke up and remembered it all over again and could barely get out of bed, except of course, that she desperately needed to pee.

She wanted to scream "It was an accident!" but no one ever gave her the chance to say anything. They just looked, judged and sentenced her, without the right to explain.

According to Jon Barker, Jack was coping extremely well. He seemed to be positive and strong, supportive of Lily and Aisha, and was holding his head high. Susie agreed that whenever there was anyone else around, he certainly appeared to be just that. It was at home, on his own with Susie, that he was so difficult. The word obnoxious jumped into her head and she guiltily swept it away.

Susie had tried to get him on his own when Henry and Fenella were out, asking Amelia to go and do some prep, talk to him calmly about it, get him to tell her what he was feeling and thinking to see if she could help.

"What the fuck would you know about it, Mum?"

Susie had winced. She eventually found out, but only from Amelia, what the main problem was. He had indeed been "seeing someone". Apparently, they were officially "in a relationship", according to Facebook. It wasn't anyone she knew; she wouldn't even have recognised her if she'd bumped into her on the street: Emily Chittenden.

Emily Chittenden, the name rang a bell.

Susie had an inkling that she could be the Emily who had come to Jack's birthday supper. The one he was snogging the face off. The bold, little miss, wearing too much make-up – the skinny girl with her hair pulled back tight?

There were no pictures of her anywhere in Jack's room, of course, she'd checked, and she assumed that it was all hidden away on good, old, inaccessible Facebook, the bane of every mother's life. She'd apparently dropped him like a hotcake after she, Jack's evil mother, had "sent Mrs Hughes to her death, leaving poor, innocent Hannah an orphan".

He was enraged when Susie had confessed that she now knew about Emily.

"Fuck off out of it, Mum. You just don't know anything." Well, she did actually. Had he forgotten that she'd lost her beloved Pete? It seemed that she was losing her beloved son too, after all.

When Susie had once again suggested that he was obviously finding it hard to talk to her about it, that perhaps some counselling was a jolly good idea, he had been equally rude and dismissive. "I don't think that I am the one who needs to go to confession and receive absolution, do you?"

Jack persisted in his belief that somehow, it was all Susie's fault. She couldn't understand how he could think that. She was so dreadfully tired. She was so terribly lonely. She missed her darling Pete. She hadn't dare tell other people about Jack and his mean gibes; that would be so, so unbearable. Henners and Fen had enough on their plates with the wholesale loss of the farm. And her friends? Jessica was gone. Leah was absent.

Susie had come upstairs for something, she couldn't remember what, once she'd got her room, but she was feeling sick again. She picked up their wedding photo – she had kept it beside her bed ever since May 25th – lay down on the bed to let the queasiness pass and idly traced a finger over Pete's handsome features.

Susie wondered whether you get catch radiation from other people. She knew that she didn't have any of the other signs of radiation sickness, but she couldn't stop vomiting. She'd felt much sicker since Mum and Moira came home, so perhaps sharing with Mum and Moira meant that she'd somehow caught some of it off them.

The papers were full of advice, full of symptom checkers, full of sad, sad stories of people becoming ill and dying. They had stated categorically that it wasn't transmissible, so she must be being paranoid. Did she dare try and make an appointment with her GP? He would probably laugh in her face at being so silly, and tell her off for having been so selfish and making a fuss when she'd survived. And Jessica hadn't. And Pete hadn't. And all those other completely innocent people...

Don't go there, Susie, you know you only upset yourself.

She was dreadfully, dreadfully concerned about her mum. It was difficult to gauge how much exposure she might have had to the radiation, and Moira, of course. Everyone had questioned Mum about it endlessly, and kept asking her how she felt, but of course, by the time they had got round to asking her, she had already completely forgotten about what had been happening that day.

Mum seemed to have recovered completely, no longer complaining of nausea or headaches, which was a great relief, but they said that she could still show signs, months or even years later.

Poor, poor Mum. What had Henners been thinking?

Susie could not believe what she must have been through, stuck in that absolutely terrifyingly-scary radiation zone for days on end. Mind you, she didn't actually seem to remember it at all.

Her mum hadn't cottoned on to the idea that Pete had gone either, or simply forgot. That really hurt, deeply, and made her want to cry every time she made one of her horrible, horrible remarks about "God". She did love her mother, but sometimes, she didn't actually like her very much these days.

Poor, poor Henners and Fen.

She only now realised what he had been putting up with for the last few years.

Susie decided to try sitting up again to see how she felt. A bit better. She could go downstairs, but actually it was really, really nice to catch some time completely on her own. She hadn't had any for ages, since giving up her room. Even when she took to the bath for a bit of peace and quiet, Mum would wander in and use the loo, which she found frankly disgusting.

She just wanted some time to herself, to collect her thoughts, or just indulge in feeling sorry for herself and reminisce about Pete.

Actually, the whole situation was getting on top of Susie. She'd attended all the memorial services and prayer groups, and absolutely everything she could, but it was so, so hard always being looked at, stared at, until she caught someone's eye and they would immediately look away. She wanted to stand up in front of them all and shout, "I didn't do anything. It was not my fault! It was the evil terrorists."

Thank heavens for Kate, who seemed to be her only ally. She seemed to be the only person in the whole wide world that didn't actually blame her for Jessica. Susie just couldn't find the right words to say to support Jack and Amelia when the blame rubbed off on them.

How could everyone be so mean? It was so unfair.

She was just as heartbroken about Jessica and all those poor, innocent children as they were, and if it hadn't been for her ridiculous chaos, both she and Jack would be dead too, and then where would Amelia be? The same place as Hannah, Susie sighed, realising her stupidity.

Poor, poor Hannah.

It was all destroyed, devastated, and they hadn't even been at the centre of it. She tried to stop the tears from tumbling down her cheeks again, and wiped them away angrily at the injustice of it all. She and her children had become exiles for the impertinence of being alive.

She was completely distraught over Pete. She missed Pete so, so much. It was even more painful than childbirth. It happened every morning when she woke up and remembered, when the brutal contractions of grief would cruelly roll right though her again and again. She had to bite the pillow so that she didn't scream out loud and wake Mum and Moira.

She still hadn't made it up with Leah. It didn't sit well – the whole "guilty dead people" thing – including Jessica, but when it came down to it, they were in the same boat as the "guilty alive people".

Why can't we find a sort of truce? Why aren't we allowed our relief at not losing our children without feeling absolutely shame-faced?

Susie knew that Leah needed all the support she could get, but she just couldn't face it. People had been absolutely monstrous. Every time the anti-Muslim protests were shown on the telly, Susie cringed. They seemed to have adopted Manchester as their new place of choice for protesting.

What did they want, for God's sake, for all Muslims to be deported?

She may not agree with Leah's interpretation of the Koran, but it wasn't anything to do with her personally. At least if she and the children moved somewhere else, anywhere else, they would be absolved, whereas Leah and

Farrukh would carry it with them for the rest of their lives, wherever they went in the world.

At least her ankle was better; the swelling had gone completely and she could keep her weight on it quite happily. Perhaps it was the stress of it all, but as well as feeling queasy, her hair had gone all floppy and greasy. Maybe it was having everyone to stay, the rich food that she conjured up to try and cheer everyone up – she knew she'd always been a feeder, but she didn't how else to show them she cared – and the continuous level of strain, but she was totally drained and kept falling asleep on the sofa at the wrong time of the day. Fen looked at her quizzically, almost in disapproval, but she really couldn't help it.

It was very hard sharing a room with Mum and Moira. Mum wandered about at night, which was unnerving and broke her sleep. She tried to put a brave face on it, but to be really and truly honest, it was driving her bonkers, nearly as bonkers as Mum herself. If Mum said, "Are you pregnant?" once more, she would seriously scream the place down. It was beyond a joke.

Her body actually felt odd enough to be pregnant, the clenching feeling in her boobs, a tight feeling in her tummy.

Perhaps my period is due? When was the last one? Seriously, when is my period due?

She thought long and hard. The queasiness, her hair all weird, the tiredness. A creeping realisation dawned on Susie.

Oh my God! Could it be really, really true?

She was working it out carefully, going back over the last seven weeks. The night of Pete's promotion dinner party. Had she used her cap or had she been too pissed? Pete normally left that side of things to her; it had been fine, she'd always been careful. But not that night.

She wondered. She hoped. She placed her hand on her tummy. If it was true, it was a miracle. She was far, far too old for this nonsense and the children would be horrified, but if it was true, it was a marvel.

Please, please let it be true.

Oh Pete, oh Pete, I so, so wish you were here, you would be so, so thrilled.

She could imagine him saying "Oh Susie", in the way he always had when she'd done something daft or clumsy, but secretly being delighted.

She smiled, feeling the joy of the moment. Hugged herself.

A new, little Pete! Wow! I'd better nip into town and buy a test, just in case. I don't want to make an absolute fool of myself, like I always seem to, if I'm wrong.

She keened and started missing Pete all over again, the tears streaming freely down her face, until another wave of nausea came over her and she had to make a dash for the loo.

Chapter 67

Henry was frustrated.

It was nearly two months since it happened and he now felt powerless, helpless, enfeebled, imprisoned, and like hitting his head against a brick wall.

Henry loved Susie, of course he did; she was so hospitable, so eager to please, irritatingly so, if the truth were to tell, feeding them endlessly with over-elaborate meals, anxiously asking them how they were feeling too many times every day, but he was finding himself just so frustrated.

Susie was making them all very welcome but it was a hell of a squash. Four bedrooms had always seemed plenty, but allocating rooms had proved uncomfortable. Susie had immediately given up the master bedroom to Fen and Henry, and insisted on sharing the spare room with Mum and Moira. It was very kind of her, but she always slightly overdid the "I really, really insist", and she then behaved like the brave sacrificial lamb.

She would burst into the bedroom, stop with an aghast look on her face: "Gosh, I keep forgetting! I'm so, so sorry. I really, really must knock." There was nowhere that he and Fen could go where they felt any real privacy.

Susie had insisted that Henry use Pete's clothes, which made him feel very uncomfortable – dead man's shoes – and they didn't smell right, not like his own clothes. It was unnerving, and he had nipped into Reading at the first opportunity with Fen to at least get a basic wardrobe and their preferred brand of washing powder, to make them smell right. Susie's clothes swamped Fen, of course, which made Mum laugh cruelly, far too loudly.

Susie didn't help the situation, always hovering over Mum, asking her how she was feeling, and making sideways glances at Henry, as if somehow, it was his fault, implying without saying so that he had abandoned Mum through choice. This coming from someone who had virtually ignored Mum for the last 10 years while he and Fen had made a home for her, included her in their family, dealt with all her eccentricities and her unkindness, supported her through her descent into lunacy, let alone paid for Moira, was somewhat galling.

He and Fen had tried so hard to be sympathetic about Pete, but Susie had a way of being dismissive about their proffered compassion, dismissing it with a conversation-stopping "I'm fine", and yet seemed to want more than she was receiving. It was confusing. Susie was the same about taking compliments, with great awkwardness, always had been.

At least while Alice and Arthur were back at school, it had helped them all from an accommodation point of view, but the summer hols had started and they were home again. Amelia seemed fine about sharing with Alice, but Jack was not exactly welcoming to poor, little Arthur. It wasn't Arthur's fault.

Henry still felt guilty about Heather Easton. There was no way they could have taken her in, it just wouldn't work, and he didn't want to raise it with Susie, who he knew would still open her arms and gushingly find a way to accommodate her. It was a blessing that Dave had finally died. It was a horrible way to die – slow, painful and ugly – and he wouldn't wish it on anybody. He shuddered at the sheer thousands of people all having to go through it, some often even worse than Dave. The dying could go on for many, many more months. Mum and Moira seemed fine, but they could still take a turn for the worse. It didn't bear thinking about.

Mum was driving them all mad. Every morning, she would greet Henry like a newly-arrived visitor, with great beams of joy on her face. "Henry, darling, I didn't know you were here. How marvellous. Have you come to take me home?" They had all agreed that it was simplest just to say that he had come to collect her but would be staying for a day or so to catch up with Susie.

Susie wasn't used to Mum's foibles – perhaps she hadn't realised just how bad she'd become. Mum was upsetting Susie, Jack and Amelia by making constant references to Pete: "Aren't you going to wait for God before we have supper?" Amelia was getting used to it now, but on the first couple of occasions, had fled from the dining room table in acute distress. Jack just became quieter and quieter. Susie tried very hard to smile, but it was a pale imitation, and again, they had finally agreed on "He's away working at the moment". It made it easier.

Mum made relentless remarks about Susie's weight. If she asked Susie just once more whether she was pregnant or just fat, he thought he might scream, and poor Susie, sharing a bedroom with Mum, was getting it on a very regular basis. Susie seemed to be taking it well and would just smile enigmatically.

The situation regarding the farm was an absolute disaster. Sitting at Pete's desk in Pete's study, he had read the latest statement with increasing horror.

He had read the Defra report three times, hoping that he had misunderstood its judgements. Defra had declared the whole farm to be within the Exclusion Zone. They had recorded "unacceptable" radiation levels. It all seemed such an over the top and nonsensical approach. They seemed to be treating the fallout area exactly the same as the blast zone. *Surely it couldn't be so bad?* The radiation in the fallout from a uranium-enriched bomb was only dangerous for 24 hours – something to do with half-lifes, Henry had read.

This isn't like Chernobyl or Japan, where a very different sort of radiation was released continuously over days and days. This was a one-off 10-kiloton device. Completely different. Devastating and destructive at the time but over and done with after a short time. Surely the amount of radiation that "might have" contaminated the cows through fallout must be negligible and would have been dissipated in a much shorter time, with its short half-life?

The Defra death squad, the ghostly white army, had already moved steadily and stealthily through the affected area, shooting all livestock, all living animals, "just in case". They had discounted the full-scale use of Prussian Blue, or any other treatment, on the grounds that they only had sufficient supplies for humans. They weren't even assessing, recording or reporting back on the status of any living creature that they had summarily killed, whether the animal had shown symptoms of being sick or not. There was "too urgent a need to contain the contamination. It must be completed forthwith".

The wholesale destruction had included everything: his whole herd of precious cows, 300 of them, each and every one nurtured and developed and bred to top quality standard, each with her own unique personality and motherly instincts; the cheeky bull, Roscoe, who had cost a fortune and relished his job; the chickens, each given ridiculous names by the children, like Fluffy, Henny Penny and suchlike; and even the dogs, Rags, Barney and Mutt. That made him desperate.

Why couldn't they have saved the dogs? How am I going to tell the children about the dogs?

Every one of his animals despatched dispassionately, their carcasses spread across an unspecified field on his farm, buried, covered in lime, not burnt, to avoid any further distribution of radiation. It was unimaginably awful.

It was mind-numbing in its sheer magnitude, its finality, its emotionless and calculated response. He knew that they had a duty to be careful, that everyone needed protecting from such a disaster on such an extraordinary scale, but he felt this was madness. He shuddered and tried not to think about it, but he felt like crying for the first time since he was a small boy.

Henry had got straight on to the helpline to protest. A blank, robotic voice answered, after three minutes and going through hundreds of menu options, who seemed to have only a limited number of responses. This faceless idiot managed to make it sound as if Henry was not only stupid but that he wanted to endanger the whole nation and deliberately poison people.

Henry had tried to be measured, as he presented the scientific assessment that he had carefully researched. He tried to make the faceless automaton listen, regarding the initial likely levels of radiation and the natural reduction in radiation in a relatively short time.

Whatever he said, even when he pleaded, the robot just continued to repeat "the Exclusion Zone was to be kept in place for the foreseeable future to safeguard public interests" – whatever that meant. If the automaton said, "That may be so, but our policy is clear" one more time, he would explode with rage. The indignant "your tone is not helpful" just made him incandescent.

Even when he challenged the fool about what were they doing about the birds and the wildlife that lurked unseen, he stayed resolute.

Did they stalk and shoot the sparrows, the badgers, the foxes, the pheasants or the deer? What would they do about all the trees, the brambles, the stinging nettles?

Henry was powerless and had put down the phone in despair.

It was frankly amazing how quickly Defra had responded when they'd been dragging their feet over everything else for years and years.

Useless bunch of bureaucratic idiots.

How was he going to tell Fen and the children, Susie and Mummy, that everything that they had ever worked for, their parents had worked for, even their parents, lived for, loved, nurtured, had been poisoned, destroyed and been given a life sentence, despite no concrete evidence of guilt?

When would they be allowed to go home? Would they ever be able to go home at all?

No one could tell him.

Everyone kept telling him that he and his family had had such a lucky escape. They went on about it as if he should be grateful.

Grateful for what?

When he told anyone that asked that he'd been away for the day, they gasped as if he'd deliberately been absent. They implied that he had somehow abandoned his mother, and the faithful Moira, to her fate, and hadn't Dave lost his life standing by his cows while he was holed up with his sister, Susie, safe?

He could see how Susie felt; the guilt, stigma, remorse and uncommunicated disgrace. There was nothing you could say to change their minds. He was just so helpless in every respect.

The future look extremely bleak and Henry needed to work out where they went from here. He had discussed it with his faithful Fen. At his instigation, Henry, Fen, Moira and Susie decided to sit round Susie's kitchen table, trying to find a way forward that would work for them all. It couldn't go on like this.

Henry had first of all read them the latest update from Defra. They had all gasped involuntarily in unison. Henry waited for the full implications to sink in; it was the first time that Moira and Susie had heard the full picture.

Having got their heads round it, it was Moira who bravely brought up the elephant in the room and asked, "Where are we all going to live in the meantime? We can't stay here indefinitely."

Susie immediately gushed, "You are truly, truly welcome to stay as long as you need to, even if it is forever, but I do did understand it if you want to go elsewhere, it isn't very cheerful here at the moment." That irritated Henry, Susie once again playing the martyr, so he ignored it.

Henry and Fen put forward their conclusion that they had reached. They would rent somewhere nearby, so that they could still be supportive of each other during this tricky time, but at the same time, have a bit more space.

They hadn't worked out how the hell they would pay for it in the long term without any income, but they still had access to their bank account, which was looking reasonably healthy for the moment, and they always had an overdraft facility in place – it was the only way to survive as a dairy farmer, in the ups and downs of supermarkets' vagaries.

The National Farmers Union, who had provided their insurance for years and years, had completely washed their hands of the whole thing. "An Act of Terrorism, Mr Hillier. It is quite clearly given as an exclusion in your policy."

Defra had been very guarded about any compensation, and if Defra ran true to form, it would be years before anything was forthcoming. In any case, they would try and wriggle out of it.

It was actually Susie who came up with the brainwave. Henry had heard Susie and her friend, Kate, twittering endlessly about Susie's old school friend, Caroline, who had unluckily chosen that very day to go to London for a hair appointment, of all things, and walked right into the heart of the conflagration.

Susie and Kate did seem to be as thick as thieves, most probably because they were parents of two of the only four surviving children from the school trip, and Kate seemed to be the only person who had decided that Susie was not responsible for Jessica Hughes' death.

Kate had rung and summoned Susie to Caroline's house just after they had moved in. Susie had excitedly reported back from their meeting some complicated story about Thomas. Apparently, they had assumed that he was staying elsewhere and was likely to return at some point in time, but it had transpired that they were absolutely certain that he had been in London.

They had concluded that he must have died too, because of a message of some sort that he had left on the answering machine. They had wittered on about it, almost relishing the gossip and their part in its discovery. Together, they had registered Thomas with the Missing Persons helpline.

To be honest, it had rather gone over Henry's head, he had been so caught up in his own misery. He had known

Caroline vaguely from all sorts of family events over the years, but barely remembered Thomas, only bringing to mind some amazing eyebrows.

Susie boldly suggested that Fen and Henry investigate moving into Thomas and Caroline's house, temporarily of course. Kate had a key.

With the enormity of the situation, the vast scale of the human disaster, the urgency of taking care of the survivors and getting the country back on track, the people who were missing, assumed dead, and had no dependants, came very much at the bottom of the list.

Susie would contact Caroline's family; she'd known them for years, and only recently written to them to commiserate in their sad loss.

"They surely, surely wouldn't mind. They would absolutely be very, very sympathetic to Fen and Henry's plight. And Mum and Moira's, of course, particularly after what they have been through."

Ouch.

Henry did wish Susie would stop those little digs, but all the same, it was actually a brilliant solution. Perhaps then he could do something for Heather as well.

Chapter 68

Leah had been so lonely since the day it all happened.

The imam at the Waylen Street Mosque had been very helpful, and had expressed the whole situation clearly, but the message was not reaching the public, however many times it was repeated on TV.

"Attributing these crimes to Islam is wrong. Dead wrong. Our Prophet, peace and blessings of Allah upon him, informed us, 'No one of you murders at the time that he kills and remains a believer. Therefore, beware, beware!' To clarify, the murderer is engaging in an act that true faith would have prevented, hence, his engaging in such a reprehensible act is a sign that he does not truly believe. Only cowards attack innocent civilians. This is nothing except evil people killing innocent humans. We pray for the victims of terror and violence, not just here in London, but around the world."

Leah thanked Allah every day for his mercy in keeping her and all her family safe, but she felt like a prisoner in her own home. Whenever she ventured out, less and less now, people looked at her. They stared with malice, as if it was she who had plotted and planned the bomb and it was all completely her fault. They spat at her. Total strangers, just spitting at her. Disgusting. The imam's voice was most definitely not heard outside the mosque.

It seemed ironic that she was the one who lived by her religion, was criticised for following her beliefs, yet all these so-called Christians, who never went to church, blasphemed freely, always taking their Lord's name in vain, and did not live by their God's laws at all, were now behaving like fanatics and looking at her sideways.

It was the whispering that was so hard to take. The whisper of words always just out of hearing, the conversations that stopped suddenly when she tried to join a group. The excuses made as people melted away on her approach. She'd done nothing, nothing at all to deserve this.

Leah sat nursing a cup of tea, alone at the kitchen table, and wrapped her sari tighter around her. She missed Jessica so much, Susie too. Despite the growing summer heat, she just couldn't get warm. Saas was happily ensconced in a chair on the patio, her nose in a book. She seemed oblivious to it all.

Leah knew that both Sara and Aisha were experiencing the same covert estrangement, but not so blatantly. It was subtle. Insidious. Children are so clever at being hostile and mean, without giving you anything to put your finger on. None of them had been near social media since 25/5. It was just too malicious. Leah had always found social media dangerous and better avoided. This was the proof of that.

Leah suspected that Aisha especially was having a terrible time of it at school, as one of the so very few survivors, let alone most obviously being a Muslim because of her hijab, and all the apocryphal hubris that had become associated with it. Her innocent, virtuous, open, friendly, non-judgemental Aisha had been vilified through no fault of her own. It was destroying her.

The meagre, little handful of surviving Year 12s looked ridiculously out of place at school, and people turned to stare at them all as if they were aliens from another planet. Susie's Jack, Kate's Lily, her Aisha, and Charlie Powell. Apparently, Charlie Powell had just vanished and not bothered to come into school at all, but at least Aisha was still attending regularly, despite the constant gibes and insults. Leah admired Aisha's strength of character.

It had been so hard for all the family to join in with all the Christian memorial services, always going together, no one lost from their unscathed family unit. It had been difficult not knowing whether to mouth along to the *Our Father* prayer or stay silent, whether to attempt to sing *The Lord is my Shepherd*, the hymns or not – either could offend. People were so easy to offend at the moment.

There had been so many services to go to. So many people that she had known and loved and been friends with. Beloved Jessica's, Mrs Davies', all the children in Year 12. She couldn't go to all the children's services, just the ones that she felt that she knew well enough, friends of Aisha.

And Pete's. She'd gone to that just with Farrukh and saas. They had hidden away at the back, behind a sea of dark blue uniforms, topped with incongruously pink, balding and shaved heads. She wasn't sure Susie even knew she was there. Hiding with her was Meredith, Gary's timid, little wife, Ellie's mum. Apparently, Gary had not been seen since 25/5. She could not feel so sad about that.

Ever since 25/5, her cherished Susie had turned against her, which hurt more than anything. Leah missed the confidences, given and received, the friendly smiles of encouragement in groups, being included, Susie's infectious giggle, her crazy accidents, and things that were always going wrong . She missed Susie reaching out to touch Leah's sleeve and her heart.

In all truth, she didn't really understand why. She knew that she had overreacted in the heat of the moment. She couldn't now remember exactly what she had said but she winced at her recollection of her accusations about Jessica. She and Susie had utterly and completely, unequivocally fallen out. There was a chasm of misunderstanding between them now.

Her heart ached too for the lovely Jessica. She wanted to turn the clock back. She wanted the Eternal Triangle back, the three of them around one or other of their tables, the laughter, the affection, the allegiance.

Leah sighed, dejected. She felt trapped, persecuted and lonely. She missed the only people who had always made her feel happy, assimilated and loved. Susie and Jessica. She sipped her tea.

Chapter 69

Pips missed Ellie so much.

It felt like years since Ellie and Dad had been missing, presumed dead. They wouldn't declare you outright dead, which seemed a bit mad, and made it so hard for both Mum and Pips. She just couldn't believe that Ellie was really gone, really dead, passed away, etcetera, etcetera.

Her counsellor had suggested that she wrote a diary to let her feelings come out, unchecked. She felt a bit stupid actually writing it down, and was worried that her mum might come and snoop at it, so she had decided to write it all to Ellie, a sort of letter, but on Facebook, where no one would ever see it. The counsellor was right – it helped a bit.

Pips sat forward and tapped away on her tablet, her messages to beyond the grave.

"I still miss you every day. I wonder how different life would be now if you were here. Mum and I have just had supper on our knees in front of the telly! We do every night now. We had pasta and, no, it doesn't taste like condoms, so there, Dad! And some yum sauce out of a jar. Did I tell you we're now veggies? Mum doesn't trust the meat. You can never tell if it isn't radioactive, she says. I don't like to point out to her that plants have been zapped too, but it makes her happy, LOL.

School is okay. End of term, Friday. I'm dreading the holidays. It is still dead strange to go in every day on the bus without you, and I miss Alfie too, even though I didn't know him that well. You must have realised I fancied him. It makes it especially hard. It is hard to miss so many people all at the same time. You almost run out of missing. It can get exhausting. Whenever I am up to something that I shouldn't, I hear Mrs Davies telling me off, even though I know that she is dead too. Dead, dead, dead. So much deadness. I just wish, wish, wish that you weren't too. Ramble, ramble. Love yer, Ellie."

Mum would never log on to Facebook and see all this crap – she didn't really know how – and with Dad missing, presumably dead, she no longer felt the need to change her password every few days, just in case he was snooping.

Pips felt dreadful that she actually rather hoped that Dad was really dead. She must be the most horrible person on the planet. She sort of loved him, but at the same time, hated him, detested him, loathed him. He was so foul to Ellie, and to Mum, but never quite as much. Life was much easier and just more peaceful now.

Every time she fed Marmite, "that incident" came back to her in a hideous rush, even though Mum had changed his food to pouches to remove the association with the canned stuff. She'd noticed that Marmite's collar had disappeared. Pips hadn't said anything, as it seemed better not to bring it up.

Mum seemed to believe that Dad really was dead. She never ever said so, but Pips could tell. She went round looking the part, the grieving widow, loud sobs and all, but Pips had noticed that Mum had started to look so much younger, happier, even though she obviously was devastated about Ellie.

Gradually, things had changed. Mum didn't bother to paint on her thick layers of make-up every day, and the washing up was left in the sink until the next morning after supper. Stupid things that Pips had never noticed that they did before, like making sure that the towels were hanging straight in the downstairs toilet, had gone to pot, and the ironing basket full of wrinkled clothes in the corner of the sitting room had been left there for days.

Pips felt more relaxed too. Not on edge all the time. She walked in and grabbed whatever she wanted from the fridge. She chucked her shoes off and deliberately let them lay in a heap, rather than on the rack inside the back door. She missed Ellie so much, but she didn't miss Dad. It appeared that the only person, well, not really a person as such, to miss Dad was Marmite.

Poor Marmite, very confusing.

Life was moving on. She felt that. At first, everyone was in shock and wallowed in it. Some people seemed to get, well, stuck into the wailing, even though they weren't affected themselves, and kept it going for as long as they could.

We have to move on sometime. Weird.

Chapter 70

Susie was very, very taken aback to see Thomas on the doorstep, and stifled a gasp.

She thought he was dead. It seemed a struggle to remember who was dead and who was alive. It still caught her by surprise that she could now think about it so calmly without going into instant meltdown.

It was a good few months after "that day", well, to be precise, three months, eleven days and three hours, but who was counting, and it seemed especially odd that he should suddenly just reappear in front of her eyes when everyone had included him in the memorial services alongside all the others, and then the special service for him, William and Caroline. She hoped she wasn't going mad and wasn't actually hallucinating.

Thomas and Caroline's house had stood empty after she and Kate had made their discovery, another confused casualty of the chaos and dangling loose ends. It had seemed perfectly alright to invite Henry, Fenella, Arthur and Alice to shelter there with Mummy and Moira. A mortified Henry had moved Heather in too – there was plenty of space.

She'd assumed that, in time, that someone, who knew who, would sell it or give it to an evacuee from the exclusion areas, so it might as well be Henry as anyone. Defra kept saying that they might eventually be able to go back to the farm, but not when. They were as vague as ever.

It suddenly dawned on her how presumptuous it had been to move her family in. *How embarrassing!* She blushed and felt horribly, horribly flustered.

"Come in, come in," she said, hoping that he hadn't read her mind. He was patently alive, and she was extremely puzzled, as well shocked rigid, so she tried to stick an "everything is absolutely normal" smile on her face. She was tempted to reach out and pinch him, just to check that he wasn't a phantom.

Hesitating, she wondered where to take him. Everything was in a bit of a muddle, and somehow, without Pete to nag her, the place had descended into chaos. Jack made remarks such as, "Mum, pull yourself together and stop living like a pig", but they just didn't carry the same weight as Pete's gentle nudges. Jack just didn't seem grateful enough that he was standing there, alive and kicking, and able to actually be there at all, and all because of her chaos and muddles.

Just keeping it in a jumble seemed to act as a talisman to keep them all safe; the more chaotic she was, the safer they would all be in the end. She kept putting back the loo roll on the stairs in the exact same place that it had been that day, even though Jack, or was it Amelia, kept moving it into their bathroom.

Susie waved Thomas through to the sitting room, removed a heap of papers, mostly correspondence from the police about Pete's pension, from the sofa, invited him to sit down, and then swooped up all the dirty coffee mugs, a half-eaten packet of choc chip cookies and a Mars bar wrapper, hoping Thomas wouldn't notice.

"Tea, coffee?"

"Yes, yes please," Thomas replied, stumbling over his words. None the wiser, Susie scuttled into the kitchen, dumped the dirty mugs on the island and put the kettle on. It gave her time to get her thoughts in order and line up the right questions. Her heart was pounding.

What on earth were the right questions when someone resurrected themselves and appeared on your doorstep? How on earth do you explain that you have moved your family into someone's home without so much as asking?

Susie could see now why Leah had reacted in that hysterical way "that day". She hadn't had the chance to be immunised by it all then. Looking back, the shock, the pain must have been so raw for Leah. It is, after all, what we all do when we are frightened, lash out in alarm, say hysterical things.

Susie felt a hint of shame; perhaps she too had overreacted, but only a slight murmur, because she had become so numb. Every drop of emotion had been squeezed out over the last few months until she was empty. Every word of sympathy had become an empty platitude, every word of comfort, hollow. The whole country had got accustomed to it, probably the whole planet.

A ridiculous thought passed through her mind like a leaping flame: *if Thomas is alive then perhaps Pete is too?* She just couldn't believe that Pete was gone. Every single day when she woke up, it hit her all over again, and she yearned for him and wanted to scream about how unfair it was and how no one seemed to care. This was always followed by the guilt of being alive herself. It had been so hard. She would clutch her belly, her precious, new life for comfort.

Everywhere she went, people still looked at her with, I don't know, just a look, a strange, almost angry, look. It was if they wished that she'd gone on the trip, and taken Jack with her, and never come back, like their children, and like Jessica, and like Pete, like everyone else. It still hurt terribly after so much time. *When would they stop?*

Since her bump had started showing, the looks had got even worse. I know I am too old for this, but it is my little miracle and I sure as hell am not going to get rid of Pete's precious gift to me just to please everyone else. She knew that they were all predicting that it wouldn't "come out right". The effects of radiation. She didn't care.

Jack and Amelia were mortified, she knew. She'd also heard the hint of whispers, questioning whose child it was. *Who else's would it be, for God's sake!*

It had been Amelia and Jack's first day back at school yesterday, and Amelia was still having a hard time at school, but what on earth could she do? It was now as if they believed that Amelia had forced Hannah to leave, but it had definitely been the right thing to do, for Hannah to go and live with her auntie up North, make a new start at a new school. They hadn't made up before she went, so sad.

Susie's heart had bled when Amelia had told her how she'd stood on the edge as all the others had made their fond farewells, the hugs, the tears as they said goodbye at the end of last term. She hadn't even looked at Amelia as she finally left. Susie knew that if she accused them of bullying Amelia, it would probably make things worse.

You know what kids are like. Poor, poor Amelia. Poor, poor Hannah.

They still looked at Leah like that too, as if it was also her fault somehow, rather than a miracle that Aisha was alive. You couldn't accuse everyone of being culpable, just because they shared a religion, but somehow, Susie and Leah had just not been able to build bridges since Leah's shocking outburst that day.

Clattering about loudly so that Thomas wouldn't hear her thoughts, Susie put together a tray of tea *and* coffee, and carried it through. She squeezed it onto the coffee table, pushing piles of stuff out of the way, and it teetered on the edge. She busied herself with the pouring of tea and coffee and all the niceties of being the renowned hostess, and waited for Thomas to speak.

"You must be surprised to see me, Susie."

"Yes," she replied, a bit too brightly, and looked at him with "go on" face. Well, she hoped it looked like a "go on" face, not a "what the bloody hell are you doing sitting on my sofa alive when Pete is dead?" face and "how do I explain why I have taken over your house?"

"I didn't know whether to come back."

"Come back?" echoed Susie, sounding, she thought, rather moronic.

"It has been difficult."

Tell me about it.

"They have all gone."

What can I say? I have run out of platitudes and things to say when people tell me this. I am exhausted. I am empty. What about me? Yes, I do have my children, both of my wonderful children, and a baby on the way, but my beloved and unique Pete has gone forever. And Jessica. And even Leah.

Why did there have to be a value, a strange comparison, a complex formula on what or how much or what age the people that you had lost had been. We could only be touched by those we knew and loved.

"I'm so, so sorry, Thomas. William was a lovely boy, and Caroline..." Susie tailed off, what else could she say that hadn't been said over and over and over again? She meant it quite genuinely, but it was muddled by his unexpected reappearance. It sounded insincere, even to her own ears.

"I thought Caroline was still here, venting her widow's weeds. I was so surprised, that sounds like a pathetic understatement, but I was, to get to the house and find that she was gone too. I walked into the kitchen and found total strangers gawping at me, as if I was in the wrong house. They were somewhat surprised to see me, not surprisingly really. I couldn't really take it in when they told me that all the occupants of our house had been recorded as PD, and then when I found out who they were, and who had registered me as PD, I was even more shocked. I don't know why. It just seemed a bit... presumptive."

Susie squirmed with embarrassment. "I'm really, really sorry, Thomas, it was just that... you know."

"William, he would have been annihilated instantly at school," Thomas interrupted, sounding bitter. Susie cringed and that guilty feeling came over her again, as she thought about Jack.

"He was in the epicentre of it, in Westminster," Thomas mumbled on. "God knows where Caroline was, but she was evidently in London, I am now told."

He doesn't sound too sad about Caroline.

"Hairdressers," Susie whispered, but Thomas didn't hear.

"I hadn't told her that I was going to North London for a meeting. Why should I? I was beside myself when I heard. It was so close and yet so far... unimaginable. My first thought was William. Disappeared in a puff of smoke. Vaporised. It was hell."

Thomas went into a reverie, staring into the distance.

Susie tried to breathe loudly to remind him that she was there.

Thomas started up again. "I hadn't thought about the whole firestorm and the radiation fallout business. It was impossible for hours to get any sense of the overall effect. It was so chaotic."

Another long pause.

"What you don't understand is that now, everyone has gone. Everyone, every single one of them has now gone."

Susie was confused. "Yes, yes, I had gathered that." She tried the "tell me more" face again. It did the trick and Thomas continued.

"You see, Susie, I had a little girl too, Valentina, born on February 14th, obviously, with Galina. She was so little, so beautiful, a perfect angel, absolutely adorable. A blonde, little cherub, she was only 15 months old."

This was not helping, what on earth was he talking about?

Her confusion obviously showed on her face. "They lived in Wimbledon, just a tiny flat, but enough. I thought that they would be fine, far enough away to escape the... the..." He hung his head in despair and shook his head, unable to voice it out loud.

"I tried to get back right away, but it was chaos, it was madness. They wouldn't let me go into that part of London, they just kept telling us to get out, to head due north. I begged and begged and pleaded with them. I didn't know where to go, other than I just wanted to get back to save them. A very sweet lady, a complete stranger, but it is amazing how strangers react in these circumstances, put me up locally so that I could try and get to them. It took days and days before I could find them, make contact with them."

Thomas continued. "They didn't die instantly, like William. I knew William would have been instantly wiped out. He would have just evaporated." Thomas winced. "Somehow, because it was instant, it was better, I know that sounds crass. When I eventually reached them, they seemed fine. I really thought they were fine.

"We were together, we were so relieved, but it didn't last. Galina started being ill again first. She was unbearably sick; she told me how they had both been as ill as this for a few days, vomiting, diarrhoea, like a really bad stomach bug, but that they had got better. But suddenly, her skin erupted into revolting lesions, the vomiting, the spontaneous bleeding... suddenly vomiting up blood... her skin... her hair fell out, and she was in dreadful agony. It was horrible. I was helpless. There was nothing they could do, even though she was moved to one of the outlying emergency centres, in Bristol. At least I could be there with her and I could look after Valentina for her."

Susie was finding it hard to make neither head nor tail of this very, very long tale, as well as being distinctly queasy at all the graphic detail ,and decided to interject, "Galina? Why Bristol? Um, who? When?"

Thomas seemed to understand her confusion and suddenly looked at her, it made her jump with its intensity. "When Caroline had her thing with Pete, I was angry, I was hurt, and I decided that rather than make a fuss, I would quietly do things my own way, exact my revenge, I suppose. I found a lovely girl, a kind girl, a self-effacing darling, Galina, who after Caroline's strong and overpowering character, was quiet, dignified, loving, and supportive. She made me so happy. I actually found love. I have been blessed with nearly three years of happiness with her."

Hang on a moment, rewind there, Thomas, please, did I miss something there? Did he say Pete? Did he or did I imagine it? Not my Pete? Another Pete?

Susie, distracted by this "Pete", who had been plopped into the conversation ever so casually, wasn't really clear where this was going.

"I really believed that perhaps Valentina would make it. She hung on for weeks after her mum, poor, little poppet, but she has gone too. It is a horrible way to die. I was so helpless, and I couldn't think where to go or what to do, so I came back here, where else could I go? I wanted to die too. Wimbledon, where our home was, is still a total exclusion zone, and I couldn't stay on at the centre in Bristol.

"My family all presumed that I was dead, I didn't actually mind terribly much, I was so wrapped up with Galina and Valentina. I didn't want to reappear out of the blue. I genuinely thought Caroline was here, you see. I assumed that she would think I was dead. I knew she would be surprised but I thought I could start again and that she would be kinder to me. I did love her once and I think, in a funny sort of way, she loved me. Ironic really."

Susie had so many questions at this point that she could only stare at Thomas with her mouth open. She shivered and tentatively asked, "Pete?"

Thomas seemed to come out of his reverie and looked at Susie, as if he was surprised to find her there at all.

"Pete?" she repeated more firmly.

"Pete?" he responded, beetling his Denis Healey eyebrows at her.

"Yes, Pete, Thomas! What did you say about Pete and Caroline?" Susie almost shouted, she wanted to shake him; had he just expected an outpouring of sympathy?

He continued to look at her, frowned, looked around the room, and eventually returned his gaze to her face. "Didn't you know? I thought you did, but it didn't last very long, it was a storm in a pan, a one-night stand, I think. It was silly, just a bit of attention seeking from Caroline. Nothing to worry about."

Susie went cold, shivered, but Thomas was burbling on. "I just didn't know what to do. I thought I would come back and find Caroline. Despite everything, I thought she would provide me with some comfort, share our shock and the loss of William. I could pick up with old friends, those that had lived through it too. I didn't know about Pete. I'm so sorry. Stupid really, but I thought with nowhere else to go that I at least had the right to move back into the house with Caroline. She didn't even have to know about Galina and Valentina really, although I suspect I would have had to let the cat out of the bag."

Who cares, Thomas! Who fucking cares!

"For God's sake, Thomas, are you absolutely sure about *Pete* and Caroline," Susie burst out.

"Mmm? Yes, absolutely." Thomas said airily, before continuing. "Now, I am not sure what to do, having found out that Caroline has died too, that was a bit of a shock. It might take some time getting used to it."

"No seriously, Thomas, are you absolutely positive?" Susie almost shouted at Thomas.

"What? Oh yes." He looked momentarily surprised, but instantly continued his rambling. "You know, I could just go and live with my family, but I will probably move in with your family, or something, they are nice people, it seems; they need all the space they can get and the house is enormous, far too big for just me. It is all just so terrible and confusing, I really don't know what to think."

Fucking, fucking Caroline, fucking Pete. How could you? How could you?

Clutching their precious, new life, to protect it from this devastating betrayal, this perfidy, this treachery, Susie screamed inside so loudly, she thought her head would explode. Suddenly, without warning, she threw up – every single loving memory of her darling, her dearest, her beloved, cherished, revered Pete, soiled and spoiled forever. She wanted to die.

Thomas raised his incredible eyebrows in surprise.

Chapter 71

Charlie came to; something had disturbed him.

Last night, he had staggered to the settee, curled up, pulled the manky throw over himself, and slept, deeply exhausted by the venting of his grief and rage. He could just see through the small gap in the feeble curtains that only just met in the middle, someone at the window, peering in and tapping on the glass, loudly. They must be using their car keys.

Fuck, they had better not break the window. Last fucking thing I need.

Charlie leapt up, his heart racing, looked down to check that he was decent, forgetting that he had slept in his pub uniform. What to do? He waited. The tapping set up again.

Couldn't be the fucking press, they were long gone. Could it be the police? Bailiffs? Should I pretend not to be here?

"Charlie. I can see you in there."

Shit, it was Mrs Pietruski.

He stood still, hoping that she was guessing. If he stood still, she wouldn't catch his movement.

But man, Mrs Pietruski?

He couldn't stop a swell of warmth pass through him. Was it happiness? He didn't think he could remember what that felt like.

"Charlie, if you won't let me in, I am going to call the police while I am standing here, and I will not leave until they arrive. Do you get me?" Charlie couldn't help but smile at her attempt at gangster speak. He stayed motionless for a minute and thought about it, breathing as quietly as he could so she wouldn't hear him, although it would be hard not to hear the hammering in his chest.

She continued. "Charlie, it is the start of a new term and I hoped that you would be back. I know that you are old enough to leave school and therefore, that it is not a matter for the local authorities, but you are a minor and therefore... therefore... Oh for God's sake, Charlie, sod all that official crap. I am here because I am beside myself with worry about you. I want to help!"

There was no way out of it. Perhaps if he spoke to her, she would lay off. He needn't say anything much. Despite the instinct to hide, he found that he was pleased, a whole lot more than pleased, that it was her and that she'd bothered to come and find him, relieved that here was a way out of his crappy zombie existence, but he was reluctant to reveal it. He hesitated.

What would she think?

He caught a whiff from his clothes. Fuck, could he face her, stinking like this. He looked around the room. It looked as if there had been a whole gang of gypsies living rough in here, and glancing through to the kitchen, he could see the sink crammed with stuff, takeaway food packaging haemorrhaging from the garbage, and the cooker looked like a volcano with lava sliding off of it. It looked like a disaster zone. Not a great analogy.

She tapped again. "Charlie, please."

Charlie took a deep breath. He could feel emotion rising into his chest, a rush of adrenalin. He made his mind up. He scuttled to the front door, fiddled stupidly with the bolts and eventually pulled them back, wrenched open the door and stepped out. He drew himself up, tried to speak, cleared his throat, which was thick from despair.

He had wanted to be fierce, to be a big man, but he fell into her motherly arms and, giving in to everything, wept like a little child.

Chapter 72

Pips was sitting on the sofa, finishing her supper.

When Mum had finally got the Presumed Dead certificate, everyone had been trying to find nice things to say about her dad. Her mum was pretending what a great guy he had been, but Pips knew that the tears streaming down both their cheeks were really only for Ellie.

Life was much more, well, relaxed without Dad around. They both missed Ellie so much, and it still hurt as deep as a bottomless chasm, but Dad? It was horrible to say so but she didn't actually miss him much at all.

Since Dad had been declared PD, it had seemed to have given Mum a new lease of life. She'd swooped around the house messing stuff up, unmaking the usually perfectly-smoothed bed, flinging damp towels onto the bathroom floor, scrumpling up the dish cloths and leaving them on the counter tops. She was acting really loopy.

But then Mr HC had reappeared and she'd seemed to calm down a bit. *Was Mum worried that Daddy might suddenly walk in too?* It seemed unlikely now. They would never know where he had gone that day, but he had to be dead. *Didn't he?* Pips couldn't help crossing her fingers, but hastily uncrossed them in case it had been noticed. Mum had relaxed again and everything got messy once more.

They had just finished supper, sitting in front of the TV, another of Mum's acts of rebellion. The novelty of eating on knees had worn off, and Pips kinda hoped that they would get back to sitting at the table. She always ended up spilling stuff down her front. She didn't like to suggest it though.

Just one of Mum's silly acts of pointless mutiny; perhaps they would never eat at a table ever again.

Putting her tray on the coffee table and shoving Marmite off it as he lunged greedily for her dirty plate – he wasn't shy in tucking into any remains that he could find – Pips turned on her tablet, touched the icon for FB. There was a notification that she had a message, flicked through to messages.

Her heart stopped. She went absolutely still, frozen, a horrible, cold feeling spread from the top of her head to her feet. Someone was playing a horrible trick on her. Alfie perhaps? Who else would have known the password?

Don't be stupid, Pips, Alfie is dead, they are all dead.

It was horrible how it could just hit you all over again without warning. Would she ever get back to feeling normal?

She was too scared to tap on the message, and spent forever just trying to breathe and looking at the screen. She looked at Mum. Oblivious. She stared at the screen.

There is only one way to find out what the fuck is going on here.

She touched the message icon.

"Pips, I'm really sorry to do this to you but I didn't know what else to do. I have just logged on to FB for the first time – I haven't dared to before in case I was traced – and read all your messages. They broke my heart. I'm okay. I'm in Manchester. I was on a train well clear of London when it happened. Is Dad really dead like you said? If he is then I will come home. Remember what I told you that morning – you won't understand what I am saying but please remember that whatever happens today, I really, really love you – that is as true today as it was then. I've put that so you know that it is truly me, in case you think I'm a fake. Love yer. xxxxx"

Pips burst into sudden, hysterical sobs. She couldn't stop. Mum leapt from her chair, her tray flew off in all directions; Marmite leapt on it, unable to believe his luck.

She enveloped Pips in her arms. "Philippa, what is wrong, what on earth is wrong?"

Pips couldn't speak, just looked at her mum, her face trying hard to smile in delight, while being contorted by the sheer volume of feeling.

She wailed, she keened, and her mum looked horrified and tried to rock it away. It took ages for Pips to find her voice. "Mummy, Ellie. Ellie is alive."

Her Mum just stared at her, pushed her away in anger, it seemed.

"Don't, Philippa, please don't, not again, you know that it can't be true."

"It's real Mummy, it is real." She thrust her tablet under Mum's nose.

Meredith was confused, didn't know what she was looking at. She was crap with tablets. Pips took it back out of her hands and, still half sobbing, half crowing, haltingly read the message to her. "You see, it is true, Mummy, only Ellie knows that."

"Knows what?"

"Knows what she said to me that day."

"Oh my God, oh my God, you're not kidding? Are you sure?" Mum leapt to her feet, doing a crazy sort of dance thing, grabbing at Pips' hands, pumping them up and down. Marmite got excited and started dancing around too.

"What shall we do? It is true, isn't it? Isn't it? Oh, Philippa, that is amazing, fantastic, wonderful." She stopped suddenly and stared at Pips, looking worried. "It couldn't be some horrible joke?"

The thought crossed Pips' mind. *Dad?* Is that what Mum was thinking? *Couldn't be. He wouldn't know about what Ellie had said. He couldn't, could he? It had to be her, really, truly, honestly.*

"It has to be real. No one else would know what she said. I haven't told anyone about that, not a soul. Honest."

Pips and her mum danced around the room together, kicking the prostrate tray and mashing ketchup joyfully into the carpet, Marmite joining in with joyous barks.

"What shall I do, Mummy?"

"Write back to her. Quickly, straight away."

"What shall I say?"

Her mum thought about it, her eyes dancing, her body wiggling with delight, just like Marmite did when he was overexcited. Pips started tapping it in. It seemed to take forever her fingers were trembling in excitement; she had to keep overriding the predictive text.

Shit, shit, it was suddenly impossible.

She did it. She touched the reply arrow, her face shone, her eyes lit up, and she burst back to life.

"Come home, Ellie. Come home as fast as you can. Love Mum and Pips."

Chapter 73

Leah arrived at the NADFAS meeting in plenty of time.

She was going to be there, just inside the door, to greet people as they arrived, so they had to be extremely and blatantly rude if they were to ignore her, as they had seemed to do over the last few meetings. She'd arrived far too early though and there wasn't a soul in sight. The chairs were all set out and the speaker's lectern was in its designated place.

She wandered up the rows and took a random orange plastic seat, it scraped with a loud squeal in the silence, and settled herself down into its hard form. She couldn't help but notice that the orange clashed horribly with her pink sari. She glanced down at her programme of events and read:

"Art and Feminism: Do women have to be naked to get into art galleries? Feminism in modern art has used various strategies, ranging from humour and irony, through to confrontation and downright belligerence. This lecture starts by looking at the difficulties women had making their voices heard in the macho world of art from 1950s, to the highly politicised works of early 1970s, and on to the more nuanced attitudes of the 1990s and beyond."

The lecturer was Rachael Thomas, not a particularly arty sort of name, neither did it sound ragingly feminist, although what a feminist looked like, Leah wasn't entirely sure.

Not really her cup of tea but she liked to show her face and make sure that she kept in touch with everybody. If she hid in fear of everybody and their slanderous stories, they would only have more opportunity to talk behind her back.

She waited and pondered. No one had said a thing, not a single thing to her face, but she knew that they were still muttering behind her back after all this time. Whispering campaigns were just so difficult. She wanted to stand up in front of them and say… say what? What did she want to say?

It isn't fair! I am just an ordinary woman who happens to be a Muslim, and I am not culpable for any of this. Stop it, please, stop it.

This hellish act was man-made by a mad extreme sect that no one had heard of before, they had just suddenly emerged out of nowhere, Fundamentalist Soldiers of Islam, claiming victory in the name of Islam, but they simply were not Muslims. They couldn't be.

Islam means peace, surrender of one's will to God. Islam's main message is to worship God and to treat all of God's creation with kindness and compassion. One is encouraged to lead a healthy, active life, with the qualities of kindness, chastity, honesty, mercy, courage, patience and politeness. This heinous act was not anything to do with Islam, absolutely not. She could feel frustrated tears threatening.

Perhaps she could sweep aside Rachael Thomas and stand in front of them all and tell them this. Tell them the truth.

The door creaked open. Leah turned and her heart leapt. It was Susie. Of all the people to get here early too. She'd been avoiding Leah and had been barely civil for months. It was as if she couldn't bring herself to speak to Leah at all. She would hardly look Leah in the eye.

Actually, Susie wouldn't look anyone in the eye. It was clear that Susie had suffered terribly from all the myths that abounded about her too. Susie was no more culpable for the tragedy of Jessica Hughes than Leah was for the whole tragedy itself. She could not have known about it in advance either, it was completely ridiculous.

Susie had lumbered in, looked about herself with glazed eyes, no make-up, frowned at her watch. She'd obviously thought the meeting was at a different time, and looked completely lost. She didn't even have the energy to register Leah's still and silent presence.

Leah saw Susie with fresh eyes. She looked dreadful, her face grey, pudgy and pasty, and she seemed to have put on even more weight. The rumour was that she was pregnant.

At her age? Extraordinary.

Leah's heart went out to her. Poor, lovely, kind, selfless Susie. She'd never, ever heard Susie say a bad word about anyone. She was her friend, always had been, the two remaining members of the Eternal Triangle. She and Jessica had been the only people that had truly invited her and Farrukh into their homes and their hearts without judgement, without analysis.

What had she been thinking?

She felt dreadful. She felt all the indignant anger and blame melt. What ran through her mind was "kindness, honesty, mercy, courage, patience and politeness". She scampered up, the chair squealing horribly again, her sari swishing across the floor, enfolded Susie in her arms, her bracelets jangling, tears cascading down her cheeks.

"Susie, Susie. I am so sorry. Forgive me. Please, forgive me."

Susie groaned like an animal in pain and leant into Leah's embrace. "Leah, Leah... I have just been to see the counsellor... I did kill Jessica, Jack is being really, really foul, Amelia hates me, I am just so lonely and I am having a baby, which is a miracle, but Pete and Caroline... my beloved Pete." Susie broke down, weeping, sobbing and wailing. Leah held her tight, rocked her gently.

When the others started drifting in, they were enormously surprised to see the two villains of the 25/5 cataclysm, the sworn enemies, standing at the speaker's lectern, locked together in unity, Susie seemingly enfolded in Leah's sari, the pink colour of forgiveness, healing and compassion.

Leah boldly raised her chin and in a commanding voice began, "Ladies, we need to speak to you, not about why women have to be naked to get into art galleries, but about the fallout of 25/5." She paused, receiving their full attention. They all stared intently.

"We need to talk to you, Susie and me, together, about truth, forgiveness, kindness and compassion, and the appropriate apportionment of blame."

Lightning Source UK Ltd.
Milton Keynes UK
UKOW08f0621210417
299602UK00002B/12/P